SHERRYL WOODS

With her roots firmly planted in the South, #1 *New York Times* bestselling author Sherryl Woods has written many of her more than one hundred books in that distinctive setting, whether it's her home state of Virginia, her adopted state, Florida, or her much-adored South Carolina. Now she's added North Carolina's Outer Banks to her list of favorite spots. And she remains partial to small towns, wherever they may be.

A member of Novelists, Inc., Sherryl divides her time between her childhood summer home overlooking the Potomac River in Colonial Beach, Virginia, and her oceanfront home with its lighthouse view in Key Biscayne, Florida. "Wherever I am, if there's no water in sight, I get a little antsy," she says.

Sherryl loves to hear from readers. You can visit her on her web site at www.sherrylwoods.com, link to her Facebook fan page from there or contact her directly at Sherryl703@gmail.com.

RAEANNE THAYNE

finds inspiration in the beautiful northern Utah mountains, where she lives with her husband and three children. Her books have won numerous honors, including four RITA® Award nominations from Romance Writers of America and a Career Achievement Award from *RT Book Reviews*. RaeAnne currently writes for Harlequin Special Edition and Harlequin HQN. RaeAnne loves to hear from readers and can be contacted through her website www.raeannethayne.com.

#1 *New York Times* Bestselling Author

SHERRYL WOODS

Safe Harbor

HARLEQUIN® BESTSELLING AUTHOR COLLECTION

If you purchased this book without a cover you should be aware that this book is stolen property. It was reported as "unsold and destroyed" to the publisher, and neither the author nor the publisher has received any payment for this "stripped book."

ISBN-13: 978-0-373-18084-4

SAFE HARBOR
Copyright © 2014 by Harlequin Books S.A.

The publisher acknowledges the copyright holders of the individual works as follows:

SAFE HARBOR
Copyright © 1987 by Sherryl Woods

A COLD CREEK HOMECOMING
Copyright © 2009 by RaeAnne Thayne

This edition published by arrangement with Harlequin Books S.A.

For questions and comments about the quality of this book, please contact us at CustomerService@Harlequin.com.

® and TM are trademarks of Harlequin Enterprises Limited or its corporate affiliates. Trademarks indicated with ® are registered in the United States Patent and Trademark Office, the Canadian Intellectual Property Office and in other countries.

Printed in U.S.A.

CONTENTS

Dear Friends,

As I was preparing to write this letter for the reissue of *Safe Harbor*, I realized it was first published way back in 1987! It still astonishes me that I've been writing for so many incredible years and getting to know so many of you along the way. It's been a blessing!

And while *Safe Harbor* wasn't my first book, it was the first one I wrote for Silhouette Special Edition, a prospect I and my editors found a little daunting at the time. You see, back then, I had a habit of running out of words. The thought of writing a longer book didn't just worry me, it had my editors in a panic that *Safe Harbor* would be the shortest Special Edition on record. I suggested we could fill any blank pages with the oddities from the zoning code in swanky Palm Beach, Florida, the setting for the book. They were not amused.

Hopefully, though, this story of widow Tina Harrington and sexy, infuriating Drew Landry will amuse and delight you in all the right ways. While I've written many books about families since this one, none of those families has been cobbled together quite the way this one was. For me it's added proof that blood isn't the only thing necessary to create strong family bonds. Even those of us most alone in the world can create a family full of love and respect. I hope you'll enjoy this one.

All best,

Sherryl

SAFE HARBOR
Sherryl Woods

Chapter One

It had all started with Sam.

That was it, Tina decided, throwing herself into one of the antique wicker chairs overlooking the pool and perfectly landscaped terrace. The palm trees with their limply hanging branches seemed to reflect her mood perfectly as she stared dolefully at the thick vellum papers in her hand. She only barely resisted the urge to crumple them up and throw them for one of the cats to bat around the lawn, possibly straight into the pool's sparkling turquoise water. It would be a fitting end to the documents. As for her bad habit, it seemed there was no end in sight.

It had all started twenty years ago, back when she was eight and that scrawny marmalade kitten she'd named Sam had made its way to her front door. It had meowed so pitifully that not even her father had been able to resist Tina's pleas to take it in. Ever since then, she'd been adopting strays.

Sam had been followed by Penelope, the gerbil who was about to be sent away to who-knew-what awful fate by her best friend, then by Sam's totally unexpected litter of kittens. Bandit, who barked as though he had laryngitis, had limped in with a thorn in his front paw and stayed for nearly ten years, bringing home friends when it suited him.

By the time she'd left for the University of Florida, the house had looked like a damned menagerie, according to her amazingly tolerant parents. They might not have known where the next mortgage payment was coming from, but they'd always found room in their hearts and food scraps for one more of Tina's pets.

They should see me now, she thought with a sigh as she reread the letter from the Florida Department of Children and Families. The letter was filled with legal jargon, but what it boiled down to was an accusation that she was taking in human strays without benefit of a license, followed by a stern admonition that she should cease and desist promptly or risk penalties meant to scare the daylights out of her. The threats only infuriated her.

She glared at the paper. Those pompous, meddling fools! Of all the ridiculous, simpleminded…

"Tina, dear, I've brought you a nice glass of iced tea," Grandmother Sarah said as she set down a tall, frosted glass, then sat herself and waved a lilac-scented, lace-edged hankie to stir the still, humid air into a slight breeze. "My, but it's a scorcher today. I'll be so glad when we get another cold front through here to cool things off."

"The minute the temperature goes below seventy you complain that your arthritis acts up," Tina reminded her with a gently teasing smile.

"Posh-tosh. My arthritis acts up all the time. I'm an old lady."

"Some days I think you're younger than I am," Tina

said with a heavy sigh that drew a sharp-eyed glance from Grandmother Sarah.

Grandmother Sarah, with her wisps of flyaway white hair surrounding a weathered face, her sparkling periwinkle blue eyes and her flowered print dress, wasn't Tina's grandmother at all. They had met a year ago while walking on the beach and had started talking. It hadn't taken long for the gregarious and unceasingly curious Tina to discover that the spirited, elderly woman with her spry manner and tart tongue was about to be thrown out of her soon-to-be-demolished rooming house and had nowhere to live. She'd invited Sarah home as casually as she'd admitted Sam all those years ago. She hadn't regretted the spontaneous suggestion for a single minute. It had been like she'd always imagined having a real grandmother would be.

Tina gazed at Grandmother Sarah fondly and took a long swallow of the cool drink. The way she was feeling, it probably should have been a mint julep at the very least. Maybe even straight bourbon. If the ominous tone of the letter she held was any indication, she had a feeling she was in for the fight of her life.

Intuitive as always, Sarah picked up on her mood.

"Dear, if you don't mind my saying so, you look a mite peaked. Is it the weather or is something wrong?"

Tina shook her head.

Grandmother Sarah regarded her critically. "Your nose is growing, child. Fibbing is not becoming."

"I didn't say a word."

"Exactly."

"Okay, there is a problem. But it's nothing for you to worry about."

Sarah's eyes narrowed and she retorted spiritedly, "Of course it is. I'm your friend, aren't I? If something has you all in a tizzy, then the rest of us certainly want to help."

Tina didn't have the heart to explain that the rest of them *were* the problem. Grandmother Sarah was only the tip of the iceberg. There was slightly dotty Aunt Juliet, also no relation, as well as little Billy and old Mr. Kelly, to say nothing of Sam's great-grandchildren, one of Bandit's descendants and Lady MacBeth, a parrot who had the vocabulary of a drunken sailor.

No matter how she looked at it, Tina admitted, it was not your typical household. But that didn't mean she was breaking the law, although clannish, well-moneyed Palm Beach seemed to have a whole encyclopedia of etiquette and a long list of specialized zoning regulations all its own.

It had been five years now, but she'd never quite gotten used to the transition she'd made from her barely middle class childhood in West Palm Beach to the wealthy island enclave across the bridge. Her three-year marriage to Gerald Harrington had given her instantaneous social status, financial security, an estate that edged the Atlantic Ocean and, most of all, a joyous, storybook love.

Gerald's accidental death in the crash of the company jet two years earlier had devastated her. At twenty-six, she was left rattling around in a huge old house, surrounded by staff who refused to even sit down and play a card game with her. They put her meals on the table, then retreated to await the tinkle of a bell. The cook would have been horrified if she'd known that Tina would have preferred to eat in the kitchen. The butler would have been equally shocked if she'd suggested he join her at the imposing dining room table. As a result of their stuffy sense of station, she'd been faced with an intolerable loneliness at the end of every long, tiring day she spent at Harrington Industries.

Then a year ago, just when she'd thought things were at their bleakest, Grandmother Sarah, Aunt Juliet and the rest had come along needing the kind of assistance and friendship she could easily offer. Now she felt as though her life were worth living again. No one was going to take that away from her.

"You got another one of those letters, didn't you?" Grandmother Sarah said, her sharp gaze falling on the paper that Tina had tossed defiantly on the table.

"Yes," she admitted, reluctantly conceding that there was no point in denying the obvious.

"Who's this one from?"

"The state."

"My, my. He is pulling out the big guns, isn't he?"

He, of course, was Drew Landry, her new neighbor and the man behind this letter and a whole series that had preceded it. The man was attacking her way of life with tactical efforts worthy of a marine commander and the persistence of a pit bull.

"I just don't understand it," Tina muttered. "What difference could it possibly make to Drew Landry if I have a few houseguests?"

Grandmother Sarah lifted her eyebrows. "Okay," Tina muttered defensively. "So you're not exactly house-guests in the traditional sense. You didn't drop in from Monte Carlo or London or Boston. You're not just here for the annual Red Cross Gala. I still don't see what business it is of his or the State of Florida."

"Why don't you talk to him, dear? Explain about all of this. I'm sure he's a reasonable man."

An image of Drew Landry flashed in Tina's mind. Her tall, dark, jet-setting neighbor with the formidable scowl and the well-toned, impressively proportioned body struck her as anything but reasonable. On the one occasion when they'd met, long enough for her to offer to pay for the window Billy had broken with the best-hit ball of his Little League career, Landry's extraordinary blue eyes had flashed angrily, the nostrils of his patrician nose had flared and his full, sensuous lips emitted a string of oaths her parrot would have envied. Tina, who was rarely intimidated, had literally quaked under the impact of his fury. It was not a scene she was anxious to repeat.

"I don't think talking to Mr. Landry will accomplish a thing. He seems pretty set in his ways."

"Fiddlesticks! How can a thirty-seven-year-old man be set in his ways?" Grandmother Sarah argued.

Tina shot her a startled look. "How do you know how old he is?"

"I read the papers. He's been in the gossip columns nearly every day since he got to town." She gave Tina a sly, assessing glance. "Quite a hunk, if you ask me."

"A hunk?" Tina snorted derisively. "Looks aren't everything, you know."

"Oh, I know that well enough, but if you ask me, you could use a hunk in your life. It's time you put Gerald behind you and got on with things. Juliet and I were discussing it just the other night. You're far too young to be shut away here with only us old folks for company."

"Billy's only thirteen," she reminded Sarah, "and my social life is just fine, thank you very much."

"If you're into—what's the word you use all the time about some of your lily-livered board members—wimps."

Tina's brown eyes flashed, but she couldn't put much spirit into her defense. "Martin is a very successful man. He is not a wimp."

"He does a fine job of impersonating one," Sarah declared. "How can you say that man's successful? He's living on his daddy's money. I'll bet he's never gone out and earned a dime himself. And the way he dresses…" She shook her head sadly. "I'll bet that man has never once gotten his hands dirty. Now what kind of a man is that?"

"We are not talking about Martin," Tina retorted in exasperation. She'd heard Sarah's opinions of her companion often enough. "We're talking about Drew Landry and his ridiculous notion that we're destroying his property value or something. He just bought the place three months ago, for heaven's sakes. He hardly needs to worry about the selling price now."

"What makes you think he's worried about his property value?"

"What other reason could he have for meddling in something that's none of his business?"

"I have no idea, but I still say you ought to talk to him and find out. You could settle this thing once and for all," Sarah suggested with a sudden gleam in her eyes. Tina eyed her nervously and waited for the rest. It didn't take long.

"In fact," Sarah said, "why don't you go over right this minute and invite him for dinner tonight? I'll bake one of my cherry pies. There's not a man alive who can resist warm cherry pie topped with homemade vanilla ice cream."

"Drew Landry strikes me as the type who'd only appreciate Cherries Jubilee and champagne."

Grandmother Sarah was obstinate as a mule. "I'm telling you, the cherry pie will do it. Go on, Christina Elizabeth," she persisted in her very best grandmotherly, don't-cross-me tone. "Before you lose your nerve."

"Lose it?" Tina muttered as she reluctantly set off across the sweeping lawn. "I don't have any nerve to lose. The man scares me out of my wits."

Then she thought about the stakes, about Sarah and Juliet and Billy and Mr. Kelly, to say nothing of the assorted pets, and a tiny flare of anger sparked to life in the pit of her stomach. She fanned it for all she was worth. By the time she'd slipped through a widening in the hedge—when Gerald had been a boy, his best friend had lived next door—she was ready to make Drew Landry rue the day he'd ever set out to destroy her perfectly happy if somewhat unorthodox household.

The gray-haired, tight-lipped butler who answered the door was so stiff she was afraid he'd shatter if he cracked a smile. He definitely was not the type to settle down and spend an evening playing gin rummy. She wondered if he and the man she'd finally fired, along with the cook, were related. They'd clearly been turned out of the same mold.

His narrowed eyes took in her skimpy, turquoise one-piece jumpsuit and he virtually sniffed his disapproval. She was surprised he didn't ask her to go around to the kitchen entrance.

"Mr. Landry is on the terrace, miss. If you'll follow me." It was less a suggestion than a command. Tina obeyed, trying to control a practically irresistible urge to giggle.

Even after five years in Palm Beach, during which she'd grown accustomed to the often ridiculous dictums of high society, it had never ceased to amaze her that the servants were sometimes even stuffier and more class conscious than their bosses. She'd seen chauffeurs stand by the family Mercedes or Cadillac or Lincoln on Worth Avenue and look down their haughty noses at each other, while their mistresses shopped in elegant boutiques or lunched together in fancy restaurants.

She didn't have time to explore this social phenomenon too closely because she was suddenly on the terrace. Mr. Landry was not sipping tea and eating fresh scones or using his cell to make million-dollar business deals as she'd half expected. Instead, he was swimming laps in a pool that curved like a lagoon amid an abundance of palm trees and bright yellow hibiscus. Her breath caught in her throat as she watched his lean, tanned body slice through the sparkling water with practiced ease, creating hardly a ripple…except along her spine, which she instinctively straightened in the hope the sensation would go away. It didn't.

Tina barely noticed when the butler left. Her eyes

traveled slowly from the shoulders that glistened in the late afternoon sun, taking in the muscles that moved with sleek grace, the long legs that kicked with controlled power. A wayward image of those legs tangling with her own in the heat of passion ripped into her mind creating a feverish tension. She sighed softly.

As the annoyingly wistful whisper of sound escaped, Drew Landry swam to the side of the pool and gazed straight into her eyes, the knowing cobalt blue of his taunting her as he lifted himself out of the water and stood before her like someone waiting to be admired.

The disarray of his damp black hair caught the sparks of afternoon sunlight like coal turned to diamonds. Rivulets of water ran down his muscled torso, lingered in the dark hairs that were matted on his chest, then continued over his flat stomach to be captured by the band of a barely decent, skin-hugging bathing suit. Tina was fascinated by those trails of water, her pulse beating ever faster as her gaze followed their path, then froze on that skimpy piece of material.

"Is there something you wanted?" The lazy drawl was filled with amused innuendo.

Tina shook her head, meeting laughing eyes.

"I mean yes," she mumbled, fighting embarrassment and a disturbing desire to run a finger along the tempting path created by that trail of water. She was not going to let Drew Landry have the upper hand for even a split second. She certainly was going to keep her hands to herself. She jammed them into her pockets, just to be sure.

"We have to talk," she said in the firm, decisive voice she'd trained herself to use when she wanted to tactfully persuade the board of directors of Harrington Industries to heed her advice.

Drew Landry lazily rubbed a towel over his awesome body, and Tina forced herself to look at the branch of lovely pale lavender orchids hanging from a tree just beyond his shoulder. In the end, though, she couldn't resist sneaking just one more peak. Grandmother Sarah was right. He was a hunk.

"We do?" he said skeptically. "Am I supposed to know why?"

"You're trying to destroy my family. I want to know what you're up to."

"My dear Mrs. Harrington..."

"So, then, you do remember me?"

He grinned, and her heart lurched in what had to be an infuriatingly Pavlovian reaction.

"How could I forget?" he was saying when she finally managed to concentrate. "Our first meeting was rather...inauspicious."

She gazed at him sharply. "You say that as though I were some sort of criminal you'd caught stealing the family silver. It was only a kitchen window, for heaven's sakes, and Billy didn't mean to do it."

"The window is forgotten. I'm more concerned with what you're doing to those poor people, to say nothing of the neighborhood. It's nothing short of criminal. My God, woman, you can't turn your home into a refuge for all the derelicts in the world. There are zoning laws, to say nothing of state regulations about that sort of thing."

"The laws are absurd and they don't apply anyway."

"The zoning laws may be ridiculous, but they exist nonetheless. As for the state regulations, they are designed to protect innocent people, no matter their background, from cranks."

"I am hardly a crank, and my friends are not derelicts," she replied heatedly. "They may have had a rough time, but they're honest, kind, wonderful people."

"Are they members of your family?"

"You mean legally?"

He grinned again, a dimple on his left cheek teasing her. Her traitorous heart skipped several beats. "That's generally the way it works," he said dryly. "Either by birth or marriage."

Captivated by the slow caress of the towel over his masculine body, Tina had trouble remembering the original question. She forced herself to concentrate on the conversation. Families. They'd been talking about families and whether she was related to Grandmother Sarah and the others.

"No. Of course not," she admitted at last, then added defiantly, "That doesn't mean I love them any less."

"Perhaps not. But it does mean they have no business living there, unless you can get a license to operate a congregate living facility."

"A congregate living facility?" she repeated in astonishment. "Is that what you think I'm doing?"

"Isn't it? How many nonfamily members do you have tucked away in the corners of that mansion of yours? Or can you even find them all?"

She shot him a scathing glare. "There are only three." She paused. "Well, four, if you count Billy, but he's only a child."

He seemed taken aback for the moment. He'd obviously thought there were dozens. "It's still three or four too many if they're not related," he finally said.

"Tell me," she said sarcastically, "is old Giles in there…?"

"Giles?"

"Giles. Henry. Whatever his name is. Your butler. Is he a member of your family?"

"Of course not, and his name is Geoffrey."

"Then I fail to see the difference."

"He's an employee."

She nodded sagely. "I see. You pay him, so that entitles him to live here. I don't pay my friends to live with me, so that's illegal. Have I got this down yet?"

"You're missing the point," he retorted impatiently, the grin fading. Her heart jolted one more time just the same. The reaction was getting downright irritating. You'd think she'd never seen a practically nude man before. Why didn't he put some clothes on?

She glared up at him. It was an incredibly long distance, even for her, and she was a taller-than-average five-foot-eight. Once her eyes met his, she was almost sorry she'd bothered. His dark eyes were very distracting, suggesting hidden depths and tantalizing mysteries. What was wrong with her? Was it possible to get sunstroke from a five-minute walk?

She forced her mind to seize yet another point that had been about to drift away and lashed back at him. "I'm not missing the point. You are. These people are my guests."

"Guests?" he repeated skeptically. "Are you trying to tell me you don't charge those poor souls to live there?"

"Mr. Landry!" Her voice rose and this time she had

absolutely no trouble staring disdainfully into his obnoxious, doubting eyes. She drew herself up to her full height and, despite her casual attire, managed to look every bit the corporate executive she was.

"My late husband built Harrington Industries into one of the top corporations in the country. Perhaps you've heard of it?" She regarded him questioningly. He nodded, his lips twitching with amusement. She continued, "I inherited that when he died. I have an M.B.A., take an active role in the day-to-day operation of the company and am chairman of the board. Our profits have doubled in the last two years. Our stock, of which I own a significant percentage, has tripled. Do you honestly think I need to earn extra pocket money by taking in boarders?"

He studied her curiously, as if he'd just discovered an alien creature on his lawn and was trying to understand its strange language. "Then why do you do it?"

"Because I like them, Mr. Landry. My parents are dead. I don't have a lot of family left in the world and the ones who are left tend to want the fortune I inherited, rather than my affection. On the other hand, the people who stay with me don't give a hang about the balance in my checking account. They buy the groceries when they can afford to. Grandmother Sarah cooks. Aunt Juliet does my correspondence, and Mr. Kelly tends to the lawn and the garden. Billy does his share of the chores, too."

"So they're servants, then. Why didn't you just say so?"

Tina stamped her foot, a purely feminine reaction that was so out of character it astonished her. The man was destroying her reason. The next thing she knew she'd be bursting into tears like some simpering female. She steeled herself against that awful possibility.

"You just don't see it, do you?" she snapped back. "They are not my servants. They are not my boarders. They are my friends, and you and your expensive legal eagles are not about to break up my home, if I have to go to court and adopt every last one of them."

She whirled around and started toward the house, then turned back and met his still-puzzled gaze. "By the way, Grandmother Sarah wants you to come to dinner tonight. God knows why, but she thinks you might like her homemade cherry pie."

"And you?"

"I think you're too damned pompous to want to eat with some people you obviously consider your inferiors."

"I'll be there at eight."

Tina stared at him in astonishment. He wasn't supposed to agree. He was supposed to laugh in her face. Maybe Grandmother Sarah was right after all. Maybe the man was a sucker for cherry pie. She noted the disconcerting gleam in his eyes as they traveled over the swell of her breasts and down to her long, slender legs, which were revealed all too enticingly by the jumper. She should have worn a demure suit and a strand of pearls. Instead, she hadn't even worn shoes. Her toes curled against the cool tiles on the shaded side of the terrace.

"Make it seven," she said at last. "Aunt Juliet goes to bed early and, if she eats too late, it upsets her stomach and keeps her up all night."

He chuckled and the sound washed over her like a cooling afternoon shower. It made her feel good. It should have made her feel rotten, she told herself stoutly. In fact, she shouldn't be affected at all. The insufferable Mr. Landry was not deserving of one more instant's worth of worry or consideration. He certainly should not be stirring up her blood this way.

She tried telling herself that again when she was soaking in scented bubble bath, and once more when she was dressing in a bright yellow cotton sundress that bared her creamy shoulders and nipped in at her tiny waist. She repeated the statement as she uncoiled her auburn hair and let it fall to her shoulders in a tangle of curls. As she touched her cheeks with blusher and swept a coral lipstick over her full, sensuous lips, she murmured it aloud at her reflection in the mirror.

"You look lovely, dear," Grandmother Sarah noted with a satisfied smile when Tina walked into the kitchen.

"Oh my, yes," Aunt Juliet concurred. Mr. Kelly whistled approvingly.

"This Landry guy must be something special, huh?" Billy said, winking at Grandmother Sarah, who winked right back. "She never looks like this when Martin's coming over."

"Like what?" Tina said, looking down at her simple dress, which she'd bought off the rack at a sale a week before. She'd thought she was dressing down for the occasion. They were acting like she'd gone on a designer binge and outfitted herself for a date with somebody really important, instead of a meal at home with a man she didn't even like.

"Sexy," Bill responded. Grandmother Sarah and Aunt Juliet nodded enthusiastic agreement.

"Absolutely perfect. He won't be able to resist you," Grandmother Sarah gushed.

"Damn it!" Tina muttered. "What is wrong with all of you? I am not interested in Drew Landry. I am only interested in ending this ridiculous vendetta of his."

"Of course you are, dear," Grandmother Sarah said, and patted her hand consolingly. Aunt Juliet, who was as romantic as her namesake, chuckled delightedly, and Billy left the room whistling an off-key version of "Here Comes the Bride."

Tina wondered if maybe Drew Landry weren't right after all. Maybe she should toss these people straight out on their ears.

Except, perhaps, for Mr. Kelly. He was very good with the garden, and his huge, home-grown tomatoes were sinfully delicious. She couldn't give those up.

As for the rest, they were flat-out meddling.

Just like family, she thought with a sigh.

Chapter Two

When the doorbell rang just as the grandfather clock in the hallway chimed seven, Tina jumped nervously and began whipping the potatoes with enough force to stir concrete. She was hoping that one of the other people who lived in the house would have enough sense to answer the door, leaving her in the kitchen where she'd be safely out of Drew Landry's sight...perhaps until after dessert had been served. If Grandmother Sarah was right, he'd be in a much more amenable mood by then. She doubted if he'd be any less intimidating.

She'd discovered this afternoon that the man didn't just scare her to death because of his temper. He also attracted her in a purely male-female sort of way that had been so totally unexpected it made her very nervous. She did not think a rational woman would be drawn to a man who'd been demonstrating the compassion and single-mindedness of a steamroller. Never in her life had she met anyone who could stir her anger and her blood at the same time. Drew Landry's bold arrogance infuriated her, yet she couldn't deny that he also stirred her heartbeat to a wild, exciting tempo. The conspiratorial matchmaking that seemed to be going on around the house tonight, and the all-too-knowing hints about her own intentions toward Drew Landry, hadn't done a thing to calm her nerves. She felt like an aging spinster faced with an unwanted blind date and surrounded by a hopeful family that was inclined to prod her toward the altar no matter the suitability of the man.

The doorbell chimed again, and this time Grandmother Sarah gave her a penetrating look. "Aren't you going to get the door, dear?"

"I'm in the middle of fixing the potatoes. Maybe Mr. Kelly…"

"He went back upstairs to change. His clothes were covered with mud from the garden."

"Billy, then."

"Do you think that's wise? I mean he did break the man's window. It might get the evening off to a bad start. I could go, but the pies…"

"Oh, darn," Tina muttered grumpily. "I'll get the door."

"Remember to smile, dear. You can catch more flies with honey than you can with vinegar."

"Does the same hold true for a snake?"

"Tina!"

"Oh, I know," she said with a sigh. "I'll be nice to the man. Just remember when this whole thing blows up in our faces that this was your idea."

Sarah chose to ignore the gibe. "Be sure to offer him a drink. A man's always more receptive after he's had a nice drink to soothe his nerves."

"Should I offer to give him a massage, too?"

"Tina!" This time Sarah, who could feign the Southern gentlewoman, sounded properly scandalized, and Tina felt guilty right down to her toes.

"Sorry. I was just joking."

The impatient chiming of the doorbell for the third time sent Tina scurrying down the hall through the tiled foyer to the door. She swung it open to find Drew Landry glaring at the magnificent, intricately carved wood with its stained-glass inserts as though it personally were responsible for holding him up. It was too much to hope that he would have gotten angry and left.

"Am I too early?"

From Tina's point of view, the twenty-second century would have been too early, however she said only, "No. Of course not. I was in the kitchen."

"Oh?" He lifted his brows with an infuriating expression of skepticism that made her want to stamp her foot again—right on top of his. "Cook's night off?"

Amber eyes immediately sparked with anger. Talk about getting things off to a bad start. "I don't have a cook," she said stiffly. "Nor do I have a butler. As I explained this afternoon, we do our own work around here."

"How very democratic of you."

She studied him curiously. "Are you always such a stuffed shirt?"

Blue eyes bored into her, and suddenly a grin appeared on his very sensuous mouth. Kissing that mouth could prove to be very exciting, she decided thoughtfully.

And absurdly dangerous, she added very quickly.

"Straightforward thing, aren't you?" he said, and she knew it wasn't exactly meant as a compliment. She smiled at him cheerfully anyway.

"I try to be."

"Do you suppose I could come in, or do you want me to dine out here?"

"Actually I could send Aunt Juliet out with a plate," Tina said after thoughtful consideration.

He shook his head with greatly exaggerated sorrow. "Mrs. Harrington, I'm truly sorry."

Tina stared at him, thoroughly puzzled by his unexpectedly sympathetic tone. "About what?"

"Your failure to graduate from finishing school."

"I didn't go to finishing school."

"Ah. That explains it, then."

"Explains what?"

"Your unorthodox manners."

At that, Tina did blush. Her parents might have grown up on the wrong side of the tracks by Drew Landry's high and mighty standards, but they would have been horrified by her behavior. For that matter, so would Grandmother Sarah and Aunt Juliet. She had invited the man to dinner, even if it had been against her better judgment. Now that he was here in her home—or on her doorstep to be more precise—she was behaving like an ill-mannered, spoiled brat.

"I'm the one who's sorry, Mr. Landry. Please," she said, holding the door open. "Come in."

She led him into the living room, which was the one room in the stately old house that she absolutely hated. It still had heavy, burgundy velvet drapes, dark Oriental carpets and solid antique furniture that was totally out of keeping with the airy, tropical Florida setting and the rambling, Spanish-style house. It had been Gerald's favorite room, though, and, while he'd allowed her to do as she pleased with the rest of the house, he'd remained adamant about keeping this room the way it was. He'd told her once that it reminded him of his grandparents' home in Boston. Because of that sentimental tie she hadn't yet been able to bring herself to redecorate in a style more suited to her own informal taste.

"What a charming room," Drew said, his gaze lingering on the mahogany bookshelves lined with expensively bound volumes of the classics. Either he had borderline taste, Tina thought, or he had gone to finishing school and passed the elementary course in polite chitchat that she'd missed.

"Isn't it?" chimed in a whispery, disembodied feminine voice.

"Aunt Juliet?" Tina said, instantly on guard. "Where are you?"

"Over here," the voice replied.

"Over where?"

"Behind the drapes."

Tina sighed. Apparently it was going to be another one of Aunt Juliet's less than conventional nights. "Why?"

Sparkling brown eyes, peering out from behind wire-rimmed glasses that had slipped to the end of a pert nose, appeared at the edge of the drapes. "I was watching for Mr. Kelly."

"Mr. Kelly is upstairs."

"Oh," Aunt Juliet said, sighing in disappointment. "I was so hoping to see him tonight."

"You will see him, Aunt Juliet," Tina said patiently, wondering just what Drew was going to make of this scene. She and the rest of the household had gotten used to Aunt Juliet's whimsical departures from reality, but to an outsider already expecting the worst she must seem decidedly odd. "He'll be down for dinner shortly."

"Oh, good," Juliet said happily, slipping into the room and catching sight of Drew. She tilted her head at an inquisitive angle to get a better look at him and smoothed her sedate black dress down over her ample figure. Aunt Juliet had dressed in mourning since her own husband's death thirty-five years earlier, and not even Tina's gaily-colored Christmas and birthday offerings had been able to tempt her out of her somber attire. The gifts were still hanging in Juliet's closet. Now she touched her fingers lightly to the wisps of fading brown hair that were escaping from the braided coil on top of her head.

"And who is this?" she asked, staring at Drew with interest.

"This is Mr. Landry, Aunt Juliet. You remember, we invited him for dinner."

"Well, of course I remember. I'm not senile yet," she grumbled. "How do you do, Mr. Landry? Tina has told us so much about you."

"Really?"

"Yes. I'm sure you'll be very happy together. Tina is such a lovely girl. We're all quite fond of her."

Tina choked and tried to think of some urgent crisis that might require her immediate attention. Unfortunately, the only crisis seemed to be right here. She glanced sideways at Drew to see how he was taking the unexpected announcement of their betrothal. His gaze was sliding over her, an appreciative gleam building in his eyes, an amused quirk playing about his lips. He looked satisfied.

"Yes, she is lovely," he said, taking her hand and bringing it to those lips. They were just as soft, just as sensuously persuasive as she'd imagined. In fact, their touch was so disturbing that Tina wanted to jerk her hand away, but he was holding it with just enough pressure to prevent her from doing it. His mouth caressed the back of her hand, then the inside of her wrist, and currents of awareness ripped unexpectedly through her like an unexpected bolt of lightning. She had the oddest sensation that the storm between them was beginning and that it was destined to be a wildly passionate one.

"A drink," she mumbled, working her hand loose from his grasp as she caught the despicable, knowing laughter in his eyes. "Aunt Juliet, would you like some sherry?"

"That would be lovely."

"Mr. Landry?"

"Scotch, please."

"With water? Soda?"

"No. Straight, on the rocks."

Naturally he'd want it straight, she thought as she went to the bar. Frankly, she wouldn't mind a straight swallow of the stuff herself, she thought, noting that if today had been any indication, the man definitely seemed to have the potential to drive her to drink. The thought held a definite appeal. Maybe then, with a strong drink under her belt, she wouldn't notice that her hand was still shaking or that there was an intense, white-hot sensation settling low in her abdomen.

Martin, damn him, had never stirred such feelings in her, she thought with an irrational surge of fury. Come to think of it, Martin had never kissed her hand.

He'd settled for ending each date with a chaste peck on the cheek.

Much as she hated to admit it, Grandmother Sarah was probably right about Martin. He wasn't the right man for her. Not after Gerald. They might share the same social circle and the same interests, but her evenings with him were less exciting than the ones she spent playing cutthroat Scrabble with Mr. Kelly and Aunt Juliet.

Already she knew that Drew Landry was definitely more exciting than a Scrabble game. He would never settle for a chaste peck on the cheek. The man was as bold and greedy as a pirate. His lips would maraud hers, his tongue plundering her mouth for every wildly stirring sensation.

As she handed him his drink and caught the predatory gleam in his eye once again, she knew that he would accept nothing less than total possession. The thought, complete with more of those enticingly sensual images, sent a shudder through her. Her brain obviously had not been speaking to her body lately. Otherwise her hormones would not be reacting with such ridiculous abandon to a man that she'd already ascertained was a domineering, class-conscious jerk, out to ruin her life and send her dearest friends packing.

Dinner, she decided, was going to be very interesting. The whole evening was potentially explosive. If the first few minutes were anything to go by, it was also going to seem interminably long.

She decided to leave Drew alone with Aunt Juliet and try to hurry dinner along. Excusing herself, she raced back to the kitchen.

"Is it ready yet?"

"Another few minutes," Sarah said. "How is it going?"

"Aunt Juliet is entertaining him."

Sarah's eyebrows lifted. "Oh, my. Perhaps you should get back."

"Don't worry. She can't do much more harm. She's already informed him that she thinks we'll be very happy together."

Sarah brightened. "That's wonderful. I must admit the thought had crossed my mind, too."

"Oh, for heaven's sakes. You don't even know the man," Tina grumbled. "Will you stop matchmaking and get dinner on the table. I want him out of here."

"Dear, he just arrived, and the whole point of this evening is to show him that he doesn't have to worry about having us for neighbors."

"I think we've already lost that argument. Aunt Juliet was hiding behind the drapes when he arrived."

Sarah shrugged. "He can't possibly make too much out of that. Now if she'd been running through the neighborhood naked…"

Tina shuddered. "Don't even say it."

"Christina, you know perfectly well I was only trying to make a point. Juliet is a lady. She would never do that," Sarah huffed indignantly. She paused thoughtfully. "And I don't think Mr. Kelly is likely to do it anymore, either. He loves those new pajamas you gave him after the first time he went for a midnight stroll in the altogether."

"Thank goodness we stopped him from sleepwalking before he got off the estate."

"No," Sarah chided. "Thank goodness we caught him before he caught his death of cold running around in the middle of the night."

She dished up a bowl of Mr. Kelly's fresh green beans and handed them to Tina. "Put these on the table, dear, and then call everyone. Dinner's ready."

Tina got Billy and Mr. Kelly first, then went back to the living room for Drew and Aunt Juliet. She found them bent over the Scrabble board.

"There is no such word, Mr. Landry," Aunt Juliet was protesting vehemently.

"Of course, there is. You're just mad because I got to use my *q* and my *x* in the same word with double points," he teased.

"Mr. Landry, don't you try to cheat an old lady. *Quick* does not have an *x* in it."

His brow creased in a frown, and he gazed at her uncertainly. Only Tina caught the gently teasing laughter in his eyes. "Are you sure?"

"It's a good thing you're an executive," Juliet consoled.

"Oh? Why is that?"

"So you can hire an assistant to spell for you."

Drew laughed heartily at the sharp retort. To Tina's amazement, he actually seemed to be having a good time. In fact, he didn't seem the least bit stuffy, which was more than a little disconcerting. She could fight an attraction to a man who disapproved of her friends. She wasn't at all sure she could do battle with a man who was fitting in like one of the family.

"I must have been thinking of *quixotic*," he said,

casting a significant glance at Tina, who scowled back at him.

"I may be a bit idealistic, but I am also very practical, Mr. Landry," Tina said. "That's why I'd like to invite you to come to dinner before it gets cold."

"Is Mr. Kelly there?" Aunt Juliet inquired in a whisper to Tina.

Tina grinned at her. From the moment that Jacob Kelly had moved in, Aunt Juliet had been smitten. So far, though, her love had gone unrequited. "He's there."

"Do I look okay?"

"You look positively lovely," Drew chimed in, gallantly offering her his arm. "Let's go make this Mr. Kelly of yours insanely jealous. Perhaps we should tell him that I've made you a proposal of marriage and that you're seriously considering it."

Aunt Juliet giggled like a schoolgirl and blushed becomingly. "Why, Mr. Landry, you devil. You know perfectly well you're much too young for an old woman like me. Besides, whatever would Tina think?"

He gazed over at Tina, his blue eyes warmly appraising, and her heart turned another somersault.

"Oh, I don't think she'd mind loaning me out to a friend just this once. Would you, dear?"

"Of course not, *dear*," she retorted sweetly, then wondered if she'd feel quite so charitable if the friend were thirty and gorgeous, instead of a slightly faded, if charming seventy-two. It was probably a question best left unanswered.

In the dining room, Tina performed the introductions and tried to ignore the way Grandmother Sarah was openly assessing Drew and nodding approvingly.

Clearly, if things were to be left up to her, Tina's fate would be sealed. Aunt Juliet might have made a slightly dazed miscalculation about the relationship between Tina and her guest, but Sarah was sound of mind and very quick. She was perfectly capable of launching a series of romantic maneuvers that would land Tina and Drew in front of a minister before brunch next Sunday. Since Drew had no way of knowing what he was up against, it was up to Tina to dodge Sarah's carefully planned snares.

She missed the first one.

No sooner had she been seated in her usual place than Sarah was nudging Billy away from his regular chair on her left and urging Drew toward it. The quickly executed maneuver put Drew's long legs within mere inches of Tina's. In fact, if she shifted only slightly toward the radiating heat of his flesh, their knees would be touching. She had the darnedest urge to slip her foot out of its sandal and run it up the hard muscle of his calf. Instead, she picked up her crystal water glass with trembling fingers and took a deep swallow, wondering if it might not be far wiser to douse herself with the icy water.

Drew suddenly gasped and jerked backward so quickly his chair almost toppled over. "What was that?"

For a horrifying instant, Tina wondered if her foot had followed her instincts after all. Then she glanced under the table and, with a sigh of relief, saw that her shoe was still on her foot where it belonged. A further survey caught Aster slinking away.

"It was the cat," she said.

"Which one?" Billy wanted to know, before Tina could shut him up.

"How many do you have?" Drew asked.

"Let's see," Billy began. "There's Jake and Lucifer and Marian and…"

"It was Aster," Tina said quickly, but not quickly enough.

"There are eight altogether," Billy said cheerfully.

"Eight?" Drew gulped, then sneezed. And sneezed again. His eyes started watering.

"Bless you," Sarah and Juliet said in unison.

"Thank you."

"Wait," Billy said. "There are nine now, aren't there, Tina? I'd forgotten about the one that Tiger brought home yesterday."

Drew appeared stunned. "My Lord!"

"Mr. Landry!" Grandmother Sarah protested.

"Sorry, ma'am," he said, and Tina had to restrain a chuckle. She wondered if Drew had been chastised that effectively since he'd left the cradle. Considering the fierce scowls of which he was capable, she doubted it.

"Don't you like cats, Mr. Landry?" Aunt Juliet said. "That could be a bit of a problem. Tina loves them so."

"It's not that I don't like them. I'm allergic to them." He sneezed again, as if to emphasize the point.

Tina briefly considered rounding every one of them up and bringing them into the dining room, but Drew's earlier assessment of her manners kept her from fueling his criticism.

"Billy, get Aster out of here, please," she requested. "And make sure the others are in one of the back rooms or upstairs someplace."

"What about Panther?"

Drew's eyes widened considerably. "You have a panther here?"

"Of course not," Billy said disgustedly. "Panther is a dog."

There was a sudden twinkle in Drew's eyes, and his lips curved into a grin. "Obviously. How foolish of me. I hesitate to ask, but is Panther the only dog?"

Tina shrugged. "He was yesterday. It's hard to say today. Sometimes he brings home friends."

"Naturally," Drew said dryly.

Once the animals had been hidden away, dinner went relatively smoothly. To Grandmother Sarah's smug satisfaction, Drew ate two helpings of everything, including the cherry pie, and exclaimed over the fresh vegetables from Mr. Kelly's garden.

"Compost," Mr. Kelly informed him. "You have to have good compost."

"I'm sure Mr. Landry isn't interested in how you fertilize the garden," Tina interrupted.

"What's that?" Mr. Kelly asked loudly, and Tina realized he'd left his hearing aid upstairs again.

"I said that Mr. Landry probably doesn't care about fertilizer."

"Course he does," Mr. Kelly retorted, scowling at her. "A man can never know too much about fertilizer. How else do you expect him to grow decent vegetables?"

"I'm sure Mr. Landry doesn't grow his own vegetables. He probably has them shipped in seasonally."

"As a matter of fact, I do," Drew said, his gaze challenging hers. Cool blue ice taunting amber fire. "From my farm in Iowa."

Tina's mouth dropped open. "You own a farm?"

"I was born on one. My father still lives there."

"Why, that's wonderful," Grandmother Sarah said, when Tina couldn't seem to think of a single thing to utter to a man who'd just destroyed every preconceived notion she had about him.

She had figured that Drew Landry had grown up attending the best schools in Europe, playing squash or polo with princes and spending his summers on the Riviera courting beautiful young heiresses. That was the lifestyle of most of her neighbors. From the late 1800s when Henry Morrison Flagler had built the first railroad into South Florida, the city had been the resort of the wealthy. Even in the early days hotel suites at the Royal Poinciana had gone for one hundred dollars a night at the height of the season. She'd figured Drew for one of those whose families had been ensconced here for generations. Instead, he was a farmer. Astonishing!

"I've always thought a man who understands the earth is much wiser than those fellows who spend all their time tinkering around with computers and that kind of nonsense," Sarah continued, ignoring Tina's increasingly stunned expression. Harrington Industries had been built on the fortunes of the tech boom, Tina groused mentally. You'd think Sarah would at least feign approval of the company that kept food on their table.

"The earth will be here long after all these mechanical gizmos break down," Sarah said, returning Tina's scowl with a defiant look of her own.

"That's just what my father used to say," Drew

agreed, still staring into Tina's flashing eyes with an amused, penetrating look that said volumes about what he was reading in her mind.

Grandmother Sarah obviously caught the flare of sparks arcing between the two, because she hopped out of her chair and began bustling around. "Come on, Juliet, let's clean up these dishes."

"I'll clean up," Tina said. "That's my job."

"Not tonight, dear. You and Mr. Landry go out on the terrace and enjoy the breeze. There's a full moon tonight," Sarah added pointedly.

Juliet sighed and gazed wistfully at Mr. Kelly. "Oh, my, yes. It's very romantic."

Tina tried one last time. "Why don't all of you go on outside then? Billy will help me with the dishes."

Billy groaned, but it didn't matter anyway. She might as well have been talking into the wind for all the attention they paid her as they scurried off to the kitchen carrying plates and glasses.

Drew stood up and offered her his hand, an all-too-enticing gleam in his eyes. "Come on, Mrs. Harrington," he said in a low, provocative voice that sent a flurry of sparks cascading down her spine. "Let's not disappoint them."

Disappoint them? She wanted to strangle them.

Chapter Three

Tina reluctantly led the way out to the terrace, where a strong ocean breeze had swept in at sunset to make the palm trees sway and whisper. The black velvet of the sky was scattered with diamond sparkles. The air smelled of salt spray and the sweetness of tropical flowers. It was a night for romance, which made it about as dangerous for her to be out here alone with Drew Landry as it had been for Adam to be in the Garden of Eden with Eve. She had one edge on Adam, though. She was aware of the potential dangers.

"Let's take a walk," Drew suggested.

"Where?" Tina's immediate caution brought an amused smile to his lips.

"Your tone's not very flattering," he taunted. "You sound as though you think I might be planning to skip the review by DCF and take you straight to the gallows myself."

Tina was not worried about the gallows. She was concerned about something far worse. In fact, by comparison, the gallows would have been a quick and easy way to go. Spending secluded time with Drew Landry in an atmosphere as ripe for seduction as this one seemed like torture.

"You haven't exactly done a lot to encourage my trust," she responded.

He gazed down at her with his blue eyes. A tanned finger reached over and gently followed the curve of her cheek, leaving behind a path of fire. She was as much startled by the touch's tenderness as by the sensation it aroused.

"Let's see if we can't change all that," he said softly. "Tonight I've discovered that I want very much for you to trust me."

Her breath caught in her throat and she asked in a choked whisper, "Why?"

"Because you intrigue me, Tina Harrington. You're not what I expected at all. You're not like any woman I've ever known. You're like fire and ice, scratchy wool and soft satin, a prickly cactus and a delicate orchid. The contradictions are fascinating."

"Is that your poetic way of saying that after the women who fall all over you, I'm a challenge?"

Her spirited response drew another high-voltage smile. "Perhaps. Couldn't we start over?"

As the promise of his words whispered over her, Tina felt an aching tug deep inside. She couldn't draw her eyes away from his gaze, though she wanted to desperately. She felt as though she were losing her will, as though she were watching her hard-won independence slip away. But when a smile revealed his wicked dimple and he added questioningly, "Deal?" she could only nod and fight the urge to kiss that dimple.

"Then let's start by taking that walk."

Silently, they walked around the house and crossed the narrow road to the beach, where the ocean pounded against the shore with the same wild turbulence that stirred Tina's blood. The wind whipped her hair about her face and teased her flesh in a way that hinted strongly at the effect Drew's deft touches might have. They went down the wooden stairs, and at the bottom, Tina braced herself on the weathered railing, slipping off her shoes before she and Drew set off across the soft, damp sand.

Their way was lit by a spectacular full moon hanging low on the horizon, reminding her once more that it was, indeed, a night made for lovers. And here she was with an attractive, surprisingly charming man who—just as surprisingly—made her blood sizzle.

Despite the pounding of her heart and the responsiveness of her reawakening body, she couldn't forget that the real reason they were together had nothing to do with love or even physical attraction. They had been brought together by his intention to force Sarah, Juliet and the rest out of her house. How could she and Drew start over with that between them?

They began walking hand in hand—she wasn't quite sure how *that* had happened—their silence a counterpoint to the crashing waves. Suddenly, Tina stopped in her tracks, determined to make him see what he was setting out to destroy. Surely there was some compassion in him, some sense of decency that would respond to her pleas. But when she looked up at him, ready to fight for her friends and her way of life, the expression in his eyes captured her and held her silent.

"Tina," he said quietly, her name floating away on a gust of wind just as his mouth came down to meet hers. His mouth was oh-so-soft yet commanding as he took gentle possession, waiting for her to relax into the kiss, persuading her lips to part. His tongue teased against her mouth until her body screamed for him to claim her more intimately. As if he'd read her mind, the moist velvet of his tongue darted inside, taunting her with yet another suggestion of the powerful, shattering intimacies that could rise between them.

From the moment that he'd taken her in his arms, Tina had sensed an inevitability that had shaken her. This man was a danger to her happiness, her serenity. Yet her body had responded to him in a way that spoke of acceptance and yearning and a desire so intense, so all-consuming it was like nothing she had ever known before, not even with Gerald. With Gerald she had felt respected, even loved, but she had never experienced this shattering femininity.

When the kiss ended at last—far too soon, yet not nearly soon enough—only his hands on her arms stilled her trembling. Nothing short of an explosive joining, however, could ease the throbbing ache she felt and she knew it. Dear Lord, how well she knew it! The realization terrified her and made her more skittish than ever.

"I'm sorry," he apologized, then shook his head, unable to keep the sparkle out of his eyes. "No, I'm not. I've wanted to do that from the minute I saw you this afternoon."

He paused thoughtfully. "Come to think of it, I think I even wanted to do it weeks ago, when you came over and stood there valiantly defending Billy in front of my shattered window, then demanded that I return his baseball. I'm fascinated by women with spirit."

The solemnity of his words reached in and captured

a tiny part of Tina's heart, but still she was puzzled. "If you felt that way, then why did you stir up all this fuss over the way I live? You had to know it would infuriate me." She tilted her head to study him more closely. "Or were you one of those kids who showed affection by pulling a girl's hair?"

He winced. "I hope my approach has always been much smoother than that. I gave my first love a bouquet of dandelions. We were seven. I've graduated to roses now."

"I'd have settled for dandelions," Tina retorted. "It would have been a whole lot better than a letter from DCF. That was not the best way you could have demonstrated your interest."

"Actually one thing has nothing to do with the other."

"It certainly does. You can't reject part of me and want the rest."

"Oh, can't I?" he said dryly. Then he sighed. "Okay. On a rational level, you're probably right. But I didn't understand before."

"Understand what?"

"What was really going on at your house. The way it was presented to me, it all sounded sinister."

Tina couldn't restrain the grin that spread over her face and lit her eyes. "Like in some gothic novel?"

"Not quite that dark and mysterious, perhaps," he admitted. "Right after I moved in, I got a couple of anonymous letters, a phone call or two. I started asking around, and a few of your other neighbors confirmed that you'd been taking in all these strange people since your husband died, giving them the run of the place. They implied they were worried about you, but now it's evident they were more concerned about what it might do to the neighborhood, if somebody didn't put a stop to it. You're a powerful lady. They weren't willing to risk your wrath. They figured I'd have nothing to lose." His expression turned grim. "I also have something of a reputation for dealing with situations like this."

"So you decided to take my lifestyle on as your own personal crusade without even talking to me?"

"Well, the evidence did seem to be pretty clear-cut. The people were living here and the zoning laws are very specific about these being single family dwellings, not some sort of glorified rooming houses."

"Except for the servants' quarters, of course," she countered.

He caught the dry note in her voice. "Of course."

"What about the state? Why did you have to drag them into it?"

"You may not believe this, but I was actually concerned about the people you have staying here. I kept thinking how I'd feel if it were my father living in some unlicensed place that nobody'd checked out."

"What?" Tina couldn't have been more shocked by his unspoken innuendo. It was as if he'd flat-out accused her of being a mass murderer. She missed the odd, faraway look that came into his eyes and shadowed their usual brightness. "That's the most ridiculous thing I've ever heard. Did you think I was holding them prisoner and starving them all to death, for heaven's sakes?"

He had the good grace to look embarrassed. "Well, I had no way of knowing what kind of crazy crank you might be, or whether they were old and rich and senile. Nobody bothered to tell me you were a feisty, sophisticated lady with a quirky sense of humor. They said you were a widow, that you'd been a little odd since your husband's death. For all I knew, you could have been getting senile, as well."

"At my age?"

"They didn't mention your age either, and Gerald, after all, was quite a bit older."

"He wasn't *that* old." She stared innocently up at him. "He was about your age, as a matter of fact."

"Touché."

"Of course, you saw no need to check any of this for yourself? You'd make a terrific journalist," she said sarcastically.

He winced as her shot hit its mark. "I knew that senility wasn't the problem when you came over to defend Billy. Still, you could have been bilking a bunch of sweet old folks for every penny they had. You wouldn't be the first person to do something like that. Some of the best con artists look absolutely harmless, but they prey on the helpless."

"Does Grandmother Sarah strike you as helpless? Or Mr. Kelly?"

"No. Of course not." His eyes sparkled wickedly. "Then, again, there is Aunt Juliet..."

"I am not bilking Aunt Juliet. She doesn't have anything to steal. And don't you kid yourself, she's not as helpless as she may seem. You saw what happened when you tried to cheat at Scrabble."

"I know that now," he said softly. "And I've seen you with those people. I know that you really do love them and that they love you."

"If you'd taken the time to find that out first before

going off half-cocked, it could have kept me out of this mess." She stared up at him with eyes that were suddenly tear-filled. She hated showing him even this tiny sign of weakness, but she was angry and frustrated and scared. Her life had been lonely for so long after Gerald died and now, just when she'd found happiness again, it was threatened.

"Now you've gone and ruined everything," she murmured.

He brushed away the single tear that rolled down her cheek. "Come now. There's no real harm done."

"No real harm?" She regarded him disbelievingly. "For one thing, do you have any idea what this kind of publicity could do to Harrington Industries? The board will think I'm off my rocker and try to yank the chairmanship away from me. There are a few of them who've already got a candidate in mind and have been looking for any excuse to push him forward. You've just given them a dandy one."

"They don't know a thing about this. It hasn't been in the papers yet."

Tina regarded him as if he'd lost his mind. "How long do you think it will take for some ambitious reporter to discover that the state thinks I'm operating an unregulated foster home for wayward kids and stray adults?"

"I'll go in tomorrow and withdraw the complaint. That should be the end of it."

"You really did grow up on some piddly little farm in Iowa, didn't you?"

"Actually, it was a pretty big farm. With hundreds of acres of corn," he retorted with that beguiling twinkle back in his eye. Tina glowered at him. He was not making her feel one bit better.

"My point is that you're naive if you believe the state will simply say thanks for telling us about the mistake and go on to something else. They've been under a lot of pressure lately for not being too thorough in the past. I'm a well-known lady. It will be a terrific publicity coup. They can show they weren't afraid to take on a big shot. Just to be safe, they're going to have a whole crew of inspectors crawling all over the place to be sure I'm not a raving lunatic and that the estate meets a zillion dumb sanitation requirements..."

He grinned at her rantings and, despite herself, her anger faded just a bit. "No problem. I'll vouch for your sanity and you must have half a dozen bathrooms in that place," he said encouragingly.

"Ten, actually, but that won't stop them from sending inspectors down here from Tallahassee to count them. What if they make Sarah and Juliet and the rest of them leave? They don't have any place to go."

"Tina, that's not going to happen. I'm sure once you explain it to them, they'll understand. I do."

She gazed at him with renewed hope. If she could convince Drew Landry then maybe she could convince the state. "You do?"

"Well, I'm not exactly sure how they all landed on your doorstep, but I understand that there's nothing illegal about what you're doing. I doubt if you're even violating the zoning code. I'll back you up one hundred percent."

"Thanks. Will that keep me out of jail?" she asked sarcastically.

He patted her arm and, if it hadn't felt so good, she'd have hit him for being so patronizing. "Don't go getting hysterical," he soothed. "Nobody's going to jail."

"I wouldn't be so sure of that if I were you. Palm Beach has some mighty peculiar laws."

"And I'm sure you have some bright lawyers on staff at Harrington Industries. If you don't, I have a few myself, but," he said emphatically, tilting her chin until her gaze met his, "it is not going to come to that. I won't let it."

Tina sighed and wondered exactly when Drew Landry had set himself up as her protector. She wasn't sure she liked him in that role any better than she'd liked him as the enemy. "*You won't let it?* Did they hold an election and name you governor?"

"I may not be governor, but I do have a certain amount of clout."

"And you're planning to rush in and save my hide, a hide which wouldn't be in danger in the first place if you'd kept your nose on your side of the hedge?"

"You don't sound appreciative."

"I prefer to fight my own battles."

"Independence can get pretty lonely."

"Maybe so, but then you have no one to blame but yourself for the outcome."

"Do you object to letting me help at least?"

"I suppose not," she said so reluctantly that it brought yet another grin to his lips.

He drew her to the stairs leading up to the road and pulled her beside him on the bottom step. "If I'm going to help, I need to know everything. Tell me, how did they all come to be living with you? I mean they don't seem to be the kind of people you'd meet at a charity gala or on a cruise."

Tina explained about her meeting on the beach with Grandmother Sarah. "We got to talking and one thing led to another and she moved in the next day."

"You invited her home just like that? Without doing a security check?" He sounded horrified. "She could have been an ax murderer."

Tina glowered at him. "Does that sweet little old lady who just baked you a cherry pie strike you as an ax murderer?"

"Well, no," he admitted. "But in your position you can't be too careful."

Tina threw up her hands. "You're prejudging again. I thought you said you liked my friends now that you've gotten to know them."

"Well, I do, but it's because I've gotten to know them."

"You've talked to them for exactly two hours," she pointed out. "Are your instincts supposed to be better than mine?"

"No, but…"

Her eyes flashed dangerously. "If you say anything about your being a man and my being a woman, I will dump sand down your trousers."

"You are a woman," he noted dryly. "As for your threat, it raises some interesting possibilities."

"Never mind."

"Okay, let's forget about our respective abilities to judge character for the moment. Where did you meet up with Mr. Kelly?"

"He was my neighbor when I was growing up. He

was always like a surrogate grandfather to me. His wife died a few months ago, and all of his kids have moved away. I couldn't bear the thought of him in that tumble-down old house all by himself. He put up quite a fuss, said he'd lived there all his life and, by golly, he wasn't going to move out now." She mimicked Mr. Kelly's grumpy tone perfectly.

Drew chuckled.

"What's so funny?"

"I was just trying to imagine how you talked him into it."

"Well, it was a rather high-spirited conversation. I started out by telling him to stop being a stubborn old mule, and he told me to quit being an obstinate brat."

"Sounds like you were off to a typically diplomatic start."

"Then I wised up and began telling him how crummy my grounds looked. If there's one thing Mr. Kelly can't stand, it's weeds messing up a perfectly good landscape. When I told him the tomato vines were practically wilting because I didn't know what to do with them, he packed up his tools and moved the next day. He said he was only going to stay till he got things straightened out around here, but that was six months ago. I think he's realized things will never be completely straightened out here and he's terrified Aunt Juliet will start dabbling in his garden."

"What about Aunt Juliet? Where did you find her?"

"Actually she and Billy came together, a few weeks after Sarah. Billy broke into one of the Harrington Industries offices, and the police called me down to the station. I found out that he and his great-aunt were living on her Social Security check in a dump that wasn't fit for the rats who shared with them."

Tina's voice shook with indignation. "You should have seen it. It was a disgrace. The landlord—an even bigger rat—was charging them practically every penny she got from the government. That's why Billy had broken into the office. He was trying to find something he could fence to buy food and medicine for Juliet."

"So, of course, you dropped the charges and brought them home."

She lifted her chin defiantly. "What else was I supposed to do? Leave them there?"

"There are agencies—"

"Which are overburdened as it is. Besides, once you get caught up in that cycle, you never get out." She stared out at the ocean, then said softly, "I saw it happen to too many of my friends when I was growing up. I wasn't going to let it happen to Juliet and Billy."

She regarded Drew hopefully. "Billy's not a bad kid. You can see that, can't you?"

"He did break my window," he reminded her, but his tone was teasing.

"It was a great hit."

Drew chuckled. "It certainly was. Right straight into my kitchen. The cook is still shaking and threatening to quit."

"Is that why you called the authorities? So you could hang on to your cook?"

"I'd starve without her."

"I'm sure Grandmother Sarah would be thrilled to pieces to feed you."

"I'll keep that in mind."

"Will you really withdraw the complaint in the morning?"

"I told you I would."

"I'm coming with you."

"Still don't trust me, huh?" he taunted.

"It's not that. They may have questions that you can't answer."

He shrugged. "If I don't know the answer, I'll make one up."

"Terrific. Then you'll land in the cell next door to mine, charged with perjury."

"We could hold hands through the bars."

Tina's heart skipped a couple of beats. "Nice try, but no dice. I'm going with you."

"I'll pick you up at nine, and we can drive over to the DCF offices together."

"Maybe Sarah, Juliet and Mr. Kelly ought to come along. They could help explain."

Drew simply stared at her. "Are you crazy?"

"They're rational adults...well, most of them are," she corrected when his brow quirked skeptically. "Anyway, they have a perfect right to live anywhere they like."

"With the possible exception of a Palm Beach estate," Drew noted dryly.

His words, meant in jest, sent a shiver of dread over Tina. He was undoubtedly right. It was better if they remained safely at home. She shivered at the possibility that her household might very well be broken up if she and Drew were unsuccessful in the morning.

"Drew, what am I going to do if they say they can't stay?"

He put an arm around her and pulled her close. For a moment she allowed herself to revel in the sensations that closeness aroused. She felt safe—and threatened— all at the same time. Her body's response was all too disturbing, so she decided to pretend she didn't notice it. After several seconds, she realized that her powers of pretense must have deserted her. The sensations were there, stronger than ever, and the look in Drew's eyes was fueling them.

"You know what I think, Tina Harrington?" he said softly.

"What?" she asked shakily.

"That you're getting as much out of this arrangement as they are."

"Of course I am. I told you that. They're like family to me."

"But why would a lovely young woman like you need to take in strays to have a family? Surely there are men ready to serenade beneath your balcony, court you with lavish gifts, tempt you with romantic trips, fill all of those bedrooms with gorgeous children."

"A few," she agreed. "But that's not enough."

His eyes sparkled back at her wickedly. "It's not? Lord, woman, what do you want?"

She chuckled. "You know what I mean."

"No. Tell me."

"I never know if it's me they want or Harrington Industries," she confessed wistfully.

"I see."

Tina wondered if he did. Even as a teenager of limited financial means, she'd never had a doubt about her attractiveness to boys. She'd known they dated her because they found her pretty, with her shining, wavy hair, wide amber eyes and slender figure, or because they enjoyed her impish humor, or were challenged by her sharp wit. It certainly wasn't because she was rich.

The same had certainly been true when she'd met Gerald. She'd had nothing to offer him but the shrewd business acumen she'd been on the verge of attaining, her gentle manner and all of her love. For him, that had been more than enough.

But now she was worth a small fortune, and it tended to get in the way. When she saw a sparkle in a man's eyes, she was never sure whether it was a reaction to her perfume or the smell of her money.

So she had filled in the empty spaces in her life with people who needed her as a friend, not a wealthy benefactor or stepping-stone to corporate greatness. It also helped her to repay in some small way the wonderful things that had come her way when she had fallen in love with Gerald. It had been too late, by then, to help her parents. She was convinced they had died from struggling too long against life's hard knocks. Once they'd seen her happily settled, they had simply given up the fight, passing away within months of each other.

There were a lot of emotions at war within her these days. Anger at her parents' sad lot in life, gratitude for her own blessings, determination to make what she could of all that Gerald had left her despite the board of directors and a tremendous fear of being used. All but the last had made her strong. The fear had made her cautious.

It was that caution that told her she should run from Drew Landry while she still could. It was the strength that told her she needn't fear him or anyone. Except, perhaps, the DCF.

Settling for détente between her conflicting emotions, she said, "I think we should be getting back," and got to her feet. "They'll be wondering what happened to us."

"Judging from the look in Grandmother Sarah's eyes when we left, she'll be hoping she already knows exactly what happened to us," he replied as they went back to the estate.

Fortunately, it was too dark for him to see the blush that spread up her cheeks. "So you noticed that?"

"How could I miss it? She practically swept us out the door with a broom."

"Don't mind her. She's a bit of a romantic."

"So's Aunt Juliet, it appears. Think there's any chance for her and Mr. Kelly?"

"Not if she tries to put petunias in his vegetable garden. He'll go after her with a trowel, and then we really will be in trouble around here."

They had reached the terrace, and Drew stood looking as though he couldn't quite decide whether to go or stay. Tina wasn't about to help him out.

"I don't suppose you're going to offer me a nightcap?"

"I hadn't planned on it," she teased.

"If I asked for one, would you deny me?"

She shook her head and saw the smile on his lips just before they brushed oh-so-lightly across her own and sent waves of delightful, pulsing heat over her.

"Are you asking?" she said breathlessly.

"Nope," he said, giving her a jaunty wave as he strolled away. "It's no fun if you have to ask. See you in the morning, angel."

"See you," she said softly, her eyes following him until he'd slipped into the shadows and was lost to her view. She wrapped her arms around her middle and hugged, wondering at the strangely empty feeling that suddenly taunted her. The howl of the wind was suddenly lonely rather than exciting. Just a minute ago, she'd felt...what? Alive? Elated? Dangerously provocative?

Dangerous. That was the operative word here. Drew Landry represented danger and excitement and all the things she'd been missing. Until now, she'd had no idea that there was an empty space in her life that Grandmother Sarah and the others couldn't fill. She hadn't realized it until Drew had vanished into the shadows and left her alone again.

She turned around quickly and ran smack into someone who let out a groan at the impact.

"Mr. Kelly, I'm sorry," she apologized, then noted his pajamas and the dazed expression in his eyes. He was sleepwalking again.

"Come on, Mr. Kelly," she said gently, taking him by the hand. "Back to bed with you."

"Damn petunias," he muttered.

"Ssh. I won't let Aunt Juliet put her petunias anywhere near your garden."

He blinked and gave Tina a sharp glance. "What's that, girl? Speak up."

"I said I'd keep Aunt Juliet away from your garden."

"You'd better. That woman's a menace with those frilly little flowers of hers. I'll dig her her own damn garden if she wants one, long as she stays away from mine."

Tina smiled. "I'm sure she'll love that. Now you come on, Mr. Kelly. Let's get you back to bed."

"I can get back to bed perfectly well on my own, young lady." He scowled at her. "And don't you forget it."

Tina sighed as he marched toward the winding staircase, his back as straight as a royal palm and twice as stiff.

"I love you, Mr. Kelly," she murmured after his retreating form.

"So," came an interested female voice from the shadows. Tina couldn't see much, but she recognized that voice and its determined tone. "What did you think?"

"About what, Sarah?" she replied innocently.

"Don't go all vague on me, young lady. About Drew Landry, of course."

"He's interesting." It seemed a safe enough description.

Sarah emerged from her hiding place and smiled smugly. "I knew it. I knew he was perfect for you. Why that man has pizzazz and sex appeal and brains. You'd have to be plum crazy to miss it."

"I only said the man was interesting, for heaven's sakes. I didn't say a thing about his sex appeal."

"It was your tone, dear. There's interesting and then there's *interesting*."

Tina groaned. She'd known this was going to happen. "I am not discussing this," she said, stomping off into the house muttering under her breath.

"Interesting." She tried the word out, once out of earshot, then tried it again. "Interesting. *Interesting.* Oh, hell."

Chapter Four

When Drew rang the doorbell in the morning, the household was in its usual state of chaos. This kept Tina from fully appreciating the knockout effect of Drew in a dark suit, crisp white shirt and pin-striped tie, which was probably just as well. It was disconcerting to discover that he had the same devastating power over her senses at the crack of dawn as he did by moonlight.

"Where's my homework?" Billy shouted from the top of the stairs just as her gaze left the Italian leather shoes, moved up over the blade-sharp crease in Drew's trousers and took in the superb fit of the jacket over his magnificent shoulders. She was on her way back for another dreamy look into Drew's eyes when she was forced to drag her attention from the dressed-for-success man on her doorstep to the disorganized kid upstairs.

Billy and homework were not compatible. It was his firm conviction that it was contrived as a punishment for sins he'd committed in a past life and that he had no obligation to pay for mistakes he didn't remember making. On the rare occasions when he actually did his assignments, he either lost them on the way to school, forgot them, or spilled orange juice all over them. His grades weren't helped one bit.

"Did you do it?" Tina asked, gesturing for Drew to come in. Two of the cats immediately wound themselves affectionately around his ankles, rubbing hair all over the dark suit, while Panther sat eyeing him hopefully. Drew grimaced at the cats, sneezed three times, then gave the dog a distracted pat. All the while his gaze was focused so intensely on Tina that she felt a flush of heat stain her cheeks.

Oblivious to the electricity that crackled in the air in the foyer, Billy scowled down at her, indignation written all over his freckled face. "Of course I did it. It was an essay for English."

In that case, Tina thought, it was probably just as well that he couldn't find it. Billy seemed to have difficulty putting the English language down on paper. Not only was his spelling unrecognizable, he'd picked up a good bit of Lady MacBeth's vocabulary and wasn't above using it on his teacher for shock value.

Sixty-three-year-old Viola Maxwell was not unlike Grandmother Sarah in her ability to convey Southern gentility at its most innocent. She and Tina had had several conversations about Billy's rather unusual and provocative impressions of the world around him. Miss Maxwell seemed to feel that Billy would benefit from a sterner hand—and perhaps several years in a military school environment.

Tina couldn't bring herself to tell Billy to stop doing his English assignments. She'd tried to channel his creative energies in a less controversial direction, but when that hadn't worked, she had, on occasion, hidden the papers. This, however, was not one of those times. She'd been too distracted last night to even go looking for his homework to inspect it.

Billy regarded her all too knowingly. "You didn't hide it somewhere, did you?"

Tina stole a quick look at Drew and noted that he was watching the exchange with interest. She coughed and stared at the chandelier. The crystals needed cleaning. She'd have to remind Mr. Kelly. She didn't want Aunt Juliet climbing any more ladders. The last time, she'd kicked it over and dangled from the chandelier for five minutes before anyone had noticed.

"Why would I steal your homework?" Tina finally muttered, wishing they hadn't had this discussion in front of Drew. He already thought she was slightly, albeit intriguingly, off balance. This might not add much strength to her cause of presenting herself as a rational, intelligent woman.

"So old straitlaced Maxwell wouldn't get embarrassed," Billy said bluntly.

"What exactly did you write about?" Drew inquired, with increased interest. He'd apparently caught the guilty gleam in Tina's eyes. That, combined with Billy's accusation, was enough mystery to rouse the curiosity of a saint, much less a man who was already known to meddle where he wasn't supposed to.

"It was sort of about sex," Billy mumbled.

Tina's brows lifted as Drew choked back a laugh. "Sort of? What exactly was the assignment?" She could not imagine Viola Maxwell assigning that particular subject. In fact, she doubted if the woman was even familiar with it. She seemed a little sheltered.

"She wanted us to write about something we knew."

"And you know about sex?"

"Well, some stuff. You know, the guys talk and all."

Tina decided the conversation had gone on long enough. If she didn't stop it now, Billy might very well enlighten Drew on exactly what the guys talked about. She, for one, didn't want to hear it, especially not in front of a man who had her thinking all too much about sex as it was.

"Billy, I think perhaps you ought to select another topic. You have a study hall this morning, don't you?" she said quickly.

"Yeah, but I was planning to use it to do my math homework."

"Why didn't you do your math last night?"

"Because I was going to do it in study hall."

Tina rolled her eyes. "Use your study hall to write a new essay," she said sternly. "And tonight we're going to have a talk about your schoolwork."

"Oh, Tina, come on," he groaned. "We talk about that all the time."

"That's because we have this problem all the time. Now get on down here for breakfast. Grandmother Sarah is waiting."

Billy ran down the stairs, gave Drew a man-to-man wink and headed straight for the dining room. Drew and Tina exchanged glances.

"Someone needs to have a talk with that boy and not about homework," Drew said, then sneezed again as the cats meowed at his feet.

"Well, I certainly can't do it," Tina grumbled, grabbing the friendly cats and putting them outside. "Maybe if you've had a kid since he was a baby you can tell him about the birds and bees, but I got this one nearly fully grown. Considering where he'd been hanging out when I met him, he probably knows more than I do."

"Want me to talk to him?"

It would mean Drew Landry would have one more toe in the door, but Tina didn't think she was up to fighting him on this one. "That might be a good idea," she agreed readily. "I can't quite see Aunt Juliet or Sarah doing it, and if Mr. Kelly talked to him, he'd probably forget to wear his hearing aid and we'd all hear every word."

"I'll do it," Drew promised as he followed her into the dining room where Mr. Kelly and Aunt Juliet were arguing heatedly about where to put her petunia bed.

"Wouldn't it be nice to have it right by your vegetable garden?" Juliet said, clasping her hands in excitement. "Then we'd be able to chat while we work."

Only an innate gentlemanly politeness kept Mr. Kelly from telling Aunt Juliet what he thought of that idea. Tina could see his gnarled fists clenching under the table, as he shot her an I-told-you-so glare.

"Nope," he growled, shaking his head adamantly. "You don't want 'em there. Too much sun. They'll wilt and die. I'll make a border 'round the gazebo. That's the place for flowers like that. Give it some color and all."

The gazebo did not need color any more than Alaska needed more snow. It had purple bougainvillea climbing all over it. But Tina knew exactly what Mr. Kelly's clever reasoning was. If Aunt Juliet were clear out by the gazebo, not even with his hearing aid would he be able to pick up her running commentary on the weather and what it might do to "her damn frilly flowers."

"I wish one of you would tell me what you want for breakfast," Grandmother Sarah inserted in the middle of the debate. "I'm not hanging around in the kitchen all day long. I have more important things to do."

"Like what?" Mr. Kelly retorted. "You gonna knit some more of those lacy things to put around on the tables so everything will slip right off? It's a wonder there's a lamp left in the place, way those things slide."

"They're crocheted, not knitted," Sarah replied stiffly, her blue eyes flashing. "And things wouldn't slide if some people were more careful."

"I'll have a cup of coffee," Drew said above the din, earning a beaming smile from Sarah. Tina gave him credit for tactful diplomacy. Another two minutes of that familiar debate and Grandmother Sarah would have left the room in a huff. She made the doilies not because she especially liked them, but because she considered crocheting therapy for her arthritic fingers. But she wasn't about to tell Mr. Kelly that, so she just suffered his gibes stoically.

"Thank goodness," Sarah murmured to Drew. "At last someone who knows his own mind. How about some scrambled eggs and toast to go with that?"

"You'd better take it," Tina urged with an impish grin. "Otherwise, you'll end up with oatmeal like the rest of us. That's what she gives us when she's mad."

"I am not mad," Sarah huffed. *"If some people..."*

"Eggs would be great," Drew interrupted, and Sarah bustled out of the room after scowling at Mr. Kelly one more time for good measure.

Then Drew turned his gaze on Tina, who'd dressed in her very best corporate image—navy suit, white linen blouse, navy and white low-heeled pumps and a strand of pearls—for their meeting with the officials at the Department of Children and Families. He tilted his head and examined her from head to toe, his wicked eyes lingering and caressing as effectively as a lover's touch. She had the distinct impression he'd liked her better in her sundress. In fact, she thought maybe he was stripping her right out of the clothes she had on. It made her heart pound a little faster, which was not the way she wanted to start the day. She wanted to be prepared for those state officials. She didn't want to be so shaken up by Drew Landry that they slipped something past her. She took a deep breath and squared her shoulders.

Suddenly Drew was grinning at her.

"What's so funny?" she grumbled.

"You look as though you're steeling yourself to go to war."

"I am."

"Want to talk strategy?"

She glanced around the table pointedly and shook her head. "Not now. We'll discuss it in the car on the way over."

"Over where?" Aunt Juliet immediately wanted to know. She was quick as a whip when she wanted to be. "Aren't you going to work today, dear?"

"Of course, but Mr. Landry and I have a meeting to go to first."

Aunt Juliet suddenly clapped delightedly, her brown eyes twinkling as though they'd just let her in on an exciting secret. "You're meeting with the minister, aren't you? Oh, Tina dear, that's just wonderful. I do hope you'll let me play the organ."

"The minister?" they both said blankly.

"About your wedding, of course. I'll start today practicing 'Oh Promise Me' or would you rather have something else? I'm sure I could find a lovely ballad."

Tina struggled for composure and absolutely refused to look Drew in the eye. She knew they'd be sparkling with laughter. She reached over and patted Aunt Juliet's hand. "We're not getting married."

"You're not? Did something happen?" Aunt Juliet's expression was so thoroughly woebegone that Tina looked at Drew helplessly.

"What Tina means is that we're not getting married right away," he said, ignoring Tina's gasp of dismay. "We thought it would be better to wait until we know each other a little better."

"I suppose that's wise," Aunt Juliet agreed, then she regarded Drew sternly. "Just don't you go breaking our Tina's heart or you'll have us to answer to. Do you understand me, young man?"

"I would never hurt Tina," he said gently. He gazed directly into Tina's eyes. "I promise."

While Drew ate his scrambled eggs, Tina stirred her oatmeal around in the bowl and wondered just when he'd gotten so sure of himself. He'd kissed her once. They weren't living in the Middle Ages, when that kiss would have been tantamount to a proposal.

She was still wondering about that when they left for the local DCF office in West Palm Beach. The drive seemed to take forever, and Tina was on the edge of her seat all the way. She wasn't sure if she was more nervous about the meeting or Drew's intentions, which were apparently far different today than they had been less than twenty-four hours ago when he'd regarded her as nothing more than a questionable neighbor.

"Are you sure you wouldn't rather let me handle this?" Drew asked again as he pulled into a parking space. "I'm the one who started it."

"I have to be there," Tina insisted, marching briskly up the walk and into the building. "If anything happened and I wasn't there, I'd never be able to forgive myself."

"Or me?"

Tina sighed. "Or you."

"What do you plan to say?"

Tina was already halfway down the hall toward the office of the man who'd sent the official letters. She stopped in her tracks and stared at him.

"I have no idea," she said blankly. She shook her head and started to turn back, muttering, "I'm not ready for this. I've never gone into a meeting without reports and statistics and graphs to prove my point."

Drew squeezed her hand. "You don't need all that stuff for this. Just tell your story. No one could ever doubt your sincerity."

"You did."

"That was before I got to know you."

"And you think this Mr. Grant is going to get to know me in the fifteen minutes he'll probably allot for this meeting?"

"If he's any good at his job, he will." He scanned her face closely. "Ready now?"

Tina managed a tremulous smile, then reminded herself that she'd handled difficult board members and corporate negotiations with aplomb. There was no reason she couldn't deal with one overworked DCF official. "I'm ready," she said firmly.

"Then let's do it."

Once Edward Grant had agreed to see them without an appointment, the meeting started out well enough. Mr. Grant was a tall, thin, bespectacled man in an ill-fitting suit that was just as gray as the few remaining strands of his hair. His smile was harried and his desk was cluttered, giving the impression of a man caught on the brink of chaos.

Tina described each of her houseguests in a way that captured Mr. Grant's full attention. He was chuckling when she finished recounting the morning's battle over the location of the ill-fated petunias. She concluded with a heartfelt little speech about how much having Grandmother Sarah and the others in her home meant to her.

"They're my family," she said simply, as Drew nodded in agreement.

"It's true, Mr. Grant. I've had a chance to spend some time with them recently, and it's a wonderful thing Mrs. Harrington is doing for these people. They would be out on the street or wards of the state if it weren't for her generosity and affection. She's not taking advantage of them, as I first feared."

Edward Grant sighed heavily. "It's true that the state has more than enough cases to deal with," he acknowledged, shuffling through a huge pile of folders on his desk in search of Tina's. When he found it, he flipped it open to Drew's letter and scanned the contents. He peered over the top of his glasses at Drew, his expression puzzled.

"But I have your letter right here, and you did seem

very certain that there was a problem. These are serious allegations. Didn't you check into them before making them, Mr. Landry?"

Drew and Tina exchanged glances. His expression was every bit as guilty as it should have been. "I'd been informed about what was going on by some individuals who obviously did not have complete information," he admitted. "Unfortunately, because of my own emotional reaction to situations like this, I'm afraid I reacted without checking out the facts. I take full responsibility for the mistake."

"And now you're satisfied that there's no problem?"

"Absolutely."

"Certainly I trust your judgment, Mr. Landry. I've done some checking. You have an excellent reputation, as does Mrs. Harrington. Still, we can't be too careful. We can't risk overlooking something. You wouldn't believe how many times we visit our clients, check to see that their living conditions are adequate, only to find later that something was amiss. We can't afford to have another black mark against our reputation. The media…" His voice trailed off and he shook his head. "Well, you both know how things can get distorted, and with a case like this, they would have a field day."

"But Mrs. Harrington is hardly operating a traditional state-regulated facility. She simply has a few friends visiting for an extended period of time," Drew argued, as Tina stifled the urge to chuckle at his blatant theft of her own words.

Edward Grant tapped the folder on his desk and stared at the ceiling. Tina guessed he was torn between getting one more case off of his obviously overcrowded desk and doing a tedious, time-consuming investigation. His brow puckered with a little frown and finally he pursed his lips and gazed at her sternly.

"You do understand that we can't have unlicensed facilities operating in this state. We have a large elderly population and we must protect their rights against unscrupulous people."

"Of course. I'm not operating such a facility. These people truly are my friends. I would never exploit them in any way. If a prominent family invited friends to spend the winter at their home a few miles away, you wouldn't question that, would you?"

Mr. Grant looked startled just as she'd anticipated he would. "Of course not!"

"This is virtually the same thing." She didn't point out that her friends were staying a little longer than the typical houseguest. As far as she could see, it shouldn't even be relevant.

"And you agree with what Mrs. Harrington is saying, Mr. Landry?"

"Absolutely."

He smiled, and Tina thought she also heard a sigh of relief. "Then perhaps we could put the case on hold for the time being."

"That would be wonderful," Tina said. "I promise you my guests will be well taken care of."

"If we get another complaint, though, I will have to take action," he said sternly. "The penalties can be quite severe."

Before he could go on, Aunt Juliet, Grandmother Sarah and Mr. Kelly came barging in, ignoring the protests of the harried receptionist. Tina stared at them with a horrified expression. Drew groaned.

"What are you doing here?" Tina gasped, hoping by some miracle she could make them vanish.

"We came to help, dear," Grandmother Sarah said. "We found that letter and just put two and two together and figured out where you and Mr. Landry must be."

"That's right," Mr. Kelly agreed and gave Mr. Grant a fierce scowl. "Can't go putting a woman in jail for what she's done."

"Nobody's going to put Tina in jail, Mr. Kelly," Drew soothed.

"What's that?"

"I said nobody's going to jail," Drew shouted, then muttered, "Oh, to hell with it."

Aunt Juliet was clinging to Mr. Kelly's arm and staring around with frightened eyes. "I don't like this place," she announced.

Tina stood up and went to her, putting an arm around her plump shoulders. "You don't have to stay here, Aunt Juliet. You can all go back home now. Everything has been taken care of."

"Wait a minute," Mr. Grant said. "As long as these folks are here, we might as well hear from them. Have a seat ladies, sir."

When chairs had been drawn up and everyone was seated, he leaned back and said, "Well, now, why don't you all tell me a bit about where you live. You all reside with Mrs. Harrington, is that right?"

"Yes, indeed," Sarah replied, her hands folded primly in her lap. "She took me in off the streets...or rather the beach. I don't know what I would have done if she hadn't come along. They were about to tear down the rooming house where I'd been living, and on my income you can't find too much, just a room with a hot plate most times. I never dreamed I could live in a house like Tina's."

"And do you pay her?"

Sarah looked wary.

"Well, do you?" Mr. Grant persisted.

"Not exactly."

"What do you do…exactly?"

Sarah scowled at him. "I give her my Social Security check every month, if that's what you mean."

"Why do you do that?"

"Why to pay for things, of course. None of us takes charity, young man. We all do what we can. Mr. Kelly does a lot of work around there. I don't know how he manages everything. You should see our vegetables. We should have brought you some. The green beans are especially good now." She beamed at Mr. Grant then and added brightly, "And he keeps the grounds absolutely beautiful. Why there's not a golf course in town that has prettier, greener grass."

"Well, don't give me too much credit now, Sarah," Mr. Kelly said. "You do a bang-up job in the kitchen, and Juliet here, she works around that house like a regular white tornado. There's not a speck of dust in the place."

"And does Mrs. Harrington pay you for taking such good care of her home?" Mr. Grant inquired with a decided edge to his voice. Tina did not like the sound of his tone or his frown. In fact, she had a feeling the direction of this meeting had just taken a sharp turn toward trouble.

"Of course not," they said in chorus.

"Let me get this straight then. You turn all of your money over to her and take care of her home, but she doesn't pay you a dime?"

"Oh, my God," Tina mumbled and rolled her eyes heavenward.

"I don't know what you're implying about Tina, young man," Grandmother Sarah said, "but I don't like the sound of it."

"I'm not implying anything. You've just admitted that this woman is ripping you off."

Tina groaned and three pairs of eyes widened in dismay as the allegation sank in. Sarah was the first to recover and her eyes flashed.

"Fiddlesticks!" she exclaimed angrily. "That is not what we said, young man, and don't you go trying to put words in our mouths. Tina doesn't have a mean bone in her body. She certainly isn't capable of ripping us off. She's like a daughter to all of us. Except Billy, of course. She's more like a mother to him." She turned her blue eyes on Drew and pleaded, "Mr. Landry, do something."

"It's okay, Sarah," he soothed. "We'll straighten this out. Mr. Grant just misunderstood." He got to his feet and leaned over the desk until he was practically nose-to-nose with Edward Grant. "Didn't you?"

"I understand perfectly," Mr. Grant said defiantly. "I will be over tomorrow morning at eight to check into this further."

Ignoring their protests, he ushered them out the door,

clucking his tongue disapprovingly. Tina felt more like a criminal than ever.

Next the five of them stood in the foyer of the building, their voices raised in a babble of questions until Tina felt like screaming. Why had Sarah, Juliet and Mr. Kelly come storming in there just when she and Drew had everything under control? True, she'd initially thought having them with her might be a good idea, but she had decided their words would get all twisted around. Drew had certainly realized it.

Now what? They had only wanted to help. She knew that. But now they were in worse shape than ever.

"Okay, everyone, calm down," she said at last.

"Tina dear, we're so sorry," Grandmother Sarah said. "Everything really is a mess now, isn't it?"

"It will be okay. You go on home. I'll think of something."

"We'll think of something," Drew corrected. Sarah and Juliet beamed at him as though he possessed some magic wand and had offered to wave it around in their behalf. It irritated the daylights out of Tina that they were relying on Drew rather than her. Why did everyone always just assume that a man could solve anything? Especially this particular man?

"What's that?" Mr. Kelly asked.

"We're going to take care of everything," Drew said more loudly. "Go on home now. Tina and I will discuss this and come up with a plan."

But as Drew drove the shaken Tina to Harrington Industries, they were both silent. Not even the clear, sparkling sky or wind-whipped water cheered her as it usually did as they drove along curving Flagler Drive.

She didn't have a single idea about how to go about convincing the state that she wasn't ripping off her friends, taking their scanty resources to pad her already extensive bank balance. The whole thing was absurd, and yet Edward Grant had taken the facts and twisted them into what he apparently considered a believable con artist's scheme.

During her childhood, Tina had seen many of her elderly neighbors affected by such unscrupulous individuals. She could understand Mr. Grant's transformation from friendliness to chilly distrust. Clearly, he too had seen all too many situations in which the elderly were abused, either financially, psychologically or both. How could she make him see that there was a difference, that their household was filled with a protective warmth and love? Would he be able to tell, as Drew had, simply by walking through the door?

And it had come to this because of a few anonymous letters and Drew's uninformed actions. She scowled over at him.

"I want you at my house at eight o'clock."

He grinned. "Great. We can talk afterward. What's Grandmother Sarah fixing for dinner tonight?"

"No dinner. No talking. I meant in the morning."

"Why?"

"Because when those inspectors start counting bathrooms and interviewing my friends, I want you to watch."

"To make sure they don't say or do anything crazy again?" he said.

"No. So you can see my world falling apart."

"Maybe we should go for coffee and talk about this now," Drew suggested. "You seem upset."

"Upset? I'm more than upset," she retorted, her eyes flashing. "In fact, if I weren't trying very hard to be a lady, I'd tell you in no uncertain terms exactly what I think of you and your meddling."

"I think you've made your point anyway," he said dryly.

"Good."

Not only was she furious and frustrated by a bureaucracy that allowed no room for human compassion, she was also mad as hell because the man who'd stirred up this hornet's nest still made her pulse race.

Then again, maybe one's pulse was supposed to race when she was contemplating murder.

When she got out of Drew's car, she glowered at him and slammed the door so hard that the sports car that could hug a curve at ninety miles an hour bounced on its expensive racing tires. Drew flinched, but she had a feeling he was smiling as she stalked away. She also thought she heard him murmur something about spunk.

Damn the man! Before this was over, she'd show him the real meaning of the word.

Chapter Five

The swift, silent ride to the penthouse of the Harrington Industries tower in West Palm Beach did nothing to soothe Tina's fury, despite the spectacular view she had from the glass elevator of the inland waterway and the pastel Palm Beach skyline. Normally that view, shimmering in the soft morning sunlight like a Monet painting, took her breath away, but today she was hardly even aware of it.

She was still seething as she marched down the hall to her office, her back ramrod straight. The language she was muttering under her breath would have appalled Grandmother Sarah.

Outside the double mahogany doors on which her name was displayed on a discreet brass plaque, she paused and took a deep breath. Determined not to carry her rotten mood through those doors, she plastered a cheerful smile on her face. It lasted approximately fifteen seconds.

"Thank God," Jennifer Kramer breathed when Tina walked in. Normally cool and self-possessed, with twenty-five years' experience as an executive assistant, Jennifer right now looked wild-eyed. Tina didn't have to ask why.

All six phone lines were ringing at once. There was already a stack of pink message slips on the corner of Jennifer's desk including, Tina noted as she flipped through them, two inquiries from reporters, thereby proving once again that it didn't take long for bad news to get around. Her encounter with DCF just might have set a speed record, though.

As if that weren't bad enough, one of the company's directors was pacing the outer office, a fierce scowl on his face. His face was beet red , indicating he'd been fuming quite a while.

Tina took one look at what was going on. She tore up the messages, put the calls on hold, ordered her frazzled assistant to take a coffee break and glowered at Mr. John J. Parsons III until his face turned to a more normal skin tone. Then she waved him into her office, gestured to a chair and took the call on the first line.

She twirled her swivel chair away from Mr. Parsons to gaze out the window at the water as she talked. She rather wished she were on one of the majestic sailboats skimming past. She didn't even much care where it was headed as long as it was away from the irritatingly sexy Drew Landry and the problems he'd brought down on her head at the worst possible time.

"Yes, Mr. Davis," she said politely to the caller's loudspoken inquiry about his minimal dividend check. The man owned a hundred shares of stock and behaved as though he held the controlling interest in the company. He always demanded to speak to her. Most of the time she could deal with him, but today he was sorely testing what remained of her patience. She was absolutely astonished that her tone was actually civil.

"No, Mr. Davis," she said. "I'm sure it will all be straightened out. I'll have my assistant check into it right away. Thank you so much for calling, Mr. Davis. It was good to talk to you."

It took every bit of willpower in her to keep from adding, "Go to hell, Mr. Davis." Only an image of Grandmother Sarah's horror and Gerald's disapproval kept her from doing it.

Gerald had believed that every stockholder, as well as every customer, deserved courtesy and prompt, reliable service. It was why Harrington Industries had survived the softening of the tech market. There were incredible, well-publicized stories of the lengths to which Harrington Industries would go to satisfy its customers, including the time Gerald had flown halfway across the country and installed the software himself to meet a deadline. Tina was not about to ruin that reputation by snapping back at a man whose calls to her were probably the highlight of his lonely day. She made a note to have David check into Mr. Davis's problem and get back to him.

She managed to be equally pleasant to Kathryn Sawyer, who had the personality of a barracuda and a more substantial five percent of Harrington Industries' stock. Tina was going to need that five percent if her ouster came to a vote at the stockholders' meeting at the end of the month. They had even moved the annual meeting to New York to accommodate Kathryn the Great, as she was referred to in the society pages. She was hosting a charity gala there the night after the meeting and couldn't possibly get away, her personal assistant had huffily informed Tina.

Thanks to Gerald, Tina held more stock than any other single stockholder, but if they all teamed up against her in a coup attempt, Kathryn Sawyer could provide the swing votes Tina needed to remain in power. Tina would have moved the meeting to the middle of the Sahara, if Kathryn had wanted it there. Kathryn, unfortunately, knew it.

"Tina, these next few weeks are critical," Kathryn warned unnecessarily. No one knew that better than Tina. "I've already been approached by some individuals from the board about whether I'd support a change at the top."

Tina sucked in her breath. "And what did you say?"

"I said I was withholding judgment, but for the moment I was inclined to continue backing you. Don't make me regret that."

"Kathryn, I assure you that I'm doing everything in my power to keep things running smoothly," she said, rubbing her temples. A dull throb had started in her head.

The thought of being ousted as head of Harrington Industries had kept Tina awake nights for months now. Although she was the only official nominee for chairman, this was not the first time she'd heard of the rumblings that she was too inexperienced to hold the job. She feared if this DCF business got out of hand, the rumblings could turn into a roar. Even before this had started, she had worriedly prowled the grounds of the estate at three in the morning almost as frequently as Mr. Kelly. She, however, was awake, though sometimes she wished she weren't.

When she'd first been promoted to the position of

Gerald's executive assistant years earlier, there had been rumors that she'd only moved up by sleeping with the boss. Many of his senior officers had resented what they considered to be her unearned access to the company's chief executive officer. When she and Gerald had married, the stories had gotten increasingly vicious.

No one stopped to take into account how hard she worked. No one considered how much Gerald loved his company. He would never have risked its well-being by putting someone incapable in charge. Tina was inexperienced, but she'd been a fast learner. It was true that she'd had to replace Gerald far too soon, but she understood his vision and she knew how to carry it out. The bottom line reflected that, but there were still those who could be swayed by her lack of experience or innuendos about her capabilities. The bottom line might not matter to those individuals whose actions were tied to emotions, rather than business sense. She could be replaced.

Tina sighed wearily as she listened only partially to Kathryn Sawyer. She had to resolve this mess Drew Landry had gotten her into before it blew up in the press. Then she could count on the company's annual report to speak for itself and her future at the helm of Harrington Industries would be assured, just as Gerald had wanted.

And just as she deserved! That vindication meant a lot to the insecure girl that still lurked inside the successful woman. Oh, she had enough faith in herself to believe that she could work her way to the top again at some other company, but Harrington Industries had been Gerald's legacy. For that reason alone, she had to succeed.

When she'd heard all of Kathryn Sawyer's monologue and promised her that the luncheon planned for the stockholders would indeed be a suitably elegant feast, she hung up the phone and turned reluctantly to Mr. Parsons.

"What can I do for you?" she asked, giving him her full attention.

"I've been hearing things, young lady."

Tina blanched. Please, God, not already. "What things, Mr. Parsons?" she asked cautiously.

"Talk is we're getting into something new, something downright un-American."

Tina closed her eyes and counted to ten, decided she needed to count to a hundred if she was to hear this conversation out and turned back toward the window. It could have been worse, she reminded herself. He could know about Sarah and the others. When she turned back at last, she asked calmly, "Mr. Parsons, I'm not aware of anything like that. Could you be more specific?"

"Germs, Mrs. Harrington. Germs."

Tina had to choke back a sudden desire to chuckle. She gulped and said, "Germs, Mr. Parsons? I don't understand."

"I hear we're selling germs to those bloody terrorists. Now you tell me, is that something a fine company like this ought to be doing?"

"Absolutely not, Mr. Parsons," she agreed wholeheartedly.

He eyed her warily. "Then there's no truth to it? You're sure about that?"

"I am absolutely certain about it. We're still in the computer business. There's not a germ in the place."

He nodded in satisfaction. "That's good, Mrs. Harrington. I must say I'm relieved." He hefted himself out of his chair and waved his cigar at her. "I'll be on my way now. Have to get to the club in time for lunch. Keep up the good work."

Fortunately he was gone before she had to manage another comment. She wasn't sure she could have gotten a single word past the laughter that was bubbling up. She was roaring when Jennifer peeked in the door, her eyes bright with curiosity.

"Are you okay?" she asked hesitantly.

Tina laughed even harder until tears were streaming down her cheeks. She tried to answer and couldn't. She gestured for her assistant to come in.

"What was that all about?" Jennifer asked as she came in.

"He was afraid we were climbing into bed with terrorists."

Jennifer blinked and stared. "Are you dating someone I need to run a security check on?"

"Hardly," Tina retorted, then thought of Drew. She wondered what a security check of him would reveal. She really knew very little about the man except what Sarah had read in the gossip columns and the occasional items she'd seen in the *Wall Street Journal*.

Drew Landry had a reputation for gobbling up failing companies and turning them into moneymakers. The possibility that he might be viewing Harrington Industries as an acquisition flitted through her mind and just as quickly was put to rest. The company was not failing, and Drew had never even mentioned Harrington Industries to her. He'd only been interested in her personal life.

Jennifer sat down in the chair Mr. Parsons had vacated and demanded, "Hey, wake up. Explain about the terrorists, please. I have grandchildren to think about."

"If I understood Mr. Parsons correctly, he was afraid we were about to sell a formula for germicidal warfare to foreign agents."

"Is that what Tim is working on in that lab?" Jennifer asked, wide-eyed.

Tina glowered at her. "Don't be cute."

"Well, you never know with an inventor."

"Our inventors still deal in computers."

"Thank God. I need this job."

"You'll keep it if you'll get me a strawberry milk shake and two aspirins in the next five minutes."

"Coming right up," she said, bustling from the room. "By the way, those reports you wanted on the software are on your desk."

"Thanks, Jen."

When the fifty-year-old woman, who'd been an enormous help to Tina in the months following Gerald's death, had gone, Tina picked up the reports, stared at them blindly and put them right back down. An image of Drew as he climbed from his pool and stared at her boldly flashed through her mind. It was an image that stirred an unsettling ache of need deep in her abdomen. After a lifetime of caution, of planning and struggling, Drew made her want to take risks.

She hadn't reacted that way to a man either before or after Gerald. He had been her first love, and the magic between them had been so sweetly satisfying that she hadn't looked at another man since his death. Not even Martin, though they'd been dating for months now.

She remembered the day she and Gerald had met as clearly as if it had been yesterday. She was already working in the Harrington Industries management training program. He'd sent for her one day, only a few months after she'd joined the firm. She'd gotten off the elevator with her knees shaking, feeling exactly like a terrified school kid who'd been ordered to the principal's office. She'd sat in his outer office, oblivious to Jennifer's smiles of encouragement, and tried to imagine what awful thing she'd done and whether it had been bad enough to get her fired.

Instead, Gerald had praised her report. He thought it showed initiative as well as an astute understanding of the computer industry's future. They had discussed it for hours, until finally he'd realized that it was past dinnertime. He'd invited her to join him for a late supper. It turned out to be the first of many such long, quiet evenings during which he built her confidence and taught her everything he knew.

When it evolved into something more, Tina had thought she'd been granted the world. It had been a rude awakening to discover that not everyone was equally thrilled with her good fortune, but Gerald had given her the strength to ignore their jealous insinuations.

"Are you happy with me?" he'd asked.

"Blissfully."

"Then what do they matter?" he'd always said, then kissed her and caressed her until her doubts were banished by his gentle loving.

Tina sighed when she heard the tap on the door. So much joy and so little time to share it, but she'd never forget. When the tap came again, she forced aside the past and returned to the present.

"Come on in, Jennifer."

Her assistant slipped through the narrowest possible opening, then shut the door behind her, her expression dazed.

"There is an absolute hunk outside and he insists that you two have an appointment," she said in a hushed voice.

"Do we?"

"There are no hunks on your calendar, but if I were you, I'd ask him in anyway."

Tina grinned. Jennifer was notoriously interested in her social life—or lack of one. "Does this hunk have a name?"

"Drew Landry."

"I should have known," Tina mumbled.

"What?"

"Never mind."

"Shall I send him in?"

"Why not? He's already ruined my morning. I might as well give him a shot at my afternoon."

The door creaked open. "I heard that and I take exception," Drew said, marching in with Tina's milk shake container and her aspirin. He grinned at Jennifer. "Thanks for pleading my case."

"Anytime. If she turns you down, I'm free for lunch."

Drew's smile widened as he gazed at Tina. "Are you going to turn me down?"

"You haven't asked me anything yet."

"True. I want you to play hooky and spend the afternoon with me."

"That didn't sound like a question."

"Actually it was more in the nature of an order. You've been working much too hard."

Tina's brows lifted quizzically as Jennifer openly listened, her eyes sparkling with interest.

"You've known me less than twenty-four hours," Tina reminded him. "How would you know how hard I work?"

"Grandmother Sarah told me when I stopped by your house."

"When did you do that?"

"After I dropped you off. She says you never get home before eight anymore. You don't get enough exercise, and she thinks you're looking peaked."

"She always thinks I look peaked just because I do not sit out in the sun and blister my skin to a disgusting shade of pink," Tina grumbled. "I'm healthy as an ox."

"Well, you do have circles under your eyes," Jennifer offered. "Maybe you are coming down with something."

"Thanks a lot." Tina was not going to explain that the man standing there looking as though he'd just returned from a week at a seaside health spa was responsible for any circles she might have.

"So, are you coming? I promise you it will be more fun than this watery milk shake, a couple of aspirin and a bunch of dreary paperwork."

She tilted her chin. "Have you forgotten that I'm mad at you?"

"How could I? If you'd slammed the door of my car any harder, it would probably have had a concussion."

"I don't think cars have concussions."

"Have you ever talked to an engine? They're very sensitive."

Tina moaned and buried her head in her arms. She peeked up at him. "You're not one of those, are you?"

"One of those what?"

"Those people who think their cars are human."

"My car is human," he said indignantly. "And we've had a long and very rewarding relationship. I expect you'll grow to love her too, once you've taken a few hairpin curves in her."

Tina shuddered. "I don't do hairpin curves."

"So we'll stay on the expressway today. Are you coming or not? Time's wasting." He leaned across her desk, just as he had Edward Grant's earlier. Tina doubted if the caseworker's heart had thudded quite the way hers was.

"Go," Jennifer urged. "I'll cancel your appointments. Besides, if you stay here, you'll have to deal with all those reporters."

"Reporters?" Drew lifted his eyebrows.

"News gets around fast," Tina said succinctly. Drew had no trouble interpreting her meaning.

"I'm sorry, Tina. I really thought we could keep this quiet."

Jennifer's eyes lit up. "You mean you two—"

"No," Tina practically shouted before Jennifer could join in Aunt Juliet's fantasy. "It's a long story." She looked at Drew, thought about the reporters, and nodded. It was definitely the lesser of two evils. "I'll go."

Once they were in Drew's sleek automobile, she regarded him curiously. The man continued to amaze her. A few days ago he'd been ready to try to convict her for abusing the elderly. Now he seemed to have set himself up as a member of the family. "Why did you stop by the house?"

"I wanted to be sure everyone had calmed down."

"Had they?"

"No. They were still very upset by what happened at DCF this morning. They felt as though they'd let you down."

"Let me down? How? By telling the truth? It's not their fault that Edward Grant managed to turn the truth into something ugly."

"That's what I told them."

"Did they buy it?"

"I'm not sure. Grandmother Sarah was crocheting like mad when I left, if that's any indication."

"It is. It means she's worried sick."

"I was afraid of that."

"How about Juliet and Mr. Kelly?"

"Mr. Kelly was up to his elbows in dirt and petunias with Juliet supervising."

"That ought to keep them distracted for a while then. I'll talk to them tonight."

Drew glanced away from the road and met her gaze. His smile was tender and filled with concern. "They're tougher than you think, Tina. They'll be just fine."

"I know that. It's just that I hate to see them worry. I thought living with me would end their worries."

"A little worrying makes you grateful for what you have."

"I'll remind you of that little bit of armchair philosophy the next time you try to drag me out of my office just to distract me from my problems."

"Ahh, but you're a different case."

"Oh, really? How so?"

"You have me to protect you from things. I could probably even give you some advice on Harrington Industries, if you wanted it. It would make Grandmother Sarah very happy if someone took some of that load off of your shoulders. She thinks you're too young to be buried under paperwork. She also thinks you're more worried than you're letting on about the stockholders' meeting."

"My shoulders are doing just fine. Did someone appoint you as my dragon slayer or did you volunteer for the role?" Tina said with an edge to her voice that Drew apparently missed.

"Grandmother Sarah hinted, but I volunteered," he said lightly. "Gladly."

"Then I hope you won't feel too bad when I fire you."

"You can't fire a dragon slayer," he countered.

"Watch me," she said tightly. "I've told you before that I like to fight my own battles."

"And I like to look out for people I care about," he said just as stubbornly.

"Then I'd say we have a definite problem, don't we?"

"Not the way I see it."

"Oh?"

"I'll just have to make very sure to maintain a low profile, sort of like one of those bodyguards who are meant to be invisible."

Tina suddenly relaxed and laughed. "Drew Landry, you couldn't stay quietly behind the scenes if you tried."

"We'll just have to see about that, won't we?" he said, staring straight at the road. Tina still caught the twinkle in his eyes and knew that the battle was far from over. Drew was a very determined man, who most likely always got what he went after. If he made up his mind that he was going to slay a few dragons for her, she had an awful feeling there wouldn't be much she could do about it. She decided to change the subject instead.

"When are you planning to talk to Billy?"

"I already have."

She regarded him with astonishment. "When on earth did you have time for that?"

"I stopped by his school after I left the house. I was just in time for his study hall."

Tina sighed in exasperation. "Drew, it could have waited. He was supposed to use that study hall to do his English assignment."

"Judging from the conversation you two had this morning, that assignment was best left undone."

The thought of Drew explaining the facts of life to Billy sent a tingling awareness scampering over her flesh. "So, umm, what exactly did you two talk about?"

"Oh, love and sex and stuff," he said, mimicking Billy. "He seemed to think he had the sex part down pretty good."

Tina's eyes widened. "Did he?"

"Let's just say that for his age he had a better than average understanding of the mechanics of it."

"Oh, my God. Has he...?"

"I don't think so," Drew said with a definitely wicked sparkle in his eyes. "I decided to concentrate on the emotions in the hope that he might stop and think before he does. The boy is only thirteen, after all."

"Do you think he got the message?"

"Well, judging from his reaction, I think he's going to be keeping a close eye on you and me."

Tina had an awful sinking feeling in the pit of her stomach. "What is that supposed to mean?"

"Well, I sort of used us for comparative purposes."

"You what!"

"Come on, Tina. You have to admit that you and I are attracted to each other. More than attracted, in fact."

"I do not have to admit any such thing," she said, despite a traitorous racing of her pulse.

"You will, if you're honest."

"Humph!"

"At any rate, my point was that you and I are not hopping in the sack just because of a mutual attraction."

"You told a thirteen-year-old boy who lives in my house that? Are you crazy?"

Drew feigned hurt. "I thought I was setting a good example. When you and I go to bed, it will be because of the way we feel about each other."

"When you and I go to bed, there will have to be an ice storm in hell," she snapped.

"Will you feel better if I tell you that it worked? Billy understood exactly what I meant."

"He did?"

"I'd say offhand that he now expects to see a marriage license before he gets the first clue that you and I are sharing more than a chaste kiss good-night. Otherwise, I'm likely to be hammered over the head with his baseball bat," Drew said ruefully. "Talk about protective. That kid has the instincts of a mother hen."

Laughter bubbled forth. "I love it," Tina said. "You built the trap, and it snared you."

He glowered at her. "You don't have to enjoy it quite so much. You're going to wind up just as frustrated as I am."

"Wanna bet?" she retorted. Before she could discover who was actually likely to have the last laugh, she decided she'd better retreat to a safer topic. "How do you manage to have all this free time on your hands to run around and offer advice and consolation? Don't you have a company to run?"

There was a wicked gleam in Drew's eyes as he answered. He obviously saw straight through her ploy. "Yes, but technically I'm on vacation. I've left some very good people in charge of things. They call when they need me, and I touch base a couple of times a day."

"What if they need you while we're out gallivanting?"

"Oh, I think they can spare me for an afternoon. Besides, we are not gallivanting. This trip is business, too."

"Terrific! You're taking me along to a business meeting."

"Not exactly."

"Then where are we going?"

"You'll see."

"Am I dressed properly?"

"If you were dressed any more properly, you could teach in a convent."

"That's not what I meant."

"Let's just say, if you don't think what you're wearing is suitable, you can always take it off."

"Drew!"

His low chuckle sent a wave of heat scampering straight down her abdomen. The memory of her rotten morning fled, and the fact that he never did answer her question sent her imagination soaring in all sorts of wicked and thoroughly inappropriate directions.

She moaned softly as she realized what was happening. It hadn't been ten minutes since Drew had dared her to remain immune to his charms and already she was succumbing. Infuriatingly enough, frustration was apparently not very far away after all.

Chapter Six

With Drew flirting outrageously during the ninety-minute drive to Miami, Tina's traitorous mind explored a whole assortment of interesting possibilities for the afternoon. Although she breathed an outward sigh of relief, she realized she was almost disappointed when he turned into the palm-lined driveway at Hialeah Park. As lovely as the place was, with its lagoons and flamingos and lush tropical plants, it was not a secluded setting for a lovers' rendezvous. There were already thousands of people yelling their heads off as a pack of gleaming Thoroughbreds turned into the homestretch.

"We're going to the races?" she asked thoroughly baffled and trying not to reveal her disappointment. It would make Drew too smug. "I thought you said this was business."

"Actually there's a little stand here that sells great pizza," Drew retorted innocently. "I thought we'd have lunch before I get to work."

She shook her head. "Nobody goes to a racetrack for lunch. You're nuts."

"That's why I fit in so well at your place. Now stop wasting time and let's get moving. I'm starved."

She stared at him. "You really did come here for lunch?"

He shrugged, his grin sending Tina's heart slamming against her ribs again. "Well, I suppose we could watch the races, as long as we're here."

"Gee, what a novel idea!"

Tina had never been closer to the races than her television screen and then only for the Triple Crown events, which Gerald had watched avidly. As soon as Drew had grabbed a couple of slices of pizza, they found seats and within moments Tina became fascinated by the spectacle around them. She insisted that Drew explain every bit of the *Racing Form* to her. He pointed out the horses' breeding, the rundown of top trainers, the owners, the current listing of winning jockeys, the speed ratings and the past-performance listings for each horse. She listened intently to every word, asked several questions, then nodded in satisfaction when she'd heard his answers.

"Got it," she said, reaching into her purse for the calculator on her phone.

"What are you doing?"

"It all seems pretty scientific. I'll just work out a quick formula based on past performance and speed rating and I should be able to calculate the winners," she said confidently, punching numbers into the calculator for the horses in the third race. She pointedly ignored Drew's expression of amused tolerance.

Oblivious to the smudges of newsprint on her fingers, she concentrated on what she was doing until, ten minutes later, she looked up and announced, "I'm betting on number seven."

"That horse hasn't won a race in the last year," Drew argued. "Don't waste your money."

"But he had one of those dots beside his last workout. You said that was important. And the number-two jockey is riding him. The top jockey isn't even in the race," she countered, airily waving off his obvious intention to argue further.

"Besides," she said with finality, "I saw him when he came on the track and I liked the color of the jockey's shirt. That shade of emerald green is one of my favorites."

"So much for scientific analysis. How much are you wagering on this sure thing?"

"I'll bet two dollars to show," she said decisively and handed him the money.

Drew's lips twitched. "It's nice to see that you have the courage of your convictions."

Tina scowled at him. "Which horse are you betting on, Mr. Know-it-all?"

"I think I'll sit this race out."

"Coward."

"A smart bettor picks his races carefully. He does not bother with a race when the favorite is a sure thing and has such low odds, he'll barely get his money back."

"Forget the favorite. I'm telling you, you should put some money on this horse of mine."

"Tina, the odds are forty-five to one. That horse will be lucky to come in by the end of the afternoon."

"Oh, go place the bet," she muttered in disgust.

Fifteen minutes later she was cashing in her ticket. The horse had cruised across the finish line three lengths ahead of the favorite.

"Don't gloat," Drew growled. "It was beginner's luck."

Tina ignored him. She was already punching numbers into her calculator again.

It wasn't until the ninth race, when her throat was already practically raw from screaming and her pocketbook stuffed with crumpled bills, that she discovered Drew owned a horse running in the day's feature race. Somehow she'd forgotten all about his claim that he had come to the track for business. This was the last thing she'd expected.

Listening to the enthusiastic comments from the crowd around them, she discovered that his stable was reputedly one of the best in the country. Drew's Serendipity Sal was going in as the favorite.

"And I thought you were just a staid old businessman. How did you get into this?" Tina asked as they walked to the paddock area for the saddling. She'd reluctantly put her phone away. She couldn't very well bet against Drew, anyway.

"I grew up riding," he said, a reflective expression on his face for just an instant. Clearly he was back in Iowa, reliving a time of which Tina knew far too little.

"I've always loved horses," he went on. "But there's something about a Thoroughbred that is almost mystical. These magnificent creatures go faster than the wind. If I weren't so big, I think I'd like to be a jockey. What a thrill it must be to skim over the ground, feeling the muscles of the horse stretch to the limit and knowing that your slightest touch is in control of all that energy."

Tina's eyes were wide and lit with amber fire. "You make it sound incredible."

He regarded her with astonishment. "Haven't you ever ridden?"

"Never. The only horse I've been on was on a merry-go-round in an amusement park."

"I'll take you riding someday, and you'll see for yourself. It won't be the same as this, but it will give you some idea."

"I'd like that." She regarded him quizzically. "I'm still not sure how you wound up as an owner. Did you just go out one day and buy a racehorse?"

Drew chuckled. "It wasn't quite that simple. With the amount of money involved, you don't go into this lightly. I found a trainer who agreed to work with me. As soon as the rest of my business was financially sound, we went to the sales and bought my first racehorse, a two-year-old colt."

His eyes were filled with distant nostalgia. "He was only mediocre on the track, but was he spectacular to watch. After that, I was hooked. I knew, though, that I had to either make a commitment to go with it all the way or drop out. I wouldn't have been satisfied to run a one-horse stable."

His enthusiasm was infectious. "Obviously you went with it. Is your obsession costing you a bundle, or did it turn out to be a good decision?"

He nodded sheepishly. "Actually, it's turned out pretty well."

"How well?"

"I have a farm in central Florida for breeding and training and I have about twenty horses on the track now. This little beauty you're about to see cost 750,000 as a yearling. She's only a four-year-old and she's already won over a million. If she wins today, we'll prob-ably retire her and breed her."

Tina was used to talking big money, but not when it came to something that seemed to her as risky and frivolous as horse racing. When she'd been growing up, her parents had scraped by. She still wasn't used to treating money casually. She shopped in the chain de-partment stores, not the elegant boutiques, and on Sun-day mornings both she and Sarah clipped food coupons from the paper.

Now, though, what had always seemed to her to be merely a rich man's hobby took on a whole new mean-ing. Grandmother Sarah's crocheting and Aunt Juliet's petunias were hobbies. This was big business.

She took a good long look at Serendipity Sal with her gleaming coat and prancing step.

"Nice horse," she commented wryly.

"Are you referring to her looks or her value?"

"I'm impressed by both."

"Just wait until you see her run. That's what it's all about."

As they went back to their box to wait for the start of the mile-and-a-quarter race, Tina's heart pounded in anticipation. Drew trained his binoculars on the starting gate when the gun went off, and when Sal broke badly, Tina could see tiny white lines edge his mouth. But the four-year-old's speed more than made up for the faulty start. By the time the horses reached the backstretch, Sal was running third and gaining.

As they rounded the turn, Sal moved into a neck and neck race with the leader. Tina was jumping up and down, clinging to Drew's arm, her throat parched and scratchy and beyond sound, even though she tried like crazy to yell. When the two horses burst across the finish line in a cloud of red dust, she had no idea which had won.

Frustrated, she caught the amused laughter in Drew's eyes.

"What's so funny?"

"You."

"Oh?"

"For a lady who knew virtually nothing about racing a couple of hours ago, you're hooked, too, aren't you?"

"It's wonderful," she enthused. "One question, though."

"What?"

"Did she win?"

"It's a photo finish. They'll announce it in a minute."

"You mean we have to wait?"

He tapped her on the nose. "Your impatience is showing, Mrs. Harrington."

Tina grimaced. "I know. Patience is not one of my virtues. Ask Grandmother Sarah."

"She did mention that it might be nice if I could slow you down a bit. Haven't you ever had to wait for something? Anticipation is part of the excitement."

"I waited for things most of my life," she replied, suddenly serious. "Now that I can make things happen, waiting makes me crazy."

Drew touched a hand to her cheek, flooding her with warmth. "I can understand that," he said gently, "but don't get so caught up in the action that you forget to stop along the way."

"And smell the roses?" she retorted with a touch of irony.

"Or savor the special moments," he said solemnly, his blue eyes capturing hers, holding her until the world vanished and it was just the two of them, alone in a timeless, reckless place all their own. Tina searched Drew's eyes and found them clear, honest and filled with warmth. The thundering of her heart resounded in her ears, and her lips parted on a soft sigh. Drew lowered his head. His mouth was only a heart-stopping hair's breadth away from hers when an explosion of sound split the air and shattered the moment.

The posting of the results had drawn the crowd to its feet. When she saw that Serendipity Sal was officially in first place, Tina impulsively threw her arms around Drew's neck and kissed him soundly, though without the sweet tension of the kiss they'd lost.

Blue eyes glittered at her dangerously. "You do that again, Tina Harrington, and I won't be responsible for my actions," he warned in a low growl. "We'll never get down to the winner's circle."

"Racing is a sport of gentlemen," she reminded him tartly.

"Actually it was the sport of kings and not all of them were gentlemen. Besides, all sorts of mavericks are into it now," he teased right back, and a tingle of anticipation danced down her spine. Anticipation. She was beginning to see what he meant.

"Like you?"

"Exactly like me."

"Have I mentioned what an enigma you are?"

Drew seemed puzzled. "In what way?"

"If I'd had to describe your personality a day or two ago, I'd have said you were a pompous, meddling, stuffed shirt with the mental diversity of a rabbit."

"How flattering." He actually grinned at her description. "And now?"

"Your mind darts in so many directions, I have trouble keeping up with you. You're filled with contradictions. On the one hand, you strike me as a man who has quite a knack with the ladies. You always know just what to say. Jennifer practically fell at your feet. You've charmed Grandmother Sarah and won Aunt Juliet's heart. On the other hand, you've convinced Mr. Kelly you're the only man in Palm Beach besides him who knows a thing about compost. You're equally at home either here, in a boardroom, or playing Scrabble."

"What about you? Have I won you over yet?"

"With all those other ladies vying for your attention, why does it matter?"

"All those other ladies, hmm? Does the competition bother you?"

"Why should it?" she retorted promptly.

He bent down and brushed a tantalizing kiss across her lips, lingering just long enough for another shock of awareness to rip through her and set her pulse to racing.

"Because you and I are going to have something very special," he said softly, his eyes locked with hers. Tina's breath caught in her throat. "If I were you, I wouldn't want any other woman interfering."

Tina blinked and tore her gaze from his. She managed a shaky laugh. "What arrogance!"

"Actually, I thought I was just being very straightforward. Someday you'll understand that it's a trait I value above all others."

After the ceremony in the winner's circle, they made a brief visit to the barn to see that Serendipity Sal had returned from the race in good condition. She'd been washed and brushed until her chestnut coat was shining in the late afternoon sun. A groom was walking her up and down in front of Drew's stalls.

While Drew chatted with his trainer, Tina leaned against a railing and took a deep breath. An earthy, pungent odor filled the air that was not at all unpleasant. This was real. She'd never been on a farm, but imagined that this must be what it was like. She tried to envision Drew's home in Iowa and couldn't. Even there, his growing-up would have been so much easier than hers. From what he'd said, it had not been a hand-to-mouth existence as hers had been, or even as so many small farmers lived, their fortunes fluctuating on the success or failure of a single crop, on a fluke of the weather.

She was still thinking that over when they stopped for dinner at a small Cajun restaurant. Once they'd both ordered the spicy, mouth-watering blackened grouper, she sat back with her glass of wine and studied the man across from her. He'd left his jacket in the car and the collar of his shirt was open, revealing a provocative shadowing of dark hairs at the base of his tanned throat.

"What were you like when you were a little boy?" she asked, suddenly feeling a need to go back to a time when Drew would have been less formidable, less boldly masculine. Even now that she'd discovered that his temper flared only under provocation, she still found him to be a bit intimidating. That feeling could merely be from his power over her senses, but it was very real.

"I was a little hellion," he admitted, that faraway look back in his eyes. "I started climbing practically before I could walk, and my dad was constantly having to pull me down from trees, the hayloft, the kitchen counters. No place was safe from my excursions."

"You miss your home, don't you?"

"Sometimes. Life was certainly less complex when I was growing up."

"Was it fun living on a farm?"

"It was incredible. Even on a farm as large as ours, it's not an easy life. You learn responsibility at an early age." He grinned at the memories. "You can't imagine what it was like in the winter, though, when the snow could block all the roads and we would sit around the fire and read or watch a movie or TV and pop popcorn in the fireplace. In the summer I went skinny-dipping in the stream or rode my horse. As much as I love it down here, I still miss watching the change of seasons."

"We have a change of seasons," Tina countered with all the defensiveness of a native.

"Sure. The temperature drops ten degrees."

"You sound like a typical northerner. Just because we don't get snow, doesn't mean we can't tell when winter comes. All you have to do is go out to the Everglades and see which birds are here or look at the flowers that bloom only in the cooler weather."

Her expression went all soft and dreamy. "And then there are the strawberries." She practically licked her lips at the thought.

"Strawberries? What do they have to do with winter?"

"You've never gone strawberry picking down here? What kind of a farmer are you? There's nothing better to do on a winter afternoon than go to a field and pick fresh strawberries."

"Why don't you just buy them in the store?"

Tina looked scandalized. "It wouldn't be the same at all. We'll go one day and you'll see. Have I convinced you we have a change of seasons yet?"

"I'm starting to be a believer, especially since there's also the mosquito test," Drew teased.

"The mosquito test?"

"Sure. If you don't have mosquitoes, then it must be winter."

"I suppose you were never bitten by a mosquito up north?"

"Maybe once or twice," he admitted. "But it was a fluke."

"A fluke, my eye."

"Okay, so we're at a standoff on mosquitoes."

"How did you wind up in Florida? Landry Enterprises is headquartered in Cedar Rapids."

"I first came to Florida because of the horses. Then a friend told me about the house, and I decided to check into it. I thought it might be nice for my father to have someplace to go during the cold weather. At his age the harsh Iowa winters get to him."

"Is he here now?"

"No, but he's due any day. He couldn't seem to make up his mind whether to fly or drive. I suppose I'll hear from him tomorrow or the next day. He's not exactly predictable," he said with fondness in his wry tone that intrigued her.

"Will you only be here through the season then?" she asked, surprised at her sense of disappointment. She'd hoped he might be settling in, that he would be a real neighbor. Maybe even more? No. She wouldn't allow herself to start thinking like that.

"I'll come and go," he said, reaching over to rub his fingers across the knuckles of her clenched fist. "I seem to be discovering a lot of reasons to stay lately."

Tina shivered and met his gaze boldly. "I'm glad," she admitted softly, contradicting her head, which was shouting that she'd only be safe from these disturbing sensations once he was back in Iowa.

"Enough about me now," he said. "I gather you're a Florida native."

"Yep. I was born in West Palm Beach, went to the local junior college and then finished at the University of Florida," she said, watching him for any subtle sign of surprise that she hadn't had a classier background. It didn't seem to faze him at all. "That doesn't bother you?"

He stared at her in astonishment. "Why should it?"

"It bothers a lot of people in Palm Beach and at Harrington Industries. Unless your pedigree is a mile long and your degree is from Harvard, you don't count for much. I mean, where else would the mayor's race involve a descendant of Charlemagne and King Louis XIV running against a descendant of Russian czars?"

"By those standards, I'm just as nouveau riche as you are. The world is full of snobs, Tina. I'm not one of them. I thought we established that last night." He regarded her closely. "Gerald Harrington wasn't a snob, either, was he?"

"No," she said quietly. Unexpected tears suddenly shimmered in her eyes. Sometimes it hit her like a blow that Gerald was truly gone. "Gerald wasn't a snob. He loved everyone. I think that's what made him such an anomaly in the business world. He didn't have a ruthless, unkind bone in his body and yet he succeeded."

"Are you still in love with him?"

Tina sensed the tension as he asked the potentially volatile question and sighed. "I suppose I'll always be in love with him. He was a wonderful man, and I owe him a great deal. He turned my life into a fairy tale. There were times when I felt exactly like Cinderella. I think that's why I want so badly to help Sarah and the others. I was extraordinarily fortunate. I don't ever want to forget that."

"I'm not sure you answered my question. Are you over your husband and ready to go on?"

"Gerald is dead, Drew. I'd be a fool if I clung to the past rather than live in the present."

The tightness around his mouth eased. "I'm glad, Tina." He reached across the table and lifted her hand to his lips. The velvet warmth spread through her, stealing into all the hidden places that had grown so cold since Gerald's fatal accident.

"Tina, maybe it's too soon for me to be saying this, but I have to. I don't want there to be any misunderstandings between us about what I want."

She gave him a puzzled glance, though her heart was skittering crazily. "I don't understand," she said,

not meaning the remark to be coy. She needed to have
him make his intentions very clear.

"I said it earlier. I want you. I've wanted to make love
to you ever since I first laid eyes on you. I don't intend
to give up until you want the same thing."

Tina gulped. That was certainly clear enough. Now
that he'd said it so plainly, she needed time to absorb
it. A lifetime or two ought to do it, but he wasn't going
to allow her nearly that long. She tried to look away,
but Drew's fingers captured her chin and forced her to
meet this gaze. "Could I talk you into coming home
with me tonight?"

"You probably could," Tina admitted softly, surprised to find that she was enjoying the purely feminine thrill of watching the heat of desire blaze to life
in his eyes. "But I hope you won't try."

"Oh."

She smiled tremulously. "I didn't say never, just not
yet, Drew. I don't think either one of us can be sure of
our feelings and I know there are too many complications in my life right now."

"And you blame me for at least one of them."

"I don't really blame you, though I still don't understand entirely why you felt you had to meddle in my
lifestyle."

The blue of his eyes darkened. There was so much
pain shadowing those eyes that Tina felt the hurt deep
inside herself.

"Someday I'll explain it to you," he promised, "but
right now I'm more interested in why you won't go
home with me when you've admitted that you want to."

"You must read the *Wall Street Journal*. You know

that I'm facing a critical board meeting in a few weeks. I have to focus all of my energies on that and on getting DCF off my back. I need some time to put things back on track before I face any sort of personal involvement."

"Am I a distraction, then?" he asked, a teasing glint in his eyes.

"That's one way of putting it."

"Is that your only reason?"

"No," she admitted candidly.

"I didn't think so. What's the rest?"

"Well, from what you said earlier, Billy would heartily disapprove of things heating up so rapidly between the two of us. After your speech on honor and respect and emotional commitment, he'd probably come after you with a shotgun."

"He probably would at that."

Tina didn't add that she also needed some time to sort out her feelings about becoming involved with a man as driven and domineering as Drew Landry, a man capable of wresting control of her life away from her. Although Drew had been supportive so far, she knew that he was also a very protective man. He'd hinted earlier at a willingness to take over Harrington Industries rather than have her worry herself to death over it. It seemed nothing more than honest concern for her well-being, but perhaps it was more.

Tina had learned from experience that too many men saw her as a shortcut to control of Harrington Industries. Things were happening too quickly between her and Drew for her to trust her feelings—or his stated ones—completely. Although she was aggressive and decisive in her business dealings, it was only today that she'd learned to gamble at all. She was not ready to bet with abandon on something as potentially hurtful as a commitment to a man she hardly knew. It would take time for Drew to convince her that his motives were entirely personal and altruistic.

Right now the look in his eyes was certainly personal. It was bold and assessing and heated with desire.

"You take as long as you like to get things back on track, Tina," he said slowly, his voice filled with lazy sensuality. "Just make sure that track leads right next door."

Tina discovered that she wanted desperately to believe he meant what he said, that he would be there when she was ready to take a chance on the future.

Chapter Seven

When Drew turned off the coastal highway into Tina's driveway, it was close to midnight. His headlights picked up Billy's forlorn, hunched figure sitting in the shadows. Lady MacBeth sat on his shoulder. For once, the normally talkative bird was absolutely silent. A flutter of dread rippled through Tina.

Anxious words tumbled out almost incoherently as she leapt from the car and ran up the walk. "Billy, what are you doing out here at this hour? Has something happened? Is somebody sick? Are you okay?"

"Sure," he mumbled, swiping at the tears on his cheeks. He didn't look at her.

Drew approached more slowly and touched a restraining hand to Tina's arm. When she would have probed further, he shook his head, then asked Billy casually, "Mind if we sit here with you for a while, then? It's a nice night."

Billy shrugged, his gaze still directed toward the ground. They sat down on either side of him, waiting for more, letting the silence go on and on, thickening with an unbearable tension.

"Where is everyone else?" Tina asked finally when she could keep her voice calm.

"Out back, I guess. Maybe they've gone to bed. I don't know."

"Were you waiting for us?"

Suddenly Billy turned to face her, his eyes no longer sad but filled with anger. He drew back a hand as though he wanted to hit her, but at the last second he stopped himself and demanded in a choked whisper, "Why didn't you tell me what was going on? How could you keep something this important from me? Don't I count around here?"

"Tell you what, son?" Drew said when Tina couldn't think of a thing to say in the face of such smoldering rage and heartrending anguish.

"That me and Aunt Juliet are going to have to go away."

"That's not so," Tina said. She reached out to Billy, but he jerked back as though he couldn't bear her touch. His rejection wrenched her heart. From the moment she'd rescued Billy and his aunt, he'd been her adoring shadow. He'd trusted her and now he obviously felt she'd not only betrayed him but was abandoning him as well.

"Billy, no one is going to make you go away. I swear to you, everything is going to work out."

He glowered at her, his eyes disbelieving. "But you didn't tell me anything, and that's not what they were saying tonight. They said some guy's coming in the morning and he's going to make us leave. It'll be just like it was before, when my folks went off and dumped me with Aunt Juliet. We won't have any money, nothing to eat. Aunt Juliet can't live like that. She gets so cold. Last winter she coughed all the time. She should have gone to the doctor, but we didn't have any money."

Billy shuddered, and Tina could only imagine what his memories must be like. He was far too young and vulnerable to have shouldered such responsibilities. She should have seen what the DCF threat would do to him and prepared him for it.

"I promise you, we're going to work this out."

"Why are they coming after all this time? It doesn't make any sense. We've been here for ages."

"It's because of me," Drew admitted. Tina could hear the guilt and sadness in his voice. He was seeing first-hand the traumatic effect of his well-meaning actions. "I filed a complaint."

Billy stared at him in stunned disbelief, his lower lip quivering. "But I thought you liked us. I mean after that talk we had and all, I even thought you and I were going to be pals. Is it because I broke your window? Are you still mad about that?"

"Of course not." Drew swore gently, briefly touching Billy's arm. Tina noticed that the boy didn't pull away from the tender, comforting gesture. "I'm only human, Billy. I made a mistake. A big one. I thought things were different than they are. The people at DCF are making the same mistake. Once they arrive, they'll know better, just like I did."

Billy's gaze swept anxiously over Tina's face. "Do you believe that?"

She embraced him. Though he didn't respond, this time he didn't move away, and her breath escaped in a tiny sigh of relief.

"I have to believe it, Billy. I don't know what I'd do if they ever took you away. You're part of my family now." She managed a tremulous smile for him and brushed the hair off his face. "Now why don't you go on up to bed. Tomorrow's an important day and we all need to be ready for it."

"Can I stay home from school?"

"I don't know. We'll talk about it in the morning."

His lip curled defiantly. "You can't make me go. I want to be here with you."

"We'll talk about it in the morning," she repeated firmly.

Billy's skinny arms wound around her and held her tight. "Don't worry, Tina. I'll tell 'em that we love you. Then they'll have to let us stay, won't they?"

"That might do it," she said, but she wondered if it would be nearly enough.

When Billy had gone inside, Drew pulled Tina into his arms. The tension eased, then fell away as she buried her face in his shoulder, the smooth fabric of his shirt soft against her cheek. His arms were so much stronger than Billy's and just as loving. She let her eyes drift shut. She felt so safe right now, but how long would that fragile feeling last? Would it survive even another twenty-four hours?

"We're only postponing things between us," Drew reminded her as though he'd read her mind. "You and I are going to have our time together someday. This won't change that."

"I hope you're right," she said wistfully, suddenly aware of just how much she needed him in her life. It was too soon to describe that emotion as love, but there was an undeniable aching desire building inside that went straight to her soul.

"I know I'm right, and it's going to be soon, because I'm not sure how long I can wait to hold you in my arms."

She gave him a faltering half smile. "You are holding me in your arms. Should I be insulted that you haven't noticed?"

"I noticed all right, but I'm trying not to think about it." His voice was rough with frustration.

"That doesn't make a lot of sense."

"It does, when you're not sure if you can control yourself."

Tina fiddled flirtatiously with his loosened tie and gazed up at him provocatively through half-lowered lashes. "I thought Drew Landry was the sort of man who was always in control."

Uttering a low groan deep in his throat, Drew stilled her roaming fingers, which were headed daringly down his chest. "He was until he met a bewitching, spirited neighbor, who seems to invite everyone to live with her except him. It's doing terrible things for his ego."

"You have a perfectly good home of your own," she retorted.

He brightened. "If that's what it takes, I'll sell it first thing in the morning."

"Nice try, but I think I'm in enough trouble with the group I've got now."

He sighed heavily, but she noted that the corners of his lips were twitching with amusement. "Okay," he said regretfully. "I guess I'll see you tomorrow."

"You are going to be here when they come, then?"

"Of course. You ordered me to be here."

"And you listened?" she said in mock astonishment. "Amazing. I'll have to remember the technique."

He kissed her lightly. "Don't let it go to your head."

Then he kissed her again, his tongue sliding over velvet softness as ripples of excitement danced along her spine. Her fingers tangled in his dark hair as she held him close, reveling in his strength and his gentleness. Problems that had seemed insurmountable vanished, caught up in a whirlwind of thrilling sensations. She hadn't wanted to feel that way in his arms, hadn't wanted to face the rush of heat and alluring tension that his touch created, but it was there, beyond her control.

Despite her intentions to the contrary, that kiss would have lasted until dawn if Tina had had her way. It would be accompanied by every nuance of lovemaking that she and Drew could explore. Part of her wanted, needed, that tonight, but once again she rejected it as coming at the wrong time. She was attracted to Drew, but she didn't know him. Loving intimacy deserved much more. It deserved a depth of feeling built on trust and sharing, things that couldn't happen overnight.

Breathless, she pulled away as far as Drew's tight embrace would allow. "I think you'd better go."

"Give me a rain check?" he asked and pressed a burning kiss at the hollow in her throat. Flesh that had been cool to the touch turned feverish, and her pulse pounded with a shattering violence. Too much, she thought with a moan. She withdrew from the heated temptation.

"You've got it," she said softly, trailing her fingers along his cheek, astonished at the possessiveness that flared inside her.

And then, just when she would have kept him with her, he was gone and the long, lonely night was all that waited for her.

It was a particularly somber group that gathered to await the arrival of the DCF inspectors. Aunt Juliet was in her usual black attire, which did nothing to brighten the mood. In her nervousness she'd drawn her hair back so tightly that her face had a pinched look.

After much heated discussion about the impression it might make on DCF, Billy had been allowed to stay home from school. Drew's vote had been the clincher. Before Billy came downstairs, he warned them that leaving Billy out would devastate him, shattering the feeling of belonging he'd finally found. The others finally agreed.

Normally, a day off from school would have thrilled Billy. Today, though, he sat next to his aunt, clutching her hand and trying valiantly not to let his own anxiety show.

"I don't suppose anyone wants breakfast," Sarah asked hopefully, twisting her lace-edged hankie with nervous fingers. Not even Drew responded.

"I'll go fix some coffee anyway. We might as well be wide awake for this." She bustled off to the kitchen.

"I can't stand this waiting around," Mr. Kelly grumbled to no one in particular. He stood up and hitched up his khaki pants. "I'm going out to pick tomatoes. Can't let 'em die on the vines just 'cause some fancy bureaucrats take it into their heads to come nosin' around where they don't belong. Anyone wants me that's where I'll be." He stomped off through the French doors. Tina could hear him muttering long after he'd disappeared from sight.

Drew, who'd arrived practically at first light, took Tina's icy hand and held it until she could feel her blood stirring to life. She smiled at him gratefully.

"Are you okay?" he asked, his voice filled with concern.

She nodded. "I'll be fine once this morning is over with. It's the waiting that's killing me. I couldn't sleep last night. Mr. Kelly and I were bumping into each other in the halls all night long."

"Let me handle things," Drew suggested again. "They may listen to me. You're all too emotionally involved."

Tina scowled at him. "Drew, you got us into this."

"Which means it's up to me to get you out."

"You already had a chance yesterday, and it didn't work. Besides, I've told you before that I don't need a protector. I'm perfectly capable of fighting my own battles." She grinned as his jaw set stubbornly. "Drew Landry, I mean it. It's my battle."

"Then what the hell am I doing here if you don't need me?"

"You're here to watch," she reminded him lightly, then sighed and gently touched his cheek. "And I do need you just to be my friend."

"Always," he promised, "but I can't swear I'll be able to keep my mouth shut."

Sarah returned with a silver coffee service just then, but before she could even pour the first cup the doorbell rang. Edward Grant and two young assistants were on the doorstep, all of them carrying battered, bulky

briefcases. The introductions were perfunctory. Mr.
Grant obviously was as anxious to get through the ordeal as Tina was.

Tina had no sooner escorted them to the living room,
than the doorbell rang again. She opened the door
this time to find several reporters outside. Most were
society-page writers in search of titillating gossip, but a
prominent business columnist from Miami was among
them, and the sight of him made Tina's blood run cold.

Before she could get the door closed, a dashing, elderly man with a shock of white hair and startlingly familiar blue eyes walked in, followed by the reporters.

"I'm Seth Landry," he told Tina, looking a little be-
mused by all the confusion. "That son of mine around
here someplace? I told him I'd be coming down for a
little visit, and he's disappeared. That tight-lipped old
butler next door seemed to think he might be here."

"Of all days," Tina muttered, but she smiled brightly
and waved Drew's father vaguely in the direction of
the living room where everyone else had gathered. She
considered boarding up that awful room with all the
combatants inside and then fleeing to Bermuda. It was
a very attractive, if cowardly notion. Instead, she took
a deep breath and jumped into the fray.

The noise level was so high, it was impossible for
Tina to hear herself think. Only Mr. Kelly, returning
from the garden and brushing dirt off his trousers,
seemed unduly complacent. Tina knew perfectly well
that was because his hearing aid was upstairs on his
dresser. She almost wished she had one too, so she could
shut out the din.

Apparently Mr. Grant was equally dismayed by the

unexpected interest in his inspection. He beckoned Tina over.

"I wasn't aware that this would attract quite so much attention," he muttered, blinking at her from behind his glasses. He didn't look nearly as sure of himself as he had yesterday. "Could we go somewhere else to talk?"

"Certainly." She started to lead the way to a cheerful room across the hall, but everyone jumped up to follow them. Mr. Grant, his eyes wide, stared at Tina helplessly. She stifled a grin and said, "Everyone, please. If you'll wait here until I conclude my meeting with the gentlemen from DCF, I'll be happy to answer any questions."

Grumbling, the reporters sat back down. Grandmother Sarah, delighted at finding a way to keep occupied, offered them coffee and fresh-baked blueberry muffins. She recruited Juliet to help.

Billy and Drew, however, were not about to let Tina go off alone with the enemy. "It's okay," she told them.

"Tina, please," Billy pleaded, running his fingers through his slicked-down hair. The gesture created rows of little spikes all over his head. He looked as though he'd stuck a finger in a light socket. "I gotta tell him how I feel."

"You'll get a chance to talk with us, young man," Edward Grant promised, smiling for the first time. That smile, as tepid as it was, gave Tina renewed hope. Billy looked at her and, when she nodded, he retreated to help in the kitchen.

Drew was less easily persuaded. Finally, Tina suggested he stay with Mr. Kelly. "I know he's more upset than he's letting on. It can't be good for his blood pressure. Please, Drew."

"Are you positive you don't need me? I'm sure Dad would be happy to keep Mr. Kelly occupied. They could go out and look at the garden. Dad's crazy about compost."

"Stay with them. I need to do this myself."

"Damn it all, woman," he muttered, but he went.

Tina took Mr. Grant and his assistants through the house. None of them said a word as they saw the rooms in which her friends were staying, each of them bright and cheerful and filled with personal memorabilia. Each also had a private bath. If the inspectors were surprised that Grandmother Sarah and the rest hadn't been banished to servants' quarters or worse, they kept it to themselves. At subtle signals from Mr. Grant, the assistants made frantic notes on forms they carried with them on clipboards.

Back downstairs, Mr. Grant asked if there was someplace where he could interview each of the guests privately. Tina showed him into a room and brought Grandmother Sarah to him. Mr. Kelly followed, and Mr. Grant agreed to interview Billy and Aunt Juliet together at the end.

Tina sat outside the door while the first interview went on and on, her hands folded in her lap. She knew that she appeared totally relaxed. She'd conditioned herself from childhood not to show her emotions and thus upset her parents. It was an ability that had been extraordinarily helpful when she'd been confronted with difficult board members as well. Never once had they been able to read her intentions or her fears.

Despite the outward appearance of calm, the inside of her stomach was churning. When Grandmother Sarah came out, the older woman's expression had brightened considerably. She sat beside Tina and patted her hand.

"Well, now, that wasn't half as bad as I'd expected. Stop fretting. Edward is really quite a nice young man."

"Edward?" Tina glanced at her sharply. "Are you referring to that emotionless automaton inside by his first name?"

"Really, Tina, I'm surprised at you," Sarah scolded. "You're normally quite a good judge of character. Edward is just trying to do his job."

"It's a lousy job," she retorted crossly. "And that's not what you were saying about him yesterday."

"That may be, but I can admit a mistake when I make one. He explained it all very carefully. He has to learn the truth. Not everyone is as lucky as we are."

"Do you think he can see that?"

"I think he'd be a fool if he didn't, and Edward is no fool. Trust me," she said and patted Tina's hand again. "Why don't I send Drew out here to keep you company?"

"I'm not sure I'm speaking to him today after all."

"Oh, posh-tosh. This will be over soon and you'll forget all about it. Don't throw away a chance at an exciting new life over a little thing like this."

"*A little thing?* You think turning our lives upside down is a *little thing?*"

"Come now, Tina. Don't go losing your perspective. I think life gets utterly boring if there's not some sort of disturbance now and again to spark things up."

"*Spark things up,* for heaven's sakes? Just tell me one good thing to come out of all this."

"Why that's easy, child. Just look how much closer

we all are now that we see we might lose each other. We appreciate things we'd been taking for granted."

Tina regarded her doubtfully. "I suppose, but I could have appreciated all of you just fine without going to this extreme."

"Maybe. Maybe not," Sarah replied, then gave her a calculated glance. "Then, of course, there's you and Drew."

"No, there's not," Tina insisted stubbornly.

Sarah said with absolute aplomb, "We'll just have to wait and see about that, won't we? I think maybe I'll send him on over to keep you company anyway. He seems to distract you better than I do."

"Humph."

When Drew entered the hallway a few minutes later, he gave her his most dazzling grin. It warmed her down to her toes in spite of her best intentions to keep him at arm's length. If she was going to wind up hating Drew for splitting up her family, she didn't want to have a taste of falling in love with him first.

"Sarah sent me out to cheer you up."

"Actually, I think she'd prefer it if you'd seduce me. She seems to be feeling particularly romantic and philosophical today."

"I'd be happy to oblige with the seduction, if you think DCF wouldn't object to our using one of the bedrooms. I'm afraid we'd draw too big a crowd down here."

Tina suddenly found herself giggling at the thought of all those society writers peeking through the curtains as she and Drew gave them enough material to gossip about for the next ten editions of their papers. The potential headlines in the business pages could be even more provocative.

"I can just see the headline on Gregory Hanks's column," she said, still chuckling. "Merger talks begin between Harrington Industries exec and Landry CEO."

"I like that," Drew agreed. "Care to merge?"

"If you're referring to us, we've already put that possibility on hold. If you're referring to our companies, don't hold your breath."

"It might not be a bad idea, you know," he said thoughtfully, as though the prospect had just occurred to him. "We'd be an unbeatable team."

Tina eyed him warily. Why this sudden talk of a merger? In an instant, Drew had reawakened her earlier doubts about why he had involved himself so deeply in her life.

"I've already got my business lineup in place. I'm not interested in joining a new team," she retorted lightly, determined not to take his idle chitchat seriously right now. Later, she might have to examine Drew's motivations more closely, but for the moment she had to focus all her energies on keeping her household together.

That, of course, was all the more frustrating because the entire situation was out of her hands. She could only sit idly by and wait.

When Mr. Grant and his assistants finally emerged, she tried to read the expressions on their faces, but they were masters of disguise. Looking at them, you'd have thought they'd just dropped in for a pleasant morning of tea and conversation.

"Will you speak to the press before you leave?" she asked. "They've been waiting."

"I'd really rather not," Mr. Grant said nervously. "We're still in the preliminary stages of this."

"Then tell them that. I'm sure they'd rather hear it from you than me."

He finally agreed.

Looking uncomfortable and running a finger around the collar of his shirt as though he were choking, Mr. Grant said tersely, "Mrs. Harrington has been extremely cooperative with this investigation. Our preliminary findings are that there are no violations of state regulations. However, we have not completed our report. We expect it to be available within the next few weeks."

He waved off questions and practically ran to the front door, leaving Tina to field the remainder of the questions. Most of them had to do with how she had met her friends and what their backgrounds were. The society reporters, although clearly somewhat aghast at their lack of social connections, were charmed by Sarah, Juliet and Mr. Kelly. Even Billy managed to delight them with comments that were actually printable.

Just when she thought it was winding up, the business writer requested a last question.

Tina nodded. "Certainly, Mr. Hanks."

He turned to Drew. "Mr. Landry, exactly what is your role in all of this? I understand that you were the one who made the report that brought this situation to the attention of the state."

"That's true. I had received some information which I felt merited further investigation. As some of you may know," he said, glancing at his father, "I have a special interest in the welfare of the elderly. I wanted to assure myself that no one here was being taken advantage of.

After meeting Mrs. Harrington and her friends, I am now reassured that I was mistaken and that this is a happy, family-style environment. I regret that I stirred all of this up unnecessarily and brought these people so much pain."

Tina looked from Drew to his father, whose eyes were surprisingly misty, and wondered what Drew had meant about his special interest in the elderly. Now that she did some thinking, he had been hinting from the very beginning, but she'd been too wrapped up in her own concerns to ask the right questions.

Even now, her appreciation and curiosity couldn't dispel the aura of gloom that seemed to weave around her. She still worried about how this could end up and what it might do to the image of Harrington Industries.

Since taking over, she had tried so hard to do the things that she thought would make Gerald proud and, while she knew he would have approved of what she'd done by taking in her friends, she wasn't sure how he would have felt about the implications for his company. Gerald had been an intensely private man who ran his business with quiet diplomacy and behind-the-scenes finesse. It appeared she was about to bring everything into the public eye with a bang.

She was drawn back from her reverie by the tail end of another question from the business writer.

"So you don't see this as increasing the opportunity for you to snap up Harrington Industries?"

Tina's breath caught in her throat as her attention was riveted on Drew, awaiting his response. The question pulled together all of the confusion and doubts that had begun to plague Tina. Drew met her gaze steadily,

and his reply was clearly directed more to her than to
Gregory Hanks.

"My interest in this situation is strictly personal. It
has nothing whatsoever to do with Harrington Industries or Landry Enterprises."

"But you must agree that adverse publicity right now
for Mrs. Harrington would make her company a prime
target for a takeover attempt."

"As a businessman, I would have to say that your
analysis is correct. However, I repeat, I am not interested in acquiring Harrington Industries."

Drew's statement was made with absolute conviction, but Tina couldn't shake the feeling that he was only
saying what he knew she wanted to hear. Trust, which
had been building slowly, suffered a severe setback.

Chapter Eight

As soon as the last of the reporters had left, Tina sagged against the front door with relief.

What an ordeal!

She wanted nothing more than a day—maybe even a whole month—all to herself to try to sort out everything that had happened, but getting time alone in this house was next to impossible. She would have settled for an hour just to think about Drew's offhand, yet disturbing private allusions to a possible merger, followed only moments later by his public denial that such a prospect had ever occurred to him.

For the last few days she had put aside her doubts about his motives, but his comments this morning had made it impossible for her to go on ignoring her suspicions. With the critical stockholders' meeting coming up soon, she had to find some way to counter all of the adverse publicity. Otherwise, Gregory Hanks's suggestion about some shark—possibly Drew?—sniffing blood was very likely to become a reality.

The one thing she didn't want to face, but knew she had to, was the possibility that Drew had initiated the DCF investigation not for his stated reasons, but because of his own interest in Harrington Industries. Was he actively pursuing her for the same reason? She had to find some way to discover the truth before it was too late.

A thought flashed through her mind. If Drew were making a move on the company, it might be showing up already in the sale of Harrington Industries stock. Checking to make sure that Drew had gone outside with the others, she took out her phone to call her assistant, David Warren, an eager young man who'd proved himself time and again. Not only was he good with the stockholders, but he was efficient, loyal and, above all, discreet. She needed to rely on all of those traits now more than ever.

"Jennifer, get David for me."

"Sure, honey. How did this morning go?"

"Don't ask. I'm sure you'll read all about it in the papers anyway."

"I can hardly wait. I just love starting my day with juicy gossip, especially when I know it's probably not true. Just a second and I'll put David on."

A moment later he picked up. "Hi, Tina. What's up?"

"David, I want you to do some checking for me."

"Sure."

"Do a little nosing around with our brokerage house contacts and see if there's been any unusual movement in our stock."

David's voice dropped to a whisper. "Have you heard something? Is there anything in particular I should be asking about?"

"No. Not yet. I just have a few unsubstantiated suspicions. For now, just check on the movement. Is the volume especially high, any large blocks selling, that sort of thing. Okay?"

"You've got it. Want me to call you back at home or will you be in later?"

"If you discover anything significant call me here. Otherwise we'll talk it over again tomorrow. I want you to stay on top of this for the next few weeks."

"Sure."

"Thanks, David."

When she'd hung up, she sat for a long time, staring pensively out the window, wondering when she had become so distrustful. Would her entire future always be filled with doubts? The possibility depressed her. There couldn't be much joy in success if it robbed her of the ability to trust, to care.

She sighed as she caught a glimpse of a laughing Drew. He, Aunt Juliet and Billy were on the lawn playing croquet. Drew was leaning down to whisper in Aunt Juliet's ear, probably suggesting strategy judging from the scowl Billy was shooting at them.

"Hey, you guys, no fair," Billy finally shouted, his voice drifting into the house on the breeze. Tina grinned at his indignation. Billy did everything with an all-out energy, and his desire to win reminded Tina of herself as a girl.

From a very early age, she'd had ambition and drive. At first it had been evidenced by little more than the typical ten-cent lemonade stand, set up on the front lawn day after day until she'd had enough money for a bright green bicycle she wanted. As she'd grown older, her goal had been refined, her determination solidified: she was going to change her life for the better, to achieve the success that had always eluded her parents.

She realized now it hadn't been so much the money or social status that had motivated her. She'd simply wanted the respect that seemed to go hand in hand with them. In Palm Beach County the separation between rich and poor wasn't a line. It was the whole damn length of the causeway. She'd wanted desperately to cross that bridge, just for the sheer joy of the challenge. Few people made it. She wanted to be one of them.

Billy responded to challenges just as she had. Although life had become easier for him since coming to live with Tina, he hadn't forgotten the past. Last night's tearful conversation had been proof enough of that. Though he had the adolescent's aversion to studying, he had enough street savvy to survive in school and the athletic ability to be a star. Billy would make a name for himself someday. She had no doubts about it.

Tina grinned as Billy moaned loudly when Aunt Juliet, hooting with glee, drove his ball far from the next wicket. Drew threw his arms around Juliet and planted a kiss on her cheek. As far away as she was, Tina could see the older woman blushing with pleasure. When wisps of her hair fell loose from her bun, Aunt Juliet didn't even notice.

"Hey, Billy," Tina called out the window. "Maybe you should stick to baseball."

Billy looked up and gave her a crooked smile. "Why don't you get out here and help? These guys are teaming up against me."

"Hold them off awhile longer. I'll be out as soon as I do something about lunch."

However, when she walked through the swinging door that separated the dining room and kitchen a few minutes later, she found that Grandmother Sarah was already pouring iced tea into a crystal pitcher and arranging sandwiches on a plate. Seth Landry was sitting at the table, his long legs stretched out in front of him, his fingers laced behind his head. As Tina watched, he reached out and snitched a piece of ham that had fallen onto the plate. Sarah smacked his hand. With a sense of amazement and delight, Tina realized that he looked perfectly at home, as though he'd been doing the same thing for years and years. The normally unflappable Sarah was as nervous and fluttery as a teenager.

Tina smiled as she caught the sparks of interest arcing between the two of them. "Need any help?" she asked brightly.

Startled, Sarah practically knocked over the pitcher of tea. She glowered at Tina. "Christina Elizabeth, stop sneaking up on me. You're going to scare me to death one of these days and you'll have that on your conscience forever. I'll probably even come back to haunt you."

Seth's blue eyes sparkled and, Tina noted, he never once turned away from Sarah. The man looked as though he'd been dazzled by a bolt of lightning.

"I only asked if you needed any help," Tina said with exaggerated innocence. She had to try very hard not to wink at Drew's father. "Your mind must have been on other things."

Sarah's scowl deepened. "Just take these things out to the others," she grumbled. "I'll be along with the pie in a minute. It's warming in the oven." Her glance skimmed over Seth, then focused on the oven door as she mumbled, "Maybe you should go on out with Tina."

"Nope," Seth said, settling down more comfortably right where he was. "Think I'll stay right here. Haven't been around a kitchen that smelled this good in a long time."

"Sarah does bake a terrific pie," Tina said agreeably, picking up the overburdened tray of food. "Take your time."

"Perceptive gal," she heard Seth say after she'd left the room.

"I don't know what you mean," Sarah retorted huffily, and Tina rolled her eyes heavenward.

If the last few minutes were any indication, Seth Landry's visit to Florida ought to be very interesting. She wondered if he needed to get back in time for the spring planting or, for that matter, the fall harvest. Sarah was not likely to be won over easily. She had an independent streak that went back more than sixty years and had survived the persuasive tactics of many an amorous suitor. Tina had no idea why she'd never married, but she knew Sarah was too warm and giving not to have had her share of love along the way.

Still grinning at the thought of the fireworks to come, Tina went back through the living room, only to discover that the croquet game had apparently ended and that Drew had come back inside. He was standing at her desk with a puzzled expression on his face, holding a piece of her stationery.

"Who won the game?" she asked neutrally, not sure she was thrilled about being alone with him now that her mind was reeling with confusing thoughts and doubts.

"What?"

"Croquet. Who won?"

"Oh. Juliet did."

"With a little help from you from the looks of it. I suspect Billy's going to be out for blood after lunch."

"Hmm," he muttered distractedly.

"Drew, is something wrong?"

"I wonder..." His mind was still a million miles away.

"Drew!" Tina said in exasperation. "What is going on?"

He looked up finally and caught the stubborn set of her chin. "Sorry. I was just trying to figure something out."

"So I noticed. Care to explain or would you prefer to keep this mystery to yourself?"

"Give me a couple more minutes." He noticed the tray in her hands for the first time. "Take that on out, why don't you, and then come back. I need to ask you something."

There was an odd edge to his voice, an unfamiliar tone she couldn't quite identify. Puzzled, she watched him for a minute, then shrugged. "Okay. I'll be right back."

But Drew was already absorbed with the note in his hand.

When she returned a few minutes later, her curiosity fully aroused, he hadn't moved an inch and he was still scanning the same piece of paper. He held it out to her.

"Is this yours?"

She regarded him oddly, still perplexed by the intensity of his tone. "You mean the stationery? Of course. It has my name engraved on it."

He arched his eyebrow meaningfully. "I was referring to the handwriting."

Tina looked at it more closely. "No. It's Aunt Juliet's. She was answering some invitations for me. Why?"

Suddenly, Drew's eyes danced with amusement and his lips started twitching. Then they quirked into a full-fledged smile followed by a roar of laughter. "Oh my. This is too much. I should have guessed."

"Mind letting me in on the joke?"

"We've been had, my dear."

"What on earth are you talking about?"

"Remember I told you about those anonymous letters, telling me about what was going on here and suggesting that I should check it out personally."

"The ones that sent you scurrying off to talk to my neighbors and interview every official in town?"

"Yep."

"How could I forget? What about them?"

"We have Aunt Juliet to thank for them."

"What!" Tina's horrified shriek wasn't muffled a bit by the thick velvet drapes. It practically shook the windows.

Drew nodded, wearing one heckuva grin, Tina thought as she tried to focus on the implications of what he was saying.

"I'm no handwriting expert," he told her, "but I'd wager my income for the next few years on it."

"But why?" Tina's amber eyes filled with confusion. "Why on earth would she do something like that? She must have known the trouble it would cause."

"Obviously she didn't." He held out his hand. "Shall we go find out what she was up to?"

The conversation that followed was like something out of a Freudian case study. As soon as everyone had assembled on the terrace, Drew gazed fondly at Juliet and said gently, "Mind if I ask you a question?"

"Of course not, young man. You're practically a part of the family."

"Were you the one who sent me those anonymous letters?" he asked bluntly.

Aunt Juliet immediately turned pale. Behind her glasses, her eyes took on a vague, faraway look, and she twisted her napkin nervously. She did not once meet Tina's incredulous gaze.

"I don't know what you mean," she said in a whispery, frightened voice.

"I think you do. It's okay. I just wanted to know if you were the one who sent them."

Tears welled up in Juliet's brown eyes and she tugged off her glasses and wiped at the dampness futilely. "I didn't mean to cause all this fuss. We only wanted to do something nice for Tina," she said, staring at Drew pleadingly. "I had no idea... Oh, I'm so sorry."

Suddenly she jumped up and ran weeping into the house.

"Now look what you've done. Thought we'd had enough of an inquisition 'round here already today," Mr. Kelly admonished and went after her. Billy glared at Drew, then followed.

"Oh, dear, it's all my fault," Grandmother Sarah wailed, as Seth Landry patted her hand.

"Now, Sarah, calm down," he said gently. "Don't get all worked up over this. I'm sure they'll understand."

"Understand what?" Tina demanded, just as Drew repeated, "Your fault?"

To Tina's astonishment, Sarah blushed furiously and clung tightly to Seth Landry's hand. She must really be in a dither if she was hanging onto a man she hardly knew.

"Well?" Tina urged. "What did you do, Sarah?"

"Leave the woman be," Seth said defensively. "Can't you see you're upsetting her?"

"If she's done something, we might as well get it out in the open," Tina countered. "Keeping things quiet has already caused enough trouble."

"It's okay, Seth," Sarah said with a resigned sigh. "Tina's right. I suppose I might as well admit to everything."

"Sarah!" Tina's patience was reaching the breaking point.

"All right. Just give me a minute to pull my thoughts together."

"Your thoughts have never been scattered for a single minute. Stop fiddling around."

Sarah's eyes twinkled with a devilish glint, then shifted to include Drew. "Okay. The truth of the matter is that I was trying to think of some way to get the two of you together. I'd seen Drew's picture in the paper and you didn't have anyone in your life to speak of."

She stared at Tina, daring her to contradict the statement. Tina simply scowled. "When he moved in next door, I thought it was too good to be true. Juliet and I discussed it, and I guess she decided to take matters into her own hands. You know how she can be when she goes all flighty and romantic. I had no idea things would get this out of hand. I doubt if she ever even thought of the consequences."

"You were trying to do *what?*" Tina still couldn't believe her ears and she didn't dare look at Drew. Of all the hare-brained, idiotic, humiliating schemes.

Drew was suddenly chuckling again. Tina glowered at him. "Are you crazy, too?"

"No crazier than anyone else around here."

"Sarah, how could you?" Tina glared at Seth Landry. "How did you know about this?"

"Sarah just mentioned that she thought something like this might have happened, but she wasn't sure. She's been worried sick about it."

"Why didn't you say something to me?" Tina demanded. "Maybe I could have done something sooner. If I'd gone right over, I could have stopped that report to DCF."

"Like Seth said, I wasn't sure, until now. I didn't want to go pointing the finger at Juliet. Besides, what good would it have done? All the wheels were already in motion. My telling you wouldn't have stopped them."

"Dear God," Tina moaned. "I don't believe this. You two and your matchmaking. I should have known that sooner or later something like this would go on. Couldn't you have tried a little harder to like Martin? Then none of this would have happened."

At the mention of Martin, Drew shot her a startled glance. Sarah lifted her chin defiantly. "You don't have to make such a fuss about it now. It might not have been the ideal solution, but it worked, didn't it?" she sniffed. "You two are together, aren't you? That's all we wanted."

Tina and Drew exchanged glances, hers resigned, his sparkling with devilment. "Not yet, we aren't," she retorted, as he nodded enthusiastically. "Don't you go encouraging her."

"Why not? I think she's got a terrific head on her shoulders."

"You're all impossible. While you're so busy manipulating my love life, the state's going to come in here and cart every one of us off to the funny farm, where," she added pointedly, "I'm not at all sure we don't belong."

She stood and ran around the corner of the house, only to run smack into Martin. The impact rocked her back on her heels. He reached out to steady her, though his gray eyes were filled with disapproval and his mouth was twisted in a way that reminded her of someone forced into doing a distasteful deed. She got the distinct impression he would have preferred to see her fall flat on her rear.

She cursed under her breath. She did not need this. Biting off every word with a minimum of politeness in her tone, she said, "Martin! What are you doing here?"

It was amazing, but until a few minutes ago she hadn't given him a thought. She'd never once considered calling on him for moral support. Now that he was here, she found his presence to be nothing more than another irritant in an already horrendous day.

"I came to see what the devil was going on over here," he replied peevishly. He looked surprisingly rumpled and distraught. Martin never appeared in public unless every hair was in place. He must be upset, she decided, then realized why when he added, "I couldn't even get in a decent game of golf at the country club because everyone kept coming up to ask if you'd gone bonkers or something."

Tina prayed for strength. "Not so far, though I am considering it," she retorted. Martin was staring at her as though he'd never really seen her before.

"I don't understand. How could you allow yourself to become the subject of public ridicule, Christina? It's certainly not good for business and it's an embarrassment to me personally."

If she'd been distracted and upset when she bumped into Martin, his remark got her full attention. "An embarrassment to you? I'm not sure I understand." Her tone would have daunted a more sensitive man. It didn't faze Martin.

"People know that you and I are involved—"

"We are not involved, Martin."

He looked at her peculiarly. "Of course, we are. Everyone expects that we'll get married one day. I'll take over Harrington Industries, if you haven't destroyed it by then..." His voice trailed off significantly.

"I beg your pardon," she said coldly. "You will never take over Harrington Industries, and you and I will never be married. It's not like you to make assumptions, Martin." In fact, it was not like Martin to make a scene, either. Obviously he figured this one was too erratic. He took her hand and patted it. She did not find the gesture comforting. If anything, it was patronizing and infuriated her even more. His words only added to her rapidly growing sense of outrage.

"Now, Christina," he began in an awful, condescending tone. "I realize all of this unpleasant notoriety has been most upsetting to you, but don't talk crazy. People will forget all about this little peccadillo as soon as another scandal comes along."

"Peccadillo? Scandal?" she said with quiet fury. "You think I'm involved in a scandal? You don't know the meaning of the word. There have been divorces in this town that scattered more dirt than what's happening here."

Martin continued as though she'd never opened her mouth. "You and I will be married as soon as everything settles down again and these people are out of here."

Shock filled Tina's eyes, followed by a sharp twisting in her stomach. "You want my friends to leave?"

Martin apparently missed the ominous edge to her voice because he blundered on. "They certainly can't live with us. I'm sure you can find them a more suitable place, perhaps a nice nursing home for the older ones and a foster home for the boy if you feel you must help them. They don't belong on a Palm Beach estate."

"Why you…you…" Words failed her. "I don't think I ever realized that you are nothing but a high-class snob! How dare you come here and insult my friends. There's not a one of them who needs to be in a damned nursing home. If anyone doesn't belong on this Palm Beach estate, it's you!"

She tried to brush past him, but he caught her arm. "Christina, don't be foolish."

"I'm not being foolish, Martin. I am seeing things very clearly. And, frankly, I don't much like what I see."

She twisted free from his grasp and stalked across

the lawn, not stopping until she was off the grounds and across the street.

She'd always believed that the sea, whether smooth as glass or whipped to a white-capped turbulence as it was now, held a sort of magic, that it could bring her serenity. After the DCF inspection, the press conference, her doubts about Drew, then Aunt Juliet's revelation and now Martin, today was going to be a real humdinger test of its powers.

Chapter Nine

Tina had gone to the beach, oblivious to the rolling clouds that were gathering to the west in the late afternoon sky, turning it to an ominous gray. The wild fury of the impending storm matched her mood perfectly. Even when torrents of rain poured down, plastering her auburn hair to her head and soaking her clothes so that they clung revealingly and uncomfortably to her body, she continued to walk, wondering how her life had gotten into such a tangle in so short a time.

As if things hadn't been bad enough, Martin's revealing outburst had shattered her few remaining illusions about his suitability for her. Oddly enough, she felt more relief than dismay. How had she ever deluded herself into thinking that they might someday become seriously involved? Worse, how had she ever thought that he was remotely comparable to Gerald?

Martin had revealed himself as an undeniable snob, one of the idle rich who had nothing to do except make judgments about other people. Talk about people destroying Harrington Industries. Martin could probably do it within a week. That's probably why his father had given him such a large trust fund, to keep him safely away from the family firm.

Tina was rounding a curve of the ocean when she spotted Drew ambling toward her. His hands were jammed into the pockets of faded, cutoff jeans he'd obviously gone home to put on. Those jeans ought to be outlawed in mixed company, Tina decided.

Water ran down his face and cascaded over his bare shoulders. It reminded her of the day she'd caught him coming out of his pool. It seemed no matter how lousy she felt, or what his role had been in creating the events affecting her mood, she was always glad to see him, always instantly aroused by him to an intriguing level of sunlight-bright expectancy.

"Mind some company?" he said as his gaze swept over her with heated intensity, finally coming to rest on her breasts, which were clearly visible through the soaked material of her blouse. Her nipples hardened.

She shrugged, feigning an indifference she most certainly did not feel.

"Want to tell me what got you so upset back there?"

"Before or after Martin?"

Drew stared at her blankly. "Who the devil is this Martin? That's the second time this afternoon his name has come up."

"According to Sarah, he's a wimp. According to him, he's the man I'm supposed to marry."

"And according to you?" he asked with tight-lipped restraint, his eyes darkening to a shade even more dangerous than the sky.

Tina grinned wryly. "I think Sarah has it pegged."

Drew's expression brightened. "That takes care of old Martin, then. What sent you scurrying off in the first place? You don't usually run away from your problems."

"I told you. I'm worried sick about what will happen to those people if the state says they can't stay. All of the meddling by Juliet and Sarah may wind up destroying our lives."

"They love you. It was well-intentioned."

She sighed. "I know that and I'm sorry I snapped at everybody, but, Drew, don't you see? They could be back on the streets or in some dump, and I could lose everything—my friends, my company."

"Your money?"

"I don't care about the money. I never have. What would I spend it on anyway, aside from the upkeep of the house? I don't travel. I don't have expensive taste. The idea of spending hundreds of dollars for a blouse or a pair of shoes appalls me. My one extravagance is..." She snapped her mouth shut and blushed. "Well, never mind what it is."

Drew was immediately intrigued by her reticence. Naturally. "Tina! What exactly do you fritter away your money on?"

"I don't fritter it away," she grumbled, furious at herself for the slip of the tongue.

"Whatever you want to call it then. What do you buy that makes your cheeks turn that attractive shade of pink?"

She heaved a disgusted sigh. She might as well admit it. Drew wasn't likely to give up until he'd wormed it out of her. The man probably would have been much happier in life as a detective.

"Lingerie," she mumbled.

Drew's lips quivered. "That's your vice? Lingerie?"

"Yes, dammit." She scowled at him defiantly.

"You mean that under those demure, businesslike suits of yours you are attired in sexy, lacy little things?" His voice was suddenly tense and he swept his gaze over her as if he were mentally disrobing her again.

Her heart slammed against her ribs. "Drew, couldn't we talk about something else?"

"Actually, I'm beginning to like this topic just fine."

"Drew!"

"Oh, okay," he grumbled. "We'll get back to that later."

"No, we won't." Her gaze locked with his, first in defiance, then in something else entirely. She felt crowded, though they were standing in the middle of a deserted beach. She felt hot, though the rain had cooled the air. But for all of the tension that knotted within her, it was Drew who finally blinked and looked away.

"So," he said, his voice thick and husky, "money doesn't matter to you. It's your grand passion for your husband that makes the thought of losing control of Harrington Industries so terrible."

"Exactly. I married Gerald because I loved him, because he was kind to me, not because of what he could do for me professionally and socially, and certainly not because of his wealth. I was already on my way up at Harrington Industries when Gerald and I met, and he was paying me very well even then. It was enough."

"He did help you along the way, though. He did speed up the process. You have to admit that."

"Of course, but I could do it again if I really had to. I love the challenge of mastering something new anyway. To tell you the truth, I've discovered that living in Palm Beach is not all it's cracked up to be or it wasn't until Sarah and Juliet and Mr. Kelly came along. They're real. Their lives are more than shopping trips to Worth Avenue or luncheon at the country club. Do you know that Sarah and Juliet spend three mornings a week volunteering at a hospital? Even when they didn't have much, they gave what they did have—their time. They know all about loving and sharing and trust. Some of my neighbors love their stockbrokers more than they do their families."

"Are you including me in that group?"

"I'm not sure," she said directly. She saw the hurt that her doubts inflicted, but she had to tell him the truth. "All this talk about mergers and takeovers this afternoon has spooked me. I'm not sure anymore what you want from me."

Drew nodded. "That's fair." He hesitated, and Tina interpreted that tiny pause as time he needed to calculate a response. Shouldn't the truth have come more easily?

"The answer's not so easy," he said at last. "You and I have just met. You've awakened desires in me I've never felt before, desires for a home of my own, a family. I want to protect you and make love to you and show you things you've never seen before.

"I'm not sure how to go about doing all that. You've certainly made it very clear that you don't want to be protected. You don't want to make love. And your experiences are probably as vast as mine. I'm terrified to bring up the subject of marriage. You'd probably scamper off to the Caribbean and hide out until I go back to Cedar Rapids."

Tina heard the raw edge of frustration and sincerity and responded to it. She wanted to believe he was telling the truth, but was it all of the truth or only a convenient portion?

"What about Harrington Industries?"

"That has nothing to do with you and me," he said firmly and without hesitation.

"Does that simply mean you are able to separate your professional and personal life?"

"No. It means precisely what I told Gregory Hanks. My interest in you is personal. My interest in Harrington Industries, except as it affects you, does not exist. I can't say it any more clearly than that."

The cards were all on the table now. She might as well play them out, even if she wasn't sure where the game would lead. "But you said something earlier about merging."

"True." He ran his fingers through his damp, wind-tousled hair. His eyes met hers and pleaded for understanding. "I suppose I was only half joking when I said that. I've already seen how much that company takes out of you, how much it dominates your life. Even now, with all that's on your mind at home, you're as concerned about the impact on Harrington Industries as you are for yourself and your friends. A part of me would like to relieve you of that pressure so that you'll have time for me. For us."

"Someone else may save you the trouble, once the news breaks about my wacky household. My friends and my company may be taken away."

Drew put an arm around her shoulder. Tina found herself feeling grateful for the warmth, responding to the comfort. "Want to hear how I see it?"

"Why not?"

"Despite the chaos that went on in there this morning, the state is not going to do a thing to disrupt your household and even if it did, those people would still be your friends. You wouldn't lose them. You could even find another way to help them, maybe get them an apartment. Mr. Kelly has his own home already. He could go back there."

"And die of loneliness?" she retorted. "I won't allow that. As for the others, they'd never accept charity like that from me. Here they feel they're making a contribution."

"Tina, you could work it out. I know you. You're an ingenious lady."

"And Harrington Industries? I wouldn't care so much for myself, but it's Gerald's company. He spent a lifetime building it into what it is today. Even Martin, who has the business acumen of a sea turtle, pointed out that all of this notoriety is bad for it and for me. I just can't lose control of it. It would mean I'd failed Gerald."

"Don't you see?" he chided. "That's exactly what I've been talking about. Your priorities are all twisted around. You've put business first, albeit in the disguise of some emotional commitment to your late husband."

Tina felt a cold knot forming in her stomach. "You don't expect me to turn my back on my obligations to the company, do you? Would you be happier if I just quit or turned it over to you?"

He apparently heard the frost in her voice and interpreted its cause correctly, because he replied quickly and with satisfying certainty. "No, of course not. Your career is obviously an important part of you, just as Gerald's memory is. I wouldn't want to change that. I just want you to keep it in perspective. Besides, Harrington Industries is not in any real danger."

"How can you be so sure? Do you have a magic wand to make wishes come true?"

"No. You're the one with the magic. I've been watching you in action. You wrapped those media people around your finger this morning. Even Edward Grant was bedazzled by your style and I doubt he's easily charmed."

"Edward Grant was bedazzled because I have more bathrooms than the average hotel."

"Whatever. If I hadn't been sure before, I would be now. I know you can handle anything the board of directors or stockholders throw your way. Trust me. I'm a terrific judge of character."

As her stomach unknotted, she realized with a tremendous sense of relief that she did. Whatever doubts she might have had about Drew's motives had been banished, perhaps only because she needed right now to believe in someone. She wanted desperately—for reasons she didn't dare analyze—to trust Drew Landry. For now if he said everything was going to be okay, then she'd just have to believe him—even if her normally healthy self-confidence seemed to be taking a royal beating.

"Care to come in out of the rain now?" he asked gently, brushing her wet hair off of her face, then cupping her chin between his hands. The touch of his lips against hers was warmer than the sun that had been lost behind the clouds. His gentle touch held a blazing promise and a raw hunger that tempted her beyond all reason. Right or wrong, she wanted all that he offered. She wanted him to banish the cold that had seeped into her bones, into her very soul. She sensed only Drew could fire such an incredible warmth in her that nothing else would matter. Not the past. Not the future.

He led her back along the edge of the water, then turned toward his home, rather than hers. She didn't hesitate. She needed one timeless afternoon with him. Tomorrow and its problems would come soon enough, especially if David found the information she feared he might. Then it would be too late and she would have lost her one chance to discover if the sensations Drew aroused were as unique as she believed them to be. Because of Gerald, she'd learned that life can be cruelly short and that joy was something to be grabbed and savored.

As she went with Drew, never had she felt more reckless, more on edge with anticipation. Never had she simply felt, without reason, without fear.

At the edge of the lawn he paused. "It's up to you," he said. The fingers curled around hers loosened ever so slightly, as though to signal his willingness to release her.

Tina tightened the grip. She could feel the wave of relief that shuddered through him. "I want you, Drew. For today, no matter what, I want you."

"For always," he countered.

She put a finger on his lips to silence him. "No, love. No promises. Just today."

His arms went around her then, holding her close,

heat spreading from the points of contact until Tina was surprised that in their damp clothes they weren't leaving a trail of steam as they walked through the gate and slowly up the graceful, curving drive.

"Upstairs, love," Drew said, the minute the door of his Spanish-style home closed behind them. They were standing in a large interior courtyard. A fountain bubbled in the middle, and a profusion of purple and pink flowers splashed a riot of hot color against the cool white stucco walls. Tina was charmed. She was also impressed with the amount of work he had done to restore the house which had fallen into disrepair after its previous owner died several years earlier, leaving his affairs in a mess that had taken months to untangle.

She concluded her rapid survey and grinned back at Drew. "You don't waste any time, do you?"

"Are you referring to my invitation upstairs or the work I've done around here?"

"Both."

"The house is coming along," he said with pride.

"As for the other, when the time comes, I guarantee you, I'll use a little more finesse," he promised, his dimple forming as he teased, then vanishing as he turned solemn again. "For now I was thinking perhaps you'd like a nice, hot bath. You're shivering."

"Is that all?" she asked, her mouth turning down in disappointment. He kissed each corner.

"Oh, I think we can work out something else, if you'd like."

She lifted her eyes boldly to meet his as her imagination soared and her pulse raced. "I'd like. But what about your father?"

"I suggested he might want to have dinner at your place."

"I see," she said dryly.

"I doubt it," Drew retorted just as quickly as he drew her along a cool corridor, then up a narrow staircase. She peeked into the rooms they passed, pleased with his choice of cheerful colors and masculine, but not oppressively heavy furniture. In the bedrooms, brightly-striped Mexican blankets lay across the foot of each bed and cool breezes streamed through sheer curtains that billowed sensuously at the windows. He led her at last to a magnificent bathroom with a sunken marble tub, pots of orchids hanging from the ceiling and mirrors everywhere except on the exterior wall, which was open to the western sky with French doors leading to a flower bedecked balcony.

Finally, Drew's remark registered. "Don't doubt it. I saw the way your father's eyes were following Sarah every time she budged an inch and the way he jumped to her defense," she said. "I don't think you could pry him away from her just yet even with the promise of one of those cutthroat poker games you say he loves."

Drew nodded as he turned on the water full force and poured in scented bath crystals. Tina wondered if he planned to join her. The tub was certainly more than big enough for two. The image sent a wave of heat through her that was torrid enough to fog up the mirrors. She tried to concentrate on the conversation and not the sultry, languid setting.

His blue eyes sparkled with amusement when he added innocently, "That's part of it."

"What more could there be?"

He winked and handed her a towel. "He wants grand-children almost as much as Sarah does," he said ca-sually, then turned and headed out the door and back down the stairs, leaving Tina wide-eyed and choking.

"Drew Landry, I am not going to sleep with you just to give your father and Sarah a baby to spoil rotten," she fumed indignantly and stomped back down the steps after him, dragging the towel along behind her like a child's security blanket. She caught him halfway down and spun him around.

"Not this afternoon, anyway," he said with infuri-ating calm.

"Not…"

"Ssh," he said, pressing a finger against her lips. "Don't make promises you can't keep."

"Oh, I can keep this one."

He swept her into his arms, and carried her right back up the stairs. "Wanna bet?" he said, as he sat her down in the steaming tub of water.

"Drew," she squealed. "You idiot. I still have my clothes on."

He shrugged. "They were soaked anyway. I'll leave something dry on the bed for you."

He was chuckling as he walked out the door. Tina sent a splash of water in his direction, but it only soaked the towel she was supposed to use to dry herself. The day was not improving by leaps and bounds.

Then she thought about Drew, about the blaze of de-sire she'd seen in his eyes, the hunger in his kiss, the tenderness of his caresses and the throbbing tension that made her body feel as though springs were coiled inside. She grinned. On the other hand, there was a definite possibility that it could get a whole lot better.

Chapter Ten

Tina soaked in the fragrant water until it turned cool and her knotted muscles were totally relaxed. She stretched languidly, enjoying the luxurious sensation of endless time. It was the first time in ages that she had pampered herself. With all that had been going on at home and at work, she was lucky if she had time for a quick shower before racing out the door. Was it possible that Drew had sensed this need in her when she herself hadn't recognized it?

Stepping out of the tub, she wrapped herself in the warm, oversize towel, then padded across the marble floor of the bathroom to the thick carpeting of Drew's bedroom. He had been true to his word. She found a velour robe waiting for her on the king-size bed. She had to roll up the cuffs, and while it was probably a knee-length size on Drew, it fell nearly to midcalf on her.

Standing in front of the mirror, the expression in her amber eyes softened by a lazy sensuality, she rubbed the thick collar across her face. Taking a deep breath, she caught the lingering scent of Drew's distinctive aftershave. The act was thoroughly innocent, yet held such a hint of intimacy that it sent a tingle racing down her spine.

Once she was enfolded in the robe, though, she wasn't quite sure what to do next. Did Drew expect her to come back downstairs? The thought of bumping into stuffy old Geoffrey in the hall and being subjected to one of his haughty, disapproving glares made her decide to wait right here. She walked around the room curiously, wondering what clues it would yield about the man who slept there.

There was a single photograph in an ornate antique silver frame on the dresser. A woman with laughing, adoring eyes and an abundance of thick, dark hair was gazing raptly at a man Tina immediately recognized as a much younger Seth Landry. He looked so much the way Drew did now that it took her breath away. Both men radiated warmth and strength and a certain air of bold self-assurance that bordered on arrogance. Impertinence, evident in the quirk of their lips, was mellowed by a gentleness that was all the more enchanting because it was not expected.

The woman in the photo had to be Drew's mother and, for all the adoration in her eyes, she too appeared strong and filled with an impish humor. It was odd that Drew never talked about her. Had she died? Were she and his father divorced? Perhaps she had been unable to take the isolation of living on a farm, though Drew had never hinted at that when he'd shared his childhood memories with her.

Tina replaced the photograph and moved on, stopping at the desk Drew had set up to face the window, its top covered with neatly arranged stacks of paper and rolls of blueprints tied into a tidy bundle. Tina grinned. She had known, somehow, that Drew would be organized, that there would be no haphazard clutter, no need for wasted motions. No wonder a man like him had been appalled by the disorganization of her household, the flighty nature of her friends. Left up to him, they'd probably be on a schedule in a week. She shuddered at the prospect. Although she ran her business with a precise attention to detail, she preferred her private life to be easy and relaxed. That's probably why it had been enhanced, rather than disrupted, by her strays.

Tina found a novel Drew had been reading on the nightstand. She curled up in the middle of the huge bed and glanced through it, wondering what kind of book would hold the interest of an intelligent, busy man. In minutes she was caught up in the story, written by a Cuban immigrant, of a man's survival in shark-infested waters after his rickety boat capsized en route to America. It was a lyrical testament to a man's will to live and his desire for freedom. It was yet another confirmation that Drew was filled with intriguing contradictions. She would have expected efficient, informative nonfiction on that nightstand. Instead, she had found the work of a man whose writing was almost poetic.

As she read, her eyes grew heavy. The next thing she knew she was dreaming that she was caught up in the middle of an earthquake. Her world shook violently, buildings crumbled around her and she woke with a sudden start, only to find that the jiggling motion had not been in her imagination. Drew was standing beside the bed, bumping it rhythmically with his knee.

Tina peered up at him balefully. "You need some work on your technique, Landry. That is not a good way to start a seduction."

"I do not seduce sleeping women, even when they are in my bed."

She sat up and tucked her legs under her, her voice sultry. "But you do plan to seduce me, don't you?"

"What if I said no?"

"Then I'd suggest you get that look out of your eyes, blow out these wonderful scented candles you've lit and get my clothes back to me right this minute."

"In that case, I suppose I'll have to seduce you," he said with feigned resignation. "Geoffrey has your clothes. Who knows how long it might be before they're ready." He waved a bucket at her. "I brought champagne just in case."

"French or California?"

"Does it matter?"

"Just checking to see if you're going for taste or snob appeal. I've had my fill of snobs today."

"Then I'm glad I chose the California."

"Are you going to stand there all day or are you going to sit down here and open the bottle?"

"I'm not sure," he said, and Tina detected an odd note of hesitancy in his voice.

"What's the problem?"

He glanced significantly at her legs, which were displayed almost to the point of indecency by a rather provocative gap in the robe. "Unless you do something about that, I'm not sure we'll get to the champagne."

Tina wriggled sensuously.

"Tina!"

"Okay, I'll behave," she said, and tied the robe more securely. She peeked at him through seductively lowered lashes. "For now."

Drew groaned and put the tray he'd been holding on the nightstand. The bottle of champagne nearly toppled over, and the two crystal glasses tilted precariously. Tina reached for them just as Drew sat down. She grabbed him instead.

"Oh," she said softly, as his arms came around her. Her laughter died in her throat, replaced by an exquisite tension as Drew buried his face in her still-damp hair.

"You smell wonderful."

"Are you suggesting I stick to shampoo and forget about fifty-dollar-an-ounce perfume?" she said, struggling to recapture the lightness she was far from feeling. There was an aching tightness in her loins. Her breasts, full and throbbing, were almost painfully sensitive as the rough texture of Drew's robe rubbed across them.

"The scent of your warm skin alone is enough to drive me wild," he confessed, drawing Tina's glance down to the evidence. Tina's eyes met his and she was lost, hardly aware of the instant when he took her hand and placed it where only a moment before she had been looking. A tiny gasp escaped as her fingers encountered denim-encased heat. Drew's eyes closed and he moaned softly. "That feels wonderful! Do you have any idea how much I've wanted to feel your touch just like that?"

His words gave Tina the courage to explore as she'd yearned to do since the moment days ago when he'd climbed out of that pool and stood before her in a proud display of all of his masculine virility. The corded muscles of his thighs were hard, his skin practically hot enough to sear her. A wild sense of abandon seized her as she touched the bare flesh above his waist, then followed the touch with a moist kiss that left the taste of him on her lips and filled her head with the sharp, musky scent of him.

"More?" she asked as a low groan rumbled through him.

"More."

It was just as well he agreed, because she wasn't sure she could have stopped now, even if he'd wanted her to. She needed to know all of him, to drive her senses mad with his essence. Her lips found masculine nipples, buried amidst dark swirls of crisp hair. She teased at them with her tongue, first one, then the other until she could feel the buds turn hard and felt Drew shudder with each new caress. His shoulders, tan and warm, were dusted with an inviting collection of freckles, each one worthy of attention and a mind-drugging kiss.

She touched her lips to the base of his neck, lost in the smooth, pulsing heat she found there. A satisfying tremor ripped through him and then with a suddenness that stunned her, she was on her back, Drew's knee between her parted thighs, his hands braced on either side of her. His eyes, glittering like rare blue topaz, were filled with laughter and a blazing excitement.

"Thought you were going to turn the tables on me, didn't you?" he teased in a husky whisper that rasped along her spine. "I invite you up here for a seduction and you take charge."

Dramatically, she threw a hand to her forehead. "I was carried away. I admit it," she murmured, her voice laced with laughter. "Never again."

"Never?" he questioned, lowering his head toward hers at the same time he began slipping his robe off her shoulders with excruciating slowness.

Laughter died as suddenly as it had begun. "Never," she said, breathless with anticipation. His lips were so close she could feel the whisper of his breath, but still the promised kiss didn't come.

"You're sure?" The question was soft, taunting. Tina moaned, put a hand behind his neck and pulled him down. "To hell with it," she muttered, just before she claimed his mouth.

It was the last conscious decision she made. After that, it was all sensation, drawing her in, tormenting her, lifting her to spectacular heights, then waiting for her to free-fall back to earth before taking her ever higher.

Drew's touch, deft and sure, was pure magic. Perhaps even black magic, it was so devilishly certain, so craftily confident. His eyes revered her, and she thrilled to the look. A hand caressed, and she soared. Hair-roughened skin chafed, and she writhed with unbearable delight. Hot lips plundered, and she burned with a flaming ecstasy. He filled her, and her world trembled and tilted on its axis, never to be quite the same again.

The culmination, so satisfyingly slow in coming, was a wild, demanding thrashing amid passion-dampened sheets. Drew's name exploded from the depths of her soul as wave after never-ending wave of pleasure rocked her.

It was the untamed fury of a storm, just as she'd expected.

It was the magnificence of heaven and the torment of hell and everything in between.

It was, God help her, love.

From the moment that she recognized that, the afternoon was timeless and filled with a joy that was almost frightening in its intensity. Tina had never expected to experience so much feeling, never known her body could respond like a finely tuned instrument, resonant with pleasure.

The afternoon was also filled with lazy talk of inconsequential things, with the discoveries and sharing of new lovers, talk that circumstances seemed to have robbed them of having sooner.

"Drew," Tina murmured sleepily as shadows crept in to magnify the intimacy, their sense of being isolated in their own private world. "What did you mean today when you told the reporters about your interest in the elderly? Did it have something to do with your father? The look you two exchanged was so…I don't know, special. Sad, maybe."

She could feel his heartbeat still beneath her cheek. When she started to lift her head to study his face, he held her in place and when he spoke at last, his voice seemed faraway and filled with incredible pain.

"It was sad. We were thinking about my mother."

"Is that why you don't talk about her? You've told me all about the farm and your dad, but you've hardly ever mentioned your mother. I saw the picture. She's very beautiful."

"Was. She was very beautiful."

"She's dead? That's why you don't talk about her?"

"I think it's because I can't bear to remember how it was at the end." Tina could feel his body tremble and she tightened the arm she had wrapped around his waist.

"Tell me."

He sighed and closed his eyes. When he opened them again, he stared straight at the ceiling. "She developed

Alzheimer's disease when I was just out of college," he began quietly, his voice tense. "At first, there were just the little signs that something was wrong. She'd forget the car keys or leave her purse someplace in the house and not be able to remember where. I don't think even she realized it was anything significant. In fact, she'd laugh about it.

"One day, though, I came home and found her in the kitchen, crying. She'd been trying all afternoon to remember her brother's name. It just wouldn't come and she had panicked. She had photographs scattered all around, trying to find one with his name on the back. She was almost hysterical."

"What did you do?"

"Once I'd calmed her down, I wanted to make an appointment with a doctor, but Dad convinced her she was making too much fuss over nothing. He said everybody forgets things. It was nothing to get all worked up about. There hadn't been quite so much attention focused on Alzheimer's back then, so it seemed reasonable. Mother wanted to believe him, so she let herself be convinced. In the end, I did, too."

"But things didn't get better," Tina guessed. Drew sighed and his hand idly stroked her bare back. Even though it was a distracted gesture, Tina was still aroused by it. Her breasts tightened at the memory of where such touches had led only a short time earlier. She pressed a kiss against Drew's chest. "Do you want to tell me the rest?"

"I don't want there to be any secrets between us. Secrets can destroy a relationship."

"That's not exactly an answer. You could tell me later, if it's still too painful."

"It will always be painful," he said and a tear slid down his cheek. Shaken by the sign of vulnerability that he was strong enough not to hide, Tina kissed the tear away. He sighed and met her gaze evenly, his jaw tightening. "I will never forget what happened. I don't want to forget."

"But, Drew…"

"No," he said harshly. "I have to remember so that I'll go on fighting to see that it never happens to anyone else." He gave her a penetrating look. "Maybe you don't want to hear this. It's ugly, and I'm not very proud of the part I played in it."

"Drew, there's nothing you can't tell me as long as you're honest. It's only lies and deception that I can't handle."

"Mother got progressively worse. It was like that case down in Miami where the devoted husband finally shot his wife after fifty years or something, because he couldn't bear to watch her suffer anymore. Dad was falling apart watching Mother deteriorate slowly, month after month. You can't imagine, seeing him now, what he was like then. He lost weight. He was pale, his eyes always shadowed by anguish."

A flicker of humor flashed in Drew's eyes. "Both of them had always been so filled with life before. It was something so wonderful to see. I had envied them the little secrets they shared, the laughter that filled the house when they thought they were alone."

Then the light was gone, as the memories once more turned sorrowful. "Now, though, Mother couldn't be left alone for a minute. She was dying by inches, and he was dying right along with her. I knew we had to do something, so I finally convinced Dad that we had to put her in a nursing home where she could get the round-the-clock care she needed."

Tina ran her hand along his cheek. "You did what you had to do, love."

"Did we? Or did we take the easy way out? All I know is that the place we chose seemed fine. It was bright and cheerful. There was a garden that was filled with lilacs in the spring and roses in the summer. There were lots of white wicker chairs under the trees. We told ourselves it wasn't all that different from the farm."

Suddenly Tina realized where the story was headed and it made her heart ache. "It wasn't like that, though, was it?"

He shook his head. "No. It wasn't like that at all. We called almost every day to check on Mother and we always got very specific, professional-sounding reports. We went to see her once a week, on Sunday afternoons. That was the official visiting day. They said it disturbed the routine to have drop-in callers. It seemed to make sense. Mother did seem agitated by our visits, though often she didn't recognize us at all.

"One week I happened to be very close to the home on a Thursday. I decided to stop by anyway. To hell with the rules. It was my mother, after all, and Dad and I were paying the enormous bills."

A shudder swept through him and he closed his eyes. His voice dropped to a whisper. "My God, you can't even begin to imagine what it was like. I had to wonder if anyone ever cared for those patients except on Sunday. Mother cried when she saw me. I took her out of there that very afternoon and filed a report with state officials. They closed the place down."

"What happened to your mother then?"

"I took her home, and we hired a private-duty nurse to be with her until she died three months later. Ever since then, I've been working with officials and groups to see that people realize that it takes more than paint and sunshine to make a good nursing home. Dad and I were lucky. We could afford home care. I still shudder to think what happens to those who can't."

With something akin to horror, Tina said in a hushed voice, "And you were afraid that's what was happening to Grandmother Sarah, Juliet and Mr. Kelly?"

"All of the anger and pain came flooding back when I got those letters from Juliet. I think if I'd discovered that someone with your resources was truly ripping off innocent old people, I'd have strangled you with my bare hands."

Tina gave him a faltering smile. "No wonder you roared into my life like an avenging angel. I'm just glad Grandmother Sarah had that cherry pie ready. It seemed to smooth things over."

"It was more than the cherry pie, Tina Harrington. There was so much love in that house. I could feel it when I walked through the door, even though you were scowling at me as though some awful creature had invaded your privacy." He grinned at her, and the somber mood lifted. "It was also that sexy little bottom of yours in that jumpsuit you wore over to my house and those bare shoulders in your yellow sundress and that stubborn tilt of your chin."

Her brows knitted, and she said with mock severity, "Are you sure you went over there to check out the living arrangements?"

"Well, there were a few distractions," he admitted, kissing her chin and then her shoulder. He was heading lower when she sighed and murmured, "If only this didn't have to end."

"It doesn't. That's what I've been trying to get through that thick little skull of yours. Marry me."

Tina's eyes widened, and she rolled away from him, tugging the sheet around her as she went. She shook her head adamantly. "You don't propose to a woman you've only known for a few days."

"Is that written down in an etiquette book someplace?"

"Knowing Palm Beach, it's probably in the city code."

"I'll check first thing in the morning, but I think you're wrong. I think I can ask and you can answer."

"I did answer."

"You did? I must have missed it. Run it by me again."

"I can't marry you, Drew. Not until things are settled."

"But you will marry me?" he persisted.

Tina grinned. "Maybe. When things are settled. Knowing my life, do you expect to be around long enough to see that happen?"

"If I have to move heaven and earth to see to it that it does."

"That might be easier," she advised.

"Well, while we wait, do you suppose we could find a little time to ourselves?"

"I have an hour between meetings tomorrow."

"Not good enough." A kiss punctuated the remark. It was a very nice kiss. She wanted another one very badly.

"I'm free for lunch on Friday."

"Not nearly good enough." Kisses rained down her shoulder, across her throbbing breasts and onto her stomach. "I need proof that you care more about me than you do about that company."

Tina looked at him oddly, noted that there seemed to be a tightening of his lips despite the teasing tone of his comment. Still, she couldn't resist those kisses. There were several spots that were feeling neglected. "I could stay now," she said breathlessly.

"That's more like it."

"Except your father is on his way up the stairs whistling something that sounds like 'Don't Fence Me In.'"

"Damn."

"Does it help to know that I share your disappointment?"

"Not much," he grumbled. "When you get home would you mind speaking to Sarah about the fine art of keeping my father distracted?"

"If you expect her to do it like this, you'll have to talk to her yourself."

"A game of chess would do."

"Sarah doesn't play chess."

"Wonderful."

"How so?"

"It ought to take Dad days to teach her."

Laughter bubbled up in Tina's throat, then faded. "Oh my gosh."

"What's wrong now?"

"Do you realize I don't have any clothes up here? What will your father think?"

"Unless you go running out into the hallways without them, I doubt he'll think a thing. Now stay still and I'll go get them."

"Drew," Tina called softly as he went out the door.

"What?"

"Try not to get caught with my lingerie in your hands."

"Don't worry about it. Dad knows I don't wear peach-colored underwear trimmed in antique French lace."

"I was worried about my reputation, not yours."

"Oh. By the way, I approve of your vice."

He started away, then he stuck his head back in. "So does Geoffrey."

Tina groaned and buried her face in the covers. She wondered if old Geoffrey had taken a vow of silence. Hopefully, it was part of the butlers' code of ethics. Otherwise, she could very well end up right back in the headlines. Palm Beach society liked nothing better than reading about a steamy romance.

Chapter Eleven

"**O**ut mighty late last night, weren't you, missy?" Mr. Kelly said with deliberate coyness at breakfast, his sharp eyes obviously catching the shadows under her eyes. Tina didn't miss the implication of his remark. It brought an immediate stain of pink to her cheeks. She was glad Billy wasn't around to witness this particular conversation. He'd probably start hunting around for a shotgun to go after Drew.

"It wasn't that late," Tina mumbled, quickly stuffing a spoonful of oatmeal into her mouth. Sarah was obviously miffed again this morning. She hadn't even emerged from the kitchen to ask what they wanted. She'd just left a chafing dish of oatmeal, a bowl of sliced bananas and raisins and a pitcher of cream on the serving table.

"You with Drew?"

"Umm-hmm."

"Speak up, missy. Was that a yes?"

Tina glared at him defiantly. "Yes," she repeated loudly.

A sudden glint of amusement sparked to life in Mr. Kelly's eyes. "Guess Juliet and Sarah didn't do so bad by you, after all, did they?"

Tina choked, then laughed in spite of herself. "No. I guess not," she admitted.

"You might want to tell them that. They've been moping around ever since you stormed out of here yesterday."

"All right," she said meekly. "I'll apologize. I was worried and angry, but I shouldn't have taken it out on them." She looked up just in time to see Juliet's nose poking around the door frame. "Aunt Juliet?"

"Yes, dear?" She inched her way cautiously into the room and waited as if poised for flight.

Tina got up and went to her. She put her arm around her and hugged her tightly, her eyes misting as she heard Juliet's sigh of relief. "I'm sorry," she whispered. "I didn't mean to get so upset yesterday."

"It's okay, dear. I was meddling, after all. My late husband used to tell me all the time that nothing good ever comes of that."

"Oh, I wouldn't say that," Mr. Kelly chimed in with a wink at Tina. "Things seem to be working out just the way you and Sarah wanted."

Juliet's nut-brown eyes sparkled with interest. "Really? Oh, Tina, that's wonderful. Have you set a wedding date finally?"

Tina scowled at Mr. Kelly. "See what you've done. You've gotten her hopes up again. Drew and I have no plans to marry."

"No plans to marry?" Mr. Kelly blustered with parental indignation. "What kind of man is he, taking advantage of a lovely gal like you? I just wonder what that father of his would have to say, if he knew?"

"There is nothing for him to know," Tina said firmly,

pushing Mr. Kelly right back into the chair he was about to vacate. All she needed was for the two men to start interfering and she and Drew would be standing before a judge with a shotgun aimed at Drew's head. "You stay out of it. I'm a grown woman. I can handle my own social life."

"You're the one who picked Martin," Mr. Kelly sniffed. "I heard what that nasal-sounding, self-indulgent scoundrel said to you yesterday. If you ask me, you ain't got the scenting ability of a bloodhound."

"I didn't ask you. Now let's just drop it. I have to get to work."

"Don't forget to talk to Sarah before you go," Juliet said. She sighed heavily, and there was a hint of censure in her tone. "She's been so upset, dear. I don't think she slept a wink all night for fear she'd driven you straight into Martin's arms."

"You can both stop worrying about that. Martin and I are definitely through. I'll go talk to Sarah right now and tell her that's one thing she doesn't need to fret about," Tina promised.

The apology to Grandmother Sarah was easier by far than she'd expected. As soon as Tina admitted that she'd been with Drew the previous evening, Sarah's eyes lit up with satisfaction.

"You don't have to look so smug," Tina chided.

Sarah paused in her dishwashing and said with feigned ferocity, "You just can't admit it, can you, Christina Elizabeth."

"Admit what?"

"That it doesn't hurt to listen to us old folks once in a while."

"I don't mind listening to you. It's when you take matters into your own hands that I object."

Sarah blushed guiltily and attacked the oatmeal-encrusted pot she'd been scrubbing with renewed purpose. "I'll try to remember that," she mumbled.

"See that you do," Tina said with severity, then grinned and hugged her. "I love you."

"I love you, too, girl. We all do. Now run along to work."

Tina gave her another squeeze, then left for Harrington Industries, dreading what she might find there. As soon as she arrived at the penthouse, she went straight to David's office. As usual, he had arrived ahead of her. Paperwork literally spilled off his cluttered desk. She moved several folders and sank down in a chair across from him, noting again that for a man of twenty-five, who radiated calm professionalism and dressed for the precise image, he was amazingly untidy otherwise.

"So," she said. "What did you find?"

"Nothing."

Her eyes widened in surprise. "Nothing?"

"The price of the Harrington Industries stock is steady. The volume is steady. There hasn't been a single thing out of the ordinary in the last few weeks. I can't figure it out. What made you think something was going on?"

"It was just a funny feeling. I guess my feminine intuition blew it this time," she said as relief flooded through her. It was true, then. Drew wasn't after the company. After their closeness yesterday, the feelings that had flourished, she couldn't believe that he was trying to use her, either. Perhaps it was just as he'd said, and his interest was only in relieving her of pressure. Now that he knew she didn't want that, he would drop all talk of a merger.

"What do you want me to do now, Tina?" David asked.

"Keep an eye on things and let me know if the situation changes. Hopefully I really was all wrong about this."

Once she'd left David's office, she pushed the issue to the back of her mind, knowing that he'd stay on top of it. She spent the morning in meetings with her art department designing the materials needed for the stockholders' meeting. It was after noon when Jennifer came in and stood in front of Tina's desk with her hands behind her back. She was fidgeting nervously. Jennifer never fidgeted unless things were really bad. It made Tina's pulse slow with dread.

"What's up, Jen?"

"Have you seen this?"

"What?"

She handed over the Miami paper. Gregory Hanks's column bore a headline forecasting Dark Days Ahead for Harrington Industries. Tina unconsciously balled her hand into a fist as she scanned the damning article, which detailed her problems with DCF and predicted trouble at the stockholders' meeting as a result.

"We're already getting calls," Jennifer said when Tina had thrown the offending newspaper on her desk. "Mr. Davis was threatening to take over the company himself."

"That might be interesting," Tina said dryly. "Why didn't you interrupt me?"

"David's been handling the calls, except for Mr. Davis's. I had the pleasure of talking to him."

"Get David in here."

He was there within minutes, his expression harried, his tie loosened. Astonishingly, he looked even more frazzled than Jennifer had a few days earlier.

"What are they saying?" she asked bluntly.

"They want to know what you plan to do about the report. They figure it'll be picked up in the *Wall Street Journal* next."

"What can I do about it? The facts are accurate. I can't very well challenge Gregory Hanks on his interpretation of them or on his predictions."

"Damn, Tina. This is going to blow up in our faces. Can't you get rid of those people until after the stockholders' meeting is over?"

Tina glared at him, and David promptly looked guilty.

"Sorry. I just thought it might help."

"It wouldn't. Then somebody would probably write that I'd cast them out into the street. Besides, I have no intention of allowing this to force me into abandoning my friends."

"Well, you'd better do something or you're going to have a mutiny on your hands in New York."

"And here?" she asked perceptively.

David sighed. "No. Not here. Jennifer and I will do the best we can. Just try to think of something, please," he pleaded.

No matter how hard she tried over the next few days,

though, Tina couldn't come up with a quick solution that would settle the nerves of the stockholders while allowing her to stand up for her principles. Drew sensed her anxiety and tried to reach her. In fact, he did everything he could think of to distract her, short of kidnapping her.

Each morning she found a fresh rose on her desk. He turned up daily at lunchtime either with a picnic basket filled with Sarah's tempting goodies or gourmet take-out for which he must have bribed the chefs at the best restaurants in town. He was back every day at five-thirty to pick her up. If she wasn't ready to leave, he sat and waited, subtly pressuring her to wrap things up and take some time for herself.

Best of all, he didn't probe. When she walked out of Harrington Industries at night, she dropped the mantle of corporate president and became a woman in love. Not that she and Drew had much time alone to be lovers. It seemed everyone who'd conspired so valiantly to get them together was now just as busily conspiring to keep them apart—or at least out of each other's arms.

Rather than attending a round of parties or going out to fancy restaurants or even hiding away by themselves, they spent their evenings playing cards or singing along to old records under the approving gazes of Seth and Sarah and the others. It had the feel of a slow, old-fashioned courtship, except for those scant occasions when they managed to slip away for hot, stolen kisses in the moonlight. One night they actually outlasted everyone else and played a raucous game of strip poker, their eyes constantly darting to the door in fear that Mr. Kelly might take one of his middle-of-the-night strolls and discover them surrounded by cards and discarded clothing.

If it hadn't been for the threat hanging over her head, Tina would have been deliriously happy. Loving Drew was as fulfilling and exciting as she'd imagined. He was tender and supportive, always ready with a pep talk or some crazy gift exactly when she needed cheering up.

Around the house, things were almost perfect. Seth helped Mr. Kelly with the gardening. They both came in to breakfast each morning moaning and holding their backs. Tina had a feeling that there wasn't a thing wrong with their backs that a little sympathy couldn't cure. They both seemed to perk right up the minute Sarah and Juliet hovered over them with hot tea and homemade coffee cake.

Mr. Kelly continued to grumble about Aunt Juliet's petunias, but he planted them just the way she wanted them. Although he blustered and fussed, there was a definite sparkle in his eyes when she threw her arms around him and kissed him on the cheek for doing it. Juliet spent the rest of the day acting thoroughly befuddled.

Whenever she'd let him, Seth tried to win Sarah over. Tina came in one afternoon and caught them dancing, spinning around in a graceful circle to an old Glenn Miller album. She stood in the doorway and watched, clapping enthusiastically when Seth ended the dance with a low dip that had Sarah's head barely two feet from the floor.

"Oh, my, you're making me dizzy," Sarah complained when she was rightside up again, but there was a genuine hint of laughter in her voice. She waved her hankie in front of her flushed face and avoided Tina's amused eyes. "I'm too old for these wild dances, Seth Landry."

"That was a waltz, Sarah, and you're only as old as you feel," he countered in his calm, easy manner.

"I feel ancient."

"You look twenty-two again with your cheeks all rosy."

Sarah scrambled out of Seth's embrace and backed toward the door. "Don't start that nonsense again. I'm sixty-seven and I look it. I spent a lot of years getting these character lines and I'm not going to deny them now. Your flattery won't make a bit of difference."

"I love every one of your character lines. What do you think, Tina?"

"I think I'll stay out of this one."

"Smart girl," Sarah grumbled as she tried to slip away. Seth grabbed her hand and whirled her neatly back into his arms. He planted a kiss soundly on her lips before chuckling and releasing her. "Think I'll go see what that son of mine is up to."

"So, what's the story?" Tina asked when he'd gone. "Are you and Seth getting serious?"

Sarah turned as pink as one of her favorite roses. "Oh, posh-tosh, girl. Don't go talking craziness. That man is never serious for more than a minute at a time."

"You know what I mean."

"Mind your own business."

"The way you did?" Tina retorted leaving a sputtering Sarah behind her as she went in search of Drew. She found him in the yard playing ball with Billy, for whom he was rapidly filling in as a surrogate father.

With Drew's assistance and encouragement Billy had even started doing his homework. Miss Maxwell had sent a note home just last week expressing astonishment—and relief, Tina suspected—at the improvement.

Tina watched the two of them together, allowing her imagination to toy with the notion of Drew as a husband and father. The thought held enchanting possibilities. A few minutes later, when Drew slammed a baseball through her kitchen window, she could only shrug. He looked so pleased with himself, she couldn't have ranted and raged even if she'd wanted to. Besides, Sarah came out of the house shouting enough for all of them. She wasn't a bit pleased about having glass all over her counter.

"I'm sorry, Sarah," Drew apologized. Just the same, he couldn't quite wipe the satisfied smirk off his face.

"I should think you would be," Sarah huffed, though Tina thought she detected the beginning of a sparkle in her eyes. "You're old enough to know better. What kind of an example are you setting for Billy?"

"I'll pay for the window," he suggested, and Sarah threw up her hands.

"Of course you will. Now go on back out there and play," she said as if she were talking to a troublesome boy. "Just be more careful."

"Yes, ma'am."

Tina smothered a grin as she sank down on a lounge chair. A few minutes later, Drew came over to join her, nudging her legs aside on the chaise lounge to sit next to her. He was mopping his face and his bare shoulders were slick with perspiration, but Tina draped an arm around his neck just the same. She needed to be close to him, to absorb just a little of his strength.

"Hey, you'll ruin that sexy dress. I'm all sticky," Drew protested.

"I don't care. I need a hug."

He looked at her sharply. "Why's that?"

She sighed. "Where do I begin? For starters, David threatened to quit today, and I suspect Jennifer will be right behind him."

"Why would they do that?"

"Ever since those stories hit the papers, the phones have gone crazy. Every stockholder in the country is convinced that I'm about to ruin Harrington Industries. One man even said he'd heard I was turning it over to charity."

Drew kissed her, nibbling lightly on her lower lip. When he did that, she couldn't think, and he knew it. It was very effective as distractions went. Unfortunately, when he stopped, the image of David standing in her office yet again today, pleading with her to do something, came back in a rush.

"David still thinks I'm going to have to throw everyone out of here before things will settle down."

Drew sighed. "He's wrong."

"That's what I told him days ago, but what if he's not?"

"Ah, my love, I sometimes wonder if you wouldn't manufacture something to worry about if things in your life went too smoothly. Your meeting will go beautifully. Take Sarah, Juliet and Mr. Kelly with you if you want to. If they're at the meeting, the stockholders will realize that they're utterly charming and harmless."

Tina's eyes lit up. "What a wonderful idea! Drew, you're a genius. We'll take them to New York with us."

His face clouded over. "I was kidding."

"I'm not. It'll be perfect."

"I was hoping we'd have some time alone up there. Do you realize we haven't had a single minute to ourselves in days?"

"Only too well," she said with heartfelt sincerity. "Don't pout, though. If all goes well, we'll send them back the day after the meeting and we can stay on."

"And do what?"

She gave him a bold wink. "Anything you'd like."

"Promise?"

"Absolutely."

"Then I'll hold you to that."

The day before the meeting all of them except a disgusted Billy, who'd been left with a friend's family, flew to New York in the company jet. Juliet's eyes were wide as saucers when they lifted off.

"Oh, my," she muttered as the ground receded below them. "Are you sure this is safe?"

"Would you like a glass of sherry, Aunt Juliet? It would calm your nerves."

"Why, yes, dear. It is a little early, but I think a glass of sherry would be very nice."

Several glasses later, Aunt Juliet was ever so slightly tipsy and having the time of her life, at least until the pilot came into the back to tell them that they'd be landing soon. Juliet looked from him to the cockpit and back again.

"Who's flying this thing?"

"I am, ma'am."

"I meant now."

"It's on automatic."

Her brow wrinkled in a puzzled frown. "You mean like one of those coffeepots you turn on the night before?"

"Something like that, ma'am."

"Well, I declare. Do you suppose I could come up there and see?"

"I think you'd better stay right here, Juliet," Tina said.

"It would be all right, ma'am," the pilot said. "That is if you don't mind."

Tina shrugged and Drew chuckled. "I think we've made a convert of her," he said.

"Five glasses of sherry would convert a saint to a sinner," Tina replied just as the plane took a sudden dip. "What the hell was that?"

The cockpit door flew open. "Sorry about that," Aunt Juliet called gaily. "I'm still getting my wings."

"Oh my God," Tina muttered.

Drew patted her hand. "See, dear. If anything happens with DCF, Juliet can always try for her pilot's license."

"Very funny."

The plane banked steeply to the left and Sarah got to her feet. "I've had just about enough of this." She marched to the cockpit door. "Juliet, you get back here. Next thing you know my stomach is going to go all queasy and you'll be up half the night with me."

"I'm sorry," Juliet said meekly, but her eyes were twinkling merrily as she came back to the passenger cabin and sat next to Mr. Kelly. "Isn't this just the most wonderful experience?"

"What's that?"

"I said isn't this the most wonderful experience?" she shouted. "Turn your hearing aid back on. You're missing all the fun."

"You call this fun?" Mr. Kelly grumbled. "I'll take my fun on the ground any day. Don't trust these things."

"We'll be on the ground soon," Tina soothed.

"Don't know why we had to come up here in the first place. Nothing in New York but a bunch of thieves."

"Oh, stop your grumbling. We came to help Tina," Sarah said. "After all she's done for us, it's the least we can do."

"Can't see how parading us around like a herd of cattle going to market will help one bit."

"It will," Tina said. "The press has made me out to be some kind of nut for taking you in. That's an insult to me and to you. It implies you're not good enough to live where you do. Do you believe that?"

"Of course not."

"Then it's time people found that out for themselves," Sarah agreed. She glanced pointedly at Juliet. "Just stay away from the sherry until Tina's stockholders get to know us."

"Why, Sarah," Juliet said, a hurt expression in her eyes. "I don't know what you mean."

"She means if you get tipsy like this again, those stockholders will think Tina's operating a retreat for drunks, instead of just a bunch of old fools," Mr. Kelly snapped.

"You are not old fools," Tina said in a horrified whisper.

"Course we're not," Mr. Kelly retorted. "But they don't know that." He shook his head. "Never thought I'd have to go proving myself to a bunch of strangers."

"I'm sorry," Tina said.

"Don't you worry about it, girl," Sarah said, shooting a scowl at Mr. Kelly. "It's not your fault. It's just the way things are. We'll all survive it. Who knows, if *some people* would stop complaining, we might even have a good time."

Tina had made the hotel reservations, asking for rooms on the same floor. She had requested adjoining rooms for her and Drew, rather than the single suite she knew he would have preferred. When he made the discovery at the registration desk, she could tell that he was biting his lip to keep from an explosion that would only add to her worries. She promised herself that once the stockholders' meeting was over, she was going to give Drew the time and attention he deserved.

When they'd finished unpacking, Drew came into her room and put his arms around her from behind. His lips burned against the soft flesh of her neck. "Let's go out on the town."

"I can't. I have too much to do. The meeting's in the morning."

"You're going to do beautifully," he reassured her, turning her around so he could face her. "You've rehearsed your statement so often, I could recite it."

"Would you?" she quipped, suddenly unsure of herself.

"Not on your life. I'm going to be watching you win this one from the sidelines." He kissed her. "And I'm going to be very, very proud. Now let's go out and do something to get your mind off of all this."

"Any ideas?"

He tightened his embrace. Tina's arms slid around his neck as his lips skimmed across her mouth in a tormentingly fleeting touch. "Quite a few," he murmured. "Unfortunately, I doubt that Sarah and the others would approve."

"What do you think they'd like to do?"

"Dad was muttering something about going to Rockefeller Center."

"To see one of the network shows? That's a great idea." She frowned. "I doubt if we can get in this late. There may not even be anything taping."

"I don't think he wants to see a show. I think he wants to go ice-skating."

Tina's face fell. "Ice-skating," she repeated blankly.

"He figures since Sarah's never done it, it would be an experience."

"It would be that," Tina said weakly, then sighed.

"What's wrong?"

"I was just wondering if Medicare covers ice-skating accidents."

"If it doesn't, I'll pay the difference," Drew offered, his eyes twinkling. "It'll be worth it to see them out there." He studied her closely. "What about you? Are you game?"

"Drew, you don't do a lot of ice-skating in Florida," she hedged.

"That raises all sorts of interesting possibilities."

"Do you want to wheel me into that meeting in the morning with my leg in a cast?"

"Nope. But I can hardly wait to get my arms around you on the ice."

"I knew you had to have an ulterior motive. Are you sure you didn't put this idea into your father's head?"

"Would I do that?"

"Darn right you would."

An hour later they were at Rockefeller Center lacing up their rented skates. Sarah was eyeing the ice with a wariness Tina could identify readily.

"I'm not so sure this is such a good idea. That stuff looks mighty hard."

"Stop dillydallying, Sarah. You're going to do just fine," Seth said, pulling her to her feet. She wobbled toward the rink, just as Mr. Kelly held out his hand to Juliet.

"Come on, gal. Let's go show these folks how to do it."

"Why, Mr. Kelly, I had no idea you could skate," Juliet whispered, her cheeks flushed with excitement.

"Oh, in my day, I tried just about everything at least once. That's the only way to weed out the things that aren't any fun. What about you, Juliet?"

A dreamy expression stole over her features. "I haven't been on skates since I was a girl, but I could do a lovely figure eight back then."

"Then let's go to it."

Tina watched the two couples with a sense of astonishment, then looked up at Drew. He was tapping his ice skates impatiently.

"Well?" he said.

"Well what?"

"Are you going to take all night?"

"Drew, I really have very weak ankles. Couldn't we just watch?"

"And hear about it for the rest of our lives? Not a chance."

"Oh, hell," she muttered and got to her feet. Her ankles promptly wobbled like a baby's. She grabbed Drew's arm and hung on.

"One time," she said between clenched teeth. "We will go around this rink one time and then you are taking me into a bar and buying me a drink. A very strong drink. Got that?"

"Anything you want."

Her face brightened. "I want to leave now."

"Except that."

She scowled at him. "Okay. Then let's get moving. If I'm going to break something, I want to get it over with."

With Drew's arm tight around her waist, Tina lost a little of her nervousness. Still, she never took her eyes off the ice, except to gaze longingly every so often toward the gate where she'd be able to leave it. She was concentrating so hard on survival, she didn't notice at first that everyone else had slowed, then come to a halt. When she heard the applause, she blinked and looked around.

In the center of the ice, Juliet and Mr. Kelly, their arms linked, were skating with a slow, easy stride that was surprisingly skilled. Juliet's hair was escaping from her bun and her cheeks were flushed becomingly from the cold air. Mr. Kelly said something to her and she laughed, then twirled around and came back into his arms in an intricate step that drew more applause.

When they stopped, Sarah and Seth skated over to them, and Tina, her fear of the ice forgotten, tugged Drew along as well.

"You two were wonderful," she said, skidding into them and almost knocking them down.

"Whoa, gal," Mr. Kelly said with a low chuckle. "Haven't quite got your skating feet yet, have you?"

"I will never have my skating feet if I have anything to say about it. Where did you learn to do that, though? I'm impressed."

"Oh, there was a time way back, when the missus and me tried just about everything. I'd forgotten how much fun it could be." He gazed down at Juliet fondly. "Thank you for reminding me of those times."

"Thank you," Juliet said, her eyes misty, her lips curved into a gentle smile of remembrance. "It took me back, too."

To Tina's amazement, they didn't sound sad about having the past brought back to them. She gazed up at Drew and wondered if, in years—or even days—to come, the memories they shared would be as happy.

Chapter Twelve

Tina was lying in bed, her head buried under her pillow, when she felt the mattress dip beside her.

"What the hell!" She sat straight up, clutching the sheet to cover herself more effectively than her apricot satin and French lace nightgown did. At the same time she grabbed for the phone to use as a weapon. Through bleary eyes, she saw the shape of her attacker. It looked astonishingly familiar.

"Morning, beautiful," Drew murmured and handed her a perfect rose the exact shade of her gown.

"How did you get in here?" she demanded furiously. "You scared me to death."

"You did get adjoining rooms."

"But the door..." Her gaze shot to the door linking the rooms. It was wide open.

"Was unlocked," he finished with an infuriatingly satisfied smile. "Exactly the way I left it when I slipped back into my own room at 2 a.m." He placed the rose on her pillow and tugged at the sheet. It fell away, along with Tina's initial anger.

"If you ask me," Drew murmured huskily, his fingers playing along her bare flesh, "it was a waste of a perfectly good night."

"I couldn't have you sleeping in here with Sarah and Juliet right down the hall. For all their romantic talk, they would have been scandalized."

"And who put them right down the hall?"

"The hotel," she retorted brightly.

"At your request," he reminded her.

"True. I wanted to be able to look out for them."

"A fine job you did of that," he teased. "They were out until four. I heard them come in, giggling and carrying on like a bunch of giddy teenagers."

"Your father was probably responsible for that. I saw him order another round of drinks just as we left the table in the bar downstairs."

"Actually, I don't think they spent all that time drinking. When Dad came in, he was muttering something about having roared through Wall Street like that brokerage house bull."

"Oh dear heaven." Tina put her hands over her eyes and groaned.

"My sentiments exactly," Drew murmured right before his gaze fell to a point considerably below discretion. "Now could we forget about my father, Sarah, etcetera and concentrate on us?"

"What did you have in mind?"

"This."

His fingers trailed along the edge of her nightgown, following the dip that revealed an unladylike amount of creamy cleavage. His touch skimmed over cool flesh, leaving it feverish and sensitive. Her nipples tightened and strained against the silky fabric. When he lowered his head and took the tip into his mouth, a moan shuddered through her. Moist heat and slick friction created a volatile sensation that jolted her heartbeat from early morning laziness into a frantic midnight tempo.

Drew pushed her back until she was reclining against the pillows, open to his marauding hands and the raw hunger of his mouth. She tried to roll away from temptation, telling herself that surely they could wait another twenty-four hours to be together, but when Drew's tongue danced across the flesh of her inner thigh, common sense and good intentions flew out the window. Her gown slid up, followed by the promise of Drew's kisses.

Tina's back arched and the throbbing he'd set off deep inside became a rhythmic demand.

"Damn you, Drew Landry," she murmured, her voice raw-edged with the unexpected passion.

He stilled his tormenting touches, but his fingers remained right where they were. The pulsing heat went on, slowing, fading, but never gone. "Do you want me to stop?" he asked innocently.

Tina groaned and put her hand over his, pressing it more tightly in place. "No." The word came out on a ragged breath and Drew's eyes smoldered in the morning light.

"Then let me take you to the top." Deft fingers probed and sensation coiled deep inside her, an unbearable tension that was destined for a wild explosion.

Determined not to make the trip over the edge alone, Tina fought against losing herself to Drew's will and countered each of his strokes with bolder and bolder caresses of her own. Subconsciously, she knew it was a battle for control and, in the end, she knew she would lose. There was no way she could hold out against

Drew's persuasion, no way to keep her body from responding to the need that was building inside her.

"Come to me, Drew," she pleaded. "Now."

"Not yet," he said, leaving one sensitive curve to pay homage to another as the tension coiled more tightly. "Not yet. I want you to let go. Please, darling. For once, just let go."

"Not without you," she said, biting her lips as she struggled beneath him. Then, as her eyes grew wide and startled, her body defied her, spinning away on a raging tide that rose and crashed with astonishing intensity.

She was still coming down from the wild ride, when Drew slowly and gently thrust into her.

"Drew?"

"Now we'll go together," he whispered, his voice husky.

"But I can't."

"You can," he promised and then she was feeling again, feeling the heat, the shock waves as strong as any quake. Her nails dug into Drew's back, her hips rose in anxious joining and together, slick with perspiration, they responded with a raw, primitive passion that left Tina shaken, exhausted and more in love than ever.

"That's it," Drew murmured some time later, propping himself on his elbow and gazing down at her approvingly.

"That's what?"

"The look I wanted to see on your face before the meeting. You look tousled and satisfied and very, very beautiful. You'll knock 'em dead."

"So this was only a sort of beauty consultation," she muttered indignantly. She tried to scowl at him, but her lips kept twitching. "Other people suggest blusher. Maybe a little eye shadow, but you could be right. There might be a major market for this sort of thing. Landry Enterprises ought to consider diversifying, hiring a stable of...what would you call them?" She lifted a brow. "Studs, perhaps?"

"What a good idea!" Drew said enthusiastically. "It would revolutionize the cosmetics industry."

She rolled her eyes. "I should have known you'd like it."

"I like all your ideas."

"Even the one about your getting out of this bed and letting me get dressed?"

He paused consideringly. "Well, that one could do with a little work."

"I suspect it's the only sensible idea, I'll have all day. Once the stockholders get started, I may not be able to think at all."

He kissed her soundly. "Now there you go again. Am I going to have to start distracting you all over again?"

"I wish," she said wistfully, but she slipped determinedly away from him. "I've got to get downstairs to be sure the luncheon is set up or Kathryn Sawyer will pitch a fit. She seems to think I can't be trusted to put the proper number of forks on the table or something. Will you make sure everyone else is down there by noon? I want them to mingle with the stockholders."

"We'll be there," he promised. "Now stop worrying. Everything is going to be just fine."

Tina went to the closet where her clothes were supposed to be hanging. Puzzled, she shut the door and opened the one next to it. She was not going to panic.

There had to be a reasonable explanation for the disappearance of her expensive new suit. Burglary was one possibility, but she wasn't wild about it.

"Drew, my clothes are missing." Her voice was amazingly steady.

"No, they're not."

"Drew, I am standing in front of the closet. The suit I planned to wear today is not here."

"Oh, well, that could be," he said agreeably.

She shot him an accusing glare. "What do you know about this?"

He cleared his throat. "Well…"

"Drew Landry, I have the most important meeting of my life in exactly two hours. I do not have time for one of your games. Where the hell is my suit?"

"I replaced it."

"You did what?" There was an ominous note in her voice.

"I knew you wanted to look just right today, so I got rid of the suit. I mean I didn't really get rid of it. It was probably an expensive suit and I knew you'd be furious if I threw it out, so I just sort of temporarily misplaced it."

"Well, you can just get it right back again."

"Nope," he said, shaking his head adamantly, a pleased gleam in his eyes. "Afraid not. But there is something else in there. You probably didn't see it. The color is just right for you. Emerald green. Remember? You told me how much you like it. I thought it would cheer you up. That dull old suit was depressing. It was exactly the same shade as mud."

"That dull old suit was businesslike. I actually made myself pay nearly three hundred dollars for it."

"Your first instinct was right. That's entirely too much for that suit." He smiled at her beguilingly. "Couldn't you just look at what I bought?"

"Do I have a choice?" she snapped.

She opened the first closet door again with such force that it slammed into the wall. Drew winced, as well he should, she noted with satisfaction. Her hand fell on the emerald-green dress with its tailored lines. The wool was softer than any she'd ever felt before. She pulled the dress out of the closet and regarded it with caution. Actually, it was lovely. It was not too daring, as she'd feared after Drew's assessment of the staid nature of her suit. Nor was it overtly feminine in a way that would have offended her desire to appear professional. And, she thought, the color was gorgeous.

"Damn," she muttered.

Drew's eyebrows shot up disbelievingly. "You don't like it?"

"No, I do. Really. It's just that I don't have any accessories for this."

"Yes, you do," Drew said, climbing out of bed and strolling back to his room. He came back and handed her a velvet box, which she barely noticed since her eyes were riveted on his naked body. She finally blinked and looked at the box he'd put in her hands.

"You didn't leave anything to chance, did you? You must really hate that suit."

"I just wanted you to go in there today filled with self-confidence. Now open the box."

Tina flipped open the lid and found an antique gold

locket and tiny gold and diamond earrings. They were so incredibly right and beautiful that they brought tears to her eyes.

"The locket was my mother's," Drew said softly. "I thought you might like it."

His words and the sentiment behind them brought a lump to her throat. She put her arms around him and met his gaze. "There's nothing you could have given me that would have meant more," she said sincerely. "I love it and..." She hesitated for just a moment. "And I love you."

Drew's body relaxed in her arms and he pressed her head into his shoulder. "You don't know how much I've wanted to hear you say that."

Tina sighed with pleasure. Suddenly everything felt very, very right. Maybe today was going to turn out to be okay after all.

The cocktail hour and the luncheon actually did go beautifully. The bartender poured the drinks with an unrestrained hand. The chef had created a gourmet meal, followed by a delicate dessert that looked tempting and highly caloric and tasted even better. By coffee everyone seemed mellow. Tina's hopes for the meeting lifted fractionally.

It took only fifteen minutes, though, for her to see how wrong she'd been about the mood of the crowd. It shifted from jovial to antagonistic in less time than it takes an actor to slip into a familiar role. From the instant she turned over the floor to the first speaker, she heard herself maligned over and over again. The speakers' opinions were based solely on irresponsible reports in the media. No one seemed the least bit interested in the facts. Although the disparaging comments about Sarah and the others were subtly phrased, they made Tina increasingly furious.

At last it was her turn. Her knees shaking, she got to her feet and faced a roomful of grim, hostile stares. A quick glance around told her that Mr. Kelly had apparently tuned out the entire unpleasant commotion. He was staring at the modern paintings on the walls with something akin to astonishment written all over his face. Sarah and Juliet appeared shell-shocked, probably more so since only a short time earlier they'd been conversing pleasantly with these same people.

Only Drew's encouraging smile from the back of the room kept Tina from telling the stockholders they could take Harrington Industries and turn it into a playground for business school drop-outs for all she cared. It was not in her to give up without a fight, especially with not only her own, but her friends' dignity at stake.

"If I understand your concerns correctly," she said in a voice so soft those in the rear of the room had to strain to hear it, "most of you feel that my personal life has become a detriment to this company. I'd like to ask you a question now."

Her gaze wandered slowly around the room, allowing the silence to build, pinning her audience in place as they waited in suspense for her question.

"What would you do if your mother or grandmother or an elderly uncle needed help?" she asked at last. "Would you turn them out because an outsider considered them socially beneath you?" Several people squirmed uncomfortably. "That's what you're asking me to do."

Tina stepped out from behind the lectern and walked to the front row. Her eyes met Drew's, drew strength from the support she saw there. She took a deep breath and went on.

"Sarah Morgan, Jacob Kelly and Juliet Burroughs and her nephew Billy are not members of my family, according to the law. I have no family to speak of, not since Gerald died. These people came into my life at a time when I needed love, when I needed more than Harrington Industries to feel complete. They may not have a listing on the society register, but how many of you have that? They are good, honest people, just as you are."

She glanced back at Drew and Seth and they gave her a thumbs up signal. She gave them a wavering smile, then continued, her voice growing stronger as she re-called the indignation she had felt on Sarah and Juliet and Mr. Kelly's behalf in recent weeks.

"I've read that they're crazy. I've read that they're poor. I've read that I treat them no better than house-hold servants. Doesn't that arouse a specific image in your mind? It does in mine." She waited for the image to settle in, then said with mounting indignation, "Let me tell you something about Sarah, Juliet, Mr. Kelly and Billy, though. They have more dignity and warmth than anyone I've ever met. They're exactly like you and me. In fact, I suspect if you were to look around this room right now, you would not be able to identify them, they fit in so well."

There was a gasp of surprise as the implications of

her words sank in and heads turned this way and that trying to identify the people who'd been made out as both victims and senile old fools in the press. Tina nodded in satisfaction.

"I see that you understand. They are here and you can't pick them out in a crowd. Many of you have chatted with them during lunch and found them to be intelligent, lively and humorous individuals. Would you have made that same judgment about them if you'd realized they were the people I've been accused of harboring for who-knows-what evil ends? I doubt it. It would be too bad, too, because they are people worth knowing," she said simply and with heartfelt conviction. She saw the tears shimmering in Juliet's eyes and the crackling, spirited humor in Sarah's. No matter how things turned out, the expression on those faces was all that mattered.

She waited for the murmuring to die down, then said briskly, "Now I'd like to change the subject for a moment and talk about why we're really here today: to discuss Harrington Industries and its progress over the last year."

With complete confidence, she used a multimedia presentation to show the company's growth in size and profits since she'd assumed command. She could hear the rumblings of surprise when she presented the strong bottom-line figures. Only the board members remained stoically silent. They'd known all of this, yet a few of them had tried to capitalize on the negative publicity to try to maneuver her out.

"I know many of you have lost faith in my leadership due to the publicity in recent days, so if my stepping down is what it will take to keep Harrington Industries on track, I'm prepared to do that," Tina said. "This was Gerald's business. He set its management style and its direction more than fifteen years ago, when he opened the first office. I've tried to carry on those traditions as I thought he would want."

She paused and looked out at the crowd, at people who'd once been her supporters and now seemed to be her enemies. She caught an occasional flush of embarrassment. Several people blinked guiltily under her penetrating assessment.

At last, she said quietly, "The floor is now open to any motions you'd care to make."

When Mr. Parsons got to his feet, Tina paled. If he started talking about germicidal warfare, the vote on her ouster would be quicker than an approving vote on a motion for adjournment after a slow-moving ten-hour meeting.

"Mr. Parsons," she acknowledged reluctantly.

"I'd like to move that we give the current chairman— uh, chairperson..."

Chuckles greeted his remark.

"I move we give her a unanimous vote of confidence," he concluded as Tina's eyes blinked wide in astonishment. "I admit I'm from the old school, one of those fellas who think women belong in the home so I can't help confessing I'm surprised at the job she's done, but figures don't lie. Those of us on the board have watched her closely and she's done her job and more. In fact, ain't nobody done more for Harrington Industries since Gerald himself headed up the operation and I say he'd be mighty proud of her. We should be, too.

"Before all this nonsense in the press, there wasn't much doubt about her remaining in charge. Ain't no reason to go changing that now," he said and sat down heavily.

"I'd like to second that," Kathryn Sawyer said. "This company has benefited from Mrs. Harrington's fresh ideas, her business acumen and her woman's instincts. All of this other nonsense is immaterial."

Tina might have fainted dead away if she hadn't recalled that Kathryn Sawyer sat on the board of several feminist groups and wasn't likely to turn Harrington Industries over to a man, unless her money was about to go down the tubes, no matter how little she thought the woman knew about setting a proper table. She knew her money was safe.

Mr. Davis promptly asked for a secret ballot.

"What's the matter, you old geezer?" Mr. Parsons demanded. "Afraid to vote your conscience out in public so's we can all see where you stand?"

"A secret ballot's the American way."

Tina stepped in. "Of course, we'll be using a secret ballot. I believe they've been prepared in accordance with the announced election today of our officers and directors. The proxy votes have also been received prior to this meeting."

When the ballots had been distributed, marked and counted, Tina remained as chairman of Harrington Industries and two of the board members who'd been most vocal in the fight against her had been ousted. A feeling of sheer exhilaration flowed through her. She'd done it. She had won them over and she had done it all on her own. It was the vindication she'd needed before she could let her love for Drew flourish the way she'd hoped it would.

That night, Tina, Drew and the others celebrated with champagne and dinner at an elegant restaurant with an appropriately commanding view of New York. Tina actually felt as if the entire world were hers for the taking.

In the morning, she and Drew took Sarah, Juliet, and Seth and Mr. Kelly to the airport and put them on the company plane back to Palm Beach. Before the engines even turned over, Sarah gave the pilot a stern warning to keep Juliet out of the cockpit.

"Sarah Morgan, you're just jealous," Aunt Juliet accused, tugging her seat belt into place around her ample figure. "You should try it. It really is a most exhilarating experience."

"If it's all that wonderful, you can take lessons when you get back home. Just don't expect me to be one of your first passengers," Sarah grumbled.

"When did you turn stodgy?" Tina teased. "I thought Seth had talked you into going ballooning when you got back?"

Juliet's eyes glittered with excitement and she clapped her hands delightedly. "Ballooning? Now that really would be marvelous. Floating around up there with the angels."

"Which is what we might wind up doing if you fly this plane again," Sarah retorted. "As for ballooning, I only said I'd consider it. If it were up to me, we'd stick to croquet."

Seth's blue eyes were sparkling wickedly. "Oh, Sarah, love, we'll have a dandy time whatever we do."

Drew stared at the two of them in astonishment, then turned to Tina helplessly. "What on earth is happening here? You catch them dancing in the parlor. Then it was ice-skating at Rockefeller Center and cavorting down Wall Street in the middle of the night. Now they want to go up in a balloon."

Tina grinned back at him. "Isn't love grand?"

"Love? I think they've both gone crazy."

"Now who's sounding stodgy? Come on, old man. Let's get out of here and let them take off. I was thinking of checking out that tattoo parlor we saw yesterday." Her amber eyes flashed at him provocatively. "I thought I might get a tiny little rose put..."

"Tina!" Drew's voice was a husky growl.

"I knew you'd like the idea," she said merrily, tugging him off the plane. For the first time in years she felt as though she could afford to be impetuous, to do exactly what she wanted.

As soon as they were on the ground and the plane had taxied down the runway, Drew whirled Tina around and stared directly into her laughing eyes. "No tattoo. I hate the idea," he said emphatically.

"Oh, really? Why is that?"

"I will not have you spoiling that beautiful, silky skin of yours with some weird little pen and ink drawing."

"But a rose is lovely, fragile."

"You're lovely and fragile enough as it is."

"Am I soft as a rose petal, though?"

Drew groaned. "I do not believe we are having this conversation. Exactly where were you planning to put this little beauty mark?"

"Oh, I was thinking about here." She lifted her skirt a

discreet, though provocative two inches and touched the back of her leg just above the knee. "Or maybe here." A finger rested just below her breast.

A choked sound emerged from deep in Drew's throat. "Do you honestly want to do this to me?"

"Do what to you?" she asked innocently.

"I'd never be able to see a dozen roses again without getting excited."

Tina chuckled at his nervous expression. Suddenly it gave way to horror. "What's wrong?" she asked, as her own laughter bubbled forth.

"Do you realize that I have a huge rose garden? Imagine what the sight of that would do to me."

She lowered her lashes and looked up at him provocatively. "What?"

He hardened his expression as if he'd decided to do his duty no matter what. "I guess I'd just have to haul you inside and make love to you every single time I ever saw a rose. Pruning would become sheer torture."

"Sounds good to me. This tattoo bit is sounding better and better."

He twirled her into his arms and gave her a hard, bruising kiss. "Get your tattoo, if you like, Tina Harrington, but be warned in advance. I will probably go mad at the sight of any rose." He kissed her again, his tongue teasing at the corners of her mouth. "Any time." Another kiss stole her breath away. "Any place." Yet another left her gasping and clinging to his shoulders.

It was the applause of several mechanics standing outside the commuter plane terminal that broke them apart. Drew looked very pleased with himself. Tina was thoroughly embarrassed. Aroused, but definitely embarrassed.

She coughed and met Drew's eyes. "I see your point."

"No tattoo?"

"I guess not," she said glumly, then her expression brightened. "How would you feel about pink stripes?"

"Pink stripes?" he asked cautiously. "Where?"

"In my hair, silly."

"I think there's probably an ordinance against it in Palm Beach. You'd be banned from the polo matches at the very least. Possibly from the country club and the Breakers as well."

"Spoilsport."

"Couldn't we just do something a little ordinary today?"

"Like what?"

"Oh, I don't know. Maybe take a walk in Central Park. Go to the Museum of Modern Art. Ride the subway."

Tina's brows arched doubtfully.

"Okay, scratch the subway. We could go to the theater. Or find some little Japanese restaurant and eat sushi." He glanced away, then added casually, "Of course, we could also make love."

"Are you saying that making love with me is ordinary?" Tina asked indignantly.

"Never. I just meant that as alternatives go, it was one of ours."

"Not if you're going to lump it in there with sushi and subway rides."

"Wouldn't you agree that our lovemaking has something a little raw and primitive about it?"

Tina scowled at him. "Is this a trick question?"

Drew grinned back at her. "And maybe a little dangerous?"

"Okay. Okay. It's right up there with sushi and the subway. You win."

"I do? What?"

She tucked her arm through his and beamed up at him. "We'll go back to the hotel," she began slowly, running her fingers up his arm. "Get rid of those adjoining rooms." Her fingers trailed along his cheek. "Take the most spectacular suite in the place." Her nail outlined his mouth, eliciting a husky moan.

"And make love, of course," she added as if it were only an afterthought. Drew's eyes seemed a little glazed, but he dragged her back to the limousine so hurriedly, her feet barely touched the ground.

For three fabulous days they did exactly as she'd suggested—making love with a joyous abandon and unbridled passion, interspersed with walks through SoHo to explore the art galleries, dinner in elegant restaurants, drinks in intimate clubs where Drew's fingers were never far from Tina's arm, her leg, her lips. That always led them back to their suite in a rush. Ignoring the complimentary champagne and a basket of fruit that could have supplied the entire produce section of a small market, they feasted on each other.

Tina was so wonderfully sated, so filled with her ability to finally express her love for Drew freely and without complications that she was hardly aware of the series of hushed business calls he always went into the other room of the suite to take.

It was on the third day of the visit that Tina received an early morning call of her own.

"There's something strange going on, Tina," David announced without preamble, obviously unattuned to the sleepily sensual sound of her voice.

Tina tried to bring her drugged senses under control, smacking Drew's playful hands away from their continuing pursuit of all of the spots he'd found that drove her to madness.

"What do you mean?" she said, instantly alert. She gasped suddenly and shot Drew a quelling glance. He stilled his hands, but he didn't withdraw them. Her flesh burned beneath his touch.

"You were right. Somebody seems to be buying up our stock. The price has been shooting up every day since the beginning of last week, and I don't think it has anything to do with the bull market this time."

"Why on earth didn't you tell me before?"

"On Monday I wasn't sure it meant anything. I thought it might be all tied in to the stockholders' meeting. Now I'm sure it's more than that."

Tina sat up in bed, every bit of her attention focused on what David was saying. "A takeover attempt?"

"That's what it's beginning to look like."

"Any idea who's behind it?" She couldn't even look at Drew, she was so afraid of what she'd see in his eyes.

"Not so far," David said cautiously. "Several people seem to be involved, since the volume is high and no one's passed the percentage that would require them to register with the SEC. So far all of them are covering their tracks well. There's no way to tell if there's a link until somebody registers."

"Of course there is," she said. "I want you to make a few discreet calls to our sources around the country. Someone must know something."

When she got off the phone, Drew was staring at the ceiling. She tried to decide if he looked guilty, but finally settled for brooding as a more apt description.

"What was that all about?" he said, his voice casual, his expression so neutral it made her want to shout.

"David seems to think there's a takeover attempt underway." Again, there was no visible reaction.

"I suppose you want to get right back to Florida."

"Actually, no. I think I'd like to make a few stops down on Wall Street."

"I see." Drew's voice was suddenly cool. Tina had already started toward the bathroom to take a shower, but she turned back as his tone registered.

"What's wrong?" She waited for the bomb to drop. It didn't. She supposed that made sense. Why would he reveal himself now, if he were behind the takeover?

She came back and sat on the edge of the bed, her fingers tangling in the dark hairs on his chest. "Drew, I asked you a question."

"There's nothing wrong."

"Don't tell me that, Drew Landry. I can read you like a book."

"I wonder," he said softly.

Tina was inexplicably hurt by the remark. "Drew, are you upset because I want to go check this out?" She hesitated, then said slowly, "Or is it something more?"

His gaze met hers, then wavered. He was staring at the ceiling again when he said, "No. There's nothing more to it. Go. It's what you have to do."

"That's right and it's exactly what you'd be doing if it were Landry Enterprises."

"I suppose."

"You know it is. Drew, I love you, but Harrington Industries matters to me, too. It's a part of who I am. You knew that when you met me. After all I've been through in the last few weeks to stay in control, you can't expect me to turn my back on it now."

"I guess I just thought now that the fight was over what we had here might be more important to you."

"Loving you is important, but so is Gerald's company."

"That's really the point, isn't it?" he said with a bitterness that stunned her. "It's Gerald's company. Gerald will always come first."

"That's absurd. He's dead, Drew," she said bluntly.

"But your love for him isn't. Are you planning to dedicate the rest of your life to his memory?"

Tina felt a slow-burning rage building inside her. How could Drew put her in this position? He was making her choose between him and Harrington Industries. As he saw it, it was a choice between him and her late husband. The whole idea was preposterous. She was in love with Drew, but she owed something to Gerald.

"Please don't make me choose, Drew. I wouldn't do that to you."

"It's not the same."

"Yes," she said softly. "Yes, it is."

She got up and went into the bathroom then. When she'd showered and dressed, she came back into the bedroom. Drew was gone. His suitcase was missing as well. Drew had made the choice for her.

In a way, she'd been prepared for the happiness to die, but now that it had, the hurt was far more devastating than she'd imagined and it only got worse.

In a matter of days Tina was able to exploit her sources and trace the apparent takeover bid to a conglomerate even bigger and more successful than Harrington Industries. It was owned by Drew Landry.

The sense of betrayal Tina felt was more painful than anything she'd ever known before in her life.

Drew, who'd always seemed so supportive.

Drew, who'd professed to love her.

Drew, who was once again trying to turn her whole world upside down.

Tina had never run from a challenge before in her life, and she didn't run from this one. She flew back to Palm Beach and called a meeting of the board, outlining the information she had uncovered.

"We'll fight him," Mr. Parsons blustered. "No question about it. We're not going to let Landry or anyone else manipulate us." He stared hard at Tina. "Thought that man was in love with you."

"I thought so, too," Tina said softly.

To her astonishment there was a look of gentle understanding in Mr. Parsons's eyes. "I'm sorry, young lady."

Tina didn't trust herself to speak. She simply nodded, took a deep breath and asked, "So what do we do?"

"We increase our own shares, pull together the stockholders and block the attempt."

"I'll spend every cent I have, if that's what it takes," Tina said.

Within days, though, the flurry of stock purchases

died down. The price stabilized in wait of news about a takeover. To everyone's surprise, no such word came.

"Tina, you're looking downright peaked again," Grandmother Sarah admonished.

"I'm fine," she said, sipping on a glass of fresh lemonade as she sat listlessly on the terrace. It was the first day off she'd had in ages, and all she wanted to do was sit and wallow in her misery. It was time she mourned for Drew and then put the whole ugly experience behind her.

"I don't mean to meddle, girl, but..."

"Please, don't."

Sarah's face took on a stubborn demeanor, and Tina knew she was in for a lecture whether she liked it or not. "I'm not going to sit by and watch you be miserable."

"I'm not miserable."

"Could have fooled me," she huffed. "You aren't eating. When you aren't at the office, you're moping around here. You scowl every time you bump into Seth, as though this were his fault."

Tina lifted her eyes at last. "I'm sorry, if I've been rude to Seth," she said sincerely. "I know he's important to you and I know none of this was his doing."

"It's just that he reminds you of his son."

"Something like that."

"Speaking of which, don't you think it's time you talked to Drew? If he trims that hedge back much further hoping to catch a glimpse of you, there won't be a leaf or branch left on it. Mr. Kelly's already having a fit."

"Tell Mr. Kelly to go ahead and replace the hedge."

"That's not the point, Christina Elizabeth, and you know it."

Tina sighed. "No. I don't suppose it is."

"What is the point of all this fussing then? You do love the man, don't you? Any fool can see that."

"Okay, yes. I love him, but *it doesn't matter.*"

"Oh, posh-tosh, girl. Of course it matters. It's the only thing that does."

"The man tried to take everything away from me. First all of you and then Harrington Industries. I hate him for that."

"There's a fine line between love and hate, isn't there?" Sarah said sagely. "Talk to Drew. You two had so much together. Don't throw it all away over what might have been just a misunderstanding."

"Thousands of shares of stock registered in his name cannot be misunderstood."

"Maybe. Maybe not. Find out for sure and then make your decision."

"Have you talked to him? What did he tell you?"

"I think he should tell you himself. I'm not going to interfere."

"Oh, really?"

Still, Grandmother Sarah had accomplished her purpose. Tina thought about the older woman's advice all during another long, lonely night through which not even the sea breeze could lull her to sleep. By morning she had made a decision. She had made several phone calls to complete the arrangements and then she ran, seeking a refuge that would allow her to think through how she could have been so wrong about a man she had loved so much. He had overcome her initial distrust, only to prove that he wasn't worthy of her love at all.

Or was it at all possible that Sarah might be right? Could she have misunderstood Drew's actions? It didn't seem likely and yet Sarah had seemed so sure that talking would resolve everything and Sarah knew her pretty well.

She would talk to Drew, she resolved at last, but first she needed time to figure out who she was and what she wanted from life. Could there have been some truth to Drew's accusation that she was clinging to the past, and if she was, why? Was she afraid of the present? Did she fear the powerful emotions that had swept through her from the very first with Drew? Had she instinctively expected, perhaps even hoped, it would end before it developed into something much more, into a commitment, a marriage that would be stormy and exciting, exactly the opposite of her placid life with Gerald?

If there were answers to all of that, she had to find them. It was something she should have done a long time ago.

Chapter Thirteen

Over the next few days Tina worked until she thought her arms would fall off and her back would never straighten out again. She'd run away to Mr. Kelly's house in her old neighborhood. There Tina swept cobwebs, scrubbed and painted walls, stripped and waxed the floors and dusted the furniture.

When she'd finished with the inside and the outside of the house, she went to work on the yard. Mr. Kelly would have been horrified by the state it was in. There were weeds everywhere. Millions of them, if her aching muscles were anything to judge by.

Tina had returned here instinctively, needing the contact with the old Tina and a way of life that might have been less filled with creature comforts, but which, in the end, had been so much simpler. People back then—even those she hadn't much liked—were always exactly what they seemed. There were few choices and they'd always seemed clear-cut, perhaps because she'd never allowed herself to see anything but black or white. She'd never allowed for the varying shades of gray that could complicate life, even as they made it more interesting.

As the week wore on, not only did the physical labor tire her out so that she could sleep at night, but the return to her old neighborhood forced her to think about her life—what it had been and what it had become. At night she sat on Mr. Kelly's porch and looked across the tiny patch of lawn to the house where she'd grown up. Its porch sagged and it was in need of paint, but it was hardly a slum. It was simply the victim of time, old and tired and well-used. It would have tucked neatly into one corner of her Palm Beach estate and yet, she was just now realizing, it had held just as much love. She was only beginning to understand that nothing else really mattered.

As a child, she had wanted so much more. She used to sit in this same rocking chair next to Mr. Kelly and tell him about her dream of being somebody someday. People were going to seek her out because she was so smart. They wouldn't be able to ignore her as they did the scrawny little kid who wore secondhand clothes from the church rummage sale and talked with a halting shyness.

She'd wanted success and recognition not just for herself, she'd always thought, but for her parents. They'd worked so hard and deserved better than what they'd been given. Now she had to face the possibility that perhaps she'd been thoroughly selfish after all, driven to distance herself from roots of which she was ashamed.

She dug her hands into the dirt to get at the roots of the weeds and wondered if she could get to the source of her problems as easily. Had it been the money—the so-called root of all evil—after all? Had the money itself, rather than the challenge of getting it, tantalized her in ways she'd never realized? That was certainly what Drew thought.

"Damn," she muttered, yanking up a clump of weeds and tossing them over her shoulder. What did it matter to her what Drew Landry thought? He'd only been using her. The pain she thought she'd seen in his eyes when he was convinced she'd chosen Harrington Industries over him must have been another lie. If her priorities were out of kilter, his were worse. He'd betrayed her love to get what he wanted. Disillusionment had sunk in and become her constant, discomforting companion.

"I will not think about that man for another single minute," she swore valiantly, but his image didn't vanish as she might have liked. It lingered on to tease and torment her like a sun-kissed spring breeze that only hinted of warmer weather. She remembered the pain, but she also remembered the moments of incredible tenderness, of loving protectiveness and of blinding passion.

When she'd first returned to the neighborhood after Mr. Kelly had agreed to let her fix the place up so he could sell it, she'd been so sure she would feel desperately alone, even more so than she had after Gerald's death. It was a sensation she craved. She had to discover if she could learn to live quietly, with only her own thoughts for company as she'd been unable to do three years earlier.

In the beginning, it had been difficult. She'd missed the commotion of home—Sarah's wise counsel, Juliet's sweetly innocent humor, Mr. Kelly's grumpiness, their quiet evenings of Scrabble and gin rummy. Most of all, she'd missed having Billy tagging around after her, plaguing her with questions about life and a world that always seemed just beyond his reach.

After a few days, though, she'd grown comfortable

with her own company and that of a straggly marmalade cat. She'd piteously meowed her way into Tina's heart and slurped up an entire quart of milk before sprawling contentedly on the sunny front porch.

With only Samantha Junior, as she called the cat, for companionship, Tina tried to analyze her relationship with Drew and with Gerald before him. Both were men of power and single-minded purpose. Both had a vitality that attracted her, but now she wondered why she had been drawn to such strength when she'd only come to resent it when it was used to protect her.

Both men were similar in other respects as well. Both had offered her their faith in her abilities—or so she had thought. Both had given her freely of their love, but again had it only seemed so? She had never had any cause to doubt Gerald's feelings for her, but she now had every reason to question Drew's, despite Sarah's seeming faith in him.

"Mind some company?" Drew's voice startled her just as she pulled another handful of weeds out of the dry soil and tossed them haphazardly over her shoulder. She looked up in time to see the messy clump land squarely in the middle of the pale blue polo shirt that hugged his broad chest.

"Is that your answer?" he teased lightly, though his blue eyes were very solemn. He looked vulnerable, something she'd never have expected from the confident Drew Landry she'd grown to love over the last few weeks. She was astonished to find that the familiar surge of desire roared through her at the sight of him. Her eyes drank in the expression in his eyes, the tilt of his lips, and worry tugged at her heart when she saw how haggard and drawn he looked.

So, she thought, she loved him still, after all, no matter what he had done. She was determined, though, not to let him see her response. At least not until she had some answers and maybe not even then. She started with the easiest question.

"How did you find me?" Her voice was cool, detached, though her insides were churning with misery at the knowledge that she still cared when she felt so strongly that she shouldn't.

"Dad wormed it out of Sarah."

"I didn't tell Sarah."

"Who'd gotten it out of Juliet."

Tina's eyes were twinkling now, despite herself, as she concluded for him, "Who'd gotten it straight from Mr. Kelly."

"Maybe he talks in his sleep as well as taking midnight strolls," Drew suggested with a shrug. "Now that I'm here, do you want to talk about what happened?"

Tina shook her head. "I'm still not convinced we have anything to talk about. It all seems pretty clear."

"Assumptions are a lousy way to communicate, Tina. Tell me what you think you see."

"For some reason, you chose to go behind my back to try to take Harrington Industries away from me. Sarah seems to think you had your reasons and they were valid."

"And you? Don't you want to know what those reasons were?"

"I know what they were. You're a smart business-man. It was a good deal, an ideal opportunity for you to expand your own company's holdings. We're ahead of the industry in the development of new products. In your position, I might have done the same thing knowing all that you did about Harrington Industries and its growth potential."

She stared at him bitterly. "Things I'd confided to you like an innocent little lamb. You must have been laughing hysterically all the way to your broker's."

Drew couldn't have looked any more shocked if she'd slapped him. "If you believe that, then you did a lousy investigation," he snapped impatiently, then clamped his mouth shut. When he was in control again, he said softly, "You also don't have very much faith in my love."

"My investigation was very thorough, but you're right about one thing. I don't have much faith in us anymore. Can you blame me?" she inquired.

"No. I don't suppose so, since you don't have all the facts." His voice was heavy with censure. "But I thought you might at least listen to the truth. Sarah seemed to think you were ready."

Tina sighed. "Okay. Talk. But it won't change anything."

"Perhaps not, but at least you'll know exactly what happened, instead of cutting me out of your life for all the wrong reasons."

"You were the one who walked out on me in New York," she reminded him.

Drew met her gaze evenly. "That was foolish. No matter how upset I was about the choice you made that morning. I should have stayed and talked it out. I'm sure leaving only made me look more guilty in your eyes."

"It certainly didn't help your case."

"Your running away hasn't helped either."

"It's helped me find some answers about myself."

"For example?"

"Maybe I have let my love for Gerald come between us. I didn't mean for that to happen, but a part of me was afraid of the depth of my feelings for you. I was scared by the intensity, by the power you had over me. You're so strong, so self-confident and protective. I thought I might get lost, let you simply take over."

"Did you really believe that could happen? You're the most independent woman I've ever known. No one will ever rob you of that. Not even me." He touched a finger to her cheek and a throbbing heat warmed her blood. "It's a funny thing about needing someone. I'd never realized until that morning in New York how badly I wanted you to need me. I'd always equated that with love."

Tina shot him a puzzled glance. "But I'd told you that I loved you."

"Yes, but when you were in trouble, when David called about the takeover attempt, you didn't turn to me. You hopped out of that bed, where we'd just spent the night making love, and set off alone to do whatever needed to be done. Not once did you ask me to come with you, to help you. You didn't want or need my advice."

"That's true," Tina said slowly. "I never really thought about it. For so many years now I've been on my own. I've had to do things for myself. My parents weren't able to help me with school. I did it myself, working nights and weekends at two jobs. When I got out of college, I didn't have terrific connections like many of my classmates. I had to be better than the rest of them just to get a chance. For just a little while with Gerald I let down my guard. I relied on someone else."

Her eyes met Drew's and they were filled with pain. "And then he died. I don't think I realized until just now that I must have subconsciously decided never again to count on anyone. I set myself up to be the strong one in any relationship."

"Could it be that's why you also felt so helpless in this crisis with DCF, because for once you weren't in charge?"

"I'm sure that had a lot to do with it. I wanted to fix it, to make it right and I couldn't. I felt powerless, just the way I did when I was a kid. I remember once trying to tell someone I'd seen an accident, but they kept brushing me off. When the police started questioning people, I tried to tell them, but it was like I didn't exist or couldn't be trusted."

"Did it occur to you that it was because you were a child, not because of who you were?"

"I realize that now, but then I just remember feeling this terrible anger and frustration. I felt the same way when Edward Grant wouldn't listen to me."

"But you wouldn't let yourself ask for help? Not even from me?"

"Especially not from you. My feelings for you were already more than I could deal with. I was terrified of reaching out to you and finding that you'd gone."

"I'm not going anywhere, Tina."

"You can't guarantee that, Drew. Things happen. Feelings change."

"And strong people cope."

Tina sighed. "I'm not sure I could cope again."

"You could if you had to."

"But could you deal with the fact that I won't ever rely on you for everything?"

"As long as you needed my love, I think I could handle it. I had a lot of time to think during the last few weeks. I've realized that need and love aren't the same after all. I just want a chance to show you that, to prove to you that I can love you without smothering you."

Tina shook her head. "I don't know, Drew. There are so many things we haven't resolved. This stock business, for example. I can't just forget about that."

"I wouldn't even want you to. I'm ready to tell you everything, if you're willing to listen."

"I told you I would."

Drew nodded and sat down on a porch step, his elbows propped on his knees, his chin resting in his hands. He watched her, his eyes boldly lingering, until Tina felt as though she'd left her clothes inside. It was a penetrating gaze, as if he might be measuring just how much she'd be willing to believe.

"I was not behind the takeover attempt," he said at last.

Anger ripped through her at the blatant lie. Even now, he was just giving her more lies.

"Oh, please." Her voice was thick with disgust and fury.

"Wait," he said, holding up a hand to wave off her expression of outraged disbelief. "I wasn't. Not at first. When I heard about it, right before the stockholders' meeting, I started using some of my resources to buy up stock on your behalf. If you'll check, you'll see that all of the shares have been transferred into your name."

"Sure. Now they are. You did that after you knew I was on to you."

"If you're talking about the date on them, yes. If you think that's the reason, you're wrong. They were always meant for you."

"Why should I believe that?"

"If I were only interested in Harrington Industries, as you seem to think, why would I give it up now?" he asked reasonably. "I have the stock, but there was no move toward a takeover. You know that."

He had a point, Tina had to admit. If he'd wanted her company and didn't give a damn about her, why would he have transferred the stock to her, rather than forcing the takeover? Was he trying to throw her off guard so he could regain her trust and take complete control in a less public way? That explanation was so convoluted even she could see it was laughable. Was it possible that he really had done it all for her?

She sighed and jabbed the trowel she was holding into the ground with such force that Drew winced. Oh, Lord, why did things have to be so confusing? She wanted so badly to believe in him, but the last few weeks had taken their toll. Trust, slow to build in the first place, had died.

"Sorry," she said finally. "I don't buy it."

"It's the truth. Put your best people on it, if you like. You'll find that a Texas billionaire with a flair for hit-and-run moves started buying your stock three days before your stockholders' meeting. When your stock started moving, my broker mentioned it to me. He thought I might want to get in on the action."

"Which you couldn't wait to do."

"You're right. David *had* been checking the stock movement, but when I realized that both you and he were so preoccupied with the stockholders' meeting and that you weren't alert to what was happening on the market, I took action," he said, then paused to add emphasis. *"But only to protect your interests."*

"Why the hell didn't you just tell me what was going on, instead of jumping into the fray yourself? I could have dealt with it, if I'd known the truth."

His lips quirked in a rueful smile. "That's the tough one. I suppose I was being selfish and protective and a whole bunch of chauvinistic things. I thought maybe for once I could do something for you. And once that stockholders' meeting was over, I wanted your mind on me while we were in New York, not on Harrington Industries. I'm not as strong or as self-confident as you think. I'm only human, and in some twisted way that company always made me feel as though I were competing with the ghost of Gerald Harrington."

Tina searched his eyes and found them filled with vulnerability. His jealousy of Gerald was something he'd hinted at before, but only now was she realizing how deep his fear of losing her or sharing her had run.

She put a hand on his arm and felt the muscles quiver and knot. "I told you this in New York, Drew. Gerald is dead. I'm not the type to live forever in the past."

"I didn't say my reaction was rational. I said it was human." He gazed into her eyes. "Before I go, I just want you to remember one thing: what I did was out of love. It might have been wrong and it might not seem that way, but I swear to you it was out of love."

He turned to leave. He was all the way at the end of the walk, his shoulders slumped in dejection, when Tina called out to him.

"Drew."

He turned, and hope flickered in his eyes. "Yes?"

"Stay."

"Why?"

"I want to try."

He didn't move an inch, but hope and desire burned more brightly in his eyes. "Try?" he repeated softly.

She nodded. "I must be crazy, but I haven't been able to think of anything else in days. As much as I didn't want to, I still love you. I want us to get back what we had before, if we can."

"And then?"

"No promises, Drew. I can't make them."

"Will you come back home?"

"Not yet. I think we need some time alone."

"Here?"

"This place may not be the answer either. I think I've made my peace with my childhood. Now I need to make my peace with you."

"Then let's go to my farm in Ocala. There won't be any distractions, and we can start over again. We can get all our problems out in the open and work on them one by one."

Tina grinned. "I knew your obsession with organization wouldn't lie idle for long."

"Do you object?"

"Not strenuously. Just put it to work on something useful."

"Such as?"

"Making the arrangements for the trip."

They flew to Orlando the next morning and were picked up by Drew's farm manager. By afternoon, Tina was riding a gentle filly around the farm.

"Drew, I am not wild about this," she said from the unsteady perch on the horse's back. Her rear end already felt as if she'd been paddled.

"Don't be silly. She's not going to hurt you."

"She may not bite me, but she's in a terrific position to dump me on my already painful derriere. Don't you care about that?"

"I thought you wanted me to stop being overly protective."

"You picked a fine time to go along with me on that," she grumbled as she bounced along the lane that wound through Drew's small orange grove.

Tina forgot all about the aches and pains a few hours later when Drew ran another steamy bath for her, then joined her in it. The man seemed to have a penchant for enormous tubs that accommodated two, even when their interest strayed from the simple act of bathing, which it did often and with astonishingly sensual results.

Late one night at the end of the week, when Tina was curled sleepily against Drew's side, her head resting on his shoulder, the phone rang.

"Ignore it," she suggested.

"You know I can't do that." He picked up the receiver, spoke briefly to the caller, then handed over the phone. "It's Sarah."

Tina sat up in bed. "Hi, Sarah. What's up?" Her face promptly clouded over.

"What's wrong?" Drew demanded.

"It's Billy."

"Is he sick? In trouble? What?"

"Hush a minute and I'll find out," she told him. "Go on, Sarah."

Tina listened, then began chuckling. "Okay. We'll be watching for him. I'll call you when he gets here."

"Billy's coming here?"

"Yes, and I'd suggest you prepare yourself."

"For what?"

"It seems he has a few questions about your intentions. Sarah tried to stop him, but he went sneaking off to the bus station tonight. He should be here in a few hours."

"Terrific."

Tina laughed at the expression of frustration on Drew's face. "Oh, don't be such a sourpuss. Maybe this is just what we need."

"I don't know about you, but I do not need a thirteen-year-old trying to manage my life."

"Not even if he's going to force us to face our situation and make some decisions?"

Drew's eyes widened appreciably at that. "Is that what he's going to do?"

"I'd say so, and unless you want him to make the decisions for us, we'd better start talking."

"Okay. I need to ask you something."

"I thought you might," she said, beginning an utterly fascinating exploration of Drew's right arm. She'd begun at the strong curve of his shoulder, worked her way along his muscled biceps, traced the blue pattern of blood vessels that ran along the soft skin of his inner arm, rubbed the dark hairs that shadowed his forearm and sucked delicately—and she'd thought provocatively—at each fingertip. She must be doing something wrong, since he seemed intent on going ahead with the conversation, rather than using the little time they had for more pleasurable pursuits.

"Have you checked on the stock transfer?"

Startled, she dropped his hand and shook her head.

"Why not?"

She sighed, reluctantly conceding that her amorous intentions had been waylaid. "It doesn't seem important anymore. I've proved I can run Harrington Industries, that Gerald's judgment in me was not misplaced. I finally realize that I don't need to prove anything anymore. If Harrington Industries and Landry Enterprises were to merge, it wouldn't be the end of the world. In fact, it might be very smart."

"As a matter of fact, it would be. My computer division's research would blend in beautifully with what you've already done. We'd become a major force to reckon with in that market." At the flash of distrust in her eyes, he grinned. His hands cupped her face, and blue eyes gazed earnestly into amber. "But for the moment, I'm not the least bit interested in Harrington Industries. That's your decision. I'm more concerned with a merger of another sort."

"What's that?"

"Are you ready to talk about marriage? Like you said, we'd better do it before Billy arrives on our doorstep."

"In the general sense or the specific? Generally, I

think it's a positive move, if made by two people who truly love each other and know the risks and are willing to work at the commitment."

"What about specifically? Will you marry me? The time we were separated was the worst time in my life. I don't ever want to be without you again. I can't swear to you that I won't try to fight your battles for you on occasion, but I'll respect your right to tell me to butt out."

"That seems like a reasonable compromise," she conceded with an impish grin. "The only issue remaining is whether you'll actually butt out."

He hesitated. "Well…"

"Drew," she said ominously, her eyes clouding.

"If it's in your best interests."

"Not good enough. I'm entitled to make my own mistakes."

"Okay. Fine," he growled. "Make all the mistakes you want. I won't say a word."

"Of course you will," she said confidently. "You're bound to say I told you so. You won't be able to resist."

"Can you live with that?"

She sighed. "I love you. I suppose I'll have to. See how good I am about compromising."

"I think I must have missed that part. Exactly how do you plan to compromise?"

Tina pondered the question for a moment, then brightened. "I know. I'll give that suit you hate to Goodwill."

"What a girl," he said, rolling his eyes as he enfolded her in his embrace.

"But I'm yours," she reminded him.

"Yes," he said, his lips hot and urgent against hers. "Yes, you definitely are."

Before they could get too engrossed in each other, the doorbell rang. Drew moaned. "We're going to have to work on that kid's timing."

They wrapped themselves in robes and went to the door together. Billy's eyes widened when he took in their rumpled appearance, and his hands balled into fists.

"I knew it," he growled, glaring at Drew. "You lied to me."

"I never lied to you."

"All that talk about commitment and stuff, it was a bunch of bull."

"Watch your language," Drew said sternly.

"Says who?"

"Says my fiancé," Tina inserted before the two could square off into a boxing stance and start throwing punches.

A glimmer of light sparked in Billy's eyes. "You're going to get married?"

"As soon as possible," Drew confirmed.

"That means you'll be my dad?"

"More or less."

"Oh, wow, that's terrific!"

"I'm glad you approve," Tina said dryly. "Now there's a little matter of your running away from home to discuss."

"I didn't exactly run away. I told Grandmother Sarah and Aunt Juliet I was coming."

"And they told you not to."

Billy shuffled his feet uneasily. "Well..."

"Exactly."

"What would be a suitable punishment?" Drew asked.

Billy's expression brightened. "You mean I get to choose?"

Tina shot a disbelieving look at Drew. "That's a rather unusual form of justice."

"These are unusual circumstances. The boy was looking out for your honor, after all."

"That's true," she conceded with a sudden grin. "So, Billy, what's it to be?"

"How about me being the best man at the wedding?"

"That's a punishment?" Drew and Tina said in unison.

"Sure. I'll have to wear a dumb tuxedo."

"Sounds to me like the punishment fits the crime," Drew agreed. He regarded Tina hopefully. "Unless we elope and get married by a justice of the peace."

"Not a chance."

Drew and Billy exchanged put-upon glances. "Women!"

Tina put her hands on her hips and stared Drew down. "Take it or leave it."

"I'll take it."

"I thought you might." She grinned at Drew. "Why don't you find Billy a place to sleep, while I call Sarah and let her know he's okay?"

"I could probably find my own room," Billy offered, suddenly staring at the floor. "I mean if you all have stuff you want to do or something."

"That's okay," Drew said. "We have a whole lifetime ahead of us to do stuff."

He stopped at the doorway and gazed back at Tina, a long, slow look that ended in a provocative wink. Her heart slammed against her ribs.

A whole lifetime. It might not be nearly long enough.

Epilogue

The announcement of an early-spring wedding between industry tycoon Drew Landry and his new business partner, Christina Elizabeth Harrington, set Palm Beach society on its collective ear.

Columnists in the newspaper speculated about exactly how the eccentric widow with the quirky sense of humor had captured the heart of the community's most eligible bachelor after they'd gotten off to such a rocky, controversial start.

Women who hadn't said a word to Tina since Gerald's death suddenly called with invitations to have the mouth-watering *Aubergines Farcie au chevre* at Café L'Europe or the delicacies at Charley's Crab by the ocean. What they wanted in return was titillating information. Tina declined on all counts.

Even though the event was to take place after the official winter season ended, invitations were in more demand than those to the annual height-of-the-season Red Cross fundraiser, probably due to an expectation that the ceremony would be something out of the ordinary. Tina suspected that half the town was hoping she'd have the cats trailing down the aisle as bridesmaids.

Partly because she delighted in the idea of keeping gossips guessing, but mostly because she wanted to keep it simple and intimate, Tina restricted the ceremony to family and special friends only.

The wedding was held on the Harrington estate under a cloudless blue sky on the first Saturday in April. Sarah cried, dabbing at her eyes with one of her lilac-scented hankies, as she served a breakfast of waffles and bacon to the excited members of the household. Juliet forgot all about being in mourning and came down for breakfast that day in a lovely dusty-blue dress. Mr. Kelly had turned the lawn into a carpet of lush green velvet and the gardens were filled with bright, fragrant blossoms. In deference to Drew's allergies, the cats had been locked inside. The bride wore an apricot silk dress beaded with pearls and carried a bouquet of apricot roses and baby's breath. The solemnly spoken wedding vows were lifted on the wind and carried away to mingle with the ocean's timeless roar.

The destination of the honeymoon was practically a state secret, at least until Seth told Sarah, who told Juliet and on and on until half the town knew that Tina and Drew were spending their days on a beach in Monte Carlo, their evenings in a glamorous casino and their nights in a romantic villa on a cliff overlooking the sea.

On the last day of the honeymoon, Tina called home to check on things and found Sarah bubbling with exciting news.

"Mr. Grant was here yesterday. The DCF report is finished and everything's just fine. We can stay."

"Oh, Sarah, I'm so glad. That's the best wedding present I could have had."

"And the city's dropping its complaint, too. Since

we're not paying you anything, they've decided we're not in violation of any zoning code."

"That's fantastic. Anything more?"

She could hear Billy's murmurings in the background as Sarah said, "Hush. I'm not going to tell her that. She'll find out soon enough."

"Please. You've got to tell her," Billy urged. "She'll want to know."

"Tell me what?" Tina finally demanded.

Sarah sighed. "Samantha Junior had kittens," she said, just as Drew picked up the extension. "Five of them."

"Oh my Lord!" Drew exclaimed.

"Drew Landry!" Sarah scolded.

"Sorry."

"And," Sarah began.

"There's more?" Tina said as Drew began to sneeze in what could only be a reflex action. Those cats were thousands of miles away.

"Well, it's nothing for you to worry about, dear."

"Sarah!"

"It's just that Mr. Parsons—"

"From the board of directors?"

"Of course, dear."

"What about him?"

"He was over the other day visiting."

"Mr. Parsons was visiting? You must mean spying. He was probably looking for the germicidal warfare lab."

"I don't think so. He just wanted to make sure your wedding took place as scheduled. He seemed genuinely concerned after what happened before. And…"

"And what?" Tina said, not at all sure she wanted to hear the rest. She recognized that tone.

"Well, the poor man seemed very lonely. I mean his wife died years ago and he's all alone in the world. I think that's why he's so cranky, and he certainly was drinking way more than was good for him. We could all see that in New York. You could see it, too, couldn't you, dear?"

"What's your point, Sarah?"

Sarah was not about to be rushed. "He looked awfully pale. I doubt if he'd been eating properly either," she added as if it were a clincher. "You should have seen how thrilled he was when I asked him to stay for pot roast."

An awful premonition raced through Tina. "Sarah, you didn't," she exclaimed. "Tell me you didn't ask that man to live with us."

"But there are all these empty rooms here. It seems such a waste not to use them. And he's a fine gin rummy player."

"Sarah, I want to hear you deny it. Tell me you didn't ask him."

"Well, I didn't exactly ask. It just sort of happened. I mean we all agreed something had to be done."

Drew was chuckling on the extension.

"Drew Landry, don't you dare laugh," Tina ordered.

"I can't help it."

"I'll get you for that, Drew. I'll let Billy keep every one of those kittens," she warned, slamming down the phone. She went into the bedroom just as he was saying goodbye to Sarah. He was still chuckling. She advanced on him with a murderous expression in her bright amber eyes.

"Just think," he said cheerfully, "now we can hold the board meetings right in the living room between Scrabble games."

She dove into the middle of the bed and tackled him, pinning him down. "You...you..." Then she started laughing, too, and leaned down to kiss him. "I love you."

"You know, Mrs. Landry, life with you will never be dull."

"And even if it is," she said with a devilish glint in her eyes, "you'll have all those other people to keep you company."

Drew sobered instantly as a horrified expression flitted across his face. "Don't tell me you actually expect me to live in that house, when I have a perfectly lovely *empty* house next door."

Tina's eyes widened innocently. "You want to be alone with me?"

"Damn right."

"Why?"

"Let me show you, and we'll see if you still want to live in the middle of that mayhem at your place."

An hour later, Drew murmured, "Well, what do you think?"

"I think I'm beginning to see your point. Do you have any other arguments you'd like to try?"

He had several, each more exquisitely sensual than the last. By the time they flew home, Tina was convinced.

Besides, if she had her way, they'd fill the bedrooms

in that house in no time, too. Nine or ten months from now seemed about the right time to start. She knew Sarah and Seth would approve.

In fact, she had a suspicion they were already busy wallpapering a nursery just in case.

* * * * *

A COLD CREEK
HOMECOMING
RaeAnne Thayne

Dear Reader,

Reunion stories are some of my absolute favorite books to write. I find something truly magical about people who have shared a sometimes strained past yet are able to connect again when they're each in a better place to find love.

Successful businessman Quinn Southerland hasn't forgotten the way Tess Jamison treated him in high school. She was a mean girl of the highest order when it came to Quinn. How can he reconcile his harsh memories of her with the soft, sweet hospice nurse now caring so diligently for his beloved foster mother?

I loved Tess and Quinn from the first page and showing the joy that can come even in difficult circumstances when two people learn to move beyond the past and trust their hearts.

All my very best,

RaeAnne

In memory of my dear aunt, Arlene Wood,
for afghans and parachutes and ceramic frogs.
I only wish I'd dedicated one to you before!
And to Jennifer Black, my sister and hero,
for helping her pass with peace and dignity.

Chapter One

"You're home!"

The thin, reedy voice whispering from the frail woman on the bed was nothing like Quinn Southerland remembered.

Though she was small in stature, Jo Winder's voice had always been firm and commanding, just like the rest of her personality. When she used to call them in for supper, he and the others could hear her voice ringing out loud and clear from one end of the ranch to the other. No matter where they were, they knew the moment they heard that voice, it was time to go back to the house.

Now the woman who had done so much to raise him—the toughest woman he had ever known—seemed a tiny, withered husk of herself, her skin papery and pale and her voice barely audible.

The cracks in his heart from watching her endure the long months and years of her illness widened a little more. To his great shame, he had a sudden impulse to run away, to escape back to Seattle and his business and the comfortable life he had created for himself there, where he could pretend this was all some kind of bad dream and she was immortal, as he had always imagined.

Instead, he forced himself to step forward to the edge of the bed, where he carefully folded her bony fingers in his own much larger ones, cursing the cancer that was taking away this woman he loved so dearly.

He gave her his most charming smile, the one that never failed to sway any woman in his path, whether in the boardroom or the bedroom.

"Where else would I be but right here, darling?"

The smile she offered in return was rueful and she lifted their entwined fingers to her cheek. "You shouldn't have come. You're so busy in Seattle."

"Never too busy for my best girl."

Her laugh was small but wryly amused, as it always used to be when he would try to charm his way out of trouble with her.

Jo wasn't the sort who could be easily charmed but she never failed to appreciate the effort.

"I'm sorry to drag you down here," she said. "I…only wanted to see all of my boys one last time."

He wanted to protest that his foster mother would be around for years to come, that she was too tough and ornery to let a little thing like cancer stop her, but he couldn't deny the evidence in front of him.

She was dying, was much closer to it than any of them had feared.

"I'm here, as long as you need me," he vowed.

"You're a good boy, Quinn. You always have been."

He snorted at that—both of them knew better about that, as well. "Easton didn't tell me you've been hitting the weed as part of your treatment."

The blankets rustled softly as her laugh shook her slight frame. "You know better than that. No marijuana here."

"Then what are you smoking?"

"Nothing. I meant what I said. You were always a good boy on the inside, even when you were dragging the others into trouble."

"It still means the world that you thought so." He kissed her forehead. "Now I can see you're tired. You get some rest and we can catch up later."

"I would give anything for just a little of my old energy."

Her voice trailed off on the last word and he could tell she had already drifted off, just like that, in mid-sentence. As he stood beside her bed, still holding her fingers, she winced twice in her sleep.

He frowned, hating the idea of her hurting. He slowly, carefully, released her fingers as if they would shatter at his touch and laid them with gentle care on the bed then turned just as Easton Springhill, his distant cousin by marriage and the closest thing he had to a sister, appeared in the doorway of the bedroom.

He moved away from the bed and followed Easton outside the room.

"She seems in pain," he said, his voice low with distress.

"She is," Easton answered. "She doesn't say much about it but I can tell it's worse the past week or so."

"Isn't there something we can do?"

"We have a few options. None of them last very long. The hospice nurse should be here any minute. She can give her something for the pain." She tilted her head. "When was the last time you ate?"

He tried to remember. He had been in Tokyo when he got the message from Easton that Jo was asking for him to come home. Though he had had two more days of meetings scheduled for a new shipping route he was negotiating, he knew he had no choice but to drop everything. Jo would never have asked if the situation hadn't been dire.

So he had rescheduled everything and ordered his plane back to Pine Gulch. Counting several flight delays from bad weather over the Pacific, he had been traveling for nearly eighteen hours and had been awake for eighteen before that.

"I had something on the plane, but it's been a few hours."

"Let me make you a sandwich, then you can catch a few z's."

"You don't have to wait on me." He followed her down the long hall and into the cheery white-and-red kitchen. "You've got enough to do, running the ranch and taking care of Jo. I've been making my own sandwiches for a long time now."

"Don't you have people who do that for you?"

"Sometimes," he admitted. "That doesn't mean I've forgotten how."

"Sit down," she ordered him. "I know where everything is here."

He thought about pushing her. But lovely as she was with her delicate features and long sweep of blond hair, Easton could be as stubborn and ornery as Jo and he was just too damn tired for another battle.

Instead, he eased into one of the scarred pine chairs snugged up against the old table and let her fuss over him for a few moments. "Why didn't you tell me how things were, East? She's withered away in the three months since I've been home. Chester probably weighs more than she does."

At the sound of his name, Easton's retired old cow dog that followed her or Jo everywhere lifted his grizzled gray muzzle and thumped his black-and-white tail against the floor.

Easton's sigh held exhaustion and discouragement and no small measure of guilt. "I wanted to. I swear. I threatened to call you all back weeks ago but she begged me not to say anything. She said she didn't want you to know how things were until…"

Her voice trailed off and her mouth trembled a little. He didn't need her to finish. Jo wouldn't have wanted them to know until close to the end.

This was it. For three long years, Jo had been fighting breast cancer and now it seemed her battle was almost over.

He *hated* this. He wanted to escape back to his own world where he could at least pretend he had some semblance of control. But she wanted him here in Cold Creek, so here he would damn well stay.

"Truth time, East. How long does she have?"

Easton's features tightened with a deep sorrow. She had lost so much, this girl he had thought of as a sister since the day he arrived at Winder Ranch two decades ago, an angry, bitter fourteen-year-old with nothing but attitude. Easton had lived in the foreman's house then with her parents and they had been friends almost from the moment he arrived.

"Three weeks or so," she said. "Maybe less. Maybe a little more."

He wanted to rant at the unfairness of it all that somebody like Jo would be taken from the earth with such cruelty when she had spent just about every moment of her entire seventy-two years of life giving back to others.

"I'll stay until then."

She stared at him, the butter knife she was using to spread mustard on his sandwich frozen in her hand. "How can you possibly be away from Southerland Shipping that long?"

He shrugged. "I might need to make a few short trips back to Seattle here and there but most of my work can be done long-distance through email and conference calls. It shouldn't be a problem. And I have good people working for me who can handle most of the complications that might come up."

"That's not what she wanted when she asked you to come home one more time," Easton protested.

"Maybe not. But she isn't making the decisions about this, as much as she might think she's the one in charge. This is what I want. I should have come home when things first starting spiraling down. It wasn't fair for us to leave her care completely in your hands."

"You didn't know how bad things were."

If he had visited more, he would have seen for himself. But like Brant and Cisco, the other two foster sons Jo and her husband, Guff, had made a home for, life had taken him away from the safety and peace he had always found at Winder Ranch.

"I'm staying," he said firmly. "I can certainly spare a few weeks to help you out on the ranch and with Jo's care and whatever else you need, after all she and Guff did for me. Don't argue with me on this, because you won't win."

"I wasn't going to argue," she said. "You can't know how happy she'll be to have you here. Thank you, Quinn."

The relief in her eyes told him with stark clarity how difficult it must have been for Easton to watch Jo dying, especially after she had lost her own parents at a young age and then her beloved uncle who had taken her in after their deaths.

He squeezed her fingers when she handed him a sandwich with thick slices of homemade bread and hearty roast beef. "Thanks. This looks delicious."

She slid across from him with an apple and a glass of milk. As he looked at her slim wrists curved around her glass, he worried that, like Jo, she hadn't been eating enough and was withering away.

"What about the others?" he asked, after one fantastic bite. "Have you let Brant and Cisco know how things stand?"

Jo had always called them her Four Winds, the three foster boys she and Guff had taken in and Easton, her niece who had been their little shadow.

"We talk to Brant over the computer every couple weeks when he can call us from Afghanistan. Our webcam's not the greatest but I suppose he still had front-row seats as her condition has deteriorated over the past month. He's working on swinging leave and is trying to get here as soon as he can."

Quinn winced as guilt pinched at him. His best friend was halfway around the world and had done a better job of keeping track of things here at the ranch than Quinn had when he was only a few states away.

"What about Cisco?"

She looked down at her apple. "Have you heard from him?"

"No. Not for a while. I got a vague email in the spring but nothing since."

"Neither had we. It's been months. I've tried everything I can think of to reach him but I have no idea even where he is. Last I heard, he was in El Salvador or somewhere like that but I'm not having any luck turning up any information about him."

Cisco worried him, Quinn had to admit. The rest of them had gone on to do something productive with their lives. Quinn had started Southerland Shipping after a stint in the Air Force, Brant Western was an honorable Army officer serving his third tour of duty in the Middle East and Easton had the ranch, which she loved more than just about anything.

Cisco Del Norte, on the other hand, had taken a very different turn. Quinn had only seen him a few times in the past five or six years and he seemed more and more jaded as the years passed.

What started as a quick trip to Mexico to visit relatives after a stint in the Army had turned into years of Cisco bouncing around Central and South America.

Quinn had no idea what he did down there. He suspected that few of Cisco's activities were legal and none of them were good. He had decided several years ago that he was probably better off not knowing for sure.

But he *did* know Jo would want one more chance to see Cisco, whatever he was up to south of the border.

He swallowed another bite of sandwich. "I'll put some resources on it and see what I can find out. My assistant is frighteningly efficient. If anyone can find the man and drag him out of whatever cantina he calls home these days, it's Kathleen."

Easton's smile didn't quite reach her eyes. "I've met the redoubtable Kathleen. She scares me."

"That makes two of us. It's all part of her charm."

He tried to hide his sudden jaw-popping yawn behind a sip of water, but few things slipped past Easton.

"Get some sleep," she ordered in a tone that didn't leave room for arguments. "Your old room is ready for you. Clean sheets and everything."

"I don't need to sleep. I'll stay up with Jo."

"I've got it. She's got my cell on speed dial and only has to hit a couple of buttons to reach me all the time. Besides, the hospice nurse will be here to take care of things during the night."

"That's good. I was about to ask what sort of medical care she receives."

"Every three hours, we have a home-care nurse check in to adjust medication and take care of any other needs she might have. Jo doesn't think it's necessary to have that level of care, but it's what her doctors and I think is best."

That relieved his mind considerably. At least Easton didn't have to carry every burden by herself. He rose from the table and folded her into a hug.

"I'm glad you're here," she murmured. "It helps."

"This is where I have to be. Wake me up if you or Jo need anything."

"Right."

He headed up the stairs in the old log house, noting the fourth step from the top still creaked, just like always. He had hated that step. More than once it had been the architect of his downfall when he and one of the others tried to sneak in after curfew. They would always try so hard to be quiet but then that blasted stair would always give them away. By the time they would reach the top of the staircase, there would be Guff, waiting for them with those bushy white eyebrows raised and a judgment-day look on his features.

He almost expected to see his foster father waiting for him on the landing. Instead, only memories hovered there as he pushed open his bedroom door, remembering how suspicious and belligerent he had been to the Winders when he first arrived.

He had viewed Winder Ranch as just another prison, one more stop on the misery train that had become his life after his parents' murder-suicide.

Instead, he had found only love here.

Jo and Guff Winder had loved him. They had welcomed him into their home and their hearts, and then made more room for first Brant and then Cisco.

Their love hadn't stopped him from his share of trouble through high school but he knew that without them, he probably would have nurtured that bitterness and hate festering inside him and ended up in prison or dead by now.

This was where he needed to be. As long as Jo hung

in, he would be here—for her and for Easton. It was the right thing—the *only* thing—to do.

He completely slept through the discreet alarm on his Patek Philippe, something he *never* did.

When he finally emerged from his exhausted slumber three hours later, Quinn was disoriented at first. The sight of his familiar bedroom ceiling left him wondering if he was stuck in some kind of weird flashback about his teenage years, the kind of dream where some sexy, tight-bodied cheerleader was going to skip through the door any minute now.

No. That wasn't it. Something bleak tapped at his memory bank and the cheerleader fantasy bounced back through the door.

Jo.

He was at the ranch and Jo was dying. He sat up and scrubbed at his face. Daylight was still several hours away but he was on Tokyo time and doubted he could go back to sleep anyway.

He needed a shower, but he supposed it could wait for a few more moments, until he checked on her. Since Jo had always expressed strongly negative feelings about the boys going shirtless around her ranch even when they were mowing the lawn, he took a moment to shrug back into his travel-wrinkled shirt and headed down the stairs, careful this time to skip over the noisy step so he didn't wake Easton.

When he was a kid, Jo and Guff had shared a big master suite on the second floor. She had moved out of it after Guff's death five years ago from an unexpected heart attack, saying she couldn't bear sleeping there anymore without him. She had taken one of the two bedrooms on the main floor, the one closest to the kitchen.

When he reached it, he saw a woman backing out of the room, closing the door quietly behind her.

For an instant, he assumed it was Easton, but then he saw the coloring was wrong. Easton wore her waterfall of straight honey-blond hair in a ponytail most of the time but this woman had short, wavy auburn hair that just passed her chin.

She was smaller than Easton, too, though definitely curvy in all the right places. He felt a little thrum of masculine interest at the sight of a delectably curved derriere easing from the room—as unexpected as it was out of place, under the circumstances.

He was just doing his best to tamp his inappropriate interest back down when the woman turned just enough that he could see her features and any fledgling attraction disappeared like he'd just jumped naked into Windy Lake.

"What the hell are you doing here?" he growled out of the darkness.

Chapter Two

The woman whirled and grabbed at her chest, her eyes wide in the dimly lit hallway. "My word! You scared the life out of me!"

Quinn considered himself a pretty easygoing guy and he had despised very few people in his life—his father came immediately to mind as an exception.

But if he had to make a list, Tess Jamison would be right there at the top.

He was about to ask her again what she thought she was doing creeping around Winder Ranch when his sleep-deprived synapses finally clicked in and he made the connection as he realized that curvy rear end he had been unknowingly admiring was encased in deep blue flowered surgical scrubs.

She carried a basket of medical supplies in one hand and had an official-looking clipboard tucked under her arm.

"*You're* the hospice nurse?" His voice rose with incredulity.

She fingered the silver stethoscope around her neck with her free hand. "That's what they tell me. Hey, Quinn. How have you been?"

He must still be upstairs in his bed, having one of

those infinitely disturbing dreams of high school, the kind where he shows up to an advanced placement class and discovers he hasn't read a single page of the textbook, knows absolutely none of the subject matter, and is expected to sit down and ace the final.

This couldn't be real. It was too bizarre, too surreal, that someone he hadn't seen since graduation night—and would have been quite content never to have to see again—would suddenly be standing in the hallway of Winder Ranch looking much the same as she had fifteen years earlier.

He blinked but, damn it all, she didn't disappear and he wished he could just wake up, already.

"Tess," he said gruffly, unable to think of another thing to say.

"Right."

"How long have you been coming here to take care of Jo?"

"Two weeks now," she answered, and he wondered if her voice had always had that husky note to it or if it was a new development. "There are several of us, actually. I usually handle the nights. I stop in about every three or four hours to check vitals and help Jo manage her pain. I juggle four other patients with varying degrees of need but she's my favorite."

As she spoke, she moved away from Jo's bedroom door and headed toward him. He held his breath and fought the instinct to cover his groin, just as a precaution.

Not that she had ever physically hurt him in their turbulent past, but Tess Jamison—Homecoming Queen, valedictorian, and all-around Queen Bee, probably for

Bitch—had a way of emasculating a man with just a look.

She smelled not like the sulfur and brimstone he might have expected, but a pleasant combination of vanilla and peaches that made him think of hot summer evenings out on the wide porch of the ranch with a bowl of ice cream and Jo's divine cobbler.

She headed down the hall toward the kitchen, where she flipped on a small light over the sink.

For the first time, he saw her in full light. She was as lovely as when she wore the Homecoming Queen crown, with high cheekbones, a delicate nose and the same lush, kissable mouth he remembered.

Her eyes were still her most striking feature, green and vivid, almond-shaped, with thick, dark lashes.

But fifteen years had passed and nothing stayed the same except his memories. She had lost that fresh-faced innocent look that had been so misleading. He saw tiny, faint lines fanning out at the edges of her eyes and she wore a bare minimum of makeup.

"I didn't know you were back," she finally said when he continued to stare. "Easton didn't mention it before she went to bed."

Apparently there were several things Easton was keeping close to her sneaky little vest. "I only arrived this evening." Somehow he managed to answer her without snarling, but it was a chore. "Jo wanted to see all of us one more time."

He couldn't quite bring himself to say *last* instead of *more* but those huge green eyes still softened.

She was a hospice nurse, he reminded himself, as tough as he found that to believe. She was probably well-trained to pretend sympathy. The real Tess Jamison didn't care about another soul on the planet except herself.

"Are you here for the weekend?" she asked.

"Longer," he answered, his voice curt. It was none of her business that he planned to stay at Winder Ranch as long as Jo needed him, which he hoped was much longer than the doctors seemed to believe.

She nodded once, her eyes solemn, and he knew she understood all he hadn't said. The soft compassion in those eyes—and his inexplicable urge to soak it in—turned him conversely hostile.

"I can't believe you've stuck around Pine Gulch all these years," he drawled. "I would have thought Tess Jamison couldn't wait to shake the dust of podunk eastern Idaho off her designer boots."

She smiled a little. "It's Tess Claybourne now. And plans have a way of changing, don't they?"

"I'm starting to figure that out."

Curiosity stirred inside him. What had she been doing the past fifteen years? Why that hint of sadness in her eyes?

This was Tess, he reminded himself. He didn't give a damn what she'd been up to, even if she looked hauntingly lovely in the low light of the kitchen.

"So you married old Scott, huh? What's he up to? All that quarterback muscle probably turned to flab, right? Is he ranching with his dad?"

She pressed her lips into a thin line for just a moment, then gave him another of those tiny smiles, this one little more than a taut stretch of her mouth. "None of those things, I'm afraid. He died almost two years ago."

Quinn gave an inward wince at his own tactlessness. Apparently nothing had changed. She had *always* brought out the worst in him.

"How?"

She didn't answer for a moment, instead crossing to the coffeemaker he had assumed Easton must have forgotten to turn off. Now he realized she must have left a fresh pot for the hospice worker, since Tess seemed completely comfortable reaching in the cabinet for a cup and pouring.

"Pneumonia," she finally answered as she added two packets of sweetener. "Scott died of pneumonia."

"Really?" That seemed odd. He thought only old people and little kids could get that sick from pneumonia.

"He was…ill for a long time before that. His immune system was compromised and he couldn't fight it off."

Quinn wasn't a *complete* ass, even when it came to this woman he despised so much. He forced himself to offer the appropriate condolences. "That must have been rough for you. Any kids?"

"No."

This time she didn't even bother to offer a tight smile, only stared into the murky liquid swirling in her cup and he thought again how surreal this was, standing in the Winder Ranch kitchen in the middle of the night having a conversation with her, when he had to fight down every impulse to snarl and yell and order her out of the house.

"Jo tells me you run some big shipping company in the Pacific Northwest," she said after a moment.

"That's right." The third biggest in the region, but he

was hoping that with the new batch of contracts he was negotiating Southerland Shipping would soon slide into the number two spot and move up from there.

"She's so proud of you boys and Easton. She talks about you all the time."

"Does she?" He wasn't at all thrilled to think about Jo sharing with Tess any details of his life.

"Oh, yes. I'm sure she's thrilled to have you home. That must be why she was sleeping so peacefully. She didn't even wake when I checked her vitals, which is unusual. Jo's usually a light sleeper."

"How are they?"

"Excuse me?"

"Her vitals. How is she?"

He hated to ask, especially of Tess, but he was a man who dealt best with challenges when he gathered as much information as possible.

She took another sip of coffee then poured the rest down the sink and turned on the water to wash it down.

"Her blood pressure is still lower than we'd like to see and she's needing oxygen more and more often. She tries to hide it but she's in pain most of the time. I'm sorry. I wish I had something better to offer you."

"It's not your fault," he said, even as he wished he could somehow figure out a way to blame her for it.

"That's funny. It feels that way sometimes. It's my job to make her as comfortable as possible but she doesn't want to spend her last days in a drugged haze, she says. So we're limited in some of our options. But we still do our best."

He couldn't imagine *anyone* deliberately choosing this for a career. Why on earth would a woman like Tess

Jamison—Claybourne now, he reminded himself—
have chosen to stick around tiny Pine Gulch and become a hospice nurse? He couldn't quite get past the
incongruity of it.

"I'd better go," she said. "I've got three more patients
to check on tonight. I'll be back in a few hours, though,
and Easton knows she can call me anytime if she needs
me. It's…good to see you again, Quinn."

He wouldn't have believed her words, even if he
didn't see the lie in her vivid green eyes. She wasn't
any happier to see him than he had been to find her
wandering the halls of Winder Ranch.

Still, courtesy drilled into him by Jo demanded he
walk her to the door. He stood on the porch and watched
through the darkness until she reached her car, then he
walked back inside, shaking his head.

Tess Jamison Claybourne.

As if he needed one more miserable thing to face
here in Pine Gulch.

Quinn Southerland.

Lord have mercy.

Tess sat for a moment outside Winder Ranch in the
little sedan she had bought after selling Scott's wheelchair van. Her mind was a jumble of impressions, all
of them sharp and hard and ugly.

He despised her. His rancor radiated from him like
spokes on a bicycle wheel. Though he had conversed
with at least some degree of civility throughout their
short encounter, every word, every sentence, had been
underscored by his contempt. His silvery-blue eyes had

never once lost that sheen of scorn when he looked at her.

Tess let out a breath, more disconcerted by the brief meeting than she should be. She had a thick enough skin to withstand a little animosity. Or at least she had always assumed she did, up to this point.

How would she know, though? She had never had much opportunity to find out. Most of the good citizens of Pine Gulch treated her far differently.

Alone in the quiet darkness of her car, she gave a humorless laugh. How many times over the years had she thought how heartily sick she was of being treated like some kind of venerated saint around Pine Gulch? She wanted people to see her as she really was—someone with hopes and dreams and faults. Not only as the tireless caretaker who had dedicated long years of her life to caring for her husband.

She shook her head with another rough laugh. A little middle ground would be nice. Quinn Southerland's outright vilification of her was a little more harsh than she really wanted to face.

He had a right to despise her. She understood his feelings and couldn't blame him for them. She had treated him shamefully in high school. Just the memory, being confronted with the worst part of herself when she hadn't really thought about those things in years, made her squirm as she started her car.

Her treatment of Quinn Southerland had been reprehensible, beyond cruel, and she wanted to cringe away from remembering it. But seeing him again after all these years seemed to set the fragmented, half-forgotten memories shifting and sliding through her mind like jagged plates of glass.

She remembered all of it. The unpleasant rumors she had spread about him; her small, snide comments, delivered at moments when he was quite certain to overhear; the friends and teachers she had turned against him, without even really trying very hard.

She had been a spoiled, petulant bitch, and the memory of it wasn't easy to live with now that she had much more wisdom and maturity and could look back on her terrible behavior through the uncomfortable prism of age and experience.

She fully deserved his contempt, but that knowledge didn't make it much easier to stomach as she drove down the long, winding Winder Ranch driveway and turned onto Cold Creek Road, her headlights gleaming off the leaves that rustled across the road in the October wind.

She loved Jo Winder dearly and had since she was a little girl, when Jo had been patient and kind with the worst piano student any teacher ever had. Tess had promised the woman just the evening before that she would remain one of her hospice caregivers until the end. How on earth was she supposed to keep that vow if it meant being regularly confronted with her own poor actions when she was a silly girl too heedless to care about anyone else's feelings?

The roads were dark and quiet as she drove down Cold Creek Canyon toward her next patient, across town on the west side of Pine Gulch.

Usually she didn't mind the quiet or the solitude, this sense in the still hours of the night that she was the only one around. Even when she was on her way to her most difficult patient, she could find enjoyment in these few moments of peace.

Ed Hardy was a cantankerous eighty-year-old man whose kidneys were failing after years of battling diabetes. He wasn't facing his impending passing with the same dignity or grace as Jo Winder but continued to fight it every step of the way. He was mean-spirited and belligerent, lashing out at anyone who dared remind him he wasn't a twenty-five-year-old wrangler anymore who could rope and ride with the best of them.

Despite his bitterness, she loved the old coot. She loved *all* her home-care patients, even the most difficult. She would miss them, even Ed, when she moved away from Pine Gulch in a month.

She sighed as she drove down Main Street with its darkened businesses and the historic Old West lamp-posts somebody in the chamber of commerce had talked the town into putting up for the tourists a few years ago.

Except for the years she went to nursing school in Boise and those first brief halcyon months after her marriage, she had lived in this small Idaho town in the west shadow of the Tetons her entire life.

She and Scott had never planned to stay here. Their dreams had been much bigger than a rural community like Pine Gulch could hold.

They had married a month after she graduated from nursing school. He had been a first-year med student, excited about helping people, making a difference in the world. They had talked about opening a clinic in some undeveloped country somewhere, about travel and all the rich buffet of possibilities spreading out ahead of them.

But as she said to Quinn Southerland earlier, sometimes life didn't work out the way one planned. Instead of exotic locales and changing the world, she had brought her husband home to Pine Gulch where she had a support network—friends and family and neighbors who rallied around them.

She pulled into the Hardy driveway, noting the leaves that needed to be raked and the small flower garden that should be put to bed for the winter. Mrs. Hardy had her hands full caring for her husband and his many medical needs. She had a grandson in Idaho Falls who helped a bit with the yard but now that school was back in session, he didn't come as often as he had in the summer.

Tess turned off her engine, shuffling through her mental calendar to see if she could find time in the next few days to come over with a rake.

Her job had never been only about pain management and end-of-life decisions. At least not to her. She knew what it was like to be on the other side of the equation and how very much it could warm the heart when someone showed up unexpectedly with a smile and a cloth and window spray to wash the winter grime she hadn't had time to clean off because her life revolved around caretaking someone else.

That experience as the recipient of service had taught her well that her job was to lift the burdens of the families as much as of her patients.

Even hostile, antagonistic family members like Quinn Southerland.

The wind swirled leaves across the Hardys' cracked

driveway as she stepped out of her car. Tess shivered, but she knew it wasn't at the prospect of winter just around the corner or that wind bare-knuckling its way under her jacket, but from remembering the icy cold blue of Quinn's eyes.

Though she wasn't at all eager to encounter him again—or to face the bitter truth of the spoiled brat she had been once—she adored Jo Winder. She couldn't let Quinn's forbidding presence distract her from giving Jo the care she deserved.

Chapter Three

Apparently Pine Gulch's time machine was in fine working order.

Quinn walked into The Gulch and was quite certain he had traveled back twenty years to the first time he walked into the café with his new foster parents. He could clearly remember that day, the smell of frying potatoes and meat, the row of round swivel seats at the old-fashioned soda fountain, the craning necks in the place and the hot gazes as people tried to figure out the identity of the surly, scowling dark-haired kid with Jo and Guff.

Not much had changed. From the tin-stamped ceiling to the long, gleaming mirror that ran the length of the soda fountain to the smell of fried food that seemed to send triglycerides shooting through his veins just from walking in the door.

Even the faces were the same. He could swear the same old-timers still sat in the booth in the corner being served by Donna Archeleta, whose husband, Lou, had always manned the kitchen with great skill and joy. He recognized Mick Malone, Jesse Redbear and Sal Martinez.

And, of course, Donna. She stood by the booth with

a pot of coffee in her hand but she just about dropped it all over the floor when she looked up at the sound of the jangling bells on the door to spy him walking into her café.

"Quinn Southerland," she exclaimed, her smoker-husky voice delighted. "As I live and breathe."

"Hey, Donna."

One of Jo's closest friends, Donna had always gone out of her way to be kind to him and to Brant and Cisco. They hadn't always made it easy. The three of them had been the town's resident bad boys back in the day. Well, maybe not Brant, he acknowledged, but he was usually guilty by association, if nothing else.

"I didn't know you were back in town." Donna set the pot down in an empty booth to fold her scrawny arms around him. He hugged her back, wondering when she had gotten frail like Jo.

"Just came in yesterday," he said.

"Why the hell didn't anybody tell me?"

He opened his mouth to answer but she cut him off.

"Oh, no. Jo. Is she..." Her voice trailed off but he could see the anxiety suddenly brim in her eyes, as if she dreaded his response.

He shook his head and forced a smile. "She woke up this morning feistier than ever, craving one of Lou's sweet rolls. Nothing else will do, she told me in no uncertain terms, so she sent me down here first thing so I could pick one up and take it back for her. Since according to East, she hasn't been hungry for much of anything else, I figured I had better hurry right in and grab her one."

Donna's lined and worn features brightened like a

gorgeous June morning breaking over the mountains. "You're in luck, hon. I think he's just pullin' a new batch out of the oven. You wait right here and have yourself some coffee while I go back and wrap a half-dozen up for her."

Before he could say a word, she turned a cup over from the setting in the booth and poured him a cup. He laughed at this further evidence that not much had changed, around The Gulch at least.

"I think one, maybe two sweet rolls, are probably enough. Like I said, she hasn't had much of an appetite."

"Well, this way she can warm another up later or save one for the morning, and there will be extras for you and Easton. Now don't you argue with me. I'm doing this, so just sit down and drink your coffee, there's a good boy."

He had to smile in the face of such determination, such eagerness to do something nice for someone she cared about. There were few things he missed about living in Pine Gulch, but that sense of community, belonging to something bigger than yourself, was definitely one of them.

He took a seat at the long bar, joining a few other solo customers who eyed him with curiosity.

Again, he had the strange sense of stepping back into his past. He could still see the small chip in the bottom corner of the mirror where he and Cisco had been roughhousing and accidentally sent a salt shaker flying.

That long-ago afternoon was as clear as his flight in from Japan the day before—the sick feeling in the pit of his gut as he had faced the wrath of Lou and Donna and the even worse fear when he had to fess up to Guff and Jo. He had only been with them a year, twelve tumul-

tuous months, and had been quite sure they would toss
him back into the foster-care system after one mess-up
too many.

But Guff hadn't yelled or ordered him to pack his
things. Instead, he just sat him down and told one of
his rambling stories about a time he had been a young
ranch hand with a little too much juice in him and had
taken his .22 and shot out the back windows of what
he thought was an old abandoned pickup truck, only to
find out later it belonged to his boss's brother.

"A man steps up and takes responsibility for his actions," Guff had told him solemnly. That was all he
said, but the trust in his brown eyes had completely
overwhelmed Quinn. So of course he had returned to
The Gulch and offered to work off the cost of replacing the mirror for the Archeletas.

He smiled a little, remembering Lou and Donna's response. "Think we'll just keep that little nick there as a
reminder," Lou had said. "But there are always dishes
around here to be washed."

He and Cisco had spent about three months of Satur-
days and a couple afternoons a week after school in the
kitchen with their hands full of soapy water. More than
he cared to admit, he had enjoyed those days listening
to the banter of the café, all the juicy small-town gossip.

He only had about three or four minutes to replay the
memory in his head before Lou Archeleta walked out
of the kitchen, his bald head just as shiny as always and
his thick salt-and-pepper mustache a bold contrast. The
delight on his rough features matched Donna's, warming Quinn somewhere deep inside.

Lou wiped his hand on his white apron before holding it out for a solemn handshake. "Been too long," he said, in that same gruff, no-nonsense way. "Hear Seattle's been pretty good to you."

Quinn shook his hand firmly, aware as he did that much of his success in business derived from watching the integrity and goodness of people like Lou and Donna and the respect with which they had always treated their customers.

"I've done all right," he answered.

"Better than all right. Jo says you've got a big fancy house on the shore and your own private jet."

Technically it was the company's corporate jet. But since he owned the company, he supposed he couldn't debate semantics. "How about you? How's Rick?"

Their son had gone to school with him and graduated a year after him. Tess Jamison's year, actually.

"Good. Good. He's up in Boise these days. He's a plumbing contractor, has himself a real good business. He and his wife gave us our first granddaughter earlier this year." The pride on Lou's work-hardened features was obvious.

"Congratulations."

"Yep, after four boys, they finally got a girl."

Quinn choked on the sip of coffee he'd just taken. "Rick has five kids?"

His mind fairly boggled at the very idea of even one. He couldn't contemplate having enough for a basketball team.

Lou chuckled. "Yep. Started young and threw in a set of twins in there. He's a fine dad, too."

The door chimed, heralding another customer, but

Quinn was still reeling at the idea of his old friend rais-
ing a gaggle of kids and cleaning out toilets.

Still, an odd little prickle slid down his spine, especially when he heard the old-timers in their regular
booth hoot with delight and usher the newcomer over.

"About time you got here," one of the old-timers in
the corner called out. "Mick here was sure you was
goin' to bail on us today."

"Are you kidding?" an alto female voice answered.
"This is my favorite part of working graveyard, the
chance to come in here for breakfast and have you all
give me a hard time every morning. I don't know what
I'll do without it."

Quinn stiffened on the stool. He didn't need to turn
to know just who was now sliding into the booth near
the regulars. He had last heard that voice at 3:00 a.m.
in the dark quiet of the Winder Ranch kitchen.

"Hey, Miss Tess." Lou turned his attention away
from bragging about his grandkids to greet the newcomer, confirming what Quinn had already known deep
in his bones. "You want your usual?"

"You got it, Lou. I've been dreaming of your veggie
omelet all night long. I'm absolutely starving."

"Girl, you need to get yourself something more interesting to fill your nights if all you can dream about is
Lou's veggie omelet," called out one of the women from
a nearby booth and everybody within earshot laughed.

Everybody but Quinn. She was a regular here, just
like the others, he realized. She was part of the community, and he, once more, was the outsider.

She had always been excellent at reminding him
of that.

He couldn't put it off any longer, he knew. With some trepidation, he turned around from the counter to the dining room to face her gaze.

Despite the mirror right in front of him, she must not have been paying attention to the other patrons in the restaurant. He could tell she hadn't known he was there until he turned. He saw the little flash of surprise in her eyes, the slight rise and fall of her slim chest as her breathing hitched.

She covered it quickly with a tight smile and the briefest of waves.

She wasn't pleased to see him. He didn't miss the sudden tension in her posture or the dismay that quickly followed that initial surprise.

Join the club, he thought. Bumping into his worst nightmare two times in less than six hours was twice too many, as far as he was concerned.

He thought he saw something strangely vulnerable flash in those brilliant green eyes for just an instant, then she turned back to the old-timers at the booth with some bright, laughing comment that sounded forced to him.

As he listened to their interaction, it was quickly apparent to him that Tess was a favorite of all of them. No surprise there. She excelled at twisting everybody around her little finger. She had probably been doing the very same thing since she was the age of Lou Archeleta's new granddaughter.

The more the teasing conversation continued, the more sour his mood turned. She sounded vivacious and funny and charming. Why couldn't anybody but him manage to see past the act to the vicious streak lurking beneath?

When he had just about had all he could stomach, Donna returned with two white bakery bags and a disposable coffee cup with steam curling out the top.

"Here you go, hon. Didn't mean to keep you waiting until Christmas but I got tied up in the back with a phone call from a distributor. There's plenty of extra sweet rolls for you and here's a little joe for the road."

He put away his irritation at Tess and took the offerings from Donna with an affectionate smile, his heart warmer than the cup in his hand at her concern. "Thanks."

"You give that girl a big old kiss from everybody down here at The Gulch. Tell her to hang in there and we're all prayin' for her."

"I'll do that."

"And come back, why don't you, while you're in town. We'll fix you up your favorite chicken-fried steak and have a coze."

"It's a date." He kissed her cheek and headed for the door. Just as he reached it, he heard Tess call his name.

"Wait a minute, will you?" she said.

He schooled his features into a mask of indifference as he turned, loathe for any of the other customers to see how it rankled to see her here still acting like the Pine Gulch Homecoming Queen deigning to have breakfast with her all of her hordes of loyal, adoring subjects.

He didn't want to talk to her. He didn't want to be forced to see how lovely and perky she looked, even in surgical scrubs and even after he knew she had been working all night at a difficult job.

She smelled of vanilla and sunshine and he didn't want to notice that she looked as bright as the morning, how her auburn curls trailed against her slender jawline or the light sprinkle of freckles across her nose or the way her green eyes had that little rim of gold around the edge you only saw if you were looking closely.

He didn't want to see Tess at all, he didn't want to feel like an outsider again in Pine Gulch, and he especially didn't want to have to stand by and do nothing while a woman he loved slipped away, little by little.

"How's Jo this morning?" she asked. "She seemed restless at six when I came to check on her."

As far as he remembered, Tess had never been involved in the high-school drama club. So either she had become a really fabulous actress in the intervening years or her concern for Jo was genuine.

He let out a breath, tamping down his antagonism in light of their shared worry for Jo. "I don't know. To me, she seems better this morning than she was last night when I arrived. But I don't really have a baseline to say what's normal and what's not."

He held up the bakery bag. "She at least had enough energy to ask for Lou's sweet rolls this morning."

"That's excellent. Eating has been hard for her the past few weeks. Seeing you must be giving her a fresh burst of strength."

Was she implying he should have come sooner? He frowned, disliking the guilt swirling around in his gut along with the coffee.

Yeah, he should have come home sooner. If Easton and Jo had been forthright about what was going on, he would have been here weeks ago. They had hid the truth from him but he should have been more intuitive and figured it out.

That didn't mean he appreciated Tess pointing out his negligence. He scowled but she either didn't notice or didn't particularly care.

"It's important that you make sure she doesn't overdo things," Tess said. "I know that's hard to do during those times when she's feeling better. On her good days, she has a tendency to do much more than she really has the strength to tackle. You just have to be careful to ensure she doesn't go overboard."

Her bossy tone brought his dislike simmering to the surface. "Don't try to manage me like you do everybody else in town," he snapped. "I'm not one of your devoted worshippers. We both know I never have been."

For just an instant, hurt flared in her eyes but she quickly blinked it away and tilted that damn perky chin up, her eyes a sudden murky, wintry green.

"This has nothing to do with me," she replied coolly. "It's about Jo. Part of my job as her hospice nurse is to advise her family regarding her care. I can certainly reserve those conversations with Easton if that's what you prefer."

He bristled for just a moment, but the bitter truth of it was, he knew she was right. He needed to put aside how much he disliked this woman for things long in the distant past to focus on his foster mother, who needed him right now.

Tess appeared to genuinely care about Jo. And while he wasn't quite buying such a radical transformation, people could change. He saw it all the time.

Hell, he was a completely different person than he'd

been in high school. He wasn't the angry, belligerent hothead with a chip the size of the Tetons on his shoulder anymore, though he was certainly acting like it right now.

It wasn't wholly inconceivable that this caring nurse act was the real thing.

"You're right." He forced the words out, though they scraped his throat raw. "I appreciate the advice. I'm... still struggling with seeing her this way. In my mind, she should still be out on the ranch hurtling fences and rounding up strays."

Her defensive expression softened and she lifted a hand just a little. For one insane moment, he thought she meant to touch his arm in a sympathetic gesture, but she dropped her arm back to her side.

"Wouldn't we all love that?" she said softly. "I'm afraid those days are gone. Right now, we just have to savor every moment with her, even if it's quietly sitting beside her while she sleeps."

She stepped away from him and he was rather horrified at the regret suddenly churning through him. All these conflicting feelings were making him a little crazy.

"I'm off until tonight," she said, "but you'll find Cindy, the day nurse, is wonderful. Even so, tell Easton to call me if she needs anything."

He nodded and pushed past the door into the sunshine.

That imaginary time machine had a few little glitches in it, he thought as he pulled out of the parking lot and headed back toward Cold Creek Canyon.

He had just exchanged several almost civil words

with Tess Jamison Claybourne, something that a dozen years ago would have seemed just as impossible as imagining that someday he would be able to move past the ugliness in his past to run his own very successful company.

Chapter Four

"Do you remember that time you boys stayed out with the Walker sisters an hour past curfew?"

"I'm going to plead the fifth on that one," Quinn said lazily, though he did indeed remember Sheila Walker and some of her more acrobatic skills.

"I remember it," Jo said. "The door was locked and you couldn't get back in so you rascals tried to sneak in a window, remember that? Guff heard a noise downstairs and since he was half-asleep and didn't realize you boys hadn't come home yet, he thought it might be burglars."

Jo chuckled. "He took the baseball bat he kept by the side of the bed and went down and nearly beaned the three of you as you were trying to sneak in the window."

He smiled at the memory of Brant's guilt and Cisco's smart-aleck comments and Guff's stern reprimand to all of them.

"I can't believe Guff told you about that. It was supposed to be a secret between us males."

Her mouth lifted a little at the edges. "Guff didn't keep secrets from me. Don't you know better than that? He used to say whatever he couldn't tell me, he would rather not know himself."

Jo's voice changed when she talked about her late husband. The tone was softer, more rounded, and her love sounded in every word.

He squeezed her fingers. What a blessing for both Guff and Jo that they had found each other, even if it had been too late in life for the children they had both always wanted. Though they married in their forties, they had figured out a way to build the family they wanted by taking in foster children who had nowhere else to go.

"I suppose that's as good a philosophy for a marriage as any," he said.

"Yes. That and the advice of Lyndon B. Johnson. Only two things are necessary to keep one's wife happy, Guff used to say. One is to let her think she is having her own way. The other, to let her have it."

He laughed, just as he knew she intended. Jo smiled along with him and lifted her face to the late-morning sunshine. He checked to make sure the colorful throw was still tucked across her lap, though it was a beautiful autumn day, warmer than usual for October.

They sat on Adirondack chairs canted just so in the back garden of Winder Ranch for a spectacular view of the west slope of the Tetons. Surrounding them were mums and yarrow and a few other hardy plants still hanging on. Most of the trees were nearly bare but a few still clung tightly to their leaves. As he remembered, the stubborn elms liked to hang on to theirs until the most messy, inconvenient time, like just before the first hard snowfall, when it became a nightmare trying to rake them up.

Mindful of Tess's advice, he was keeping a careful

eye on Jo and her stamina level. So far, she seemed to be managing her pain. She seemed content to sit in her garden and bask in the unusual warmth.

He wasn't used to merely sitting. In Seattle, he always had someone clamoring for his attention. His assistant, his board of directors, his top-level executives. Someone always wanted a slice of his time.

Quinn couldn't quite ascertain whether he found a few hours of enforced inactivity soothing or frustrating. But he did know he savored this chance to store away a few more precious memories of Jo.

She lifted her thin face to the sunshine. "We won't have too many more days like this, will we? Before we know it, winter will be knocking on the door."

That latent awareness that she probably wouldn't make it even to Thanksgiving—her favorite holiday— pierced him.

He tried to hide his reaction but Jo had eyes like a red-tailed hawk and was twice as focused.

"Stop that," she ordered, her mouth suddenly stern.

"What?"

"Feeling sorry for me, son."

He folded her hand in his, struck again by the frailty of it, the pale skin and the thin bones and the tiny blue veins pulsing beneath the papery surface.

"You want the truth, I'm feeling more sorry for myself than you."

Her laugh startled a couple of sparrows from the bird feeder hanging in the aspens. "You always did have a bit of a selfish streak, didn't you?"

"Damn right." He managed a tiny grin in response to

her teasing. "And I'm selfish enough to wish you could stick around forever."

"For your sake and the others, I'm sorry for that. But don't be sad on my account, my dear. I have missed my husband sorely every single, solitary moment of the past three years. Soon I'll be with him again and won't have to miss him anymore. Why would anyone possibly pity me?"

He would have given a great deal for even a tiny measure of her faith. He hadn't believed much in a just and loving God since the nightmare day his parents died.

"I only have one regret," Jo went on.

He made a face. "Only one?" He could have come up with a couple dozen of his own regrets, sitting here in the sunshine on a quiet Cold Creek morning.

"Yes. I'm sorry my children—and that's what you all are, you know—have never found the kind of joy and love Guff and I had."

"I don't think many people have," he answered. "What is it they say? Often imitated, never duplicated? What the two of you had was something special. Unique."

"Special, yes. Unique, not at all. A good marriage just takes lots of effort on both parts." She tilted her head and studied him carefully. "You've never even been serious about a woman, have you? I know you date plenty of beautiful women up there in Seattle. What's wrong with them all?"

He gave a rough laugh. "Not a thing, other than I have no desire to get married."

"Ever?"

"Marriage isn't for me, Jo. Not with my family history."

"Oh, poof."

He laughed at the unexpectedness of the word.

"Poof?"

"You heard me. You're just making excuses. Never thought I raised any of my boys to be cowards."

"I'm not a coward," he exclaimed.

"What else would you call it?"

He didn't answer, though a couple of words that came immediately to mind were more along the lines of *smart* and *self-protective*.

"Yes, you had things rough," Jo said after a moment. "I'm not saying you didn't. It breaks my heart what some people do to their families in the name of love. But plenty of other people have things rough and it doesn't stop them from living their life. Why, take Tess, for instance."

He gave a mental groan. Bad enough that he couldn't seem to stop thinking about her all morning. He didn't need Jo bringing her up now. Just the sound of her name stirred up those weird, conflicting emotions inside him all over again. Anger and that subtle, insistent, frustrating attraction.

He pushed them all away. "What do you mean, *take Tess?*"

"That girl. Now *she* has an excuse to lock her heart away and mope around feeling sorry for herself for the rest of her life. But does she? No. You'll never find a happier soul in all your days. Why, what she's been through would have crushed most women. Not our Tess."

What could she possibly have been through that Jo deemed so traumatic? She was a pampered princess, daughter of one of the wealthiest men in town, the town's bank president, apparently adored by everyone.

She couldn't know what it was like to have to call the police on your own father or hold your mother as she breathed her last.

Before he could ask Jo to explain, she began to cough—raspy, wet hacking that made his own chest hurt just listening to it.

She covered her mouth with a folded handkerchief from her pocket as the coughing fit went on for what seemed an eon. When she pulled the cloth away, he didn't miss the red spots speckling the white linen.

"I'm going to carry you inside and call Easton."

Jo shook her head. "No," she choked out. "Will pass. Just…minute."

He gave her thirty more seconds, then reached for his cell phone. He started to hit Redial to reach Easton when he realized Jo's coughs were dwindling.

"Told you…would pass," she said after a moment. During the coughing attack, what little color there was in her features had seeped out and she looked as if she might blow away if the wind picked up even a knot or two.

"Let's get you inside."

She shook her head. "I like the sunshine."

He sat helplessly beside her while she coughed a few more times, then folded the handkerchief and stuck it back into her pocket.

"Sorry about that," she murmured after a painful moment. "I so wish you didn't have to see me like this."

He wrapped an arm around her frail shoulders and pulled her close to him, planting a kiss on her springy gray curls.

"We don't have to talk. Just rest. We can stay for a few more moments and enjoy the sunshine."

She smiled and settled against him and they sat in contented silence.

For those few moments, he was deeply grateful he had come. As difficult as it had been to rearrange his schedule and delegate as many responsibilities as he could to the other executives at Southerland, he wouldn't have missed this moment for anything.

With his own mother, he hadn't been given the luxury of saying goodbye. She had been unconscious by the time he could reach her.

He supposed that played some small part in his insistence that he stay here to the end with Jo, as difficult as it was to face, as if he could atone in some small way for all he hadn't been able to do for his own mother as a frightened kid.

Her love of sunshine notwithstanding, Jo lasted outside only another fifteen minutes before she had a coughing fit so intense it left her pale and shaken. He didn't give her a choice this time, simply scooped her into his arms and carried her inside to her bedroom.

"Rest there and I'll find Easton to help you."

"Bother. She...has enough...to do. Just need water and...minute to catch my breath."

He went for a glass of water and returned to Jo's bedroom with it, then sent a quick text to Easton explaining the situation.

"I can see you sending out an SOS over there," Jo muttered with a dark look at the phone in his hand.

"Who, me? I was just getting in a quick game of solitaire while I wait for you to stop coughing."

She snorted at the lie and shook her head. "You didn't need to call her. I hate being so much of a nuisance to everyone."

He finished the text and covered her hand with his. "Serves us right for all the bother we gave you."

"I think you boys used to stay up nights just thinking about new ways to get into trouble, didn't you?"

"We had regular meetings every afternoon, just to brainstorm."

"I don't doubt it." She smiled weakly. "At least by the middle of high school you settled down some. Though there was that time senior year you got kicked off the baseball team. That nonsense about cheating, which I know you would never do, and so I tried to tell the coach but he wouldn't listen. You never did tell us what that was really all about."

He frowned. He could have told her what it had been about. Tess Jamison and more of her lies about him. If anyone had stayed up nights trying to come up with ways to make someone else's life harder, it would have been Tess. She had made as much trouble as she could for him, for reasons he still didn't understand.

"High school was a long time ago. Why don't I tell you about my latest trip to Cambodia when I visited Angkor Wat?"

He described the ancient temple complex that had been unknown to the outside world until 1860, when a French botanist stumbled upon it. He was describing the nearby city of Angkor Thom when he looked down and saw her eyes were closed, her breathing regular.

He arranged a knit throw over her and slipped off her shoes, which didn't elicit even a hint of a stir out of her. That she could fall asleep so instantaneously worried him and he hoped their short excursion outside hadn't been too much for her.

He closed the door behind him just as he heard the bang of the screen door off the kitchen, then the thud of Easton's boots on the tile.

Chester rose from his spot in a sunbeam and greeted her with delight, his tired old body wiggling with glee.

She stripped off her work gloves and patted him. "Sorry it took me a while. We were up repairing a fence in the west pasture."

"I'm sorry I called you in for nothing. She seems to be resting now. But she was coughing like crazy earlier, leaving blood specks behind."

Easton blew out a breath and swiped a strand of hair that had fallen out of her long ponytail. "She's been doing that lately. Tess says it's to be expected."

"I'm sorry I bugged you for no reason."

"I was ready to break for lunch. I would have been here in about fifteen minutes anyway. I can't tell you what a relief it is to have you here so I know someone is with her. I'm always within five minutes of the house but I can't be here all the time. I hate when I have to leave her, but sometimes I can't help it. The ranch doesn't run itself."

Though Winder Ranch wasn't as huge an operation as the Daltons up the canyon a ways, it was still a big undertaking for one woman still in her twenties, even if she did have a couple ranch hands and a ranch foreman who had been with the Winders since Easton's father died in a car accident that also killed his wife.

"Why don't I fix you some lunch while you're here?" he offered. "It's my turn after last night, isn't it?"

She sent him a sidelong look. "The CEO of Southerland Shipping making me a bologna sandwich? How can I resist an offer like that?"

"Turkey is my specialty but I suppose I can swing bologna."

"Either one would be great. I'll go check on Jo and be right back."

She returned before he had even found all the ingredients.

"Still asleep?" he asked.

"Yes. She was smiling in her sleep and looked so at peace, I didn't have the heart to wake her."

"Sit down. I'll be done here in a moment."

She sat at the kitchen table with a tall glass of Pepsi and they chatted about the ranch and the upcoming roundup in the high country and the cost of beef futures while he fixed sandwiches for both of them.

He presented hers with a flourish and she accepted it gratefully.

"What time does the day nurse come again?" he asked.

"Depends on the nurse, but usually about 1:00 p.m. and then again at five or six o'clock."

"And there are three nurses who rotate?"

"Yes. They're all wonderful but Tess is Jo's favorite."

He paused to swallow a bite of his sandwich then

tried to make his voice sound casual and uninterested. "What's her story?" he asked.

"Who? Tess?"

"Jo said something about her that made me curious. She said Tess had it rough."

"You could say that."

He waited for Easton to elucidate but she remained frustratingly silent and he had to take a sip of soda to keep from grinding his back teeth together. The Winder women—and he definitely counted Easton among that number since her mother had been Guff's sister—could drive him crazy with their reticence that they seemed to invoke only at the most inconvenient times.

"What's been so rough?" he pressed. "When I knew Tess, she had everything a woman could want. Brains, beauty, money."

"None of that helped her very much with everything that came after, did it?" Easton asked quietly.

"I have no idea. You haven't told me what that was."

He waited while Easton took another bite of her sandwich before continuing. "I guess you figured out she married Scott, right?"

He shrugged. "That was a foregone conclusion, wasn't it? They dated all through high school."

He had actually always liked Scott Claybourne. Tall and blond and athletic, Scott had been amiable to Quinn if not particularly friendly—until their senior year, when Scott had inexplicably beat the crap out of Quinn one warm April night, with veiled references to some supposed misconduct of Quinn's toward Tess.

More of her lies, he had assumed, and had pitied the bastard for being so completely taken in by her.

"They were only married three or four months, still newlyweds, really," Easton went on, "when he was in a bad car accident."

He frowned. "Car accident? I thought Tess told me he died of pneumonia."

"Technically, he did, just a couple of years ago. But he lived for several years after the accident, though he was permanently disabled from it. He had a brain injury and was in a pretty bad way."

He stared at Easton, trying to make the jaggedly formed pieces of the puzzle fit together. Tess had stuck around Pine Gulch for *years* to deal with her husband's brain injury? He couldn't believe it, not of her.

"She cared for him tirelessly, all that time," Easton said quietly. "From what I understand, he required total care. She had to feed him, dress him, bathe him. He was almost more like her kid than her husband, you know."

"He never recovered from the brain injury?"

"A little but not completely. He was in a wheelchair and lost the ability to talk from the injury. It was so sad. I just remember how nice he used to be to us younger kids. I don't know how much was going on inside his head but Tess talked to him just like normal and she seemed to understand what sounded like grunts and moans to me."

The girl he had known in high school had been only interested in wearing her makeup just so and buying the latest fashion accessories. And making his life miserable, of course.

He couldn't quite make sense of what Easton was telling him.

"I saw them once at the grocery store when he had

a seizure, right there in frozen foods," Easton went on. "It scared the daylights out of me, let me tell you, but Tess just acted like it was a normal thing. She was so calm and collected through the whole thing."

"That's rough."

She nodded. "A lot of women might have shoved away from the table when they saw the lousy hand they'd been dealt, would have just walked away right then. Tess was young, just out of nursing school. She had enough medical experience that I have to think she could guess perfectly well what was ahead for them, but she stuck it out all those years."

He didn't like the compassion trickling through him for her. Somehow things seemed more safe, more ordered, before he had learned that perhaps she hadn't spent the past dozen years figuring out more ways to make him loathe her.

"People in town grew to respect and admire her for the loving care she gave Scott, even up to the end. When she moves to Portland in a few weeks, she's going to leave a real void in Pine Gulch. I'm not the only one who will miss her."

"She's leaving?"

He again tried to be casual with the question, but Easton had known him since he was fourteen. She sent him a quick, sidelong look.

"She's selling her house and taking a job at a hospital there. I can't blame her. Around here, she'll always be the sweet girl who took care of her sick husband for so long. Saint Tess. That's what people call her."

He nearly fell off his chair at that one. Tess Jamison

Claybourne was a saint like he played center field for the Mariners.

Easton pushed back from the table. "I'd better check on Jo one more time, then get back to work." She paused. "You know, if you have more questions about Tess, you could ask her. She should be back tonight."

He didn't want to know more about Tess. He didn't want anything to do with her. He wanted to go back to the safety of ignorance. Despising her was much easier when he could keep her frozen in his mind as the manipulative little witch she had been at seventeen.

Chapter Five

"You haven't heard a single word I've said for the past ten minutes, have you?"

Tess jerked her attention back to her mother as they worked side by side in Ed Hardy's yard. Her mother knelt in the mulchy layer of fallen leaves, snipping and digging to ready Dorothy Hardy's flower garden for the winter, while Tess was theoretically supposed to be raking leaves. Her pile hadn't grown much, she had to admit.

"I heard some of it." She managed a rueful smile. "The occasional word here and there."

Maura Jamison raised one delicately shaped eyebrow beneath her floppy gardening hat. "I'm sorry my stories are so dull. I can go back to telling them to the cat, when he'll deign to listen."

She winced. "It's not your story that's to blame. I'm just…distracted today. But I'll listen now. Sorry about that."

Her mother gave her a careful look. "I think it's my turn to listen. What's on your mind, honey? Scott?"

Tess blinked at the realization that except for those few moments when Quinn had asked her about Scott the night before, she hadn't thought about her husband in several days.

A tiny measure of guilt niggled at her but she pushed it away. She refused to feel guilty for that. Scott would have wanted her to move on with her life and she had no guilt for her dealings with her husband.

Still, she didn't think she could tell her mother she was obsessing about Quinn Southerland.

"Mom, was I a terrible person in high school?" she asked instead.

Maura's eyes widened with surprise and Tess sent a tiny prayer to heaven, not for the first time, that she could age as gracefully as her mother. At sixty-five, Maura was active and vibrant and still as lovely as ever, even in gardening clothes and her floppy hat. The auburn curls Tess had inherited were shot through with gray but it didn't make Maura look old, only exotic and interesting, somehow.

Maura pursed her lips. "As I remember, you were a very good person. Not perfect, certainly, but who is, at that age?"

"I thought I was. Perfect, I mean. I thought I was doing everything right. Why wouldn't I? I had 4.0 grades, I was the head cheerleader, the student body president. I volunteered at the hospital in Idaho Falls and went to church on Sundays and was generally kind to children and small pets."

"What's happened to make you think about those days?"

She sighed, remembering the antipathy in a certain pair of silvery blue eyes. "Quinn Southerland is back in town."

Her mother's brow furrowed for a moment, then smoothed again. "Oh, right. He was one of Jo and Guff's foster boys, wasn't he? Which one is he?"

"Not the army officer or the adventurer. He's the businessman. The one who runs a shipping company out of Seattle."

"Oh, yes. I remember him. He was the dark, brooding, cute one, right?"

"Mother!"

Maura gave her an innocent sort of look. "What did I say? He *was* cute, wasn't he? I always thought he looked a little like James Dean around the eyes. Something in that smoldering look of his."

Oh, yes, Tess remembered it well.

After leaning the rake against a tree, she knelt beside her mother and began pulling up the dead stalks of cosmos. Every time she worked with her hands in the dirt, she couldn't help thinking how very much her existence the past eight years was like a flower garden in winter, waiting, waiting, for life to spring forth.

"I was horrible to him, Mom. Really awful."

"You? I can't believe that."

"Believe it. He just… He brought out the absolute worst in me."

Her mother sat back on her heels, the gardening forgotten. "Whatever did you do to the poor boy?"

She didn't want to correct her mother, but to her mind Quinn had never seemed like a boy. At least not like the other boys in Pine Gulch.

"I don't even like to think about it all," she admitted. "Basically I did whatever I could to set him down a peg or two. I did my best to turn people against him.

I would make snide comments to him and about him and started unsubstantiated rumors about him. I played devil's advocate, just for the sake of argument, whenever he would express any kind of opinion in a class."

Her mother looked baffled. "What on earth did he do to you to make you act in such a way?"

"Nothing. That's the worst part. I thought he was arrogant and disrespectful and I didn't like him but I was...fascinated by him."

Which quite accurately summed up her interaction with him in the early hours of the morning, but she decided not to tell her mother that.

"He was a handsome boy," Maura said. "I imagine many of the girls at school had the same fascination."

"They did." She grabbed the garden shears and started cutting back Dorothy's day lily foliage. "You know how it is whenever someone new moves into town. He seems infinitely better-looking, more interesting, more *everything* than the boys around town that you've grown up with since kindergarten."

She had been just as intrigued as the other girls, fascinated by this surly, angry, rough-edged boy. Rumors had swirled around when he first arrived that he had been involved in some kind of murder investigation. She still didn't know if any of them were true—she really couldn't credit Jo and Guff bringing someone with that kind of a past into their home.

But back then, that hint of danger only made him seem more appealing. She just knew Quinn made her feel different than any other boy in town.

Tess had tried to charm him, as she had been effortlessly doing with every male who entered her orbit since she was old enough to bat her eyelashes. He had at first ignored her efforts and then actively rebuffed them.

She hadn't taken with grace and dignity his rejection or his grim amusement at her continued efforts to draw his attention. She flushed, remembering.

"He wasn't interested in any of us, especially not me. I couldn't understand why he had to be so contrary. I hated it. You know how I was. I wanted everything in my life to go exactly how I arranged it."

"You're like your father that way," Maura said with a soft smile for her husband of thirty-five years whom they both missed dearly.

"I guess. I just know I was petty and spiteful to Quinn when he wouldn't fall into line with the way I wanted things to go. I was awful to him. Really awful. Whenever I was around him, I felt like this alien life force had invaded my body, this manipulative, conniving witch. Scarlett O'Hara with pom-poms."

Her mother laughed. "You're much prettier than that Vivien Leigh ever was."

"But every bit as vindictive and self-absorbed as her character in the movie."

For several moments, she busied herself with garden shears. Maura seemed content with the silence and her introspection, which had always been one of the things Tess loved best about her mother.

"I don't even want to tell you all the things I did," she finally said. "The worst thing is, I got him kicked off the baseball team when he was a senior and I was a junior."

"Tessa Marie. What on earth did you do?"

She burned with shame at the memory. "We had advanced placement history together. Amaryllis Wentworth."

"Oh, I remember her," her mother exclaimed. "Bitter and mean and suspicious old bat. I don't know why the school board didn't fire her twenty-five years before you were even in school. You would think someone who chooses teaching as an avocation would at least enjoy the company of young people."

"Right. And the only thing she hated worse than teenage girls was teenage boys."

"What happened?"

She wished she could block the memory out but it was depressingly clear, from the chalkboard smell in Wentworth's room to the afternoon spring sunlight filtering through the tall school windows.

"We both happened to have missed school on the same day, which happened to be one of her brutal pop quizzes, so we had to take a makeup. We were the only ones in the classroom except for Miss Wentworth."

Careful to avoid her mother's gaze, she picked up an armload of garden refuse and carried it to the wheelbarrow. "I knew the material but I was curious about whether Quinn did so I looked at his test answers. He got everything right except a question about the Teapot Dome scandal. I don't know why I did it. Pure maliciousness on my part. But I changed my answer, which I knew was right, to the same wrong one he had put down."

"Honey!"

"I know, right? It was awful of me. One of the worst things I've ever done. Of course, Miss Wentworth accused him of cheating. It was his word against mine.

The juvenile delinquent with the questionable attitude or the student body president, a junior who already had offers of a full-ride scholarship to nursing school. Who do you think everybody wanted to believe?"

"Oh, Tess."

"My only defense is that I never expected things to go that far. I thought maybe Miss Wentworth would just yell at him, but when she went right to the principal, I didn't know how to make it right. I should have stepped forward when he was kicked off the baseball team but I...was too much of a coward."

She couldn't tell her mother the worst of it. Even she couldn't quite believe the depths to which she had sunk in her teenage narcissism, but she remembered it all vividly.

A few days later, prompted by guilt and shame, she had tried to talk to him and managed to corner him in an empty classroom. They had argued and he had called her a few bad names, justifiably so.

She still didn't know what she'd been thinking—why this time would be any different—but she thought she saw a little spark of attraction in his eyes when they were arguing. She had been hopelessly, mortifyingly foolish enough to try to kiss him and he had pushed her away, so hard she knocked over a couple of chairs as she stumbled backward.

Humiliated and outraged, she had then made things much, much worse and twisted the story, telling her boyfriend Scott that Quinn had come on to her, that he had been so angry at being kicked off the baseball team that he had come for revenge and tried to force himself on her.

She screwed her eyes shut. Scott had reacted just as she had expected, with teenage bluster and bravado and his own twisted sense of chivalry. He and several friends from the basketball team had somehow separated Quinn from Brant and Cisco and taken him beneath the football bleachers, then proceeded to beat the tar out of him.

No wonder he despised her. She loathed that selfish, manipulative girl just as much.

"So he's back," Maura said. "Is he staying at the ranch?"

She nodded. "I hate seeing him. He makes me feel sixteen and stupid all over again. If I didn't love Jo so much, I would try to assign her to another hospice nurse."

Maura sat back on her heels, showing her surprise at her daughter's vehemence. "Our Saint Tess making a selfish decision? That doesn't sound like you."

Tess made a face. "You know I hate that nickname."

Her mother touched her arm, leaving a little spot of dirt on her work shirt. "I know you do, dear. And I'll be honest, as a mother who is nothing but proud of the woman you've become and what you have done with your life, it's a bit refreshing to find out you're subject to the occasional human folly just like the rest of us."

Everyone in town saw her as some kind of martyr for staying with Scott all those years, but they didn't know the real her. The woman who had indulged in bouts of self-pity, who had cried out her fear and frustration, who had felt trapped in a marriage that never even had a chance to start.

She had stayed with Scott because she loved him

and because he needed her, not because she was some saintly, perfect, flawless angel.

No one knew her. Not her mother or her friends or the morning crowd at The Gulch.

She didn't like to think that Quinn Southerland might just have the most honest perspective around of the real Tess Jamison Claybourne.

That evening, Tess kept her fingers crossed the entire drive to Winder Ranch, praying she wouldn't encounter him.

She had fretted about him all day, worrying what she might say when she saw him again. She considered it a huge advantage, at least in this case, that she worked the graveyard shift. Most of her visits were in the dead of night, when Quinn by rights should be sleeping. She would have a much better chance of avoiding him than if she stopped by during daylight hours.

The greatest risk she faced of bumping into him was probably now at the start of her shift than, say, 4:00 a.m.

Wouldn't it be lovely if he were away from the ranch or busy helping Easton with something or tied up with some kind of conference call to Seattle?

She could only dream, she supposed. More than likely, he would be right there waiting for her, ready to impale her with that suspicious, bad-tempered glare the moment she stepped out of the car.

She let out a breath as she turned onto the long Winder Ranch access drive and headed up toward the house. She could at least be calm and collected, even if he tried to goad her or made any derogatory comments.

He certainly didn't need to discover he possessed such power to upset her.

He wasn't waiting for her on the porch, but it was a near thing. The instant she rang the doorbell of Winder Ranch, the door jerked open and Quinn stood inside looking frazzled, his dark hair disheveled slightly, his navy blue twill shirt untucked, a hint of afternoon shadow on his cheeks.

He looked a little disreputable and entirely yummy.

"It's about time!" he exclaimed, an odd note of relief in his voice. "I've been watching for you for the past half hour."

"You…have?"

She almost looked behind her to see if someone a little more sure of a welcome had wandered in behind her.

"I thought you were supposed to be here at eight."

She checked her watch and saw it was only eight-thirty. "I made another stop first. What's wrong?"

He raked a hand through his hair, messing it further. "I don't know the hell I'm supposed to do. Easton had to run to Idaho Falls to meet with the ranch accountant. She was supposed to be back an hour ago but she just called and said she'd been delayed and won't be back for another couple of hours."

"What's going on? Is Jo having another of her breathing episodes? Or is it the coughing?"

Tess hurried out of her jacket and started to rush toward her patient's room but Quinn grabbed her arm at the elbow.

Despite her worry for Jo, heat scorched her nerve endings at the contact, at the feel of his warm hand against her skin.

"She's not there. She's in the kitchen."

At her alarmed look, he shook his head. "It's none of those things. She's fine, physically, anyway. But she won't listen to reason. I never realized the woman could be so blasted stubborn."

"A trait she obviously does not share with anyone else here," she murmured.

He gave her a dark look. "She's being completely ridiculous. She suddenly has this harebrained idea. Absolute insanity. She wants to go out for a moonlight ride on one of the horses and it's suddenly all she can talk about."

She stared, nonplussed. "A horseback ride?"

"Yeah. Do you think the cancer has affected her rational thinking? I mean, what's gotten into her? It's after eight, for heaven's sake."

"It's a bit difficult to go on a moonlit ride in the middle of the afternoon," she pointed out.

"Don't you take her side!" He sounded frustrated and on edge and more than a little frazzled.

She hid her smile that the urbane, sophisticated executive could change so dramatically over one simple request. "I'm not taking anyone's side. Why does she suddenly want to go tonight?"

"Her window faces east."

That was all he said, as if everything was now crystal clear. "And?" she finally prompted.

"And she happened to see that huge full moon coming up an hour or so ago. She says it's her favorite kind of night. She and Guff used to ride up to Windy Lake during the full moon whenever they could. It can be clear as day up in the mountains on full moons like this."

"Windy Lake?"

"It's above the ranch, about half a mile into the forest service land. Takes about forty minutes to ride there."

"And Tess is determined to go?"

"She says she can't miss the chance, since it's her last harvest moon."

The sudden bleakness in the silver-blue of his eyes tugged at her sympathy and she was astonished by the impulse to touch his arm and offer whatever small comfort she could.

She curled her fingers into a fist, knowing he wouldn't welcome the gesture. Not from her.

"She's not strong enough for that," he went on. "I *know* she's not. We were sitting out in the garden today and she lasted less than an hour before she had to lie down, and then she slept for the rest of the day. I can't see any way in hell she has the strength to sit on a horse, even for ten minutes."

Her job as a hospice nurse often required using a little creative problem-solving. Clients who were dying could have some very tricky wishes toward the end. But her philosophy was that if what they wanted was at all within reach, it was up to her and their family members to make it happen.

"What if you rode together on horseback?" she suggested. "You could help her. Support her weight, make sure she's not overdoing."

He stared at her as if she'd suddenly stepped into her old cheerleader skirt and started yelling, "We've got spirit, yes we do."

"Tell me you're not honestly thinking she could handle this!" he exclaimed. "It's completely insane."

"Not completely, Quinn. Not if she wants to do it. Jo is right. This is her last harvest moon and if she wants to enjoy it from Windy Lake, I think she ought to have that opportunity. It seems a small enough thing to give her."

He opened his mouth to object, then closed it again. In his eyes, she saw worry and sorrow for the woman who had taken him in, given him a home, loved him.

"It might be good for her," Tess said gently.

"And it might finish her off." He said the words tightly, as if he didn't want to let them out.

"That's her choice, though, isn't it?"

He took several deep breaths and she could see his struggle, something she faced often providing end-of-life care. On the one hand, he loved his foster mother and wanted to do everything he could to make her happy and comfortable and fulfill all her last wishes.

On the other, he wanted to protect her and keep her around as long as he could.

The effort to hold back her fierce urge to touch him, console him, almost overwhelmed her. She supposed she shouldn't find it so surprising. She was a nurturer, which was why she went into nursing in the first place, long before she ever knew that Scott's accident would test her caregiving skills and instincts to the limit.

"You don't have to take her, though, especially if you don't feel it's the right thing for her. I'll see if I can talk her out of it," she offered. She took a step toward the kitchen, but his voice stopped her.

"Wait."

She turned back to find him pinching the skin at the bridge of his nose.

"You're right," he said after a long moment, dropping his hand. "It's her choice. She's a grown woman, not a child. I can't treat her like one, even if I do want to protect her from…the inevitable. If she wants this, I'll find a way to make it happen."

The determination in his voice arrowed right to her heart and she smiled. "You're a good son, Quinn. You're just what Jo needs right now."

"You're coming with us, to make sure she's not overdoing things."

"Me?"

"The only way I can agree to this insanity is if we have a medical expert close at hand, just in case."

"I don't think that's a good idea."

"Why not? Can't your other patients spare you?"

That would have been a convenient excuse, but unfortunately in this case, she faced a slow night, with only Tess and two other patients, one who only required one quick check in the night, several hours away.

"That's not the issue," she admitted.

"What is it, then? Don't you think she would be better off to have a nurse along?"

"Maybe. Probably. But not necessarily this particular nurse."

"Why not?"

"I'm not really much of a rider," she confessed, with the same sense of shame as if she were admitting stealing heart medicine from little old ladies. Around Pine Gulch, she supposed the two crimes were roughly parallel in magnitude.

"Really?"

"My family lived in town and we never had horses," she said, despising the defensive note in her voice. "I haven't had a lot of experience."

She didn't add that she had an irrational fear of them after being bucked off at a cousin's house when she was seven, then later that summer she had seen a cowboy badly injured in a fall at an Independence Day rodeo. Since then, she had done her best to avoid equines whenever possible.

"This is a pretty easy trail that takes less than an hour. You should be okay, don't you think?"

How could she possibly tell him she was terrified, especially after she had worked to persuade him it would be all right for Jo? She couldn't, she decided. Better to take one for the team, for Jo's sake.

"Fine. You saddle the horses and I'll get Jo ready."

Heaven help them all.

Chapter Six

"Let me know if you need me to slow down," Quinn said half an hour later to the frail woman who sat in front of him astride one of the biggest horses in the pasture, a rawboned roan gelding named Russ.

She felt angular and thin in his arms, all pointed elbows and bony shoulders. But Tess had been right, she was ecstatic about being on horseback again, about being outside in the cold October night under the pines. Jo practically quivered with excitement, more alive and joyful than he had seen her since his return to Cold Creek.

It smelled of fall in the mountains, of sun-warmed dirt, of smoke from a distant neighbor's fire, of layers of fallen leaves from the scrub oak and aspens that dotted the mountainside.

The moon hung heavy and full overhead, huge and glowing in the night and Suzy and Jack, Easton's younger cow dogs, raced ahead of them. Chester probably would have enjoyed the adventure but Quinn had worried that, just like Jo, his old bones weren't quite up to the journey.

"This is perfect. Oh, Quinn, thank you, my dear. You have no idea the gift you've given me."

"You're welcome," he said gruffly, warmed despite his lingering worry.

In truth, he didn't know who was receiving the greater gift. This seemed a rare and precious time with Jo and he was certain he would remember forever the scents and the sounds of the night—of tack jingling on the horses and a great northern owl hooting somewhere in the forest and the night creatures that peeped and chattered around them.

He glanced over his shoulder to where Tess rode behind them.

Among the three of them, she seemed to be the one *least* enjoying the ride. She bounced along on one of the ranch's most placid mares. Every once in a while, he looked back and the moonlight would illuminate a look of grave discomfort on her features. If he could see her hands in the darkness, he was quite certain they would be white-knuckled on the reins.

He should be enjoying her misery, given his general dislike for the woman. Mostly he just felt guilty for dragging her along, though he had to admit to a small measure of glee to discover something she hadn't completely mastered.

In school, Tess had been the consummate perfectionist. She always had to be the first one finished with tests and assignments, she hated showing up anywhere with a hair out of place and she delighted in being the kind of annoying classmate who tended to screw up the curve for everybody else.

Knowing she wasn't an expert at everything made her seem a little more human, a little more approachable.

He glanced back again and saw her shifting in the saddle, her body tight and uncomfortable.

"How are you doing back there?" he asked.

In the pale glow of the full moon, he could just make out the slit of her eyes as she glared. "Fine. Swell. If I break my neck and die, I'm blaming you."

He laughed out loud, which earned him a frown from Jo.

"You didn't need to drag poor Tess up here with us," she reprimanded in the same tone of voice she had used when he was fifteen and she caught him teasing Easton for something or other. He could still vividly remember the figurative welts on his hide as she had verbally taken a strip off him.

"She's a big girl," Quinn said in a voice too low for Tess to overhear. "She didn't have to come."

"You're a hard man to say no to."

"If anyone could do it, Tess would find a way. Anyway, we'll be there in a few more moments."

Jo looked over his shoulder at Tess, then shook her head. "Poor thing. She obviously hasn't had as much experience riding as you and Easton and the boys. She's a good sport to come anyway."

He risked another look behind him and thought he heard her mumbling something under her breath involving creative ways she intended to make him pay for this.

Despite the lingering sadness in knowing he was fulfilling a last wish for someone he loved so dearly, Quinn couldn't help his smile.

He definitely wouldn't forget this night anytime soon.

"She's doing all right," he said to Jo.

"You're a rascal, Quinn Southerland," she chided. "You always have been."

He couldn't disagree. He couldn't have been an easy kid to love when he had been so belligerent and angry, lashing out at everyone in his pain. He hugged Jo a little more tightly for just a moment until they reached the trailhead for Windy Lake, really just a clearing where they could leave the horses before taking the narrow twenty-yard trail to the lakeshore.

"This might get a little bit tricky," he said. "Let me dismount first and then I'll help you down."

"I can still get down from a horse by myself," she protested. "I'm not a complete invalid."

He just shook his head in exasperation and slid off the horse. He grabbed the extra rolled blankets tied to the saddle and slung them over his shoulder, then reached up to lift her from the horse.

He didn't set her on her feet, though. "I'll carry you to Guff's bench," he said, without giving her an opportunity to argue.

She pursed her lips but didn't complain, which made him suspect she was probably more tired than she wanted to let on.

"Okay, but then you'd better come back here to help Tess."

He glanced over and saw that Tess's horse had stopped alongside his big gelding but Tess made no move to climb out of the saddle; she just gazed down at the ground with a nervous kind of look.

"Hang on a minute," he told her. "Just wait there in the saddle while I settle Jo on the bench and then I'll come back to help you down."

"I'm sorry," she said, sounding more disgruntled than apologetic.

"No problem."

He carried Jo along the trail, grateful again for the pale moonlight that filtered through the fringy pines and the bare branches of the aspens.

Windy Lake was a small stream-fed lake, probably no more than two hundred yards across. As a convenient watering hole, it attracted moose and mule deer and even the occasional elk. The water was always ice cold, as he and the others could all attest. That didn't stop him and Brant and Cisco—and Easton, when she could manage to get away—from sneaking out to come up here on summer nights.

Guff always used to keep a small canoe on the shore and they loved any chance to paddle out in the moonlight on July nights and fish for the native rainbow trout and arctic grayling that inhabited it.

Some of his most treasured memories of his teen years centered around trips to this very place.

The trail ended at the lakeshore. He carried Jo to the bench Guff built here, which had been situated in the perfect place to take in the pristine, shimmering lake and the granite mountains surrounding it.

He set Jo on her feet for just a moment so he could brush pine needles and twigs off the bench. Contrary to what he expected, the bench didn't have months worth of debris covering it, which made him think Easton probably found the occasional chance to make good use of it.

He covered the seat with a plastic garbage bag he

had shoved into his pocket earlier in case the bench was damp.

"There you go. Your throne awaits."

She shook her head at his silliness but sat down gingerly, as if the movement pained her. He unrolled one of the blankets and spread it around her shoulders then tucked the other across her lap.

In the moonlight, he saw lines of pain bracketing her mouth and he worried again that this ride into the mountains had been too much for her. Along with the pain, though, he could see undeniable delight at being in this place she loved, one last time.

He supposed sometimes a little pain might be worthwhile in the short-term if it yielded such joy.

As he fussed over the blankets, she reached a thin hand to cover his. "Thank you, my dear. I'm fine now, I promise. Go rescue poor Tess and let me sit here for a moment with my memories."

"Call out if you need help. We won't be far."

"Don't fuss over me," she ordered. "Go help Tess."

Though he was reluctant to leave her here alone, he decided she was safe with the dogs who sat by her side, their ears cocked forward as if listening for any threat.

Back at the trailhead, he found Tess exactly where he had left her, still astride the mare, who was placidly grazing on the last of the autumn grasses.

"I tried to get down," she told him when he emerged from the trees. "Honestly, I did. But my blasted shoe is caught in the stirrups and I couldn't work it loose, no matter how hard I tried. This is so embarrassing."

"I guess that's the price you pay when you go horseback riding in comfortable nurse's shoes instead of boots."

"If I had known I was going to be roped into this, I would have pulled out my only pair of Tony Lamas for the occasion."

Despite her attempt at a light tone, he caught something in her stiff posture, in the rigid set of her jaw.

This was more than inexperience with horses, he realized as he worked her shoe free of the tight stirrup. Had he really been so overbearing and arrogant in insisting she come along that he refused to see she had a deep aversion to horses?

"I'm sorry I dragged you along."

"It's not all bad." She gazed up at the stars. "It's a lovely night."

"Tell me, how many moonlit rides have you been on into the mountains around Pine Gulch?"

She summoned a smile. "Counting tonight? Exactly one."

He finally worked her shoe free. "Let me help you down," he said.

She released the reins and swiveled her left leg over the saddle horn so she could dismount. The mare moved at just that moment and suddenly his arms were full of warm, delicious curves.

She smelled of vanilla and peaches and much to his dismay, his recalcitrant body stirred to life.

He released her abruptly and she wobbled a little when her feet met solid ground. Out of instinct, he reached to steady her and his hand brushed the curve of her breast when he grabbed her arm. Her gaze flashed to his and in the moonlight, he thought he felt the silky cord of sexual awareness tug between them.

"Okay now?"

"I...think so."

That low, breathy note in her voice had to be his imagination. He was almost certain of it.

He couldn't possibly be attracted to her. Sure, she was still a beautiful woman on the outside, but she was still Tess Claybourne, for heaven's sake.

He noticed she moved a considerable distance away but he wasn't sure if she was avoiding him or the horses. Probably both.

"I'm sorry I dragged you up here," he said again. "I didn't realize how uncomfortable riding would be for you."

She made a face. "It shouldn't be. I'm embarrassed that it is. I grew up around horses—how could I help it in Pine Gulch? Though my family never had them, all my friends did, but I've had an...irrational fear of them since breaking my arm after being bucked off when I was seven."

"And I made you come anyway."

She mustered a smile. "I survived this far. We're halfway done now."

He remembered Jo's words suddenly. *You'll never find a happier soul in all your days. Why, what she's been through would have crushed most women. Not our Tess.*

Jo thought Tess was a survivor. If she weren't, could she be looking at this trip with such calm acceptance, even when she was obviously terrified?

"That's one way of looking at it, I guess."

She didn't meet his gaze. "It's not so bad. After the way I treated you in high school, I guess I'm surprised you didn't tie me onto the back of your horse and drag me behind you for a few miles."

His gaze narrowed. What game was this? He never, in a million years, would have expected her to refer to her behavior in their shared past, especially when she struck exactly the right note of self-deprecation.

For several awkward seconds, he couldn't think how to respond. Did he shrug it off? Act like he didn't know what she was talking about? Tell her she ought to have *bitch* tattooed across her forehead and he would be happy to pay for it?

"High school seems a long time ago right now," he finally said.

"Surely not so long that you've forgotten."

He couldn't lie to her. "You always made an impression."

Her laughter was short and unamused. "That's one way of phrasing it, I suppose."

"What would you call it?"

"Unconscionable."

At that single, low-voiced word, he studied her in the moonlight—her long-lashed green eyes contrite, that mouth set in a frown, the auburn curls that were a little disheveled from the ride.

How the hell did she do it? Lord knew, he didn't want to be. But against his will, Quinn found himself drawn to this woman who was willing to confront her fears for his aunt's sake, who could make fun of herself, who seemed genuinely contrite about past bad behavior.

He liked her and, worse, was uncomfortably aware

of a fierce physical attraction to her soft curves and classical features that seemed so serene and lovely in the moonlight.

He pushed away the insane attraction, just as he pushed away the compelling urge to ask her what he had ever done back then to make her hate him so much. Instead, he did his best to turn the subject away.

"Easton told me about Scott. About the accident."

She shoved her hands in the pocket of her jacket and looked off through the darkened trees toward the direction of the lake. "Did she?"

"She said you had only been married a few months at the time, so most of your marriage you were more of a caregiver than a wife."

"Everybody says that like I made some grand, noble sacrifice."

He didn't want to think so. He much preferred thinking of her as the self-absorbed teenage girl trying to ruin his life.

"What would you consider it?"

"I didn't do anything unusual. He was my husband," she said simply. "I loved him and I took vows. I couldn't just abandon him to some impersonal care center for the rest of his life and blithely go on with my own as if he didn't exist."

Many people he knew wouldn't have blinked twice at responding exactly that way to the situation. Hell, the Tess he thought she had been would have done exactly that.

"Do you regret those years?"

She stared at him for a long moment, her eyes wide

with surprise, as if no one had ever asked her that before.

"Sometimes," she admitted, her voice so low he could barely hear it. "I don't regret that I had that extra time with him. I could never regret that. By all rights, he should have died in that accident. A weaker man probably would have. Scott didn't and I have to think God had some purpose in that, something larger than my understanding."

She paused, her expression pensive. "I do regret that we never had the chance to build the life we talked about those first few months of our marriage. Children, a mortgage, a couple of dogs. We missed all that."

Not much of a sacrifice, he thought. He would be quite happy not to have that sort of trouble in his life.

"I'll probably always regret that," she went on. "Unfortunately, I can't change the past. I can only look forward and try to make the best of everything that comes next."

They lapsed into a silence broken only by the horses stamping and snorting behind them and the distant lapping of the water.

She was the first to break the temporary peace. "We'd better go check on Jo, don't you think?"

He jerked his mind away from how very much he wanted to kiss her right this moment, with the moonlight gleaming through the trees and the night creatures singing an accompaniment. "Right. Will you be okay without a flashlight?"

"I'll manage. Just lead the way."

He headed up the trail toward Jo, astonished that

his most pressing regret right now was the end of their brief interlude in the moonlight.

Though Tess loved living in the Mountain West for the people and the scenery and the generally slower pace of life, she had never really considered herself a nature girl.

As a bank manager and accountant, her father hadn't been the sort to take her camping and fishing when she was younger. Later, she'd been too busy, first in college and then taking care of Scott, to find much time to enjoy the backcountry.

But she had to admit she found something serene and peaceful about being here with the glittery stars overhead and that huge glowing moon filtering through the trees and the night alive with sounds and smells.

Well, it would have been serene if she weren't so intensely aware of Quinn walking just ahead of her, moving with long-limbed confidence through the darkness.

The man exuded sensuality. She sighed, wishing she could ignore his effect on her. She disliked the way her heart picked up a beat or two, the little churn of her blood, the way she couldn't seem to keep herself from stealing secret little glances at him as they made their way toward the lake and Jo.

She hadn't missed that moment of awareness in his eyes back there, the heat that suddenly shivered through the air like fireflies on a summer night.

He was attracted to her, though she had a strong sense he found the idea more than appalling.

Her gaze skidded to his powerful shoulders under

his denim jacket, to the dark hair that brushed his collar under his Stetson, and her insides trembled.

For a moment there, she had been quite certain he wanted to kiss her, though she couldn't quite fathom it. How long had it been since she knew the heady, exhilarating impact of desire in a man's eyes? Longer than she cared to remember. The men in town didn't tend to look at her as a woman with the very real and human hunger to be cherished and touched.

In the eyes of most people in Pine Gulch, that woman had been somehow absorbed into the loving, dutiful caretaker, leaving no room for more. Even after Scott's death, people still seemed to see her as a nurturer, not the flirty, sexy, fun-loving Tess she thought might still be buried somewhere deep inside her.

Seeing that heat kindle in his eyes, replacing his typical animosity, had been both flattering and disconcerting and for a moment, she had been mortified at her little spurt of panic, the fear that she had no idea how to respond.

She just needed practice, she assured herself. That's why she was moving to Portland, so she could be around people who saw her as more than just Pine Gulch's version of Mother Teresa.

They walked the short distance through the pines and aspens, their trail lit only by pale moonlight and the glow of a small flashlight he produced from the pocket of his denim jacket. When they reached the lake a few moments later, Tess saw Jo on a bench on the shore, the dogs at her feet. She sat unmoving, so still that for a moment, Tess feared the worst.

But Quinn's boot snapped a twig at that moment and

Jo turned her head. Though they were still a few yards away, Tess could see the glow on her features shining through clearly, even in the moonlight. Her friend smiled at them and for one precious instant, she looked younger, happier. Whole.

"There you are. I was afraid the two of you were lost."

Quinn slanted Tess a sidelong look before turning his attention back to his foster mother. "No. I thought you might like a few moments to yourself up here."

Jo smiled at him as she reached a hand out to Tess to draw her down beside her on the bench. When she saw the blankets tucked around Jo's shoulders and across her lap, everything inside her went a little gooey that Quinn had taken such great care to ensure his foster mother's comfort.

"Isn't it lovely, my dear?"

"Breathtaking," Tess assured her, her hand still enclosed around Jo's thin fingers.

They sat like that for a moment with Quinn standing beside them. The moon glowed off the rocky face of the mountains ringing the lake, reflecting in water that seethed and bubbled as if it was some sort of hot springs. After several moments of watching it, Tess realized the percolating effect was achieved by dozens of fish rising to the surface for night-flying insects.

"It's enchanting," she said to Jo, squeezing her fingers. She didn't add that this moment, this shared beauty, was almost worth that miserable horseback ride up the mountainside.

"This is such a gift. I cannot tell you how deeply it touches me. I have missed these mountains so much these past weeks while I've been stuck at home. Thank you both so very much."

Jo's smile was wide and genuine but Tess didn't miss the lines of pain beneath it that radiated from her mouth.

Quinn must have noticed them as well. "I'd love to stay here longer," he said after a moment, "but we had better get you back. Tess has other patients."

Jo nodded, a little sadly, Tess thought. A lump rose in her throat as the other woman rose, her face tilted to the huge full moon. Jo closed her eyes, inhaled a deep breath of mountain air, then let it out slowly before turning back to Quinn.

"I'm ready."

Her chest felt achy and tight with unshed tears watching Jo say this private goodbye to a place she loved. It didn't help her emotions at all when Quinn carefully and tenderly scooped Jo into his arms and carried her back toward the waiting horses.

She pushed back the tears as she awkwardly mounted her horse, knowing Jo wouldn't welcome them at all. The older woman accepted her impending passing with grace and acceptance, something Tess could only wish on all her patients.

The ride down was slightly easier than the way up had been, though she wouldn't have expected it. In her limited experience on the back of a horse, gravity hadn't always been her friend.

Perhaps she was a tiny bit more loose and relaxed than she had been on the way up. At least she didn't grip the reins quite so tightly and her body seemed to more readily pick up the rhythm of the horse's gait.

She had heard somewhere that horses were sensitive

creatures who picked up on those sorts of things like anxiety and apprehension. Maybe the little mare was just giving her the benefit of the doubt.

As she had on the way up the trail, she rode in the rear of their little group, behind the two black and white dogs and Quinn and Jo, which gave her the opportunity to watch his gentle solicitude toward her.

She found something unbearably sweet—disarming, even—at the sight of his tender care, such a vivid contrast to his reputation as a ruthless businessman who had built his vast shipping company from the ground up.

That treacherous softness fluttered inside her. Even after she forced herself to look away—to focus instead on the rare beauty of the night settling in more deeply across the mountainside—she couldn't ignore that tangled mix of fierce attraction and dawning respect.

As they descended the trail, Winder Ranch came into view, sprawling and solid in the night.

"Home," Jo said in a sleepy-sounding voice that carried across the darkness.

"We're nearly there," he assured her.

When they arrived at the ranch house, Quinn dismounted and then reached for Jo, who winced with the movement.

Worry spasmed across his handsome features but she watched him quickly conceal it from Jo. "Tess, do you mind holding the horses for a few moments while I carry Jo inside and settle her back in her bedroom?"

This time, she was pleased that she could dismount on her own. "Of course not," she answered as her feet hit the dirt.

"Thank you. I'll trade places with you in a few moments so that you can get Jo settled for bed while I take care of the horses."

"Good plan."

She gave him a hesitant smile and was a little astonished when he returned it. Something significant had changed between them as a result of one simple horseback ride into the mountains. They were working together, a team, at least for the moment. He seemed warmer, more approachable. Less antagonistic.

They hadn't really cleared any air between them, other than those few moments she had tried to offer an oblique apology for their history. But she wanted to think perhaps he might eventually come to accept that she had become a better person.

Chapter Seven

After Quinn carried Jo inside, Tess stood patting the mare, savoring the night before she went inside to take care of Jo's medical needs. Quiet moments of reflection were a rare commodity in her world.

She had gotten out of the habit when she had genuinely had no time to spare with all of Scott's medical needs. Perhaps she needed to work at meditation when she moved to Portland, she thought. Maybe yoga or tai chi.

She was considering her options and talking softly to the horses when Quinn hurried down the porch steps a few moments later.

"How's Jo?"

"Ready for pain meds, I think, but she's not complaining."

"You gave her a great gift tonight, Quinn."

He smiled a little. "I hope so. She loves the mountains. I have to admit, I do as well. I forget that sometimes. Seattle is beautiful with the water and the volcanic mountains but it's not the same as home."

"Is it? Home, I mean?"

"Always."

He spoke with no trace of hesitation and she wondered again at the circumstances that had led him to Winder Ranch. Those rumors about his violent past swirled through her memory and she quickly dismissed them as ridiculous.

"I'm sorry. Let me take the horses." He reached for the reins of both horses and as she handed them over, their hands brushed.

He flashed her a quick look and grabbed her fingers with his other hand. "Your fingers are freezing!"

"I should have worn gloves."

"I should have thought to get you some before we left." He paused. "This was a crazy idea, wasn't it? I apologize again for dragging you up there."

"Not a crazy idea at all," she insisted. "Jo loved it."

"She's half-asleep in there and I know she's in pain but she's also happier than I've seen her since I arrived."

She smiled at him, intensely conscious of the hard strength of his hand still curled around her fingers. Her hands might still be cold from the night air but they were just about the only thing not heating up right about now.

He gazed at her mouth for several long seconds, his eyes silvery-blue in the moonlight, and for one effervescent moment, she thought again that he might kiss her. He even angled his head ever so slightly and her gaze tangled with his.

Her pulse seemed abnormally loud in her ears and her insides jumped and fluttered like a baby bird trying its first awkward flight.

He eased forward slightly and her body instinctively rose to meet his. She caught her breath, waiting for the brush of his mouth against hers, but he suddenly jerked back, his expression thunderstruck.

Tess blinked as if awakening from a long, lovely nap as cold reality splashed over her. Of course he wouldn't kiss her. He despised her, with very good reason.

With ruthless determination, she shoved down the disappointment and ridiculous sense of hurt shivering through her. So what if he found the idea of kissing her so abhorrent? She didn't have time for this anyway. She was supposed to be working, not going for moonlit rides and sharing confidences in the dark and fantasizing about finally kissing her teenage crush.

Since he now held the horses' reins, she shoved her hands in the pocket of her jacket to hide their trembling and forced her voice to sound cool and unaffected.

"I'd better go take care of Jo's meds."

"Right." He continued to watch her out of those seductive but veiled eyes.

"Um, good night, if I don't see you again before I leave."

"Good night."

She hurried up the porch steps, feeling the heat of his gaze following her. Inside, she closed the door and leaned against it for just a moment, willing her heart to settle down once more.

Blast the man for stirring up all these hormones she tried so hard to keep contained. She *so* did not want to be attracted to Quinn. What a colossal waste of energy on her part. Oh, he might have softened toward her a little in the course of their ride with Jo, but she couldn't delude herself into thinking he was willing to forgive and forget everything she had done to him years ago.

She had work to do, she reminded herself. People who needed her. She didn't have time to be obsessing over the past or the person she used to be or a man like Quinn Southerland, who could never see her as anything else.

She did her best the rest of the night to focus on her patients and not on the little thrum of desire she hadn't been able to shake since that almost-kiss with Quinn.

Still, she approached Winder Ranch for her midnight check on Jo with a certain amount of trepidation. To her relief, when she unlocked the door with the key Easton had given her and walked inside, the house was dark. Quinn was nowhere in sight, but she could still sense his presence in the house.

Jo didn't stir when Tess entered her room, which worried her for a moment until she saw the steady rise and fall of the blankets by the glow of the small light in the attached bathroom that Jo and Easton left on for the hospice nurses.

The ride up to the lake must have completely exhausted her. She didn't even wake when Tess checked her vitals and gave her medicine through the central IV line that had been placed after her last hospitalization.

When she was done with the visit, she closed the door quietly behind her and turned to go, then became aware that someone else was in the darkened hallway. Her heart gave a quick, hard kick, then she realized it was Easton.

She wasn't sure if that sensation coursing through her was more disappointment or relief.

"I hope I didn't wake you," Tess said.

The other woman's sleek blond ponytail moved as she shook her head. "I've still got some pesky accounts to finish. I was in the office working on the computer and heard the door open."

"I tried to be quiet. Sorry about that." She smiled at her friend. "But then, Jo didn't even wake up so I couldn't have been *too* loud."

"You weren't. I'm just restless tonight."

"I'm sorry."

Easton shrugged. "It sometimes knocks me on my butt if I think about what things will be like in a month or so. I'm trying to get as much done now on ranch paperwork so I have time to…to grieve."

Tess placed a comforting hand on her arm and Easton smiled, making a visible effort to push away her sadness. "Quinn told me about your adventure tonight," she said.

Tess made a rueful face. "I'm nowhere near the horsewoman you are. I felt like an idiot up there, but at least I didn't fall off."

"Jo was so happy when I checked on her earlier. I haven't seen her like that in a long time."

"Then I suppose my mortification was all for a good cause."

Easton laughed a little but her laughter quickly faded. "It won't be much longer, will it?"

Tess's heart ached at the question but she didn't pretend to misunderstand. "A week, maybe a little more. You know I can't say exactly."

Her friend's blue eyes filled with a sorrow that was raw and real. "I don't want to lose her, Tess. I'm not ready. What will I do?"

Tess set her bag on the floor and hurried forward to pull Easton into her arms. She knew that ache, that deep, gnawing fear and loss.

"You'll go on. That's all you can do. All any of us can do."

"First my parents, then Guff and now Jo. I can't bear it. She's all I have left."

"I know, sweetheart."

Easton didn't cry aloud, though Tess could feel the quiet shuddering of her shoulders. After a moment, the other woman pulled away.

"I'm sorry. I'm just tired."

"You need to sleep, honey. Everything will seem a little better in the morning, I promise. Midnight is the time when our fears all grow stronger and more vicious."

Easton drew in a heavy breath, then stepped away, swiping at her eyes. "Brant called from Germany earlier. He's hoping to get a flight any time now."

She remembered Brant Western as a tall, serious-minded boy who had always seemed an odd fit to be best friends with both Quinn, the rebellious kid with the surly attitude, and Cisco Del Norte, the wild, slightly dangerous troublemaker.

"Jo will be thrilled to have him home. What about Cisco?"

Easton's mouth compressed into a tight line and she focused on a spot somewhere over Tess's shoulder. "No word yet. We think he's somewhere in El Salvador but we can't seem to find anything out for sure. He's moving around a lot. Seems like everywhere we try, we just keep missing him by a day or even a few hours. It's so aggravating. Quinn has his assistant in Seattle trying to pull some strings with the embassy down there to find him."

"I hope it doesn't take much longer."

Easton nodded, her features troubled. "Even if we find him, there's no guarantee he can make it back in time. Quinn has promised to send a plane down to bring him home, even if he's in the middle of the jungle, but we have to find him first."

Her stomach gave a strange little quiver at the idea of Quinn having planes at his disposal.

"I'll keep my fingers crossed," she said, then picked up her bag and headed for the front door. Easton followed to let her out.

"Get some rest, honey," she said again. "I'll be back for the next round of meds around three. You'd better be asleep when I get back!"

"Yes, Nurse Ratched."

"I mean it."

Easton smiled a little, even past the lingering sadness in her eyes. "Thanks, Tess. For everything."

"Go to sleep," she ordered again, then walked out into the night, with that same curious mix of relief and disappointment that she had avoided Quinn, at least for a few more hours.

He awoke to the sound of a door snicking softly closed and the dimmer switch in the bathroom being turned up just enough to jar him out of dreams he had no business entertaining.

In a rather surreal paradigm shift, he went from dreaming about a heated embrace on a warm blanket under starry skies near the lake to the stark reality of a sickroom, where his foster mother lay dying.

Oddly, the same woman appeared in both scenes. Tess stepped out of the bathroom, looking brisk and professional in her flowered surgical scrubs.

He feigned sleep and watched her through his lashes as she donned a pair of latex-free gloves.

He could pinpoint the instant she saw him sprawled in the recliner, purportedly asleep. Her steps faltered and she froze.

Probably the decent thing would be to open his eyes and go through the motions of pretending to awaken. But he wasn't always crazy about doing the decent thing. Instead, he gave a heavy-sounding breath and continued to spy on her under his lashes.

She gazed at him for several seconds as if trying to ascertain his level of sleep, then she finally turned away from him and back to her patient with a small, barely perceptible sigh he wondered about.

For the next few minutes, he watched her draw medicine out into syringes, then she quietly began checking Jo's blood pressure and temperature.

Though her movements were slow and careful, Jo still opened her eyes when Tess put the blood pressure cuff on her leg.

"I'm so sorry to wake you. I wish I didn't have to," Tess murmured.

"Oh, poof," Jo whispered back. "Don't you worry for a single moment about doing your job."

"How is your pain level?"

Jo was silent. "I'm not going to tell you," she finally said. "You'll just write it down in your little chart and the next thing I know, Jake Dalton will be increasing my meds and I'll be so drugged out I won't be able to think straight. My Brant is coming home. Should be any day now."

As Jo whispered to her, Tess continued to slant careful looks in his direction.

"Easton told me earlier that he was on his way," she said in an undertone.

"They'll be good for Easton. The four of them, why, they were thicker than thieves. I can't tell you how glad I am they'll still have each other."

Quinn swallowed hard, hating this whole situation all over again.

Tess smiled, relentlessly cheerful. "It's a blessing, all right. For all of them and especially for your peace of mind."

He listened to their quiet conversation as Tess continued to take care of Jo's medical needs. He was still trying to figure out how much of her demeanor he was buying. She seemed to be everything that was patient and calm, a serene island in the middle of a stormy emotional mess. Was it truly possible that this dramatic change in her could be genuine?

He supposed he was a cynical bastard but he couldn't quite believe it. This could all be one big show she was putting on. He had only been here a few days. If he stuck around long enough, she was likely to revert to her true colors.

On the other hand, people could change. He was living testimony to that. He was worlds away from the bitter, hot-tempered punk he'd been when he arrived at the Winders' doorstep after a year in foster care and the misery that came before.

He pushed away the past, preferring instead to focus on today.

Tess finished with Jo a few moments later. After fluffing her pillow and tucking the blankets up around her, she dimmed the light in the bathroom again and moved quietly toward the door out into the hallway.

He rose and followed her, careful not to disturb Jo, who seemed to have easily slipped into sleep again.

"I'll walk you out," he said, his voice low, just as she reached the door.

She whirled and splayed a hand across her chest. She glared at him as she moved out of the room to the hallway. He followed her and closed the door behind him.

"Don't do that! That's the second time you've nearly scared the life out of me. How long have you been awake?"

"Not long. Here, let me help you with your coat."

He took it off the chair in the hallway where she had tossed it and stood behind her. Her scent teased him, that delectable peach and vanilla, that somehow seemed sweet and sultry at the same time, like a hot Southern night.

She paused for a moment, then extended her arm through the sleeve. "Thank you," she said and he wondered if he was imagining the slightly husky note to her voice.

"You're welcome."

"You really don't need to walk me out, though. I'm sure I can find the way to my car by myself."

"I could use the fresh air, to be honest with you."

She looked as if she wanted to argue but she only shrugged and turned toward the door. He held it open for her and again smelled that seductive scent as she moved past him on her way out.

The scent seemed to curl through him, twisting and tugging an unwelcome response out of him, which he did his best to ignore as they walked out into the night.

The moon hung huge over the western mountains now, the stars a bright glitter out here unlike anything to be found in the city.

The October night wasn't just cool now in the early morning hours, it was downright cold. This time of year, temperatures in these high mountain valleys could show a wide range in the course of a single day. Nights were invariably cool, even in summer. In spring and fall, the temperature dropped quickly once the sun went down.

His morning spent in the garden soaking up sunshine with Jo seemed only another distant memory.

"Gorgeous night, isn't it?" Tess said. "I don't ever get tired of the view out here."

He nodded. "I've lived without it since I left Cold Creek Canyon, but something about it stays inside me even when I'm back in Seattle."

She smiled a little. "I know I'm going to miss these mountains when I move to Portland in a few weeks."

"What's in Portland?" he asked, curious as to why she would pick up and leave after her lifetime spent here.

"A pretty good basketball team," she answered. "Lots of trees and flowers. Nice people, from what I hear."

"You know what I mean. Why are you leaving?"

She was silent for a moment, the only sound the

wind whispering through the trees. "A whole truck-load of reasons. Mostly, I guess, because I'm ready for a new start."

He could understand that. He had sought the same thing in the Air Force after leaving Pine Gulch, hadn't he? A place where no one knew his history in the foster-care system or as the rough-edged punk who had found a home here with Jo and Guff.

"Will you be doing the same thing? Providing end-of-life care?"

She smiled and in the moonlight, she looked fresh and lovely and very much like the teenage cheerleader who had tangled the hormones of every boy who walked the halls of Pine Gulch High School.

"Just the opposite, actually. I took a job in labor and delivery at one of the Portland hospitals."

"Bringing life into the world instead of comforting those who are leaving it. There's a certain symmetry to that."

"I think so, too. It's all part of my brand-new start."

"I suppose everybody could use that once in a while."

"True enough," she murmured, with an unreadable look in her eyes.

"Will you miss this?"

"Pine Gulch?"

"I was thinking more of the work you do. You seem… very good at it. Do you give this same level to all your patients as you have to Jo?"

She looked startled at the question, though he wasn't sure if was because she had never thought about it before or that she was surprised he had noticed.

"I try. Everyone deserves to spend his or her last

days with dignity and respect. But Jo is special. I can't deny that. She used to give me piano lessons when I was young and I've always adored her."

Now it was his turn to be surprised. Jo taught piano lessons for many years to most of the young people in Pine Gulch but he had never realized Tess had once had the privilege of being one of her students.

"Do you still play?"

She laughed. "I hardly played then. I was awful. Probably the worst student Jo ever had, though she tried her best, believe me. But yes, I still play a little. I enjoy it much more as an adult than I did when I was ten."

She paused for a moment, then gave a rueful smile. "When he was…upset or having a bad day, Scott used to enjoy when I would play for him. It calmed him. I've had more practice than I ever expected over the years."

"You should play for Jo sometime when you come out to the house. She gets a real kick out of hearing her old students play. Especially the hard ones."

"Maybe. I'm worried her hearing is a little too fragile for my fumbling attempts." She smiled. "What about you? Did Jo give you lessons after you moved here?"

He gave a short laugh at the memory. "She tried. I'm sure I could have taught you a thing or two about being difficult."

"I don't doubt that for a moment," she murmured.

She gazed at him for a moment, then she shifted her gaze up and he could swear he saw a million constellations reflected in her eyes.

"Look!" she exclaimed. "A shooting star, right over the top of Windy Peak. Quick, make a wish."

He tilted his neck to look in the direction she pointed. "Probably just a satellite."

She glared at him. "Don't ruin it. I'm making a wish anyway."

With her eyes screwed closed, she pursed her mouth in concentration. "There," she said after a moment. "That should do it."

She opened her eyes and smiled softly at him and he forgot all about the cold night air. All he could focus on was that smile, that mouth, and the sudden wild hunger inside him to taste it.

"What did you wish?" he asked, a gruff note to his voice.

She made a face. "If I tell you, it won't come true. Don't you know anything about wishes?"

Right now, he could tell her a thing or two about wanting something he shouldn't. That sensuous heat wrapped tighter around his insides. "I know enough. I know sometimes wishes can be completely ridiculous and make no sense. For instance, right now, I wish I could kiss you. Don't ask me why. I don't even like you."

Her eyes looked huge and green in her delicate face as she stared at him. "Okay," she said, her voice breathy.

"Okay, I can kiss you? Or, okay, you won't ask why I want to?"

She let out a ragged-sounding breath. "Either. Both."

He didn't need much more of an invitation than that. Without allowing himself to stop and think through the insanity of kissing a woman he had detested twenty-four hours earlier, Quinn stepped forward and covered her mouth with his.

Chapter Eight

She gave a little gasp of shock but her mouth was warm and inviting in the cold air and he was vaguely aware through the haze of his own desire that she didn't pull away, as he might have expected.

Instead, she wrapped her arm around his waist and leaned into his kiss for more.

A low clamor in his brain warned him this was a crazy idea, that he would have a much harder time keeping a safe distance between them after he had known the silky softness of her mouth, but he ignored it.

How could he possibly step away now, when she tasted like coffee and peaches and Tess, a delectable combination that sizzled through him like heat lightning?

Her lips parted slightly, all the invitation he needed to deepen the kiss. She moaned a little against his mouth and he could feel the tremble of her body against him, the confused desire in the slide of her tongue against his.

The night disappeared until it was only the two of them, until he was lost in the unexpected hunger for this woman in his arms. Her kiss offered solace and surrender, a chance to put away for a moment his sadness and embrace the wonder of life in all its tragedy and glory.

He lost track of time there in the moonlight. He forgot about Jo and about his efforts to find his recalcitrant foster brother and his worries for Easton. He especially refused to let himself remember all the reasons he shouldn't be kissing her—how, as he'd told her, he wasn't even sure he liked her, how he still didn't trust that she wasn't hiding a knife behind her back, ready to gut him with it at the first chance.

The only thing that mattered for this instant was Tess and how very perfect she felt in his arms, with her mouth eager and warm against his.

A coyote howled from far off in the distance, long and mournful. He heard it on the edge of his consciousness but he knew the instant the spell between them shattered and Tess returned to reality. In the space between one ragged breath and the next, she went from kissing him with heat and passion to freezing in his arms like Windy Lake in a January blizzard.

Her arms fluttered away from around his neck and he sensed she would have backed farther away from him if she hadn't been pressed up against her car door.

Though he wanted nothing more than to crush her to him again and slide into that stunning heat once more, he forced himself to step back to give them both a little necessary space.

Her breathing was as rough and quick as his own and he could see the rapid rise and fall of her chest.

Despite the chill in the air, the night seemed to wrap around them in a sultry embrace. From the trees whispering in the wind to the carpet of stars overhead, they seemed alone here in the darkness.

Part of him wanted to step toward her and sweep her into his arms again, but shock and dismay began to seep through his desire. What kind of magic did she wield against him that he could so easily succumb to his attraction and kiss her, despite all his best instincts?

He shouldn't have done it. In the first place, their relationship was a tangled mess and had been for years. Sure, she had been great with Jo tonight and he had been grateful for her help on the horseback ride into the mountains. But one night couldn't completely transform so much animosity into fuzzy warmth.

In the second place, he had enough on his plate right now. His emotions were scraped raw by Jo's condition. He had nothing left inside to give anything else right now, especially not an unwanted attraction to Tess.

Maybe that's why he had kissed her. He needed the distraction, a few moments of oblivion. Either way, it had been a monumentally stupid impulse, one he was quite certain he would come to regret the moment she climbed into her little sedan and drove down Cold Creek Canyon.

She continued to gaze at him out of those huge green eyes, as if she expected him to say something. He would be damned if he would apologize for kissing her. Not when she had responded with such fierce enthusiasm.

He had to say something, though. He scrambled for words and said the first thing that came to his head.

"If I had known you were such an enthusiastic kisser, I wouldn't have worked so hard to fight you off in high school."

The moment he said the words, he wished he could call them back. The comment had been unnecessarily cruel and made him sound like an ass. Beyond that, he didn't like revealing he remembered anything that had happened in their long-ago past. Apparently she still tended to bring out the worst in him.

He couldn't be certain in the darkness but he thought she paled a little. She grabbed her car door and yanked it open.

"That's funny," she retorted. "If I had known you would turn out to be such a jerk, I wouldn't have spent a moment since you returned to Pine Gulch regretting the way I treated you back then."

He deserved that, he supposed. *Now* he wanted to apologize—for his words at least, not the kiss—but the words seemed to clog in his throat.

She slid into her driver's seat, avoiding his gaze. "It would probably be better for both our sakes if we just pretended the past few moments never happened."

He raised an eyebrow. "You think you can do that? Because I'm not at all sure I have that much imagination."

She cranked the key in her ignition with just a little more force than strictly necessary and he felt a moment's pity that she was taking out her anger against him on her hapless engine.

"Absolutely," she snapped. "It shouldn't be hard at all. Especially since I'm sorry to report the reality didn't come close to measuring up to all my ridiculous teenage fantasies about what it might be like to kiss the bad boy of Cold Creek."

Before he could come up with any kind of rejoinder—sharp or otherwise—she thrust her car into gear and shot around the circular driveway.

He stared after her, wondering why the cold night only now seemed to pierce the haze of desire still wrapped around him.

Her words about teenage fantasies seemed to echo through his head. He supposed on some level, he must have known she had wanted to kiss him all those years ago. She had tried it, after all. He could still remember that day in the empty algebra classroom when he had been so furious with her over the false cheating allegations and then she had made everything much worse by thinking she could reel him in with a few flirtatious words.

He had always assumed her fleeting interest in him, her attempts to draw his attention, were only a spoiled fit of pique that he didn't fall at her feet like every other boy in school. Now he had to wonder if there might have been something more to it.

Trust him to make a mess out of everything, as usual. She had been kind to Jo and he had responded by taking completely inappropriate advantage. Then he had compounded his sins by making a stupid, mocking comment for no good reason.

She was furious with him, and she had every right to be, but he couldn't help thinking it was probably better this way. He didn't like having these soft, warm feelings for her.

Better to remember her as that manipulative little cheerleader looking so sweet-faced and innocent as she lied through her teeth to their history teacher and the principal than as the gentle caregiver who could suppress her own fears about horseback riding to help a dying woman find a little peace.

Tess waited until she drove under the arch at the entrance to Winder Ranch and had turned back onto the main Cold Creek road, out of view of the ranch house, before pulling her car over to the side and shifting into Park with hands that still trembled.

She was such an idiot.

Her face burned and she covered her hot cheeks with her hands.

She couldn't believe her response to him, that she had kissed him with such heat and enthusiasm. The moment his mouth touched hers, she had tossed every ounce of good sense she possessed into the air and had fallen into his kiss like some love-starved teenage girl with a fierce crush.

Oh, mercy. What must he think of her?

Probably that she was a love-starved thirty-two-year-old who hadn't known a man's touch in more years than she cared to remember.

How had she forgotten that incredible rush of sensations churning through her body? The delicious heat and lassitude that turned her brain to mush and her bones to rubber?

She had nearly burst into tears at how absolutely perfect it had felt to have his arms around her, his mouth sure and confident on hers. Wouldn't *that* have been humiliating? Thank the Lord she at least had retained some tiny modicum of dignity. But she had wanted to lose herself inside that kiss, to become so tangled up in him that she could forget the hundreds of reasons she shouldn't be kissing Quinn Southerland on a cold October night outside Winder Ranch.

If I had known you were such an enthusiastic kisser, I wouldn't have worked so hard to fight you off in high school.

His words seemed to echo through her car and she wanted to sink through the floorboards in complete mortification.

What was she thinking? Quinn Southerland, for heaven's sake! The man despised her, rightfully so. If she wanted to jump feet-first into the whole sexual attraction thing, shouldn't she *try* to have the sense God gave a goose and pick somebody who could at least stand to be in the same room with her?

The unpalatable truth was, she hadn't been thinking at all. From the first instant his mouth had touched hers with such stunning impact, she felt like that shooting star she had wished upon, bursting through the atmosphere.

She had been rocked to her core by the wild onrush of sensations, his hands sure and masculine, his rough, late-evening shadow against her skin, his scent—of sleepy male and the faint lingering hint of some expensive aftershave—subtle and sexy at the same time.

To her great shame, she had wanted to forget everything sensible and sound and just surrender to the heat of his kiss. Who knew how long she would have let him continue things if she hadn't heard the lonely sound of a coyote?

Blast the man. She had everything planned out so perfectly. Her new job, relocating to Portland. It wasn't fair that he should come back now and stir up her insides like a tornado touching down. She didn't need this sort of complication just as she was finally on the brink of moving on with her life.

She scrubbed at her cheeks for another moment, then dropped her hands and took a deep, cleansing breath. The tragic truth was, he wouldn't be around much longer and she wouldn't have to deal with him. Jo was clinging by her fingernails but she couldn't hold on much longer. When she passed, Quinn would return to Seattle and she would be starting her new life.

For a few weeks, she would just have to do her best to deal with this insane reaction, to conceal it from him.

He didn't like her and she would be damned if she would pant after him like she was still that teenage girl with a crush.

"Thanks a million for taking a look at the Beast," Easton said. "I really didn't want to have to haul it to the repair place in town."

Four days after his startling encounter with Tess, Quinn stood with his hands inside Easton's temperamental tractor, trying to replace the clutch. "No problem," he answered. "It's good to know I can still find my way around the insides of a John Deere."

"If Southerland Shipping ever hits the skids, you can always come back home and be my grease monkey."

He grinned. "It's always good to have options, isn't it?"

She returned his smile, but it faded quickly. "Guff wanted you to stay and do just that, didn't he? You could always find your way around any kind of combustion engine."

True enough. He never minded other ranch work—roundup and moving the cattle and even hauling hay. But he had always been happiest when he was up to his elbows in grease, tinkering with this or that machine.

"Remember that old '66 Chevy pickup truck you used to work on? The blue one with the white top and all those curves?"

"Oh, yeah. She was a sweet ride. I imagine Cisco drove her into the ground after I left for the Air Force."

Something strange flashed in her mind for a moment, before she blinked it away. "You could have stayed. You would have been more than welcome," Easton said after a moment. "But I knew all along you never would."

He raised an eyebrow. Had he been so transparent? "Pine Gulch is a nice place and I love the ranch. Why were you so certain I wouldn't stick around? I might have been happy running a little place of my own nearby."

She shook her head. "Not you. Brant, maybe. He loves his ranch, though you would have to use that crowbar in the toolbox over there to get him to admit it. But you and Cisco had wanderlust running through your veins even when we were kids."

Maybe Cisco, Quinn thought. He had always talked about all the places he wanted to see when he left Idaho. Sun-drenched beaches and glittering cities and beautiful, exotic women who would drop their clothes if you so much as smiled at them.

That had been Francisco Del Norte's teenage dream. Quinn had no idea how close he had come to reaching it, since the man was wickedly skillful at evading any questions about his wandering life.

Quinn had his suspicions about what Cisco might be involved with, but he preferred to keep them to himself, especially around Easton. While she might love him and Brant like brothers, he had always sensed her feelings for Cisco were far different.

"I haven't wandered that far," he protested, instead of dwelling on Cisco and his suitcase full of secrets. "Not since I left the Air Force, anyway. I've been settled in Seattle for eight years now."

"Your dreams were always bigger than a little town like Pine Gulch could hold. I think deep down, Guff and Jo knew that, even if they were disappointed you didn't come home after you were discharged."

"They didn't need me here. They always had you to run the ranch." He sent her a careful look. "I always figured you were just fine with that. Was I wrong? You left for a while there, but you came back."

She had that strange look in her eyes again when he mentioned the eight months she had moved away from the ranch after Guff died. She didn't like to talk about it much, other than to say she had needed a change for a while. He supposed, like Cisco, she had her share of secrets, too.

"Yes. I came back," she said.

"Do you regret that?"

She raised her eyebrows. "You mean do I feel stuck here while the rest of you went off and conquered the world?"

He made a face. "I haven't *completely* conquered it. Still have a ways to go there but I'm working on it."

She smiled, though her expression was pensive. "I can't deny that sometimes I wonder if there's something more out there for me than a cattle ranch in Pine Gulch, Idaho. But I'm happy here, for the most part. I can't bear the thought of selling the ranch and leaving. Where would I go?"

"You could always come to Seattle. The company could always use somebody with your organizational skills."

"That world's not for me. You know that. I'm happy here."

Even as she said it, he caught the wistful note in her voice and he wondered at it. It wouldn't be easy to just pick up and make a new start somewhere. As had been the case more often than he cared to admit, he couldn't help thinking about Tess. In a few weeks, she was off to make a new start somewhere away from Pine Gulch.

As he worked on the clutch, his mind replayed that stunning kiss a few days earlier: the taste of her, like coffee and cinnamon, the sweet scent of her surrounding him, the imprint of her soft curves burning through layers of clothing.

He could go for long stretches of time without thinking about it as he went about the routine of visiting with Jo, helping Easton with odd jobs and trying to run Southerland Shipping from hundreds of miles away.

But then something would spark a memory and he would find himself once more caught up in reliving every moment of that heated embrace.

He let out a breath, grateful he had seen Tess just a few times since, when she came out to take care of Jo—and then only briefly, in the buffering presence of Easton or Jo. He had wanted to apologize but hadn't been alone with her to do it and hadn't wanted to bring up the kiss in the presence of either of the other women.

That hadn't stopped him from obsessing more than he should have about her when she wasn't around, wondering which was the real Tess—the selfish girl he remembered or the soft, caring woman she appeared to be now.

The sound of an approaching vehicle drew his attention from either the mystery of Tess or the tractor's insides.

"Looks like company." Through the wide doors of the ranch's equipment shed, he watched a small white SUV approach the house. "Isn't it too early in the afternoon for any caregivers? The nurse was just here."

Easton followed his gaze outside. "I don't recognize the vehicle. Maybe it's one of Jo's friends."

They watched for a moment from their vantage point of a hundred yards away as the door opened, then a tall, brown-haired man in uniform stepped out.

"Brant!" Easton exclaimed, her delicate features alight with joy.

With a resounding thud that echoed through the building, she dropped the wrench to the concrete equipment shed floor and ran full-tilt toward the new arrival.

Quinn followed at an easier pace and arrived just as Brant Western scooped East into his arms for a tight hug.

"I'll get grease all over your pretty uniform," she warned.

"I don't care. You are a sight, Blondie."

"Back at you." She kissed his cheek and Quinn watched her dash tears away with a surreptitious finger swipe. He remembered again the little tow-headed preteen who used to follow them around everywhere. He couldn't believe her parents had let them drag her along on all their adventures but she had always been a plucky little thing and they had all adored her.

After another tight hug, Brant set her down, then turned to Quinn with a long, considering glance.

"Look at you. A few days back on the ranch and Easton has you doing all the grunt work."

He looked down at the oil and grime that covered his shirt. "I don't mind getting my hands a little dirty."

"You never did." Brant smiled, though his eyes were red-rimmed with exhaustion. He looked not just fatigued but emotionally wrung-out.

Quinn considered Brant and Cisco his best friends, his brothers in every way that mattered. And though they had never been particularly demonstrative with each other, he was compelled now to step forward and pound the other man's back.

"Welcome home, Major."

"Thanks, man."

"Now I'm the one who's going to get grease all over your uniform."

"It will wash." Brant stepped away and Quinn was happy to see he seemed a little brighter, not quite as utterly exhausted. "On the flight over, I was trying to remember how long it's been since we've been together like this."

"Four years ago January," Easton said promptly.

Quinn combed through his memory bank and realized that must have been when Guff had died of a heart attack that had shocked all of them. By some miracle, they had all made it back from the various corners of the world for his funeral.

"Too damn long, that's for sure," he said.

Brant smiled for a moment but quickly sobered. "Like the last one, I wish this reunion could be under happier circumstances. How is she?"

"Eager to see you." Easton slipped her arm through his. "She'll be so happy you could make it home."

"I can't stay long. I was able to swing only a week. I'll have my regular leave in January and will have a couple more weeks home then if I can make it back."

Jo wouldn't be around for that and all of them knew it.

Easton forced a smile. "A day or a week, it won't matter to Jo. She'll just be so happy she had a chance to see you one last time. Come on, I'll take you inside. I want to see her face when she gets a load of you."

"You two go ahead," Quinn said. "I'm almost done out here. Since I'm already dirty, think I'll finish up out here first and come inside in a few."

Brant and Easton both nodded and headed for the house while Quinn returned to the tractor. A few minutes later, he was just tightening the last nut on the job when he heard the front door to the house bang shut.

"Quinn! Come quick!"

He jerked his gaze toward the ranch house at the urgency in Easton's voice and his blood ran cold.

He dropped the wrench and raced toward the house. Not yet, he prayed as he ran. Not when Brant had only just arrived at Winder Ranch and when his people hadn't managed to find Cisco yet.

His heart pounded frantically as he thrust open the

door to Jo's room. The IV pump was beeping and the alarm was going off on the oxygen saturation monitor.

He frowned. Jo was lying against her pillow but wild relief pulsed through him that her eyes were open and alert, though her features were pale and drawn.

Just now, Easton looked in worse shape than Jo. She stood by the bedside, the phone in her hand.

"I don't care what you say. I'm calling Dr. Dalton. You were unconscious!"

"All this bother and fuss," Jo muttered. "You're making me feel like a foolish old woman."

Despite her effort to downplay her condition, he could see the concern in the expressions of both Brant and Easton.

"She was out cold for five solid minutes," Easton explained to Quinn. "She was hugging Brant one moment, then she fell back against her pillows the next and wouldn't wake up no matter what we tried."

"I should have called to let you know I was on my way." Brant's voice was tight with self-disgust. "It wasn't right to rush in like that and surprise you."

"I wasn't expecting you today, that's all," Jo insisted. "Maybe I got a little excited but I'm fine now."

Despite her protestations, Jo was as pale as her pillow.

"The clinic's line is busy. I'm calling Tess," Easton declared and walked from the room to make the call.

"Tess?" Brant asked.

Just when his heart rate started to slow from the adrenaline rush, simply the mention of Tess's name kicked it right back up again.

"Tess Claybourne. Used to be Jamison. She's one of the hospice nurses."

The best one, he had to admit. After several days here, he knew all three of the home-care nurses who took turns seeing to Jo. They were all good caregivers and compassionate women but as tough as it was for him to swallow, Tess had a knack for easing Jo's worst moments and calming everybody else in the house.

Brant's blue eyes widened. "Tess Jamison. Pom-pom Tess? Homecoming queen? That Tess?"

Okay, already. "Yeah. That Tess."

"You're yanking my chain."

"Not this time." He couldn't keep the grimness out of his voice.

"She still hotter than a two-dollar pistol?"

"Brant Western," Jo chided him from her bed. "She's a lovely young woman, not some…some pin-up poster off your Internet."

When they were randy teenagers, Jo had frequently lectured them not to objectify women. Brant must have remembered the familiar refrain as well, Quinn thought, as the deep dimples Quinn despised flashed for just a moment with his smile.

"Sorry, Jo. But she was always the prettiest girl at PG High. I used to get tongue-tied if she only walked past me in the hall."

She was still the prettiest thing Quinn had seen in a long time. And he didn't even want to think about how delectable she tasted or the sexy little sounds she made when his mouth covered hers….

Easton walked in, jarring him from yet another damn flashback.

"I reached Tess on her cell phone. She's off today but she's going to come over anyway. And I talked to Jake Dalton and he's stopping by on his way up to Cold Creek."

Pine Gulch's doctor had been raised on a huge cattle ranch at the head of Cold Creek Canyon, Quinn knew.

"Shouldn't we take her to the hospital or something?" Brant asked.

Quinn and Easton exchanged glances since they had frequently brought up the subject, but Jo spoke before he could answer.

"No hospital." Jo's voice was firm, stronger than he had heard it since he arrived. "I'm done with them. I'm dying and no doctor or hospital can change that. I want to go right here, in the house I shared with Guff, surrounded by those I love."

Brant blinked at her bluntness and Quinn sympathized with him. It was one thing to understand intellectually that her condition was terminal. It was quite another to hear her speak in such stark, uncompromising terms about it. He at least had had a few days to get used to the hard reality.

"But it's not going to happen today or even tomorrow," she went on. "I won't let it. Not until Cisco comes home. I just need to rest for a while and then I want to have a good long talk with you about what you've been doing for the army."

Brant released a heavy breath, his tired features still looking as if he had just been run over by a Humvee.

Quinn could completely sympathize with him. He could only hope Jo held out long enough so his people could track down the last of the Four Winds.

Chapter Nine

"What's the verdict?" Jo asked. "Is my heart still beating?"

Tess pulled the stethoscope away from Jo's brachial artery and pulled the blood pressure cuff off with a loud ripping sound.

She related Jo's blood pressure aloud to Jake Dalton, who frowned at the low diastolic and systolic numbers.

"Let's take a listen to your ticker," Pine Gulch's only doctor said, pulling out his own stethoscope.

Jo responded by glaring at Tess. "Dirty trick, bringing Jake along with you."

"I told you I called him," Easton said from the doorway of the room, where she stood with Quinn and the very solemn-looking Major Western. Tess purposely avoided looking at any of them, especially Quinn.

It was a darn good thing Jake wasn't checking her heart rate right about now. She had a feeling it would be galloping along faster than one of the Winder Ranch horses in an open pasture on a sunny afternoon.

Knowing Quinn was only a few feet away watching her out of those silver-blue eyes was enough to tangle her insides and make her palms itch with nerves.

"And I told you I don't need a doctor," Jo replied.

"Be careful or you'll hurt my feelings," Jake teased.

"Oh, poof. Your skin is thicker than rawhide."

"Yet you can still manage to break my heart again and again."

Jo laughed and Tess smiled along with her. Jake Dalton was one of her favorite people. He had been a rock to her after she moved back to Pine Gulch with Scott. Though her husband had a vast team of specialists in Idaho Falls, Jake had always been her first line of defense whenever she needed a medical opinion about something.

He was a good, old-fashioned small-town doctor, willing to make house calls and take worried phone calls at all hours of the day and night and treat all his patients like family.

She had been thrilled four years earlier when he married Maggie Cruz, a nurse practitioner who often volunteered with hospice. She now considered both of them among her dearest friends.

"This is all a lot of nonsense for nothing," Jo insisted. "I was a little overexcited when Brant arrived, that's all."

Jake said nothing, only examined her chart carefully. He asked Jo several questions about her pain level and whether she had passed out any other times she had neglected to tell them all about.

When he was finished, he smoothed a gentle hand over her hair. "I'm going to make a few changes in your meds. Why don't you get some rest and I'll explain what I want to do with Tess, okay?"

Tess knew it was an indication of Jo's weakened condition that she didn't argue, only nodded and closed her eyes.

Jake led the way out into the hall where the others waited. He closed the door behind him and headed for the kitchen, which Tess had learned long ago was really Command Central of Winder Ranch.

"What's happening?" Easton was the first to speak.

Jake's mouth tightened and his eyes looked bleak. "Her organs are starting to shut down. I'm sorry."

Even though Tess had been expecting it for days now, she was still saddened by the stark diagnosis.

"Which means what?" Brant asked. He looked very much the quintessential soldier with his close-cropped brown hair, strong jaw and sheer physical presence.

"It won't be long now," Jake said. "A couple of days, maybe."

Easton let out a long breath that wasn't quite a sob but probably would have been if she had allowed it.

Tess reached out and gripped her hand and Easton clutched her fingers tightly.

"I think it's time to think about round-the-clock nursing," Jake said. "I'm thinking more of her comfort and, to be honest, yours as well."

"Of course," Quinn said. "Absolutely. Whatever she needs."

Tess's chest ached at his unhesitating devotion to Jo.

Dr. Dalton nodded his approval. "I'll talk to hospice and see what they can provide."

Tess knew what the answer would be. Hospice was overburdened right now. She knew the agency didn't have the resources for that level of care.

"I'll do it. If you'll let me."

"You?" Brant asked, and she gave an inward flinch at the shock in his voice. Here was yet another person who only saw her as the silly girl she had been and she wondered if she would ever be able to escape her past.

"Right now the agency is understaffed," she answered. "I know they don't have the resources to have someone here all the time, as much as they would like to. They're going to recommend hospitalization in Idaho Falls for her last few days."

"She so wants to be here." Easton's voice trembled on the words.

"Barring that, they're going to tell you you'll have to hire a private nurse. I'd like to be that private nurse. I won't let you pay me but I want to do this for Jo. I'll make arrangements for the others to cover all my shifts and stay here, if that's acceptable to you all."

Tess refused to look at Quinn as she made the offer, though she could feel the heat of his gaze on her.

Part of her wondered at the insanity of offering to put herself in even closer proximity with him, but she knew he would be far too preoccupied to spend an instant thinking about a few regrettable moments of shared passion.

"I think it's a wonderful idea, if you're sure you're up to it," Brant said, surprising her. "Quinn and Easton both tell me you're the best of her nurses."

"Are you sure?" Easton asked with a searching look.

"Absolutely. Let me do this for her and for you," she said to her friend.

"What do you think?" Easton turned to Quinn, and Tess finally risked a glance in his direction. She found him watching the scene with an unreadable expression in his silver-blue eyes.

"It seems a good solution if Tess is willing. Better than bringing in some stranger. But we *will* pay you."

She didn't argue with him, though she determined she would donate anything the family insisted on back to hospice, which had been one of Jo's favorite charities even before she had need of their services.

"I'll need a little time to make all the arrangements but I should be back in a few hours," she said.

"Thank you." Easton squeezed her fingers. "I don't know how we'll ever repay you."

"I'll see you in a few hours."

She said goodbye to Dr. Dalton and headed for the door. To her shock, Quinn followed her.

"I'll walk you out," he said gruffly, and her mind instantly filled with images from the last time he had walked her outside, when they had given into the intimacy of the night and the heat simmering between them.

She wanted to tell him she didn't need any more of his escorts, thanks very much, but she didn't want to remind him of those few moments.

"Why?" Quinn asked when they were outside.

She didn't need to ask what he meant. "I love her," she said simply.

His gaze narrowed and she could tell he wasn't convinced.

"Have you done this before? Round-the-clock nursing?"

She arched an eyebrow. "You mean besides the six years I cared for my husband?"

"I keep forgetting that."

She sighed, knowing he was only concerned for his foster mother. "I won't lie to you, it's always difficult at the end. The work is demanding and the emotional toll can be great. But if I can bring Jo a little bit of comfort and peace, I don't care about that."

"I don't get you," he muttered.

"I'm not that complicated."

He made a rough sound of disbelief low in his throat. He looked as if he wanted to say more but he finally just shook his head and opened the car door for her.

Two hours later, Tess set her small suitcase down in the guest room on the first floor, right next door to Jo's sickroom.

"This should work out fine," she said to Easton. It was a lovely room, one she hadn't seen before, filled with antiques and decorated in sage and pale peach.

She found it restful and calm and inherently feminine, with the lacy counterpane on the bed and the scrollwork on the bed frame and the light pine dresser.

Where did the others sleep? she wondered. Her insides trembled a little at the thought of Quinn somewhere in the house.

Why did sharing a house with him feel so different, so much more intimate, than all those other days when she had come in and out at various hours to care for Jo?

"I hope I'm not kicking someone else out of a bed."

"Not at all." Easton smiled, though she wore the shadow of her grief like a black lace veil. "No worries. We've got room to spare. There are plenty of beds in this place, plus the bunkhouse and the foreman's house, which are empty right now since my foreman has his own place down the canyon."

"That's where you were raised, wasn't it? The foreman's house?"

Easton nodded. "Until I was sixteen, when my parents were killed in a car accident and I moved here with Aunt Jo and Uncle Guff. The boys were all gone by then and it was only me."

"You must have missed them."

Easton smiled as she settled on the bed, wrapping her arms around her knees. "The house always seemed too empty without them. I adored them and missed them like crazy. Even though I was so much younger—Quinn was five years older, Brant four and Cisco three—they were always kind to me. I still don't know why but they never seemed to mind me tagging along. Three instant older cousins who felt more like brothers was heady stuff for an only child like me."

"I was always jealous of my friends who had older brothers to look out for them," Tess said.

"I loved it. One time, Quinn found out an older boy at school was teasing me because I had braces and glasses. Roy Hargrove. Did you ever know him? He would have been a couple years younger than you."

"Oh, right. Greasy hair. Big hands."

Easton laughed. "That's the one. He used to call me some terrible names and one day Quinn found me crying about it. To this day, I have no idea what the boys said to him. But not only did Roy stop calling me names, he went out of his way to completely avoid me and always got this scared look in his eyes when he saw me, until his family moved away a few years later."

Easton smiled a little at the memory. "Anyway, there's plenty of room here at the house. Eight bedrooms, counting the two down here."

Tess stared at her friend. "Eight? I've never been upstairs but I had no idea the house was that big!"

"Guff and Jo wanted to fill them all with children but it wasn't to be. Jo was almost forty when they met and married and she'd already had cancer once and had to have a hysterectomy because of it. I think they thought about adopting but they ended up opening the ranch to foster children instead, especially after Quinn came. His mother and Jo were cousins, did you know that? So we're cousins by marriage, somehow."

"I had no idea," she exclaimed.

"Jo and his mother were good friends when they were younger but then they lost track of each other. From what I understand, it took Jo a long time to get custody of him after his parents died."

"How old were you when they moved here?"

"I was almost ten when Quinn came. He would have been fourteen."

Tess remembered him, all rough-edged and full of attitude. He had been dark and gorgeous and dangerous, even back then.

"Brant moved in after Quinn had been here about four months, but you probably already knew him from school."

She knew Brant used to live on a small ranch in the canyon with his family. He had been in her grade and Tess always remembered him as wearing rather raggedy clothes and a few times he had come to school with an arm in a sling or bruises on his arms. Just like

Quinn, Brant Western hadn't been like the other boys, either. He had been solemn and quiet, smart but not pushy about it.

She had been so self-absorbed as a girl that she hadn't known until years later that the Winders had taken Brant away from his abusive home life, though she had noticed around middle school that he started dressing better and seemed more relaxed.

"And then Cisco moved in a few months after Brant." Easton spoke the words briskly and rose from the bed, but not before Tess caught a certain something in her eyes. Tess had noticed it before whenever Easton mentioned the other man's name but she sensed Easton didn't want to discuss it.

"Jo and Guff had other foster children over the years, didn't they?"

"A few here and there but usually only as a temporary stopping point." She shrugged. "I think they would have had more but…after my parents died, I was pretty shattered for a while and I think they were concerned about subdividing their attention among others when I was grieving and needed them."

Her heart squeezed with sympathy for Easton's loss. She couldn't imagine losing both parents at the same time. Her father's death a few years after Scott's accident had been tough enough. She didn't know how she would have survived if her mother had died, too.

"They have always been there for me," Easton said quietly.

Tess instinctively reached out and hugged her friend. Easton returned the embrace for only a moment before she stepped away.

"Thank you again for agreeing to stay." Her voice wobbled only a little. "Let me know if you need anything."

"I will. Right back at you. Even just a shoulder to cry on. I might be here as Jo's nurse but I'm your friend, too."

Easton pulled open the door. "I know. That's why I love you. You're just the kind of person I want to be when I grow up, Tess."

Her laugh was abrupt. "You need to set your sights a little higher than me. Now Jo, that's another story. There's something for both of us to shoot for."

"I think if I tried the rest of my life, I wouldn't be able to measure up to her. She's an original."

Chapter Ten

The entire ranch seemed to be holding its collective breath.

Day-to-day life at the ranch went on as usual. The stock needed to be watered, the human inhabitants needed food and sleep, laundry still piled up.

But everyone was mechanically going through the motions, caught up in the larger human drama taking place in this room.

Forty-eight hours later, Tess sat by the window in Jo's sickroom, her hands busy with the knitting needles she had learned to wield during the long years of caring for Scott. She had made countless baby blankets and afghans during those years, donating most of them to the hospital in Idaho Falls or to the regional pediatric center in Salt Lake City.

Jo coughed, raspy and dry, and Tess set the unfinished blanket aside and rose to lift the water bottle from the side of the bed and hold the straw to Jo's mouth.

Her patient sipped a little, then turned her head away.

"Thank you," she murmured.

"What else can I get you?" Tess asked.

"Cisco. Only Cisco."

Her heart ached for Jo. The woman was in severe

pain, her organs failing, but she clung to life, determined to see her other foster son one more time. Tess wanted desperately to give her that final gift so she could at last say goodbye.

A few moments later, Jo rested back against the pillow and closed her eyes. She didn't open them when Easton pushed open the door.

Tess pressed a finger to her mouth and moved out into the hall.

"I came to relieve you for a few moments. Why don't you go outside and stretch your legs for a while? Go get some fresh air."

She nodded, grateful Easton could spell her for a few moments, though she had no intention of going outside yet. "Thanks. I'll be back in a few moments."

"Take your time. I'm done with the morning chores and have a couple hours."

When Easton closed Jo's door behind her, Tess turned toward the foyer. Instead of going outside, though, she headed up the stairs toward the empty bedroom Quinn had taken over for an office while he was in Pine Gulch.

She approached the open doorway, mortified that her heart was pounding from more than just the fast climb up the stairs.

She heard Quinn's raised voice before she reached the doorway, sounding more heated than she had heard him since that long-ago day she had accused him of cheating.

He sat with his back to the door at a long writing desk near the window. From the angle of the doorway, she could see a laptop in front of him with files strewn across the surface of the desk.

He wore a soft gray shirt with the sleeves rolled up and she could see his strong, muscled forearm flex. His dark hair looked a little tousled, as if he had run his fingers through it recently, which she had learned was his habit.

She wasn't sure which version of the man she found more appealing. The rugged cowboy who had ridden to Windy Lake, his hands sure and confident on the reins and his black Stetson pulled low over his face. The loving, devoted son who sat beside Jo's bedside for long hours, reading to her from the newspaper or the Bible or whatever Jo asked of him.

Or this one, driven and committed, forcing himself to put aside the crisis in his personal life to focus on business and the employees and customers who depended on him.

She gave an inaudible sigh. The truth was, she was drawn to every facet of the dratted man and was more fascinated by him with every passing hour.

Jo. She was here for Jo, she reminded herself.

"Look, whatever it takes," he said into the phone. "I'm tired of this garbage. Find him! I don't care what you have to do!"

After pressing a button on the phone, he threw it onto the desk with such force that she couldn't contain a little gasp.

He turned at the sound and something flared in his eyes, something raw and intense, before he quickly banked it. "What is it? Is she…"

"No. Nothing like that. Was that phone call about Cisco?"

"Supposed to be. But as you can probably tell, I'm

hitting walls everywhere I turn. That was the consulate in El Salvador. He was there a few weeks ago but nobody knows where he is now. I have tried every contact I have and I can't manage to find one expatriate American in Latin America."

She walked into the room, picking her words carefully. "I don't think she's going to be able to hang on until he gets here, though she's trying her best."

"I hate that I can't give her this."

"It's not your fault, Quinn." She curled her fingers to her palm in an effort to fight the impulse to touch his arm in comfort, as she would have done to Easton and even Brant, who, except for those first few moments when he arrived, had treated her with nothing but kindness and respect.

Quinn was different. Somehow she couldn't relax in his company, not with their shared past and the more recent heat that unfurled inside her whenever he was near.

She let out a breath, wishing she could regard him the same as she did everyone else.

"Sometimes you have to accept you've tried your best," she said.

"Have I?" The frustration in his voice reached something deep inside her and this time she couldn't resist the urge to touch his arm.

"What else can you do? You can't go after him."

He looked down at her pale fingers against the darker skin of his arm for a long moment. When he lifted his gaze, she swallowed at the sudden intensity in his silver-blue gaze.

She pulled her hand away and tucked it into the pocket of her scrubs. "When you've done all you can, sometimes you have no choice but to put your problems in God's hands."

His expression turned hard, cynical. "A lovely sentiment. Did that help you sleep at night when you were caring for your husband?"

She drew in a sharp breath then let it out quickly, reminding herself he was responding from a place of pain she was entirely familiar with.

"As a matter of fact, it did," she answered evenly.

"Sorry." He raked a hand through his hair again, messing it further. "That was unnecessarily harsh."

"You want to fix everything. That's understandable. It's what you do, isn't it?"

"Not this time. I can't fix this."

The bleakness in his voice tore at her heart and she couldn't help herself, she rested her fingers on his warm arm again. "I'm sorry. I know how terribly hard this is for you."

He looked anguished and before she quite realized what he was doing, he pulled her into his arms and clung tightly to her. He didn't kiss her, only held her. She froze in shock for just a moment then she wrapped her arms around him and let him draw whatever small comfort she could offer from the physical connection with another person. Sometimes a single quiet embrace could offer more comfort than a hundred condolences, she knew.

They stood for several moments in silence with his arms around her, his breath a whisper against her hair. Something sweet and intangible—and even tender— passed between them. She was afraid to move or even breathe for fear of ruining this moment, this chance to provide him a small measure of peace.

All too soon, he exhaled a long breath and dropped his arms, moving away a little, and she felt curiously bereft.

He looked astonished and more than a little embarrassed.

"I... Sorry. I don't know what that was about. Sorry."

She smiled gently. "You're doing your best," she repeated. "Jo understands that."

He opened his mouth to answer but before he could, Brant's voice sounded from downstairs, loud and irate.

"It's about damn time you showed up."

Tess blinked. In her limited experience, the officer was invariably patient with everyone, a sea of calm in the emotional tumult of Winder Ranch. She had never heard that sort of harshness from him.

In response, she heard another man's voice, one she didn't recognize.

"I'm not too late, am I?"

Quinn's expression reflected her own shock as both of them realized Francisco Del Norte had at last arrived.

Quinn took the stairs two at a time. She followed with the same urgency, a little concerned the men might come to blows—at least judging by Brant's anger and that hot expression in Quinn's eyes as he had rushed past her.

In the foyer, she found Brant and Quinn facing off against a hard-eyed, rough-looking Latino who bore little resemblance to the laughing, mischievous boy she remembered from school.

"Where the hell have you been?" Quinn snapped.

Fatigue clouded the other man's dark eyes. Tess wasn't sure she had ever seen anyone look so completely exhausted.

"Long story. I could tell you, but you know the drill. Then I'd have to kill you and I'm too damn tired right now to take on both your sorry asses at the same time."

The three men eyed each other for another moment and Tess held her breath, wondering if she ought to step in. Then, as if by some unspoken signal, they all moved together and gave that shoulder-slap thing men did instead of hugging.

"Tell me I'm not too late." Cisco's voice was taut with anguish.

"Not yet. But she's barely hanging on, man. She was just waiting to say goodbye to you."

Tears filled Cisco's eyes as he uttered a quick prayer of gratitude in Spanish.

She was inclined to dislike the man for the worry he had put everyone through these past few days and for Jo's heartache. But she couldn't help feeling compassion for the undisguised sorrow in his eyes.

"They didn't... I didn't get the message until three days ago. I was in the middle of something big and it took me a while to squeeze my way out."

Brant and Quinn didn't look appeased by the explanation but they didn't seem inclined to push him either.

"Can I see her?"

Both Brant and Quinn turned to look at Tess, still standing on the stairs, as if she was Jo's guardian and gatekeeper.

"Easton's in with her. I'll go see if she's awake."

She turned away, but not before she caught an odd

expression flicker across his features at the mention of Easton's name.

She left the three men and walked down the hall to Jo's bedroom. When she carefully eased open the door, emotions clogged her throat at the scene she found inside.

Easton was the one asleep now, with her head resting on the bed beside her aunt. Jo's frail, gnarled hand rested on her niece's hair.

Jo pressed a finger to her mouth. Though she tried to shake her head, she was so weak she barely moved against the pillow.

"It's not time for more meds, is it?" she murmured, her voice thready.

Though Tess could barely hear the woman's whisper, Easton still opened her eyes and jerked her head up.

"Sorry. I must have just dozed off."

Jo smiled. "Just a few minutes ago, dear. Not long enough."

"It's not time for meds," Tess answered her. "I was only checking to see if you were awake and up for a visitor."

Though she thought she spoke calmly enough, some clue in her demeanor must have alerted them something had happened. Both women looked at her carefully.

"What is it?" Easton asked.

Before she could answer, she heard a noise in the doorway and knew without turning around that Cisco had followed her.

Easton's features paled and she scrambled to her feet. Tess registered her reaction for only an instant, then she was completely disarmed when the hard, dangerous-looking man hurried to Jo's bedside, his eyes still wet with emotion.

The joy in Jo's features was breathtakingly beautiful as she reached a hand to caress his cheek. "You're here. Oh, my dear boy, you're here at last."

Quinn and Brant followed Cisco into the room. Tess watched their reunion for a moment, then she quietly slipped from the room to give them the time and space they needed together.

Chapter Eleven

The woman Quinn loved as a mother took her last breath twelve hours after Cisco Del Norte returned to Winder Ranch.

With all four of them around her bedside and Tess standing watchfully on the edge of the room, Jo succumbed to the ravages cancer had wrought on her frail body.

Quinn had had plenty of time to prepare. He had known weeks ago her condition was terminal and he had been at the ranch for nearly ten days to spend these last days with her and watch her inexorable decline.

He had known it was coming. That didn't make it any easier to watch her draw one ragged breath into her lungs, let it out with a sigh and then nothing more.

Beside him, Easton exhaled a soft, choked sob. He wrapped an arm around her shoulder and pulled her close, aware that Cisco, on her other side, had made the same move but had checked it when Quinn reached her first.

"I'll call Dr. Dalton and let him know," Tess murmured after a few moments of leaving them to their shared sorrow.

He met her gaze, deeply grateful for her quiet calm. "Thank you."

She held his gaze for a moment, her own filled with an echo of his grief, then she smiled. "You're welcome."

He had fully expected the loss, this vast chasm of pain. But he hadn't anticipated the odd sense of peace that seemed to have settled over all of them to know Jo's suffering was finally over.

A big part of that was due to Tess and her steady, unexpected strength, he admitted over the next hour as they worked with the doctor and the funeral home to make arrangements.

She seemed to know exactly what to say, what to do, and he was grateful to turn these final responsibilities over to her.

If he found comfort in anything right now, it was in the knowledge that Jo had spent her last days surrounded by those she loved and by the tender care Tess had provided.

He couldn't help remembering that embrace with Tess upstairs in his office. Those few moments with her arms around him and her cheek resting against his chest had been the most peaceful he had known since he arrived at the ranch.

He had found them profoundly moving, for reasons he couldn't explain, anymore than he could explain how the person he thought he despised most in the world ended up being the one he turned to in his greatest need.

He was lousy at doing nothing.

The evening after Jo's funeral, Quinn sat at the kitchen table at the ranch with a heaping plate of leftovers in front of him and an aching restlessness twisting through him.

The past three days since Jo's death had been a blur of condolence visits from neighbors, of making plans with Southerland Shipping for the corporate jet to return for him by the end of the week, of seeing to the few details Jo hadn't covered in the very specific funeral arrangements she made before her death.

Most of those details fell on his shoulders by default, simply because nobody else was around much.

He might have expected them to all come together in their shared grief but each of Jo's Four Winds seemed to be dealing with her death in a unique way.

Easton took refuge out on the ranch, with her horses and her cattle and hard, punishing work. Brant had left the night Jo died for his own ranch, a mile or so up the canyon and had only been back a few times and for the funeral earlier. Cisco slept for a full thirty-six hours as if it had been months since he closed his eyes. As soon as the funeral was over earlier that day, he had taken one of the ranch horses and a bedroll and said he needed to sleep under the stars.

As for Quinn, he focused on what work he could do long-distance and on these last few details for Jo. Staying busy helped push the pain away a little.

He sipped at his beer as the old house creaked and settled around him and the furnace kicked in with a low whoosh against the late October cold. Forlorn sounds, he thought. Lonely, even.

Maybe Cisco had the right idea. Maybe he ought to just get the hell out of Dodge, grab one of the horses and ride hard and fast into the mountains.

The thought did have a certain appeal.

Or maybe he ought to just call his pilot and move up his departure. He could be home by midnight.

What would be the difference between sitting alone at his house in Seattle or sitting alone here at Winder Ranch? This aching emptiness would follow him everywhere for a while, he was afraid, until that inevitable day when the loss would begin to fade a little.

Hovering on the edge of his mind was the awareness that once he left Winder Ranch this time, he would have very few reasons to return. With Jo and Guff gone, his anchor to the place had been lifted.

Easton would always be here. He could still come back to visit her, but with Brant in the military and Cisco off doing whatever mysterious things occupied his time, nothing would ever be the same.

The Four Winds would be scattered once more.

Jo had been their true north, their center. Without her, a chapter in his life was ending and the realization left him more than a little bereft.

He rose suddenly as that restlessness sharpened, intensified. He couldn't just sit here. He didn't really feel like spending the night on the hard ground, but at least he could take one of the horses out for a hard moonlit ride to work off some of this energy.

The thought inevitably touched off memories of the other ride he had taken into the mountains just days ago—and of the woman he had been doing his best not to think about for the past few days.

Tess had packed up all the medical equipment in Jo's room and had left the ranch the night Jo died. He had seen her briefly at the funeral, a slim, lovely presence in a bright yellow dress amid all the traditionally dark mourning clothes. Jo would have approved, he remembered thinking. She would have wanted bright colors and light and sunshine at her funeral. He only wished he'd been the one to think of it and had put on a vibrant tie instead of the muted, conservative one he had worn with his suit.

To his regret, Tess had slipped away from the service before he had a chance to talk to her. Now he found himself remembering again those stunning few moments they had shared upstairs in his office bedroom, when she had simply held him, offering whatever solace he could draw from her calm embrace.

He missed her.

Quinn let out a breath. Several times over the past days, as he dealt with details, he had found himself wanting to turn to her for her unique perspective on something, for some of her no-nonsense advice, or just to see her smile at some absurdity.

Ridiculous. How had she become so important to him in just a matter of days? It was only the stress of the circumstances, he assured himself.

But right now as he stood in the Winder Ranch kitchen with this emptiness yawning inside him, he had a desperate ache to see her again.

She would know just the right thing to say to ease his spirit. Somehow he knew it.

If he just showed up on her doorstep for no reason, she would probably think he was an idiot. He couldn't say he only wanted her to hold him again, to ease the restlessness of his spirit.

His gaze fell on a hook by the door and fate smiled

on him when he recognized her jacket hanging next to his own denim ranch coat. He had noticed it the day before and remembered her wearing it a few nights when she had come to the ranch, before she moved into the spare room, but he had forgotten about it until just this moment.

If he gave it a moment's thought, he knew he would talk himself out of seeing her while his heart was still raw and aching.

So he decided not to think about it.

He shrugged into his own jacket, then grabbed hers off the hook by the door and headed into the night.

The nature of hospice work meant she had to face death on a fairly consistent basis but it never grew any easier—and some losses hit much harder than others.

Tess had learned early, though, that it was best to throw herself into a project, preferably something physical and demanding, while the pain was still raw and fresh. When she could exhaust her body as much as her spirit, she had half a chance of sleeping at night without dreams, tangled-up nightmares of all those she had loved and lost.

The evening of Jo's funeral, she stood on a stepladder in the room that once had been Scott's, scraping layers of paint off the wide wooden molding that encircled the high ceiling of the room.

Stripping the trim in this room down and refinishing the natural wood had always been in her plans when she bought the house after Scott's accident but she had never gotten around to it, too busy with his day-to-day care.

She supposed it was ironic that she was only getting

around to doing the work she wanted on the room now that the house was for sale. She ought to leave the re-decorating for the new owners to apply their own tastes, but it seemed the perfect project to keep her mind and body occupied as best she could.

The muscles of her arms ached from reaching above her head but that didn't stop her from scraping in rhythm to the loud honky-tonk music coming from her iPod dock in the corner of the empty room.

She was singing along about a two-timin' man so loudly she nearly missed the low musical chime of her doorbell over the wails.

Though she wasn't at all in the mood to talk to any-one, she used any excuse to drop her arms to give her aching muscles a rest.

She thought about ignoring the doorbell, certain it must be her mother dropping by to check on her. She knew Maura was concerned that Jo's death would hit her hard and she wasn't sure she was in the mood to deal with her maternal worry.

Her mother would have seen the lights and her car in the driveway and Tess knew she would just keep stub-bornly ringing the bell until her daughter answered.

She sighed and stepped down from the ladder.

"Coming," she called out. "Hang on."

She took a second before she pulled open the door to tuck in a stray curl slipping from the folded bandanna that held her unruly hair away from her face while she worked.

"Sorry, I was up on the ladder and it took me a min-ute…"

Her voice trailed off and she stared in shock. That

definitely wasn't her mother standing on her small porch. Her heart picked up a beat.

"Quinn! Hello."

"Hi. May I come in?" he prompted, when she continued to stare at him, baffled as to why he might be standing on her doorstep.

"Oh. Of course."

She stepped back to allow him inside, fervently wishing she was wearing something a little more presentable than her scruffiest pair of jeans and the disreputable faded cropped T-shirt she used for gardening.

"Were you expecting someone else?"

"I thought you might be my mother. She still lives in town, though my father died a few years back. He had a heart attack on the golf course. Shocked us all. Friends have tried to talk my mother into moving somewhere warmer but she claims she likes it here. I think she's really been sticking around to keep an eye on me. Maybe she'll finally move south when I take off for Portland."

She clamped her mouth shut when she realized she was babbling, something she rarely did. She also registered the rowdy music coming from down the hall.

"Sorry. Let me grab that music."

She hurried back to the bedroom and turned off the iPod, then returned to her living room, where she saw him looking at the picture frames clustered across the top of her upright piano.

He looked gorgeous, she thought, in a Stetson and a denim jacket that made him look masculine and rough.

Her insides did a long, slow roll but she quickly pushed back her reaction, especially when she saw the slightly lost expression in his eyes.

"I'm sorry," she said. "I was stripping paint off the wall trim in my spare bedroom. I...needed the distraction. What can I do for you?"

He held out his arm, along with something folded and blue. "You left your coat at the ranch. I thought you might need it."

She took it from him and didn't miss the tiny flicker of static that jumped from his skin to hers. Something just as electric sparked in his eyes at the touch.

"You didn't need to drive all the way into town to return it. I could have picked it up from Easton some other time."

He shrugged. "I guess you're not the only one who needed a distraction. Everybody else took off tonight in different directions and I just didn't feel like hanging around the ranch by myself."

He didn't look at her when he spoke, but she recognized the edgy restlessness in his silver-blue eyes. She wanted to reach out to him, as she might have done with anyone else, but she didn't trust herself around him and she didn't know if he would welcome her touch. Though he had that day at the ranch, she remembered.

"How are you at scraping paint?" she asked on impulse, then wanted to yank the words back when she realized the absurdity of putting him to work in her spare room just hours after his foster mother's funeral.

He didn't look upset by the question. "I've scraped the Winder Ranch barn and outbuildings in my day but never done room trim. Is this any different?"

"Harder," she said frankly. "This house has been through ten owners in its seventy-five years of existence and I swear every single one of them except me has left three or four layers of paint. It's sweaty, hard, frustrating work."

"In that case, bring it on."

She laughed and shook her head. "You don't know what you're getting into, but if you're sure you're willing to help, I would welcome the company."

It wasn't a lie, she thought as she led him back to the bedroom after he left his jacket and hat on the living-room couch. She had to admit she was grateful to have someone to talk to and for one last opportunity to see him again before he left Pine Gulch.

"You don't really have to do this," she said when they reached the room. "You're welcome to stay, even if you don't want to work."

Odd how what she had always considered a good-size space seemed to shrink in an instant. She could smell him, sexy and masculine, and she wished again that she wasn't dressed in work clothes.

"Where can I start?"

"I was up on the ladder working on the ceiling trim. If you would like to start around the windows, that would be great."

"Deal."

He rolled up the sleeves of his shirt that looked expensive and tailored—not that she knew much about men's clothes—and grabbed a paint scraper. Without another word, he set immediately to work.

Tess watched him for a moment, then turned the music on again, switching to a little more mellow music.

For a long time, they worked without speaking. She didn't find the silence awkward in the slightest, merely contemplative on both their parts.

Quinn seemed just as content not to make aimless conversation and though she was intensely aware of him on the other side of the room, she wasn't sure he even remembered she was in the room until eight or nine songs into the playlist.

"My father killed my mother when I was thirteen years old."

He said the abrupt words almost dispassionately but she heard the echo of a deep, vast pain in his voice.

She set down her scraper, her heart aching for him even as she held her breath that he felt he could share something so painful with her now, out of the blue like this.

"Oh, Quinn. I'm so sorry."

He released a long, slow breath, like air escaping from a leaky valve, and she wondered how long he had kept the memories bottled deep inside him.

"It happened twenty years ago but every moment of that night is as clear in my mind as the ride we took to Windy Lake last week. Clearer, even."

She climbed down the ladder. "You were there?"

He continued moving the scraper across the wood and tiny multicolored flakes of paint fluttered to the floor. "I was there. But I couldn't stop it."

She leaned against the wall beside him, hesitant to say the wrong word that might make him regret sharing this part of his past with her.

"What happened?" she murmured, sensing he needed to share it. Perhaps this was all part of his grieving process for Jo, the woman who had taken him in and helped him heal from his ugly, painful past.

"They were fighting, as usual. My parents' marriage

was…difficult. My father was an attorney who worked long hours. When he returned home, he always insisted on a three-course dinner on the table, no matter what hour of the day or night, and he wanted the house completely spotless."

"That must have been hard for a young boy."

"I guess I was lucky. He didn't take his bad moods out on me. Only on her."

She held her breath, waiting for the rest.

"Their fighting woke me up," Quinn said after a moment, "and I heard my dad start to get a little rough. Also usual. I went down to stop it. That didn't always work but sometimes a little diversion did the trick. Not this time."

He scraped harder and she wanted to urge him to spare himself the anguish of retelling the story, but again, she had that odd sense that he needed to share this, for reasons she didn't understand.

"My dad was in a rage, accusing her of sleeping with one of the other attorneys in his firm."

"Was she?"

He shrugged. "I don't know. Maybe. My father was a bastard but she seemed to delight in finding and hitting every one of his hot buttons. She laughed at him. I'll never forget the sound of her laughing, with her face still bruised and red where he had slapped her. She said she was having a torrid affair with the other man, that he was much better in bed than my father."

She drew in a sharp breath, hating the thought of a thirteen-year-old version of Quinn witnessing such ugliness between his parents.

"I don't know," he went on. "She might have been

lying. Theirs was not a healthy relationship, in any sense of the word. He needed to be in control of everything and she needed to be constantly adored."

She thought of Quinn being caught in the middle of it all and her chest ached for him and she had to curl her fingers into her palms to keep from reaching for him.

"My father said he wasn't going to let her make a fool out of him any longer. He walked out of the room and I thought for sure he was going to pack a suitcase and leave. I was happy, you know. For those few moments, I was thinking how much better things would be without him. No more yelling, no more fights."

"But he didn't leave."

He gave a rough laugh and set the scraper down and sat beside her on the floor, his back against the wall and their elbows touching. "He didn't leave. He came out of the bedroom with the .38 he kept locked in a box by the side of his bed. He shot her three times. Twice in the heart and then once more in the head. And then he turned the gun on himself."

"Oh, dear God."

"I couldn't stop it. For a long time, I kept asking myself if I could have done something. Said something. I just stood there."

She couldn't help herself, she covered his hand with hers. After a long moment, he turned his hand and twisted his fingers with hers, holding tight. They sat that way, shoulders brushing while the music on her playlist shifted to a slow, jazzy ballad.

She kept envisioning that rough-edged, angry boy he had been when he first came to Pine Gulch. He must have been consumed with pain and guilt over his parents' murder-suicide. She could see it so clearly, just as she saw in grim detail her own awful behavior toward him, simply because he had refused to pay any attention to her.

"I am so, so sorry, Quinn," she murmured, for everything he had survived and for her own part in making life harder for him here.

"The first year after was…hellish," he said, his voice low. "That's the only word that fits. I was thrown into the foster-care system and spent several months bouncing from placement to placement."

"None of them stuck?"

"I wasn't an easy kid to love," he said. "You knew me when I first came to Pine Gulch. I was angry and hurting and hated the world. Jo and Guff saw past all that. They saw whatever tiny spark of good might still be buried deep inside me and didn't stop until they helped me see it, too."

"I'm so happy you found each other."

"Same here." He paused, looking a little baffled. "I don't know why I'm telling you this. I didn't come here to dump it all on you. The truth is, I don't talk about it much. I don't think I've ever shared it with anybody but Brant and Cisco and Easton."

"It's natural to think about the circumstances that brought you into Jo's world. I imagine it's all connected for you."

"I was on a path to nowhere when Jo finally found me up in Boise and petitioned for custody. I was only the kid of a cousin. I'd never even met her but she and Guff still took me on, with all that baggage. She was a hell of a woman."

"I'm going to miss her dearly," Tess said quietly. "But I keep trying to focus on how much better a person I am because I knew her."

Their hands were still entwined between them and she could feel the heat of his skin and the hard strength of his fingers.

"I don't know what to make of you," he finally said.

She gave a small laugh. "Why's that?"

"You baffle me. I don't know which version of you is real."

"All of it. I'm like every other woman. A mass of contradictions, most of which I don't even understand myself. Sometimes I'm a saint, sometimes I'm a bitch. Sometimes I'm the life of the party, sometimes I just want everybody to leave me alone. But mostly, I'm just a woman."

"That part I get."

The low timbre of his voice and the sudden light in his eyes sent a shower of sparks arcing through her. She was suddenly intensely aware of him—the breadth of his shoulder nudging hers, the glitter of silvery blue eyes watching her, the scent of him, of sage and bergamot and something else that was indefinable.

Her insides quivered and her pulse seemed to accelerate. "I don't regret many things in my life," she said, her voice breathy and low. "But I wish I could go back and change the way I treated you when we were younger. I hate that I gave you even a moment's unhappiness when you had already been through so much with your parents."

His shoulder shrugged beside her. "It was a long time

ago, Tess. In the grand scheme of life, it didn't really mean anything."

"I was so awful to you."

"I wasn't exactly an easy person to like."

"That wasn't the problem. The opposite, actually. I…liked you too much," she confessed. "I hated that you thought I was some silly, brainless cheerleader. I wanted desperately for you to notice me."

His mouth quirked a little. "How could I help it?"

"You mean, when I was getting you kicked off the baseball team for cheating and then lying to my boyfriend and telling him you did something I only *wanted* you to do?"

"That's why Scott and his buddies beat me up that night? I had no idea."

"I'm so sorry, Quinn. I was despicable to you."

"Why?" he asked. "I still don't quite understand what I ever did to turn your wrath against me."

She sighed. "Every girl in school had a crush on you, but for me, it went way past crush. I didn't know your story but I could tell you were in pain. Maybe that's why you fascinated me, more than anyone I had ever known in my sheltered little life. I guess I was something of a healer, even then."

He gazed at her as the music shifted again, something low and sultry.

"I was fiercely attracted to you," she finally admitted. "But you made it clear you weren't interested. My pride was hurt. But I have to say, I think my heart was a little bruised, too. And so I turned mean. I wanted you to hurt, too. It was terrible and small of me and I'm so, so sorry."

"It was a long time ago," he said again. "We're both different people."

She smiled a little, her pulse pounding loudly in her ears. "Not so different," she murmured, still holding his hand. "I'm still fiercely attracted to you."

Chapter Twelve

Her breath snagged in her throat as she waited for him to break the sudden silence between them that seemed to drag on forever, though it was probably only several endless, excruciating seconds.

She braced herself, not sure she could survive another rejection. Nerves shivered through her as she waited for him to move, to speak, to do *anything*.

Just when she thought she couldn't endure the uncertainty another moment and was about to scramble away and tell him to ignore every single thing she had just said, he groaned her name and then his mouth captured hers in a wild kiss.

At that first stunning brush of his lips, the slick texture of his mouth, heat exploded between them like an August lightning storm on dry tinder. She returned his kiss, pouring everything into her response—her regret for the hurt she had caused him, her compassion for his loss, the soft tenderness blooming inside her.

And especially this urgent attraction pulsing to every corner of her body with each beat of her heart.

This was right. Inevitable, even. From the moment she heard him ring the doorbell earlier, some part of her had known they would end up here, with his arms around her and his heartbeat strong and steady under her fingers.

She wanted to help him, to heal him. To soak his pain inside her and ease his heart, if only for a moment.

She wrapped her arms more tightly around his neck, relishing the contrast between her curves and his immovable strength, between the cool wall at her back and all the glorious heat of his arms.

"While we're apologizing," he murmured against her mouth, "I'm sorry I was such an idiot the last time I kissed you. I don't have any excuse, other than fear."

She blinked at him, wondering why she had never noticed those dark blue speckles in his eyes. "Of what?"

"This. You." His mouth danced across hers again and everything feminine inside her sighed with delight.

"I want you." His voice was little more than a low rasp that sent every nerve ending firing madly. "I want you more than I've ever wanted another woman in my life and it scares the hell out of me."

"I'm just a woman. What's to be scared about?"

He laughed roughly. "That's like a saber-toothed tiger saying I'm just a nice little kitty. You are no ordinary woman, Tess."

Before she could figure out whether he meant the words as a compliment, he deepened the kiss and she decided she didn't care, as long as he continued this delicious assault on her senses.

He lowered her to the floor and she held him tightly as all the sleepy desires she had buried deep inside for years bubbled to the surface. It had been so long—so very, very long—since she had been held and cherished like this and she wanted to savor every second.

The taste of him, the scent of him, the implacable strength of his arms around her. It all felt perfect. *He* felt perfect.

She supposed that was silly, given the slightly unromantic circumstances. Instead of candlelight and rose petals and soft pillows, they were on the hard floor of her spare room with bright fluorescent lights gleaming.

But she wouldn't have changed any of it, especially at the risk of shattering this hazy, delicious cocoon of desire wrapped around them.

Okay, she might wish she were wearing something a little more sensual, especially when his hands went to the buttons of her old work shirt. But he didn't seem to mind her clothing, judging by the heavy-lidded hunger in his eyes after he had worked the buttons free and the plackets of her shirt fell away.

She should have felt exposed here in the unforgiving light of the room. Instead, she felt feminine and eminently desirable as his eyes darkened.

"You're gorgeous," he murmured. "The most beautiful thing I've ever seen."

"I'm afraid I'm not the tight-bodied cheerleader I was at sixteen."

"Who wants some silly cheerleader when he could have a saber-toothed tiger of a woman in his arms?"

She laughed but it turned into a ragged gasp when he slowly caressed her through the fabric of her bra, his fingers hard and masculine against her breast.

He groaned, low in his throat, and his thumb deftly traced the skin just above the lacy cup. Everything tightened inside her, a lovely swell of tension as he worked the clasp free, and she nearly arched off the floor when his fingers covered her skin.

He teased and explored her body while his mouth tantalized hers with deep, silky tastes and her hands explored the hard muscles of his back and the thick softness of his hair.

"This is crazy," he said after long, delirious moments. "It's not what I came here for, I swear."

"Don't think about it," she advised him, nipping little kisses down the warm column of his neck. "I know I'm not."

His laugh turned into a groan as she feathered more kisses along his jawline. "Well, when you put it that way…"

She smiled, then gasped when he began trailing kisses down the side of her throat. Every coherent thought skittered out of her head when his mouth found her breast. She tangled her hands in his hair, arching into his mouth as he tasted and teased.

Oh, heaven. She felt as if she had been waiting years just for this, just for him, as if everything inside her had been frozen away until he came back to Pine Gulch to thaw all those lonely, forgotten little corners of her heart.

She thought again how very perfect, inevitable, this was as he pulled her shirt off and then removed his own.

He was beautiful. The rough-edged, rebellious boy had grown into a hard, dangerous man, all powerful muscles and masculine hollows and strength. She wanted to explore every single inch of that smooth skin.

She would, she vowed. Even if it took all night. Or

several nights. It was a sacrifice she was fully willing to make.

Again she had that sense of inescapable destiny. They had been moving toward this moment since that first night he had startled her in the hallway of Winder Ranch. Longer, even. Maybe all that dancing around each other they had done in high school had just been a prelude to this.

A few moments later, no clothing barriers remained between them and she exulted in the sheer delicious wonder of his skin brushing hers, his strength surrounding her softness.

He kissed her and a restless need started deep inside her and expanded out in hot, hungry waves. She couldn't get enough of this, of him. She traced a hand over his pectoral muscles, feeling the leashed strength in him.

And then she forgot everything when he reached a hand between their bodies to the aching core of her hunger. She gasped his name, shifting restlessly against his fingers, and everything inside her coiled with a sweet, urgent ache of anticipation.

She felt edgy, panicky suddenly, as if the room were spinning too fast for her to ride along, but his kiss kept her centered in the midst of the tornado of sensation. She wrapped her arms around his neck, her breathing ragged.

He kissed her then, his mouth hot, insistent, demanding. That was all it took. With a sharp cry, she let go of what tiny tendrils of control remained and flung herself into the whirling, breathtaking maelstrom.

Even before the last delicious tremors had faded,

he produced a condom from his wallet and entered her with one swift movement.

Long unused muscles stretched to welcome him and he groaned, pressing his forehead to hers.

"So tight," he murmured.

"I'm sorry."

His laugh was rough and tickled her skin. "I don't believe I was complaining."

He kissed her fiercely, possessively, and just like that, she could feel her body rise to meet his again.

With her hands gripped tightly in his, he moved inside her and she arched restlessly against him, her body seeking more, burning for completion. And then she could sense a change in him, feel the taut edginess in every touch. Her mouth tangled with his and at the slick brush of his tongue against hers, she climaxed again, with a core-deep sigh of delight.

He froze above her, his muscles corded, and then he groaned and joined her in the storm.

He came back to earth with a powerful sense of the surreal. None of this seemed to be truly happening. Not the hard floor beneath his shoulders or the soft, warm curves in his arms or this unaccustomed contentment stealing through him.

It was definitely genuine, though. He could feel her pulse against his arm where her head lay nestled and smell that delectable scent of her.

"How could I have forgotten?" she murmured.

He angled his head to better see her expression. "Forgotten what?"

She smiled and he was struck again by her breathtaking beauty. She was like some rare, exquisite flower that bloomed in secret just for him.

"This radiant feeling. Total contentment. As if for a few short moments, everything is perfect in the world."

He smiled, enchanted by her. "You don't think everything would be a tad more perfect if we happened to be in a soft bed somewhere instead of on the bare floor of your ripped-apart spare room? I think I've got paint chips in places I'm not sure I should mention."

She made a face, though he saw laughter dancing in her eyes. "Go ahead. Ruin the moment for me."

"Sorry. It's just been a long time since I've been so… carried away."

"I know exactly what you mean."

He studied her. "How long?"

Her lovely green-eyed gaze met his, then flickered away. "Since the night before Scott's accident. So that would be eight years, if anyone's counting."

"In all that time, not once?"

As soon as his shocked words escaped, he realized they weren't very tactful, but she didn't seem offended.

"I loved my husband," she said solemnly. "Even if he wasn't quite the man I expected to spend the rest of my life with when I married him, I loved him and I honored my wedding vows."

He pulled her closer, stunned at her loyalty and devotion. She had put her life, her future, completely on hold for years to care for a man who could never be the sort of husband a young woman needed.

Most women he knew would have felt perfectly justified in resuming their own lives after such a tragic accident. They might have mourned their husband for a while but would have been quick to put the past behind them.

He thought of his own mother, selfish and feckless, who wasn't happy unless she was the center of attention. She wouldn't have had the first idea how to cope after such a tragedy.

Not Tess. She had stayed, had sacrificed her youth for her husband.

"Scott was an incredibly fortunate man to have you."

Her eyes softened. "Thank you, Quinn." She kissed him gently, her mouth warm and soft, and he was astonished at the fragile tenderness that fluttered through him like dry leaves on the autumn wind.

"Can I stay?" he asked. "It's…harder than I expected to hang out at the ranch right now."

She smiled against his mouth and her kiss left no question in his mind about what her answer would be.

"Of course. I would love you to stay. And I even have a bed in the other room, believe it or not."

He rose and pulled her to her feet, stunned all over again at the peace welling inside him. He didn't think he had come here for this on a conscious level, but perhaps some part of him knew she would welcome him, would soothe the ache in his heart with that easy nurturing that was such a part of her.

"Show me," he murmured.

Her smile was brilliant and took his breath away as she took him by the hand and led him from the room.

She was having a torrid affair.

Two days later, Tess could hardly believe it, even when the evidence was sprawled beside her, wide shoulders propped against her headboard, looking rugged and masculine against the dainty yellow frills and flowers of her bedroom.

The fluffy comforter on her bed covered him to the waist and she found the contrast between the feminine fabric and the hard planes and hollows of his muscled chest infinitely arousing.

She sighed softly, wondering if she would ever get tired of looking at him, touching him, laughing with him.

For two days, they hadn't left her house, except for sneaking in one quick trip to Winder Ranch in the middle of the night for him to grab some extra clothes and toiletries.

What would the rest of the town think if news spread that the sainted Tess Claybourne was engaged in a wild, torrid relationship with Quinn Southerland, the former bad boy of Pine Gulch?

Enthusiastically engaged, no less. She flushed at the memory of her response to him, of the heat and magic and connection they had shared the past few days. The sensual, passionate woman she had become in his arms seemed like a stranger, as if she had stored up all these feelings and desires inside her through the past eight years.

She didn't know whether to be embarrassed or thrilled that she had discovered this part of herself with him.

"You're blushing," he said now with an interested look. "What are you thinking about?"

"You. This. I was thinking about how I had no idea I could…that we could…"

Her voice trailed off as she struggled with words to finish the sentence. Her own discomfort astounded her. How could she possibly possess even a hint of awkwardness after everything they had done together within these walls, all the secrets they had shared?

He didn't seem to need any explanation.

"You absolutely can. And we absolutely have."

He grinned, looking male and gorgeous and so completely content with the world that she couldn't help laughing.

This was the other thing that shocked her, that she could have such fun with him. He wasn't at all the intense, brooding rebel she had thought when they were younger. Quinn had a sly sense of humor and a keen sense of the ridiculous.

They laughed about everything from a silly horror movie they watched on TV in the middle of the night to the paint flecks in her hair after they made one half-hearted attempt to continue working on the trim in the guest room to a phone call from Easton the day before, wondering if Tess had kidnapped him.

And they had talked, endlessly. About his memories of the other Four Winds, about growing up on the ranch, about her friends and family and the miracle of how she had been led to become a nurse long before Scott's accident when those skills would become so vital.

They had also talked a great deal about his foster mother and also about Guff. He seemed to find great comfort in sharing memories with her. That he would trust her with those memories touched and warmed her, more than she could ever express. She hoped his sorrow eased a little as he brought those events and people to life for her.

"I wish it didn't have to end," she murmured now, then wished she could recall the words.

No regrets, she had promised herself that first night. She intended only to seize every ounce of happiness she could with him and then let him go with a glad heart that she had this chance to share a few wonderful days with him.

He traced a hand along her bare arm. "I wish I could put off my return to Seattle. But I've been away too long as it is. My plane's coming tomorrow."

"I know."

Her smile felt tight, forced, as she fought to hide the sadness hovering just out of reach at his impending departure.

How had he become so very important to her in just a few short weeks? Even the idea of moving to Portland, starting over with new friends and different employment challenges, had lost much of its luster.

Ridiculous, she told herself. She couldn't let herself fall into a funk over the inevitable end of a passionate, albeit brief, affair, even one with the man who had fascinated her for two decades.

"We should do something," he said suddenly.

She took in the rumpled bedclothes and the hard muscles of his bare chest. "I thought we *had* been doing something."

His sensual smile just about took her breath away. "I meant go to dinner or something. It's not fair for me to keep you chained up in the bedroom for two days without even offering to feed you."

"We haven't tried the chained-up thing."

"Yet."

Her insides shivered at the single word in that low growl of a voice.

"We could go to The Gulch," he suggested, apparently unaffected by the same sudden vivid fantasies that flashed across her mind.

She pushed them away, wondering what the regulars or Lou and Donna Archeleta would think if she showed up in the café with Quinn looking rumpled and well-loved. What did she care? she thought. She deserved some happiness and fun in her life and if she found that with Quinn, it was nobody's damn business but theirs.

"What about the others?" she asked. "Easton and Brant and Cisco? Don't you think you ought to spend your last night in town with them?"

He made a face, though she thought he looked struck by the reminder of his friends and the shared loss that had brought them all together.

"I should," he finally admitted. "I stayed an extra few days after the funeral to spend time with them but I ended up a little...distracted."

She pulled away from him and slipped her arms through her robe. "I should never have monopolized all your time."

"It was a mutual monopoly. I wanted to be here."

"If you want to spend your last evening at the ranch with them, please don't feel you can't because of me. Because of this."

"Why do I have to choose? We should all go to dinner together."

She frowned. "I'm not one of you, Quinn."

"After the past two weeks, you feel as much a part of the family as any of us."

She wanted to argue that the others would probably want him to themselves and she couldn't blame them. But she had discovered she had a selfish streak hiding inside her. She couldn't give up the chance to spend at least a few more hours with him.

Chapter Thirteen

In her heart, Tess knew she didn't belong here with the others but she couldn't remember an evening she had enjoyed more.

Several hours later, she sat at the table in the Winder Ranch dining room and sipped at her wine, listening to the flow of conversation eddy around her.

When they weren't teasing Easton about something, they were reminiscing about some camping trip Guff took them on into Yellowstone or the moose that chased them once along the shores of Hayden Lake or snowmobiling into the high country.

In every word and gesture, it was obvious they loved each other deeply, despite a few rough moments in the conversation.

Most notably, something was definitely up between Easton and Cisco, Tess thought. Though outwardly Easton treated him just as she did Brant and Quinn, with a sisterly sort of affection, Tess could sense braided ropes of tension tugging between the two of them.

They sat on opposite sides of the table and Easton was careful to avoid looking at him for very long.

What was it? she wondered. Had they fought about something? She had a feeling this wasn't something recent in origin as she remembered Easton's strange reaction whenever Cisco's name had been mentioned, before he made it back to the ranch. Obviously, her feelings were different for him than for Brant and Quinn and Tess wondered if anybody else but her was aware of it.

They all seemed so different to her and yet it was obvious they were a unit. Easton, who loved the ranch and was the only one of the Four Winds not to wander away from it. Brant, the solemn, honorable soldier who seemed to be struggling with internal demons she couldn't begin to guess at. Cisco, who by his demeanor appeared to be a thrill-seeking adventurer type, though she sensed there was much more to him than he revealed.

And then there was Quinn.

Around the others, these three people who were his closest friends and the only family he had left, he was warm and affectionate as they laughed and talked and shared memories and she was enthralled by him all over again.

She was the odd person out but Quinn had insisted she join them, even after Easton suggested they grill steaks at the ranch instead of going out to dinner.

The ranch house seemed empty without Jo. She wondered how Easton endured it—and how her friend would cope when she was alone here at the ranch after the men went their respective ways once more.

"Do you remember that snow prank?" Cisco said with a laugh. "That was classic, man. A masterpiece."

"I still can't believe you guys drove all the way into Idaho Falls just to rent a fake snow machine," Easton said, still not looking at Cisco.

"Hey, I tried to talk them out of it," Brant defended himself.

Quinn gave a rough laugh. "But you still drove the getaway car after we broke into the gymnasium and sprayed the Sweetheart Dance decorations with six inches of fake snow."

Tess set down her fork and narrowed her gaze at the men. "Wait a minute. That was you?"

"Uh-oh. You are so busted." Easton grinned at Quinn.

"I worked on that dance planning committee for weeks! I can't believe you would be so blatantly destructive."

"We were just trying to help out with the theme," Quinn said. "Wasn't it something about snuggling in with your sweetheart for Valentine's Day? What better time to snuggle than in the middle of a blizzard and six inches of snow?"

She gave him a mock glare. "Nice try."

"It was a long time ago. I say we all forgive and forget," Brant said, winking at Tess.

"Do you have any idea how long it takes to clean up six inches of snow from a high-school gymnasium?"

"Hey, blame it all on Quinn. I was an innocent sophomore he dragged along for the ride," Cisco said with a grin.

"You were never innocent," Easton muttered.

He sent her a quick look out of hooded dark eyes. "True enough."

Tess could feel the tension sizzle between them, though the other two men seemed oblivious to it. She wondered if any of them saw the anguished expression in Easton's eyes as she watched Cisco.

The other woman suddenly shoved her chair away from the table. "Anybody up for dessert?" she asked, a falsely bright note to her voice. "Jenna McRaven owed me a favor so I talked her into making some of her famous turtle cheesecake."

"That would be great," Brant said. "Thank you."

"Quinn? Cisco?"

Both men readily agreed and Easton headed for the kitchen.

"I'll help," Tess offered, sliding her chair away from the table. "But don't think I've forgotten the snow prank. As to forgiving, I don't believe there's a statute of limitations on prosecution for breaking the spirit of the high-school dance committee."

All three of the men laughed as she left the room, apparently unfazed by her empty threat.

In the kitchen, she found Easton reaching into the refrigerator. She emerged holding a delectable-looking dessert drizzled in chocolate and caramel and chopped nuts.

"All right, out with it," Easton said as she set the cheesecake on the counter, and Tess realized this was the first chance they'd had all evening to speak privately.

"With what?" Tess asked in as innocent a voice as she could muster, though she had a feeling she sounded no more innocent than Cisco had.

"You and Quinn. He's been gone from the ranch for two entire days! What's going on with you two?"

She turned pink, remembering the passion and fun of the past two days.

"Nothing. Not really. We're just… He's just…"

"You're right. It's none of my business," Easton said as she sliced the cheesecake and began transferring it to serving plates. "Sorry I asked."

"It's not that, I just… I can't really explain it."

Easton was silent for a long moment. "Are you sure you know what you're dealing with when it comes to Quinn?" she finally asked with a searching look. "I wouldn't be a friend if I didn't ask."

"He's leaving tomorrow. I completely understand that."

"Do you?"

Tess nodded, even as her heart gave a sad little twist. "Of course. These past few days have been…magical, but I know it's only temporary. His life is in Seattle. Mine is here, at least for the next few weeks until I move to Portland."

"Seattle and Portland aren't so far apart that you couldn't connect if you wanted to," Easton pointed out.

She wouldn't think about that, especially after she had worked so hard to convince herself their relationship was only temporary, born out of shared grief and stunning, surprising hunger.

"I care about you," Easton said when Tess didn't answer. "We owe you so much for these past weeks with Aunt Jo. You carried all of us through it. I mean that, Tess. You always knew exactly what to say and what to do, no matter what was happening, and I'll be forever grateful to you for all you did for her. That's why I'll be absolutely furious if Quinn takes advantage of your natural compassion and ends up hurting you."

"He won't. I promise."

Easton didn't look convinced. Not surprising, she supposed, since Tess couldn't even manage to convince herself.

"It's just…he doesn't have a great track record when it comes to women," her friend said quietly.

Tess tried hard to make her sudden fierce interest in that particular subject seem casual. "Really?"

"I love him like a brother and have since he came to the ranch. But I'm not blind to his faults, especially when it comes to women. I don't think Quinn has ever had a relationship that has lasted longer than a few weeks. To be honest, I'm not sure he's capable of it."

"Never?"

"I can't be certain, I suppose. He's been away for a long time. But every time I ask about his social life when we talk on the phone or email, he mentions he's dating someone new."

"Maybe he just hasn't met anyone he wants to get serious with. There's nothing wrong with that."

"I think it's more than that, Tess. If I had to guess, I would assume it has something to do with his parents' marriage. He didn't have an easy childhood and I think it's made him gun-shy about relationships and commitment."

"I'm sure it did. He told me about his parents and his messed-up home life."

Surprise flashed in her blue eyes. "He did?"

She nodded. "It can't be easy getting past something like that."

"When we were kids, he vowed over and over that he was never going to get married. To be honest, judging by his track record, I don't think he's changed his mind one bit. It broke Jo's heart, if you want the truth. She wanted to see us all settled before she died, but that didn't happen, did it?"

Tess forced a smile, though the cracks in her own heart widened a little more. "Easton, it's okay. I'm not interested in something long-term right now with Quinn or anyone else. We both needed...peace for a while after Jo's death and we enjoy each other's company. That's all there is to it."

Easton didn't look at all convinced and Tess decided to change the uncomfortable subject.

"What time does Cisco leave tomorrow?" she asked.

The diversion worked exactly as she hoped. Easton's expression of concern slid into something else entirely, something stark and painful.

"A few hours." Her hand shook a little as she set the last slice of cheesecake on a small serving plate. "He's catching a plane out of Salt Lake City to Central America at noon tomorrow, so he'll be leaving in the early hours of the morning."

Tess covered her hand and Easton gave her an anguished look.

"Without Jo here, I don't know if he'll ever come back. Or Quinn, for that matter. Brant at least has his own ranch up the canyon so I'm sure I'll at least see him occasionally. But the other two..." Her voice trailed off. "Nothing will be the same without Aunt Jo."

Tess pulled Easton into a hug. "It won't be the same,"

she agreed. "But you're still here. They'll come back for you."

"I don't know about that."

"They will." Tess gave her friend a little shake. "Anyway, Jo would be the first one to tell you to seize every moment. They might not be back for a while but they're here now. Don't sour the joy you can find tonight with them by stewing about what might be coming tomorrow."

"You must be channeling Jo now. I can almost hear her in my head saying exactly those same words."

"Then you'd better listen." Tess smiled.

Easton sighed. "We'd better get this cheesecake out there before they come looking for us."

"Can you give me a minute? I need some water, but I'll be right out."

Easton gave her a searching look. "Are you sure you're all right?"

Tess forced a smile. "Of course. You've got three men waiting for dessert out there. You'd better hurry."

After a pause, Easton nodded and carried the tray with the cheesecake slices out to the dining room.

When she was alone in the bright, cheery kitchen, Tess leaned against the counter and fought the urge to cover her face with her hands and weep.

She was a terrible liar. Lucky for her, Easton was too wrapped up in her own troubles to pay close attention.

She absolutely *wasn't* okay, and she had a sinking feeling she wouldn't be for a long, long time.

I'm not interested in something long-term right now with Quinn or anyone else.

It was a wonder Jo didn't rise up and smite her for telling such a blatant fib in the middle of her kitchen.

Finally, she admitted to herself the truth she had been fighting for two days. Longer, probably. The truth that had been hovering just on the edges of her subconscious.

She was in love with him.

With Quinn Southerland, who planned to blow out of her life like the south wind in the morning.

She loved the way his mouth quirked up at the edges when he teased her about something. She loved his tender care of Jo in her final days and his deep appreciation of the family and home he had found here. She loved the strength and honor that had carried him through incredible trauma as a boy.

She loved the way he made her feel, cherished and beautiful and *wanted,* and the heat and abandon she experienced in his arms.

And she especially loved that he knew the very worst parts of her and wanted to spend time with her anyway.

Whatever was she going to do without him in her world? Just the thought of going through the motions after he returned to Seattle left her achy and heartsore.

She knew she would survive. What other choice did she have?

That didn't mean she wanted to. Hadn't she faced enough heartache? Just once in her life, couldn't things work out the way she wanted?

Fighting back a sob, she moved to the sink and poured a glass of water so she could convince herself she hadn't completely prevaricated to Easton.

She thought of her advice to her friend a few moments earlier.

Don't sour the joy you can find in today by stewing about what might be coming tomorrow.

She couldn't ruin these last few hours with him by anticipating the pain she knew waited for her around the corner.

Something was wrong.

He never claimed to be the most perceptive of men when it came to the opposite sex, but even *he* could tell Tess was distracted and troubled after dinner when he drove her back from the ranch to town.

She said little, mostly gazed out the window at the lights flickering in the darkness, few and far between in Cold Creek Canyon and becoming more concentrated as he approached the town limits.

He glanced over at her profile, thinking how serenely lovely she was. He supposed her pensiveness was rubbing off on him because he still couldn't quite process the surreal twist his life had taken these past few days.

If Brant or Cisco—or Easton, even—had told him before he came back to town that he would wrap up his visit to Pine Gulch in Tess Jamison Claybourne's bed, he would have thought it was some kind of a strange, twisted joke.

Until he showed up at the ranch a few weeks ago, he honestly hadn't thought of her much in years. He was too busy working his tail off building his business to waste much time or energy on such an unimportant— though undeniably aggravating—part of his past.

On the rare occasions when thoughts of her did filter

through his mind for whatever reason, they were usually tainted with acrimony and disdain.

In these past weeks, she had become so much more to him.

Quinn let out a breath. He had tried to avoid examining those fragile, tender feelings too carefully. He appreciated her care for Jo, admired the strength she had demonstrated through her own personal tragedy, found her incredibly sexy.

He didn't want to poke and prod more deeply than that, afraid to unravel the tangled mess of his feelings.

He did know he didn't want to leave her or the haven he had found in her arms.

His hands tightened on the steering wheel as he turned down the street toward her house. For two weeks, his associates had taken the helm of Southerland Shipping. Quinn ought to be ecstatic at the idea of jumping right back into the middle of the action. Strategizing, making decisions, negotiating contracts. It was all in his blood, the one thing he found he was good at, and he had certainly missed the work while he had been at Winder Ranch.

But every time he thought about saying goodbye to Tess, he started to feel restless and uneasy and he had no idea why.

He pulled into the driveway and turned off the engine to his rented SUV.

"You probably want to be with the others," she said, her voice low. "I don't mind if we say goodbye now."

Something remarkably like panic fluttered through him. "Are you that anxious to be rid of me?"

She turned wide green eyes toward him. "No. Nothing like that! I just… I assumed you would want to spend your last few hours in town with your friends," she said, a vulnerable note to her voice that shocked him.

Though he had already said his farewells to the others when he left the house, with lots of hugs and back-slapping, he considered taking the out she was offering him. Maybe he ought to just gather his few belongings from her house and head back to bunk at the ranch for the night. That made perfect sense and would help him begin the process of rebuilding all those protective walls around his emotions.

But he had a few more hours in Pine Gulch and he couldn't bear the thought of leaving her yet.

"I'd like to stay."

He said the words as more of a question than a statement. After an endless moment when he was quite certain she was going to tell him to hit the road, she nodded, much to his vast relief, and reached for his hand.

A soft, terrifying sweetness unfurled inside him at the touch of her hand in his.

How was he going to walk away in a few hours from this woman who had in a few short weeks become so vitally important to him? He didn't have the first idea.

Chapter Fourteen

She didn't release his hand, even as she unlocked her door to let them both inside. When he closed the door behind him, she kissed him with a fierce, almost desperate, hunger.

They didn't even make it past her living room, clawing at clothes, ripping at buttons, tangling mouths with a fiery passion that stunned him.

They had made love in a dozen different ways over the past few days—easy, teasing, urgent, soft.

But never with this explosive heat that threatened to consume them both. She climaxed the instant he entered her and he groaned as her body pulsed around him and followed her just seconds later.

He kissed her, trying to memorize every taste and texture as she clutched him tightly to her. To his amazement, after just a few moments, his body started to stir again inside her and he could feel by her response that she was becoming aroused again.

He carried her to the bedroom and took enough time to undress both of them, wondering if he would ever get enough of her silky curves and the warm, sweet welcome of her body.

This time was slow, tender, with an edge of poignancy to it that made his chest ache. Did she sense it, too? he wondered.

They tasted and touched for a long time, until both of them were breathless, boneless. She cried out his name when she climaxed and he thought she said something else against his shoulder but he couldn't understand the words.

When he could breathe again and manage to string together two semi-coherent thoughts, he pulled her close under the crook of his arm, memorizing the feel of her—the curves and hollows, the soft delight of her skin.

"I wish I didn't have to go," he murmured again.

Instead of smiling or perhaps expressing the same regret, she froze in his arms and then pulled away.

Though her bedroom was well-heated against the October chill, he was instantly cold, as he watched her slip her slender arms through the sleeves of her silky green robe that matched her eyes.

"Are you lying for my sake or to appease your own guilt?" she finally asked him.

He blinked, disoriented at the rapid-fire shift from tender and passionate to this unexpected attack that instantly set him on the defensive.

"Why do I have to be lying?"

"Come on, Quinn," she said, her voice almost sad. "We both know you're not sorry. Not really."

He bristled. "When did you become such an expert on what's going on inside my head?"

"I could never claim such omnipotent power. Nor would I want it."

Okay. He absolutely did not understand how a woman's mind worked. How could she pick a fight with him after the incredible intensity they just shared? Was she just trying to make their inevitable parting easier?

"If you could see inside my head," he answered carefully, "you would see I meant every word. I *do* wish I didn't have so many obligations waiting for me back in Seattle. These past few days have been…peaceful and I don't have much of that in my life."

She gazed at him, her features tight with an expression he didn't recognize. After a moment, her prickly mood seemed to slide away and she smiled, though it didn't quite push away that strange, almost bereft look in her eyes.

"I'm happy for that, Quinn. You deserve a little peace in your life and I'm glad you found it here."

She paused and looked away from him. "But we both knew from the beginning that this would never be anything but temporary."

Whenever he let himself think beyond the wonder of the moment, the shared laughter and unexpected joy he found with her, he had assumed exactly that—this was supposed to be a short-term relationship that wouldn't extend beyond these few magical days.

Hearing the words from her somehow made the reality seem more bluntly desolate.

"Does it have to be?"

"Of course," she answered briskly. "What other option is there?"

He told himself that wasn't hurt churning through him at her dismissal of all they had shared and at the potential for them to share more.

"Portland is only a few hours from Seattle. We could certainly still see each other on the weekends."

She tightened the sash on her robe with fingers that seemed to tremble slightly. From the cold? he wondered. Or from something else?

"To what end?" she asked. "Great sex and amusing conversation?"

Despite his turmoil, he couldn't resist arching an eyebrow. "Something wrong with either of those?"

Her laugh sounded rough. "Not at all. Believe me, I've become a big fan of both these past few days."

She shoved her hands in the pockets of her robe and drew in a deep breath, as if steeling herself for unpleasantness. "But I'm afraid neither is enough for me."

That edgy disquiet from earlier returned in full force and he was aware of a pitiful impulse to beg her not to push him from her life.

He wouldn't, though. He had a sudden, ugly flashback of his mother at the dinner table trying desperately to catch his father's attention any way she could. New earrings, new silverware, a difficult new recipe. Only until she managed to push one of his father's hot buttons would he even notice her, and then only to rant and rail and sometimes worse.

He pushed it away. He certainly wasn't his mother trying desperately in her own sick way to make someone care who wasn't really capable of it. Tess was not like his father. She had a deep capacity for love. He had seen it with Jo, even Easton and Brant and Cisco.

Why else would she have stayed with an invalid husband for so long?

But maybe she couldn't care for *him*. Maybe he didn't deserve someone like her....

"I want more," she said quietly, interrupting the grim direction of his thoughts. "All I wanted when I was a girl was a home and a family and a husband who cherished me. I wanted what my parents had. They held hands in the movies and whispered secrets to each other in restaurants and hid love notes for each other all around the house. My mom's still finding them, years after Dad died. That's what I wanted."

He was silent. If not for the years he spent with Jo and Guff seeing just that sort of relationship, he would have had absolutely no frame of reference to understand what she was talking about, but the Winders had shared a love like that, deep and rich and genuine.

"I thought I found that with Scott," Tess went on, "but fate had other plans and things didn't turn out quite the way I dreamed."

"I'm sorry." He meant the words. He hated thinking of her enduring such loss and pain as a young bride.

"I'm sorry, too," she said quietly. "But that time in my life is over. I'm ready to move forward now."

"I can understand that. But why can't you move forward with me? We have something good here. You know we do."

She was silent for a long time and he thought perhaps he was making progress on getting her to see his point of view. But when she spoke, her voice was low and sad.

"Easton told me tonight that when you were younger, you vowed you were never getting married."

"What a guy says when he's fifteen and what he says when he's thirty-four are two very different things," he said, though he had said that very same sentiment to Jo in the garden at Winder Ranch just a few weeks ago.

She sat on the bed and he didn't miss the way she was careful to keep plenty of space between them. "Okay, tell me the truth. Say we continue to see each other for those weekends you were talking about. Look ahead several months, maybe a year, with a few days a month of more of that great sex and amusing conversation."

"I can do that," he said, and spent several very pleasant seconds imagining kissing her on the dock of his house on Mercer Island, of taking her up in his boat for a quick run to Victoria, of standing beside the ocean on the Oregon Coast at a wonderfully romantic boutique hotel he knew in Cannon Beach.

"So here it is a year in the future," she said, dousing his hazy fantasies like a cold surf. "Say we've seen each other exclusively for that time and have come to... to care about each other. Where do you see things going from there?"

"I don't know. What do you want me to see?"

"Marriage. Family. Can you ever even imagine yourself contemplating a forever sort of relationship with me or anyone else?"

Marriage. Kids. A dog. Panic spurted through him. Though Jo and Guff had shared a good marriage and he had spent a few years watching their example, for most of his childhood, marriage had meant cold silences alternated with screaming fights and tantrums, culminating in terrible violence that had changed his world forever.

"Maybe," he managed to say after a moment. "Who's

to say? That would be a long way in the future. Why do we have to jump from here to there in an instant?"

Her sigh was heavy, almost sad. "I saw that panic in your eyes, Quinn. You can't even consider the idea of it in some long-distant future without being spooked."

"That could change. I don't see why we have to ruin this. Why can't we just enjoy what we have in the moment?"

She didn't answer him right away. "You know, brain injuries are peculiar, unpredictable things," she finally said, baffling him with the seemingly random shift in topic.

"Are they?"

"The same injury in the same spot can affect two people in completely different ways. For the first two or three years after Scott's accident, all the doctors and specialists kept telling me not to give up hope, that things would get better. He could still improve and start regaining function some day."

Through his confusion, Quinn's heart always ached when he thought of Tess facing all that on her own.

"I waited and hoped and prayed," she went on. "Through all those years and promises, I felt as if I were frozen in the moment, that the world went on while I was stuck in place, waiting for something that never happened."

She paused. "He did improve, in minuscule ways. I don't want you to think he didn't. Near the end, he could hold his head up for long periods of time and even started laughing at my silly jokes again. But it was not nearly the recovery I dreamed about in those early days."

"Tess, I'm very sorry you went through that. But I don't understand your point."

She swallowed and didn't meet his gaze. "My point is that I spent years waiting for reality to match up to my expectations, waiting for him to change. Even being angry when those expectations weren't met, when in truth, he simply wasn't capable of it. It wasn't his fault. Just the way things were."

He stared. "So you're comparing me to someone who was critically brain-injured in a car accident?"

She sighed. "Not at all, Quinn. I'm talking about myself. One of the greatest lessons Scott's accident taught me was pragmatism. I can't hang on to unrealistic dreams and hopes anymore. I want marriage and children and you don't. It's as simple as that."

"Does it have to be?"

"For me, yes. Your views might change. I hope for your sake they do. Caring for Scott all those years taught me that the only way we can really find purpose and meaning in life is if we somehow manage to move outside ourselves to embrace the chances we're offered to care for someone else."

She lifted moist eyes to his. "I hope you change your mind, Quinn. But what if you don't? Say we see each other for six months or a year and then you decide you're still no closer to shifting your perspective about home and family. I would have spent another year moving further away from my dreams. I can't do that to myself or to you."

That panic from before churned through him, icy and sharp. He didn't want to lose what they had shared these past few days.

Or maybe it didn't mean as much to her. Why else would she be so willing to throw it all away? Maybe he *was* just like his mother, trying desperately to keep her from pushing him away.

No. This wasn't about that. The fear and panic warring inside him took on an edge of anger.

"This is it, then?" His voice turned hard, ugly. "I was here to scratch an itch for you and now you're shoving me out the door."

Her lovely features paled. "Not fair."

"Fair? Don't talk to me about fair." He jumped out of the bed and reached for his Levis, still in a heap on the floor. He couldn't seem to stop the ugly words from spilling out like toxic effluent.

"You know what I just realized? You haven't changed a bit since your days as Queen Bee at Pine Gulch High. You're still the spoiled, manipulative girl you were in high school. You want what you want and to hell with anybody else and whatever they might need."

"This has nothing to do with high school or the person I was back then."

"Wrong. This has *everything* to do with Tess Jamison, Homecoming Queen. You can't have what you want, your little fantasy happily-ever-after, and so kicking me out of your life completely is your version of throwing a pissy little temper tantrum."

His gazed narrowed as another repugnant thought occurred to him.

"Or wait. Maybe that's not it at all. Maybe this is all some manipulative trick, the kind you used to be so very good at. Don't forget, I had years of experience watching you bat your eyes at some poor idiot, all the while you're tightening the noose around his neck without him having the first clue what you're doing. Maybe you think if you push me out now, in a few weeks I'll come running back with tears and apologies, ready to give you anything you want. Even that all-important wedding ring that's apparently the only thing you think matters."

"You're being ridiculous."

"You forget, I was the chief recipient of all those dirty tricks you perfected in high school. The lies. The rumors you spread. This is just one more trick, isn't it? Well, guess what? I'm not playing your games now, any more than I was willing to do it back then."

She stood on the other side of the room now, her arms folded across her chest and hurt and anger radiating from her.

"You can't get past it, can you?" She shook her head. "I have apologized and tried to show you I'm a different person than I was then. But you refuse to even consider the possibility that I might have changed."

He had considered it. He had even believed it for a while.

"Only one of us is stuck in the past, Quinn. Life has changed me and given me a new perspective. But somewhere deep inside you, you're still a boy stuck in the ugliness of his parents' marriage."

He stared at her, angry that she would turn this all back around on him when she was the one being a manipulative bitch.

"You're crazy."

"Am I? I think the reason you won't let yourself have more than casual relationships with women is because you're so determined not to turn into either one of your parents. You're not about to become your powerless, emotionally needy mother or your workaholic, abusive father. So you've decided somewhere deep in your psyche that your best bet is to just keep everyone else at arm's length so you don't have to risk either option."

He was so furious, he couldn't think straight. Her assessment was brutal and harsh and he refused to admit that it might also be true.

"Now you're some kind of armchair psychiatrist?"

"No. Just a woman who…cares about you, Quinn."

"You've got a hell of a way of showing it by pushing me away."

"I'm not pushing you away." Her voice shook and he saw tears in her eyes. Either she was a much better actress than he could possibly imagine or that was genuine regret in her eyes. He didn't know which to believe.

"You have no idea how hard this is for me," she said and one of those tears trickled down the side of her nose. "I've come to care about you these past few weeks. Maybe I always did, a little. But as much as I have loved these past few days and part of me wants nothing more than to continue seeing you after I move to Portland, it wouldn't be fair to either of us. You can't be the kind of man I want and I'm afraid I would eventually come to hate you for that."

His arms ached from the effort it took not to reach for her but he kept his hands fisted at his sides. "So that's it. See you later, thanks for the good time in the sack and all that."

"If you want to be crude about it."

He didn't. He wanted to grab her and hang on tight

and tell her he would be whatever kind of man she wanted him to be. He had discovered a safety, a serenity, with her he hadn't found anywhere else and the idea of leaving it behind left him hollow and achy.

But she was right. He couldn't offer her the things she needed. He could lie and tell her otherwise but both of them would see through it and end up even more unhappy.

"I suppose there's nothing left to say, then, is there?"

She released a shuddering kind of breath and he supposed he should be somewhat mollified that her eyes reflected the same kind of pain shredding his insides.

"I'm sorry."

"So am I, Tess."

He grabbed his things and walked out the door, hoping despite himself that she would call him back, tell him she didn't mean anything she'd said.

But the only sound as he climbed into his rental car was the mournful October wind in the trees and the distant howl of a coyote.

Tess stood at the window of her bedroom watching Quinn's taillights disappear into the night.

She couldn't seem to catch her breath and she felt as if she'd just been bucked off one of the Winder Ranch horses, then kicked in the chest for good measure.

Had she been wrong? Maybe she should have just taken whatever crumbs Quinn could offer, to hell with the inevitable pain she knew waited for her in some murky future.

At least then she wouldn't have this raw, devastating feeling that she had just made a terrible mistake.

With great effort, she forced herself to draw in a deep breath and then another and another, willing her common sense to override the visceral pain and vast emptiness gaping inside her.

No. She hadn't been wrong, as much as she might wish otherwise. In the deep corners of her heart, she knew it.

She wanted a home and a family. Not today, maybe not even next year, but someday, certainly. She was ready to move forward with her life and go on to the next stage.

She had already fallen in love with him, just from these few days. If she spent a year of those weekend encounters he was talking about, she wasn't sure she would ever be able to climb back out.

Better to break things off now, when she at least had half a chance of repairing the shattered pieces of her heart.

She would survive. She had been through worse. Scott's death and the long, difficult years preceding it had taught her she had hidden reservoirs of strength.

She supposed that was a good thing. She had a feeling she was going to need all the strength she could find in the coming months as she tried to go on without Quinn.

Chapter Fifteen

"Tess? Everything okay?"

Three months after Jo Winder's death, Tess stood at the nurses' station, a chart in her hand and her mind a million miles away.

Or at least several hundred.

She jerked her mind away from Pine Gulch and the tangled mess she had made of things and looked up to find her friend and charge nurse watching her with concern in her brown eyes.

"I'm fine," she answered Vicki Ballantine.

"Are you sure? You look white as a sheet and you've been standing there for at least five minutes without moving a muscle. Come sit down, honey, and have a sip of water."

The older woman tugged her toward one of the chairs behind the long blue desk. Since Vicki was not only her friend but technically her boss, Tess didn't feel as if she had a great deal of choice.

She sipped at the water and crushed ice Vicki brought her in a foam cup. It did seem to quell the nausea a little, though it didn't do much for the panic that seemed to pound a steady drumbeat through her.

"You want to tell me what's bothering you?" Vicki asked.

She drew in a breath then let it out slowly, still reeling from confirmation of what she had begun to suspect for a few weeks but had only just confirmed an hour ago on her lunch break.

This sudden upheaval all seemed so surreal, the last possible development she had expected to disrupt everything.

"I don't... I haven't been sleeping well."

Vicki leaned on the edge of the deck, her plump features set into a frown. "You're settling in okay, aren't you? The house you rented is nice enough, right? It's in a quiet neighborhood."

"Yes. Everything's fine. I love Portland, you know I do. The house is great and everyone here at the hospital has been wonderful."

"But you're still not happy."

At the gentle concern in her friend's eyes and the warm touch of her hand squeezing Tess's arms, tears welled up in her eyes.

"I am," she lied. "I'm just..."

She couldn't finish the sentence as those tears spilled over. She pressed her hands to her eyes, mortified that she was breaking down at work.

Only the hormones, she assured herself, but she knew it was much, much more. Her tears stemmed from fear and longing and the emptiness in her heart that kept her tossing and turning all night.

Vicki took one look at her emotional reaction and pulled Tess back to her feet, this time ushering her into the privacy of the empty nurses' lounge.

"All right. Out with it. Tell Auntie Vick what's wrong. This is about some man, isn't it?"

Through her tears, Tess managed a watery laugh. "You could say that."

Oh, she had made such a snarled mess of everything. That panic pulsed through her again, harsh and unforgiving, and her thoughts pulsed with it.

"It always is," Vicki said with a knowing look. "Funny thing is, I didn't even know you were dating anybody."

"I'm not. We're…" Her voice trailed off and she drew in a heavy breath. Though she wanted to protect her own privacy and give herself time to sort things out, she was also desperate to share the information with *someone.*

She couldn't call her mother. Oh, mercy, there was another reason for panic. What would Maura say?

Her mother wasn't here and she wasn't anywhere close to ready to tell any of her friends in Pine Gulch. Vicki had become her closest friend since moving to Portland and on impulse, she decided she could trust her.

"I'm pregnant," she blurted out.

Vicki's eyes widened in shock and her mouth made a perfect little *O* for a moment before she shut it with a snap. She said nothing for several long moments.

Just when Tess was kicking herself for even mentioning it in the first place, Vicki gave her a careful look. "And how do you feel about that?"

"You're the one who said I'm pale as a sheet, right? That's probably a pretty good indication."

"Your color's coming back but you still look upset."

"I don't know how I feel yet, to tell you the truth," she admitted. "I just went to the doctor on my lunch hour to verify my suspicions. I...guess I'm still in shock. I've wanted a child—children—for so long. Scott and I talked about having several and then, well, things didn't quite work out."

Though she didn't broadcast her past around, she had confided in Vicki after her first few weeks in Portland about the challenging years of her marriage and her husband's death.

"And the proud papa? What's his reaction?"

Tess closed her eyes, her stomach roiling just thinking about how on earth she would tell Quinn.

"I haven't told him yet. Actually, I...haven't talked to him in three months."

"If my math is right, this must be someone from Idaho since you've only been here for two months."

She sighed. "His foster mother was my last patient."

"Did you two have a big fight or something?"

She thought of all the accusations they had flung at each other that night. *You can't have what you want, your little fantasy happily-ever-after, and so kicking me out of your life completely is your version of throwing a pissy little temper tantrum.*

Now she was pregnant—*pregnant!*—and she didn't have the first idea what to do about it. She cringed, just imagining his reaction. He would probably accuse her of manipulating the entire thing as some Machiavellian plot to snare him into marriage.

Maybe you think if you push me out now, in a few weeks I'll come running back with tears and apologies, ready to give you anything you want. Even that all-important wedding ring that's apparently the only thing you think matters.

She pushed away the bitter memory, trying to drag her attention back to the problem at hand, this pregnancy that had completely knocked the pins out from under her.

She didn't even know how it had happened. Since hearing the news from her doctor, she had been wracking her brain about their time together and she could swear he used protection every single time. The only possibility was one time when they were in the shower and both became a little too carried away to think about the consequences.

She had been a nurse for ten years and she knew perfectly well that once was all it took but she never expected this to happen to her.

"You could say we had a fight," she finally answered Vicki. "We didn't part on exactly amiable terms."

"If you need to take a little time, I can cover your shift. Why don't you take the rest of the day off?"

"No. I'm okay. I just need a moment to collect my thoughts. I promise, I can put it out of my head and focus on my patients."

"At least take a quick break and go on out to the roof for some fresh air. I think the rain's finally stopped and it might help you clear your head."

She wanted to be tough and insist she was fine. But the hard truth was she felt as if an atomic bomb had just been dropped in her life.

"Clearing my head would be good. Thanks."

When she rose, Vicki gathered her against her ample breast for a tight hug. "It will be okay, sweetheart. If this is what you want, I'm thrilled for you. I know if anyone can handle single motherhood, you can."

She had serious doubts right now about her ability to handle even the next five minutes, but she still appreciated the other woman's faith in her.

As she walked outside into the wet and cold January afternoon, she gazed out at the city sprawled out below her. So much for the best-laid plans. When she left Pine Gulch, she had been certain that she had everything figured out. Her life would be different but she had relished the excitement of making changes and facing new challenges.

In her wildest dreams, she never anticipated this particular challenge.

She pressed a hand to her abdomen, to the tiny life growing at a rapid pace there.

A child.

Quinn's child.

Emotions choked her throat, both joy and fear.

This pregnancy might not have been in her plans, but no matter what happened, she would love this child. She already did, even though she had only known of its existence for a short time.

She pressed her hand to her abdomen again. She had to tell Quinn. Even if he was bitter and angry and believed she had somehow manipulated circumstances to this end, she had to tell him. Withholding the knowledge of his child from him would be wrong, no matter how he reacted.

She only hoped she could somehow find the courage.

Two weeks later, she was still searching desperately for that strength. With each day that passed, it seemed more elusive than sunshine in a Portland winter.

Every morning since learning she was pregnant, she

awoke with the full intention of calling him that day. But the hours slipped away and she made excuse after excuse to herself.

He was busy. She was working. She would wait until evening. She didn't have his number.

All of them were only pitiful justification for her to give in to her fears. That was the hard truth. She was afraid, pure and simple. Imagining his response kept her up at night and she was quite certain was contributing to the nausea she faced every morning.

That she continued to cater to that fear filled her with shame. She wasn't a weak woman and she hated that she was acting like it.

The night before, she had resolved that she couldn't put it off any longer. It was past time for her to act as the pregnancy seemed more real each day. Already, she was beginning to bump out and she was grateful her work scrubs had drawstring waists, since all her other slacks were starting to feel a little snug.

No more excuses. The next day was Saturday and she knew she had to tell him. Though she wanted nothing more than to take the coward's way out and communicate via phone—or, even better, email—she had decided a man deserved to know he was going to become a father in person.

But figuring out how to find the man in Seattle was turning into more of a challenge than she expected.

She sat once more on the rooftop garden of the hospital on her lunch break, her cell phone in her hand as she punched in Easton Springhill's phone number as a last resort.

Easton's voice rose in surprise when she answered. "Tess! I was just thinking about you!"

"Oh?"

"I've been meaning to check in and see how life in the big city is treating you."

She gazed out through the gray mist at the buildings and neighborhoods that had become familiar friends to her during her frequent rooftop breaks. "Good. I like it here. I suppose Pine Gulch will always be home but I'm settling in."

"I'm so glad to hear that. You deserve some happiness."

And she would have it, she vowed. No matter what Quinn Southerland had to say about their child.

"How are you?" she stalled. "I mean really."

Easton was silent for a moment. "All right, I guess. I'm trying to stay busy. It's calving time so I'm on the run all the time, which I suppose is a blessing."

"I'm sorry I haven't called to check on you before now. I've thought of you often."

"No problem. You've been busy starting a new life. By the way," Easton went on, "I checked in on your morning coffee klatch crowd the other day and they all miss you like crazy. I never realized old Sal Martinez had such a thing for you."

She laughed, thinking of the dearly familiar old-timers who could always be counted on to lift her spirits. "What can I say? I'm pretty popular with eighty-year-old men who have cataracts."

Maybe she was making a mistake in her decision to stay in Portland and raise her baby. Moving back to Pine Gulch would give her child structure, community.

Instant family. She had time to make that particular decision, she told herself. First things first.

"Listen, I'm sorry to bother you but I'm trying to reach Quinn and I can't find his personal contact information."

"You can't?" Easton's shock filtered clearly through the phone and Tess winced. She had never told her friend that she and Quinn had parted on difficult terms. She supposed she had assumed Quinn would have told her.

"No. I tried to call his company and ended up having to go through various gatekeepers who weren't inclined to be cooperative."

"He can be harder to reach than the Oval Office sometimes. I've got his cell number programmed on mine so I don't have it memorized but hang on while I look it up."

She returned in a moment and recited the number and Tess scribbled it down.

"Can you tell me his home address?" she said, feeling awkward and uncomfortable that she had to ask.

Easton paused for a long moment. "Is something wrong, Tess?"

If you only knew the half of it, she thought.

"Not at all," she lied. "I just… I wanted to mail him something," she improvised quickly.

She could tell her friend didn't quite buy her explanation but to her vast relief, Easton recited the address.

"You'll have to find the zip code. I don't know that off the top of my head."

"I can look it up. Thanks."

"Are you sure nothing's wrong? You sound distracted."

"Just busy. Listen, I'm on a break at the hospital and really need to get back to my patients. It was great talking to you. I'll call you next week sometime when we both have more time to chat."

"You do that."

They said their goodbyes, though she could still hear the questions in Easton's voice. She was happy to hang up the phone. Another moment and she would be blurting it all out. Easton was too darned perceptive and Tess had always been a lousy liar.

She certainly couldn't tell Easton about her pregnancy until she'd had a chance to share the news with Quinn first.

She gazed at the address in her hand, her stomach tangled in knots at the encounter that loomed just over the horizon.

Whatever happened, her baby would still have her.

Talk about acting on the spur of the moment.

Quinn cruised down the winding, thickly forested street in Portland, wondering what the hell he was doing there.

He wasn't one for spontaneity and impulsive acts of insanity, but here he was, trying to follow his GPS directions through an unfamiliar neighborhood in the dark and the rain.

She might not even be home. For all he knew, she could be working nights or even, heaven forbid, on a date.

At the thought, he was tempted to just turn his car

around and drive back to Seattle. He was crazy to just show up at her place out of the blue like this. But then, when it came to Tess and his behavior toward her, sanity hadn't exactly been in plentiful supply.

He felt edgy and off balance, as if he didn't even know himself anymore and the man he always thought he'd been. He was supposed to be a careful businessman, known for his forethought and savvy strategizing.

He certainly *wasn't* a man who drove a hundred and fifty miles on a whim, all because of a simple phone call from Easton.

When she called him he had just been wrapping up an important meeting. The moment she said Tess had called her looking for his address and phone number, his brain turned to mush and he hadn't been able to focus on anything else. Not the other executives still in the room with him or the contract Southerland Shipping had just signed or the route reconfiguration they were negotiating.

All he could think about was Tess.

His conversation with Easton played through his mind now as he followed the GPS directions.

"Something seemed off, you know?" she had said. "I couldn't put my finger on it but she sounded upset. I just wanted to give you a heads-up that she might be trying to reach you."

As it had then, his mind raced in a hundred different directions. What could be wrong? After three months of empty, deafening silence between them, why was she suddenly trying to make contact?

He only had the patience to wait an hour for her

call before he couldn't stand the uncertainty another moment.

In that instant, as he made the call to excuse himself from a fundraiser he'd been obligated to attend for the evening, he had realized with stark clarity how very self-deceptive he had been for the past three months.

He had spent twelve weeks trying to convince himself he was over Tess Claybourne, that their brief relationship had been a mistake but one that he was quite certain had left no lasting scars on his heart.

The moment he heard her name, a wild rush of emotion had surged through him, like water gushing from a dam break, and he realized just how much effort it had taken him to shove everything back to the edges of his subconscious.

Only in his dreams did he let himself remember those magical days he and Tess had shared, the peace and comfort he found in her arms.

He had definitely been fooling himself. Their time together had had a profound impact on his world. Since then, he found himself looking at everything from a different perspective. All the things he used to find so fulfilling—his business pursuits, his fundraising engagements, boating on the Sound—now seemed colorless and dull. Tedious, even.

Southerland was expanding at a rapid pace and he should have been thrilled to watch this company he had created begin at last to attain some of the goals he had set for it. Instead, he found himself most evenings sitting on his deck on Mercer Island, staring out at the lights reflecting on the water and wondering why all the successes felt so empty.

No doubt some of the funk he seemed to have slipped into was due to the grieving process he was still undergoing for Jo.

But he had a somber suspicion that a large portion of that emptiness inside him was due to Tess and the hole she had carved out in his life.

He sighed. Might as well be completely frank—with himself, at least. Tess hadn't done any carving. He had been the one wielding the butcher knife by pushing her away the first chance he had.

He couldn't blame her for that last ugly scene between them. At least not completely. At the first obstacle in their growing relationship, he had jumped on the defensive and had been far too quick to shove her away.

In his business life, he tried to focus most on the future by positioning his company to take advantage of market trends and growth areas. He didn't like looking back, except to examine his mistakes in an effort to figure out what he could fix.

And he had made plenty of mistakes where Tess was concerned. As he examined what had happened three months earlier in Pine Gulch, he had to admit that he had been scared, pure and simple.

He needed to see her again. He owed her an apology, a proper goodbye without the anger and unfounded accusations he had hurled at her.

That's why he was here, trying to find her house in the pale, watery moonlight.

His GPS announced her address a moment later and he pulled into the driveway of a small pale rose brick house, a strange mix of dread and anticipation twisting around his gut as he gazed through the rain-splattered windshield.

Her house reminded him very much of the one in Pine Gulch on a slightly smaller scale. Both were older homes with established trees and gardens. The white shutters and gable gave it a charming seaside cottage appeal. It was surrounded by shrubs and what looked like an extensive flower garden, bare now except for a few clumps of dead growth.

He imagined that in the springtime, it would explode with color but just now, in early February, it only looked cold and barren in the rain.

He refused to think about how he could use that same metaphor for his life the past three months.

Smoke curled from the chimney and lights gleamed from several windows. As he parked in the driveway, he thought he saw a shadow move past the window inside and his breathing quickened.

For one cowardly moment, he was tempted again to put the car in Reverse and head back to Seattle. Maybe Easton had her signals crossed and Tess wasn't really looking for him. Maybe she only wanted his address to send him a kiss-off letter telling him how happy she was without him.

Even if that was the case, he had come this far. He couldn't back out now.

The rain had slowed to a cold mist as he walked up the curving sidewalk to her front door. He rang the doorbell, his insides a corkscrew of nerves.

A moment later, the door opened and the weeks and distance and pain between them seemed to fall away.

She looked fresh and bright, her loose auburn curls

framing those lovely features that wore an expectant look—for perhaps half a second, anyway, until she registered who was at her doorstep.

"Quinn!" she gasped, the color leaching from her face like old photographs left in the desert.

"Hello, Tess."

She said nothing, just continued to stare at him for a good thirty seconds. He couldn't tell if she was aghast to find him on her doorstep or merely surprised.

Wishing he had never given in to this crazy impulse to drive two and a half hours, he finally spoke. "May I come in?"

She gazed at him for another long moment. When he was certain she would slam the door in his face, she held it open farther and stepped back so he had room to get through. "I... Yes. Of course."

He followed her inside and had a quick impression of a warm space dominated by a pale rose brick fireplace, blazing away against the rainy night. The living room looked comfortable and bright, with plump furniture and colorful pillows and her upright piano in one corner, still covered with photographs.

"Can I get you something to drink?" she asked. "I'll confess, I don't have many options but I do have some wine I was given as a housewarming gift when I moved here."

"I'm fine. Thanks."

The silence stretched out between them, taut and awkward. He had a sudden vivid memory of lying in her bed with her, bodies entwined as they talked for hours.

His chest ached suddenly with a deep hunger to taste that closeness again.

"You're pale," he said, thrusting his hands in the pockets of his jacket and curling them into fists where she couldn't see. "Are you ill? Easton said you called her and she was worried."

She frowned slightly, as if still trying to make sense of his sudden appearance. "You're here because Easton asked you to check on me?"

For a moment, he thought about answering yes. That would be the easy out for both of them, but he couldn't do it.

Though he had suspected it, he suddenly knew with relentless clarity that *she* was the reason for the emptiness of the past three months.

He had never felt so very solitary as he had without Tess in his world to share his accomplishments and his worries. To laugh with, to maybe cry with. To share hopes for the future and help him heal from the past.

He wanted all those things she had talked about, exactly what she had created for herself here.

He wanted a home. He wanted to live in a house with carefully tended gardens that burst with color in the springtime, a place that provided a warm haven against the elements on a bitter winter night.

And he wanted to share that with Tess.

He wanted love.

Like a junkie jonesing for his next fix, he craved the peace he had found only with Tess.

"No," he finally admitted hoarsely. "I'm here because I missed you."

Chapter Sixteen

She stared at him, her eyes wide and the same color as a storm-tossed sea. "You…what?"

He sighed, cursing the unruly slip of his tongue. "Forget I said that. Yeah, I'm here because Easton asked me to check on you."

"You're lying." Though the words alone might have sounded arrogant, he saw the vulnerability in her eyes and something else, something that almost looked like a tiny flicker of hope.

He gazed at her, his blood pulsing loudly in his ears. He had come this far. He might as well take a step further, until he was completely out on the proverbial limb hanging over the bottomless crevasse.

"All right. Yes. I missed you. Are you happy now?"

She was quiet for a long moment, the only sound in the house the quiet murmuring of the fire.

"No," she finally whispered. "Not at all. I've been so miserable, Quinn."

Her voice sounded small and watery and completely genuine. He gave a low groan and couldn't take this distance between them another second. He yanked his hands out of his pockets and reached for her and she wrapped her arms fiercely around his neck, holding on for dear life.

Emotions choked in his throat and he buried his face in the crook of her shoulder.

Here. This was what he had missed. Having her in his arms again was like coming home, like heaven, like everything good he had ever been afraid to wish for.

How had he ever been stupid enough to push away the best thing that had ever happened to him?

He kissed her and a wild flood of emotions welled up in his throat at the intense sweetness of having her in his arms once more.

"I'm sorry," he murmured against her mouth. "So damn sorry. I've been a pathetic wreck for three lousy months."

"I have, too," she said. "You ruined *everything*."

He gave a short, rough laugh. "Did I?"

"I had this great new job, this new life I was trying to create for myself. It was supposed to be so perfect. Instead, I've been completely desolate. All I've been able to think about is you and how much I…" Her voice trailed off and he caught his breath, waiting for her to finish the sentence.

"How much you what?" he said when she remained stubbornly silent.

"How much I missed you," she answered and he was aware of a flicker of disappointment thrumming through him as he sensed that wasn't what she had intended to say at all.

He kissed her again and she sighed against his mouth, her arms tight around him.

Despite the cold February rain, he felt as if spring was finally blooming in his heart.

"Everything you said to me that last night was exactly right, Tess. I've given the past too much power in my life."

"Oh, Quinn. I had no right to say those things to you. I've been sorry every since."

He shook his head. "You were right."

"Everyone handles their pain differently. The only thing I know is that everyone has some in his or her life. It's as inevitable as…as breathing and dying."

"Well, you taught me I didn't have to let it control everything I do. Look at you. Your dreams of a happily-ever-after came crashing down around you with Scott's accident. But you didn't become bitter or angry at the world."

"I had my moments of despair, believe me."

His chest ached for her all over again and he cringed at the memory of how he had lashed out at her their last night together in Pine Gulch, accusing her of being the same spoiled girl he had known in high school.

He hadn't meant any of those ugly words. Even as he had said them, he had known she was a far different woman.

He had been in love with her that night, had been probably since that first moment she had sat beside him on the floor of her spare room and listened to him pour out all the ugly memories he kept carefully bottled up inside.

No. Earlier, he admitted.

He had probably been a little in love with her in high

school, when he had thought he hated her. He had just been too afraid to admit the truth to himself.

"But despite everything you went through, you didn't let your trials destroy you or make you cynical or hard," he said gently, holding her close. "You still open your heart so easily. It's one of the things I love the most about you."

Tess stared at him, her heart pulsing a crazy rhythm in her chest. He couldn't have just said what she thought he did. Quinn didn't believe in love. But the echo of his words resounded in her head.

Still, she needed a little confirmation that she wasn't completely hearing things.

"You...what?"

His mouth quirked into that half grin she had adored since junior high school.

"You're going to make me say it, aren't you? All right. That's one of the millions of things I love about you. Right up there at the top of the list is your big, generous, unbreakable heart."

"Not unbreakable," she corrected, still not daring to believe his words. "It has felt pretty shattered the past three months."

He let out a sound of regret just before he kissed her again, his mouth warm and gentle. At the devastating tenderness in his kiss, emotions rose in her throat and her eyes felt scratchy with unshed tears.

"I'm sorry," he murmured between kisses. "So damn sorry. Can you forgive me? I've been a stupid, scared idiot."

He paused, his eyes intense. "You have to cut me a little slack, though."

"Do I?"

Her arch tone drew a smile. "It's only fair. I'm a man who's never been in love before. If you want the truth, it scares the hell out of me."

I'm a man who's never been in love before.

The words soaked through all the pain and loneliness and fear of the past three months.

He loved her. This wasn't some crazy dream where she would wake up once more with a tear-soaked pillow wrapped in her arms. Quinn was standing here in her living room, holding her tightly and saying things she never would have believed if she didn't feel the strength of his arms around her.

He loved her.

She pulled his mouth to hers and kissed him hard, pouring all the heat and joy and wonder spinning around inside her into her kiss. When she at last drew away, they were both breathing raggedly and his eyes looked dazed.

"I love you, Quinn. I love you so much. I wanted to make a new life for myself here in Portland, a new start. But all I've been able to think about is how much I miss you."

"Tess—" He groaned her name and leaned down to kiss her again but she gathered what tiny spark of strength remained and stepped slightly away from him, desperate for a little space to gather her thoughts.

"I love you. But I have to tell you something..."

"Me first." He squeezed her fingers. "I know you think we want two different things out of life. I'll admit, it would probably be a bit of a stretch to say I've had some sudden miraculous change of heart and I'm now completely ready to rush right off to find a wedding chapel."

Well, that would certainly make what she had to tell him a little more difficult. Some of her apprehension must have showed in her eyes because he brought their clasped fingers to his mouth and pressed a kiss to the back of her hand.

"But the thought of being without you scares me a hell of a lot more than the idea of hearts and flowers and wedding cake. I want everything with you. I know I can get there with your help. It just might take me a few months."

"We have a few months."

"I hope we have a lot longer than that. I want forever, Tess."

She gazed at him, dark and gorgeous and male, with clear sincerity in his stunning eyes. He meant what he said. He wasn't going to use his past as an excuse anymore.

She couldn't quite adjust to this sudden shift. Only an hour ago, she had been sitting at her solitary dining table with a TV dinner in front of her, lonely and achy and frightened at the prospect of having to face his reaction the next day to the news of the child they had created together.

And here he was using words like *forever* with her.

She still hadn't told him the truth, she reminded herself. Everything might change with a few simple words. And though she wanted to hang on to this lovely feeling for the rest of her life, she knew she had to tell him.

Though it was piercingly difficult, she pulled her hands away from his and crossed her arms in front of her.

"I need to tell you something first. It may...change your perspective."

He looked confused and even a little apprehensive, as if bracing himself for bad news. "What's wrong?"

"Nothing. At least I don't think so. I hope you don't, either."

She twisted her fingers together, trying to gather her nerves.

"Tell me," he said after a long pause.

With a deep breath, she plunged forward. "I don't know how this happened. Well, I know how it happened. I'm a nurse, after all. But not *how* it happened, if you know what I mean. I mean, we took precautions but even the best precautions sometimes fail..." Her voice trailed off.

"Tess. Just tell me."

"I'm pregnant."

The words hung between them, heavy, dense. He said nothing for a long time, just continued to stare at her.

She searched his gaze but she couldn't read anything in his expression. Was he happy, terrified, angry? She didn't have the first idea.

She pressed her lips together. "I know. I was shocked, too. I only found out a few weeks ago and I've been trying to figure out how to tell you. That's why I called Easton for your address. I was going to drive to Seattle tomorrow. I've been so scared."

That evoked a reaction from him—surprise.

"Scared? Why?"

She sighed. "I didn't want you to think it was all part of some grand, manipulative plan. I swear, I didn't expect this, Quinn. You have to believe me. We were careful. I know we were. The only thing I can think is that...that time in the shower, remember?"

Something flickered across his features then, something that sent heat scorching through her.

"I remember," he said, his voice gruff.

He didn't say anything more and after a moment, she wrapped her arms more tightly around herself, cold suddenly despite the fire blazing merrily in her hearth.

"I know this changes everything. You said yourself you're not ready quite yet for all of that. I completely understand. I don't want you to feel pressured, Quinn. But I...I love her already. The baby and I will be fine on our own if you decide you're not ready. I'll wait as long as it takes. I have savings. I won't ask anything of you, I swear."

Again, something sparked in his gaze. "I thought you said you love me."

"I did. I do."

"Then how can you think I would possibly walk away now?"

His eyes glittered with a fierce emotion that suddenly took her breath away. Hope began to pulse through her and she curled her fingers into fists, afraid to let it explode inside her.

"A baby." He breathed out the word like a prayer or a curse, she couldn't quite tell. "When?"

"Sometime in early July."

"An Independence Day baby. We can name her Liberty."

Her laugh was a half sob and she reached blindly for him. He swept her into his arms and pulled her close as that joy burst out like fireworks in the Pine Gulch night sky.

"Liberty Jo," she insisted.

His eyes softened and he kissed her with more of that heart-shaking tenderness. "A baby," he murmured after a long while. His eyes were dazed as he placed a hand over her tiny bump and she covered his hand with hers.

"You're not upset?" she asked.

"*Numb* is a better word. But underneath the shock is…joy. I don't know how to explain it but it feels right."

"Oh, Quinn. That was my reaction, too. I was scared to death to find out I was pregnant. But the idea of a child—*your* child—filled me with so much happiness and peace. That's a perfect word. It feels *right*."

"I love you, Tess." He pressed his mouth to hers again. "You took a man who was hard and cynical, who tried to convince himself he was happy being alone, and showed him everything good and right that was missing in his world."

He pressed his mouth to hers and in his kiss she tasted joy and healing and the promise of a brilliant future.

* * * * *

We hope you enjoyed reading
SAFE HARBOR
by #1 *New York Times* bestselling author
SHERRYL WOODS and

**A COLD CREEK
HOMECOMING**
by *New York Times* bestselling author
RAEANNE THAYNE

Both were originally
Harlequin Special Edition stories!

Discover more heartfelt tales of family, friendship and
love from the **Harlequin Special Edition** series.
Romance is for life, and these stories show that every
chapter in a relationship has its challenges and delights
and that love can be renewed with each turn of the page!

⊞HARLEQUIN®

SPECIAL EDITION
Life, Love and Family

When you're with family, you're home!

Look for six *new* romances every month
from **Harlequin Special Edition!**

Available wherever books are sold.

www.Harlequin.com

NYTHSE0914

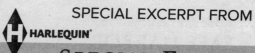
***

Just for an instant, Gabriel worried about putting Michelle in the line of fire, considering his line of work. He had enemies. Dangerous enemies who wouldn't hesitate to threaten anyone close to him. Of course, there was his sister, Sara, but she'd lived in Wyoming for the past few years, away from him, on a ranch they co-owned. Now he was putting her in jeopardy along with Michelle.

But what could he do? The child had nobody. Now that her idiot stepmother, Roberta, was dead, Michelle was truly on her own. It was dangerous for a young woman to live alone, even in a small community. And there was also the question of Roberta's boyfriend, Bert.

Gabriel knew things about the man that he wasn't eager to share with Michelle. Bert was part of a criminal organization, and he knew Michelle's habits. He also had a yen for her, if what Michelle had blurted out to Gabriel once was true—and he had no indication that she would lie about it. Bert might decide to come try his luck with her now that her stepmother was out of the picture. That couldn't be allowed.

Gabriel was surprised by his own affection for Michelle. It wasn't paternal. She was, of course, far too young for anything heavy. She was a beauty, kind and generous and sweet. She was the sort of woman he usually ran from. No, strike that, she was no woman. She was still unfledged, a dove without flight feathers. He had to keep his interest hidden. At least, until she was grown up enough that it wouldn't hurt his conscience to pursue her. Afterward...well, who knew the future?

***

Don't miss TEXAS BORN
by New York Times *bestselling author Diana Palmer,*
the latest installment in
THE LONG, TALL TEXANS *miniseries.*

Available October 2014 wherever
Harlequin® Special Edition books and ebooks are sold.

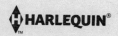

SPECIAL EDITION

Life, Love and Family

Save $1.00 on the purchase of
TEXAS BORN
by Diana Palmer,
available September 16, 2014, or on any other
Harlequin® Special Edition book.

Available wherever books are sold, including most bookstores,
supermarkets, drugstores and discount stores.

Save $1.00
on the purchase of
TEXAS BORN
by Diana Palmer,
available September 16, 2014,
or on any other Harlequin® Special Edition book.

Coupon valid until November 19, 2014. Redeemable at participating retail outlets
in the U.S. and Canada only. Limit one coupon per customer.

52611937

5 65373 00076 2 (8100)0 11980

NYTCOUP0914